# STRUCK
# DEAD

# ANDREA KANE

ISBN-13 9781682320631 (Hardcover)
9781682320662 (Trade Paperback)
9781682320648 (ePub)
9781682320655 (Kindle)

LCCN:   2023940708

Struck Dead

For questions and comments about the quality of this book, please contact us at:

CustomerService@bonniemeadowpublishing.com

BonnieMeadowPublishing.com

Printed in USA

### Publisher's Cataloging-In-Publication Data
### (Provided by Cassidy Cataloguing Services, Inc.)

Names: Kane, Andrea, author. | Kane, Andrea. Forensic Instincts novels.
Title: Struck dead / Andrea Kane.
Description: Warren, NJ : Bonnie Meadow Publishing, [2024]
Identifiers: ISBN: 9781682320631 (hardcover) | 9781682320662 (trade
          paperback) | 9781682320648 (ePub) | 9781682320655 (Kindle) |
          LCCN: 2023940708
Subjects: LCSH: Millionaires--New York (State)--New York--Fiction. | Hit-and-run
          drivers--New York (State)--New York--Fiction. | Murder--Investigation-
          -Fiction. | Forensic sciences--Fiction. | Deception--Fiction. | LCGFT:
          Thrillers (Fiction) | Psychological fiction. | Detective and mystery
          fiction. | BISAC: FICTION / Thrillers / Suspense. | FICTION / Thrillers /
          Psychological.
Classification: LCC: PS3561.A463 S78 2024 | DDC: 813/.54--dc23

With thanks to all Trauma Center health care workers. I hope *Struck Dead* reflects the level of your skill and commitment in saving lives every day.

# 1

*Offices of Forensic Instincts*
*Main Conference Room, Second Floor*
*Tribeca, New York*
*Monday, 9:40 a.m.*

Casey Woods, the president of Forensic Instincts, stood at the head of the oval table, her jaw having dropped. She pressed her iPhone closer to her ear and tried to reconcile herself, both to who the caller was and the reason for her call.

She certainly didn't sound like the Angela King that Casey knew. And why in the name of heaven was she reaching out to Casey, of all people?

Angela repeated her original demand: "I need you to meet me *now*—as in drop everything and get over here." This time her voice was commanding but shaken.

*Shaken? Angela King?*

Casey's mind raced.

Angela was a high-powered and aggressive criminal defense attorney at Harris, Porter, & Donnelly. A virtual barracuda. Rumor had it that she was next up to make partner. No surprise. She successfully defended the richest of the rich, from corporate executives, to wealthy entrepreneurs, to "businessmen" with rumored links to organized crime—a fact she chose to overlook since they were affluent enough to pay her fees. She and Forensic Instincts were on opposite sides of law enforcement. They'd battled it out more than once, the criminals that FI had helped catch becoming the very criminals Angela would defend.

Needless to say, the FI team and Angela weren't friends.

And yet, here she was, calling Casey on an urgent, time-is-of-the-essence matter—one she sounded incredibly high-strung about.

"Casey?" Angela repeated. "Did you hear me?"

Casey lowered herself into a chair. "I heard you. What is this about? And why me, of all people?"

"You'll see for yourself," Angela replied. She rattled off the address of a luxury skyscraper on Manhattan's Upper East Side. "Hurry. I'm jeopardizing my career by waiting to call 9-1-1. I can't wait much longer, but you have to view the scene first and later provide me with some answers. No more questions. Just come. I have a key to the building's back door, and I'll let you in. We'll use the freight elevator."

Casey's common sense was urging her to refuse. Nine-one-one meant a crime scene, and questions meant involving her. Both those things were screaming for her to stay away. She pushed aside that inner voice—she was too intrigued to refuse. "I'm on my way."

She shrugged into her wool winter coat as she called John Nickels, Forensic Instincts' number one on their security team. Then, she blew out the front door, not waiting to fill the FI team in on where she was going. There was no time. Plus, they'd only try to talk her out of it.

Holiday decorations were glistening everywhere, and tiny snow-flakes danced in the air.

Casey didn't notice any of it.

John pulled around a few minutes later, and Casey hopped into the car, gave him the address, and urged him to hurry.

With a brief nod, John was on his way, navigating the FDR Drive in record time. He got Casey to her destination in thirteen minutes. He dropped her off around back, far from the doorman's view. Then, he waited to return her to the brownstone once her meeting was over, as per her instructions.

Angela was pacing inside the building and opened the door to let Casey in the moment she saw her. No matter how dire the occasion, Angela always looked stunning. A cobalt blue Armani pantsuit that set off her dark skin, matching four-inch Louboutin heels, and long wavy black hair styled at the highest end salon. She carried herself like a queen. In short, she was a knockout.

Now she looked more rattled than Casey had ever seen her.

"Let's go," she said. She led the way to the freight elevator, where she and Casey rode up.

"Tell me what's going on," Casey stated flatly.

Angela didn't answer. She glanced at her Apple Watch, her gaze snapping up as the elevator stopped on the twenty-first floor.

The doors slid open.

Angela paused only long enough to ensure that Casey was right behind her. Then, she strode down the hall, made a turn, and halted in front of apartment 21B. She unlocked the door, pulled Casey inside, and faced her to offer the first few words of an explanation.

"This is the home of my client Christopher Hillington. We had a nine-thirty meeting scheduled to be held here."

Casey's brows rose. Christopher Hillington was a renowned and phenomenally wealthy managing director of the private equity firm YNE. He was also a major suspect in a vehicular homicide, and Casey knew through various news sources that he'd been questioned several times by the NYPD and was on the verge of arrest.

"I see you know of him," Angela said. "Given the circumstances, I'm not surprised." She gestured toward a breathtaking sunken living room. "In here."

Casey bit back her question about what Angela had just said. She sensed she was about to get her answers, so she remained silent.

The two women stepped down, and Angela stood to the side and waited.

Casey got the full view immediately.

Christopher Hillington's body was crumpled on the Oriental carpet beside his desk, blood pooling out around him. His head was bashed in, clearly having been struck multiple times by a heavy object. The bloodied sledgehammer lying next to the body was obviously the murder weapon. Judging from the damage done, the killer had been not only determined, but brutal.

Casey eyeballed the horrific scene, feeling sickened as well as confused. She was about to ask Angela what this had to do with her when she spotted the letters, written in blood, on the lower edge of the desk, right beside Hillington's outstretched arm.

She walked over, careful not to touch anything, squatted down, and squinted. The two words were completely legible, and they made Casey's blood run cold.

*Casey Woods.*

# 2

Casey walked back into the brownstone filled with questions and no answers. She'd taken a slew of pictures at several angles. Then, she and Angela had agreed to meet later in the day for a drink—as soon as Angela could break away from what was bound to be a law enforcement and media frenzy. Quickly, Casey had ducked out of the apartment as Angela called 9-1-1. John had taken one look at her face as she jumped into the passenger seat, and zoomed off back to the brownstone.

Casey wondered how long it would take for the detectives to show up at FI's door, given the lettering on the desk. She could hardly wait.

\*\*\*

As soon as she crossed the threshold of the brownstone, she was greeted by Yoda, FI's almost-human, almost-omniscient AI system, who'd actually shown a surge in human traits over the past month. He was extraordinary and could do almost anything, leaving the entire FI team in awe. As a result, he'd become a vital member of the team, even though no one but Ryan—the team's tech genius who'd created him—had a clue how he worked.

"Did you have a fruitful outing, Casey?" Yoda asked.

Before Casey had time to respond, Marc Devereaux saved her by heading straight down the stairs to the entranceway, eyeing her curiously.

"Hey," she said, slipping off her coat, and shaking the first winter snowflakes out of her shoulder-length red hair. She bent to scratch the ears of the sleek bloodhound who padded over to greet her.

"Hello, boy," she murmured. Hero was a former FBI human scent evidence dog who now belonged to Casey, but he was also a respected member of the FI team. He'd sniffed out more than one victim since he'd joined FI.

"Hey," Marc replied. He was studying Casey quietly in that penetrating, brooding way of his. "You okay?"

Casey rose, shaking her head. There was almost nothing she kept from Marc. He was her right hand at Forensic Instincts, and had been with her from the day she opened FI's doors. His credentials were beyond impressive. Former FBI, former Behavioral Analysis Unit, and former Navy SEAL. Given his heritage—Asian grandparents on his mother's side, and an extensive French lineage on his father's—he spoke Mandarin and French fluently, in addition to the Spanish he'd learned and perfected along the way. No wonder the FBI had snatched him up and were more than unhappy when he resigned. But Marc had grown bored with the red tape and the strict rule-following. FI had represented a change from them both, and Casey had hired him in a nanosecond.

Now, after all this time, he and Casey could practically read each other's minds.

"Casey?" he prompted her. "You look like hell. What's going on?"

"I'm in real trouble, and I have no idea why," she replied.

Marc pointed to the stairs. "Your office or mine?"

"Yours" was her immediate response. "It's quieter. And I don't want a full team meeting, not yet."

She wouldn't have one anyway. Ryan McKay, the team's intelligence analyst and creative problem solver, and Claire Hedgleigh, their amazingly accurate claircognizant, were in Maui on a two-week romantic getaway. Just last month, they'd realized what the rest of the team had known for ages—that they were head over heels in love. And after the intense, twenty-four-seven case that FI was just coming off of, the two lovebirds were entitled to the break they'd requested.

Maui would never be the same.

Still, Patrick and Emma were somewhere in the building. Patrick Lynch, retired FBI, was head of security for the team, and the one who also yanked the team's kite strings in order to keep them from going too far over the fine line between legal and illegal. And Emma Stirling, the bouncy newest team member, who was as deft at pickpocketing as the Artful Dodger, and who was also becoming a seasoned—and often covert—investigator for FI.

Casey needed to talk this through with Marc first, to hear his objective and pragmatic viewpoint, and to get her head on straight.

Silently, they climbed the two flights of stairs to his third-floor office, and hurried inside, shutting the door before anyone could see them.

Marc perched one hip against his desk, folded his arms across his chest, and leveled his gaze at Casey.

"What happened?" he asked.

Casey sucked in her breath, and then blurted out the whole scenario.

Marc's brows rose. "That's quite a story—and an all-around shocker. It's hard for me to picture Angela King as anything but a bulldozer. And the rest…" He paused. "You don't think she was trying to frame you, do you?"

Casey shook her head. "I thought of that. But I heard her on the phone, and, more importantly, checked out her tells at the crime scene. She was a wreck. If anything, she wanted my help."

Casey was a trained behaviorist who, before forming Forensic Instincts, had worked in the private sector as well as with law enforcement. They'd liked her a whole lot better back then.

"Remember," she continued, "it's one thing to draw blood in a courtroom. It's another to see a brutally murdered man. When she deals with homicide, it's from the legal end. She deals with the prosecutor and the NYPD. Bludgeoned victims are not her forte."

Marc nodded. "Good point." He reached out for Casey's cell phone, which Casey handed over, and began viewing the photos she'd taken.

He scowled. "A fair amount of blood spatter. Cast-off bloodstains on the wall and desk. Blows delivered at an angle that suggests the killer was at least Hillington's height. Not to mention the pool of blood around Hillington's head." He looked up. "You didn't walk anywhere near there, did you?"

"Of course not," Casey replied.

Marc shifted his gaze to a photo that showed another angle of the gruesome scene. "Given the name Kobalt is sprawled across the weapon, it's obvious they're the manufacturer of what's clearly a sledgehammer. I'm guessing it weighs about four pounds. Very common tool. They're sold everywhere, from home improvement stores to Amazon. So that tells us nothing more about the killer. But your written name—that certainly looks incriminating."

"I know. I called our legal team on the way back and put them on high alert."

"Smart," Marc replied, handing back Casey's iPhone. "Because the cops will be here shortly to bombard you with questions. Obviously, our lawyers won't be on the scene until you 'realize' you're being interrogated. Then make your official phone call and go silent."

Casey nodded her agreement. "This is insane," she said. "I never even met Christopher Hillington."

"Exactly. So when you do answer the detectives' questions, be frank. The only things you have to omit are showing up at the crime scene and any crime scene evidence you saw—neither of which they'd grill you on unless they had solid evidence to go on, which they don't. The rest is as big a question mark for you as it is for them. You have no idea why Hillington would write your name in blood as he died."

Casey began pacing around, massaging her temples as she did. "That's all well and good, except that obviously there *was* a reason why Hillington wrote my name. And, given FI's less-than-chummy relationship with the NYPD, they'll be champing at the bit to paint me in the worst light. I normally handle them from a position of power, lawyers or not. But in this case…"

Marc answered the question before Casey had finished asking it. "Present yourself to them as you always do—as the president of Forensic Instincts. Composed and confident, which is who you are. In the interim, we're short on time. I think we should call for a team meeting and get started on our research."

Casey nodded. "You're right. We have to check out any case in which Hillington made even a minor appearance, and every contact we have that might have even the most remote connection to him."

"Personal included," Marc replied. "You have to go through your own records to see if you ever rubbed elbows with Hillington at some event you're forgetting. Maybe one you attended with Hutch."

Kyle "Hutch" Hutchinson was Casey's significant other. They'd moved in together a while ago into a lovely apartment in Battery Park City. Hutch was brilliant. That's why the Bureau had selected him to be the BAU coordinator as well as the squad supervisor of the FBI's New York field office's NCAVC—the National Center for the Analysis of Violent Crimes. The internal competition for the job had been fierce, but Hutch had stood heads and tails above the rest, so the job had been his. Prior to that, he'd worked in the BAU in Quantico—both in crimes against children and then in crimes against adults. Marc had introduced him to Casey—something he took great pleasure in reminding them of—and their relationship had been long-distance for way too long. Now, things were great.

Except that Hutch followed the letter of the law.

Casey and Forensic Instincts didn't.

Thus, came the couple's agreement to share only information that was on the up-and-up—although Hutch had pushed that boundary more than once when Casey's life was in danger.

"I'll call Hutch now," she said. "Please Slack the team and have them meet us in the conference room."

"Done." Marc whipped out his iPhone. So did Casey.

\*\*\*

Seeing Casey's unblocked number, Hutch answered right away.

"Hi, beautiful."

"Hey," Casey replied, unable to do anything but get straight to the point. "We need to talk."

Hutch snapped into professional mode. "What's wrong?"

Casey fought to keep her voice steady and summed up the situation.

"Shit," Hutch swore, not even bothering to lecture Casey for going to the crime scene. Nor did he mince words. "What can I do?"

"First, you can tell me if you remember any occasion when we interacted with, or even met, Christopher Hillington."

Hutch was quiet, and Casey could picture his brow furrowed in concentration.

"No," he finally replied. "But that's an off-the-top-of-my-head response. Let me dig a bit, check out events we recently attended and cross-check them with any major media events that Hillington did. I'll even go through my separate activities and see if I can find any overlap."

"Thanks," she said. "I'm getting the team together and doing the same. We'll research as much as we can before the detectives come banging at our door. This is insane."

"Stay calm. Go hash things out with your team. You'll have a head start, since the detectives won't know you already set this process in motion—and why. In the meantime, I'll jump on this."

*** 

*Offices of Forensic Instincts*
*Main Conference Room, Second Floor*
*Tribeca, New York*
*Monday, 11:15 a.m.*

Patrick and Emma both looked puzzled and concerned as they settled themselves around the oval table, at which Casey and Marc were already seated.

"What's going on?" Emma blurted out in her customary forthright manner. She looked like Alice in Wonderland, and was young and exuberant—until she was in investigative mode. Then, she was all pro.

"Marc's message said it was urgent," she continued. "It must be, because our plan was to meet in the small conference room downstairs while Ryan and Claire were in Maui."

Patrick was studying Casey. He was the father figure of the team—sharp and seasoned, and as dedicated as they came. He brought wisdom and balance, plus over thirty years of violent crimes experience at the FBI, to the team.

Now, he took in Casey's demeanor—pale and tense as she sat stiffly at the head of the table. "Emma," he said, "let's give Casey the floor so we can find out the answer to your question."

Emma nodded and stopped talking.

Patrick tipped his head toward Casey. "All ears," he said.

"Thanks." Casey gave them a rueful smile. "It looks like it's me this time, coming to you guys, hat in hand, frantic to be taken on as a client."

Marc didn't laugh. "We'll give you a discount. Now go on."

Casey didn't waste another moment. She told them everything she'd seen and heard, plus all that she and Marc had discussed.

"Wow," Patrick said with a whistle. "Talk about coming out of left field."

"On all counts," Casey agreed.

Marc took over with no time to lose. "We've got a shitload of work to do, none of which we're going to complete before the NYPD gets here. But we can make a dent. Casey and I are going to review whatever public information—newsfeeds, blog and social media posts—there are on the vehicular homicide case Hillington was on the verge of being charged with. Emma, you'll work with Yoda. Yoda, call up our entire contact list—all of it, back to when FI was founded. It's already saved on the cloud. We'll have to go over it by hand, looking for the slightest reminder of Hillington."

"Yes, at once, Marc," Yoda replied, his voice reverberating throughout the conference room.

"I'll delve into Christopher Hillington overall," Patrick said. "He's a colorful figure. Let me see what I can find."

Emma frowned. "Don't we need Ryan for all this?"

Casey gave an adamant shake of her head. "No. This is on us. Claire and Ryan's flight just took off yesterday. I promised them that their vacation would be uninterrupted, and I intend to keep that promise. If things get truly dire, I'll rethink it, but definitely not now."

Marc arched a brow. "Besides, Ryan might be our tech wizard, but we're perfectly capable of doing a cursory investigation without him."

At that moment the front doorbell sounded.

"We know who that is," Casey said in a tight voice as Yoda simultaneously announced, "Law enforcement has arrived."

Casey slid back her chair. "I'll start the show."

"No." Marc put a restraining hand on her arm. "Business as usual. Let Emma open the door. She'll seat the detectives in one of the first-floor offices. Then, she'll come get you."

He turned to Emma. "Calm and curious. No signs of anxiety."

Emma was already on her feet. "I'm an A-plus actress. You know that, Marc. This will be smooth and easy." She looked at Casey. "I'll be right back."

"Don't hurry," Casey muttered.

**3**

Emma had shown Detectives Lorraine Banks and Burt Ogden of the Nineteenth Precinct into one of the team's most professional-looking interview rooms. She'd provided them each with a cup of coffee and announced that Ms. Woods would be in shortly, before leaving them alone, door partially open.

Casey waited upstairs for three minutes.

"You got this," Marc said.

She nodded, crossing her fingers and heading to the stairs.

She walked down and turned into the room with an inquisitive look on her face. She'd interacted with both these detectives before. Detective Banks was in her forties, but you'd never know it. She clearly worked out extensively and cared about her appearance. She was slim but wellmuscled, with just a light dusting of makeup and a perpetually straight face. Casey sometimes wondered if her face would crack if she smiled. Ogden was older, fiftyish, and looked a lot like Sigmund Freud. Together, they made a formidable team.

Casey greeted them, keeping that same questioning look on her face. "Lorraine. Burt. What can I do for you?"

"Hello, Casey," Detective Ogden acknowledged her. "You can have a seat, please."

Casey tried not to smile. Burt Ogden had a way of making everything sound like a hardcore interrogation. Then again, maybe in their minds this was.

Casey complied, lowering herself into a chair across the table from the two homicide detectives. She remained silent. Silence had a way of making people uncomfortable.

Detective Banks didn't look uncomfortable now. "We'll get right to the point. Are you familiar with Christopher Hillington?"

Casey's brows rose in surprise. "Of course," she replied. "He's the managing director of the private equity firm YNE, whose name has appeared in the news quite a bit lately, with regard to a vehicular homicide." She spread her hands wide, palms up. "I'm not sure how far the investigation has gone, but my team and I are not representing anyone associated with it."

"But you don't know him personally?" Banks asked.

"We've never met. Why?"

Ogden began laying out a series of photos on the table, all zoomed-in versions of Hillington, and all facing Casey. "Because sometime around dawn this morning, he was bludgeoned to death in his own apartment."

Casey's eyes widened as she studied the photos. "This is tragic," she said. "Do you have any suspects? Murder weapon? Motive—?" She broke off. "I have no right to ask those questions, so, instead I'll ask: what does all this have to do with Forensic Instincts?"

"Not Forensic Instincts," Banks corrected her. "*You.*"

"Excuse me?" Casey appeared visibly startled.

Ogden pulled out one final photo, zoomed in to the lower part of Hillington's desk. "Can you explain this?"

Casey leaned forward, seeing exactly what she'd expected. She knew that Ogden and Banks were carefully watching her reaction, and she had no intention of giving them what they were hoping to see.

Stunned disbelief shot across her face. "My name? In blood?" She shook her head. "I'm totally clueless."

"I doubt that," Ogden replied. "The two words are written in Hillington's handwriting, and his index finger was saturated with blood. So there's no doubt he's leading us to you. Why do you think that is?"

This time, Casey leaned back in her chair, arms folded across her breasts. "I have no idea," she said, but then added, "I'm a public figure and the president of a top investigative company. Maybe he wanted my attention, or even my assistance." Even as she tossed out that possibility, she wondered if it could be true. "I mean, if I were dying and sought justice, I might write Benoit Blanc's name in blood to make sure he investigated and avenged me."

"Where were you between six and seven this morning?" Ogden fired at her.

"Right here at Forensic Instincts," Casey replied. "Working. And no, none of my colleagues had arrived yet, so I was alone." She pushed back her chair. "And, as this has now become an interrogation rather than a few casual questions, I'm finished talking to you. It's time I give my lawyers a call." She rose. "Make yourselves comfortable. I'll be back with my legal representation."

Without waiting for a response, she left the room.

***

A half hour later, Casey walked back inside, accompanied by two sharp members of their legal team—Shannon Grazier and Robert Cateman—flanking her.

"Our client has filled us in." With no further greeting, Shannon set down her briefcase beside the chair she'd just claimed. "As of now, she has nothing to say to you. Any questions you have can be directed at us."

Detective Ogden leaned back and met her gaze. "That sounds like someone who has something to hide."

"No," Robert said. "It sounds like someone who's been bombarded with incriminating questions she can't answer."

"Can't or won't?"

"Can't," he stressed. "I believe our client told you all she knows. She never met the victim and clearly had no ties to his murder."

"Then how do you explain the victim writing her name in his own blood just before he died?"

Shannon's gaze was icy. "I believe that's *your* job to figure out. Ms. Woods has nothing to offer. She's as taken aback as you are." She rose and handed the detectives her firm's business card. "If you have any further questions, feel free to contact us. As of now, this meeting is over."

Both detectives rose.

"Tell your client not to make any travel plans," Ogden warned.

"Duly noted," Robert replied with a nod.

Banks shot Casey a shrewd look. "If you don't know anything now, I'm quite sure you will soon. You'll put your entire team on investigative alert."

Robert picked up his briefcase. "There's nothing illegal in that. You've just all but accused my client of being tied to a murder—which she vehemently denies. If she has the resources to investigate this matter, it's her right to do so."

Detective Ogden fired back, "Not without sharing her findings with us and not by interfering with a homicide investigation."

"You've made yourself quite clear, Detective," Shannon said. "You can see yourselves out now."

\*\*\*

*Vicario Residence*
*South Bayside, Queens, New York*
*Monday, 12:35 p.m.*

Isabel Vicario lived on a quiet street in a small brick house with a tiny garage and a green overhang—a home that, until three weeks ago, she'd shared with Frank, her beloved husband of thirty-two years. Given he was a store associate and she was a homemaker, they'd had to scrimp and save to buy it. After which, they'd raised their children there, watched them grow, and now, as empty nesters, were settling into a quieter lifestyle of peaceful companionship.

All that had been snatched away in one horrifying moment.

She'd never forget that night. The drenching rain. The expression on the police officer's face when he arrived to tell her the news. The sincerity in his voice as he offered his condolences, and his assurances that the NYPD would find the animal who, driving at top speed, had slammed into her husband's Camry, killing him on impact, and taking off without slowing down or stopping.

A part of Isabel had died that night, too.

The funeral. The gathering. The tears. The endless nightmarish nights, despite doses of the prescribed sedatives. Even the presence of her blessed son, Franklin, and her daughter, Mia. It was all a blur. And nothing could ease the anguish.

The investigation had crawled like an odious insect as the days passed and Isabel grieved. Video footage had been located and confiscated. Apparently, it had revealed evidence of the crash, although the police at the NYPD's 111th Precinct had stressed that the rain and the darkness had inhibited their ability to make out much of the car that had struck Frank's. They didn't share further details with her. Not at this point.

They'd interviewed potential suspects, although Isabel doubted that Frank had an enemy in the world. And suddenly, although they wouldn't tell her why, they'd centered on Christopher Hillington.

The more times he was brought in for questioning—accompanied by his wicked witch of a lawyer—the more Isabel loathed him. She knew he was guilty. She watched his face in media coverage on TV. Cold. Indifferent. Self-assured. Not a shred of remorse or compassion. He was a multimillionaire and the life he'd extinguished was that of a common store worker—inconsequential and written off.

Oh, how Isabel hated him. And how she longed for the day when he'd pay for his crime.

Now, she hovered in the living room recliner—the recliner that used to be Frank's—tears streaming down her cheeks and fingers tightly clenched. She continued staring at the TV, even though the NYPD press conference had long since concluded.

There would be no more waiting.

Christopher Hillington was gone.

Divine justice, was all she could think.

# 4

*Offices of Forensic Instincts*
*Main Conference Room, Second Floor*
*Tribeca, New York*
*Monday, 3:05 p.m.*

Casey was rereading the details of the vehicular homicide that she and Marc had assembled a few hours ago. It was a thin compilation of facts and speculation. November 17 at approximately nine fifteen p.m. A main street in South Bayside, Queens, with two lanes coming and two lanes going. Pouring rain. A lethal collision, no witnesses. Frank Vicario, an innocent, wrong place, wrong time victim. News leaks alleging to the existence of video footage showing the victim's maroon Toyota Camry heading up the right lane. Struck from the left with enough impact to crunch the victim's car into parked vehicles on the side of the street and to annihilate the Camry. Alleged offending car: a luxury sedan speeding up the left lane and abruptly shifting to the right. Interrogations of the man who was determined to be the owner of that sedan: Christopher Hillington.

Casey couldn't help but wonder about those interrogations. How had the cops figured out that it was Hillington's car? License plate? Make and model? Clearly, they'd seen enough on the video footage to draw that conclusion. And had the luxury sedan sustained visible damage? Did the two things add up to enough evidence to arrest Hillington? If so, why the delay in his arrest?

As usual, Casey's wheels kept turning, maybe unnecessarily so, but that's who she was. Why was Hillington in Bayside, Queens, to begin with? It wasn't exactly a multimillionaire's hangout. And was he such an evil, hardhearted man as to cruelly bulldoze past the scene of the crime? Was he drunk? Did he have something to hide?

The police must have thought so, because they came back to him again and again as the prime suspect. If they checked out potential enemies of the victim, or even interviewed his wife, those things were under wraps.

Whatever pieces were missing, she and Marc would unearth them. Ryan had taught them enough about the shadier side of obtaining information for them to make that happen.

In the interim, they were each poring over the list of contacts that Emma had compiled, Marc in his office and Casey in hers. Mind-numbing work, and with no positive return.

As she pushed on with her review, Marc returned to the conference room—which was also Casey's office of choice—and dropped a paper bag in front of her.

"A turkey sandwich," he said. "You haven't eaten all day, and your much-loved Cobb salad requires two hands to eat. This requires one, so there's no excuse to turn it down. You can eat and work at the same time."

Casey gave him a grateful smile. "I was starting to see black spots, so thanks." She opened the bag, unwrapped the turkey sandwich, and took a big bite.

"No problem." Marc lowered himself into the chair adjacent to hers. "Hear back from Hutch?"

"Five minutes ago. So far nothing. And at my end, I've reviewed our contact list, so far from *A* to *F*. All clients, client contacts, victims, suspects, you name it. Not a thing that even touches on Hillington." Casey ran both hands through her hair. "I'm going crazy, and I know in my gut that I'm going to keep coming up empty. I've got close to a photographic memory. I'd never forget any aspect of a case that involved such a high-profile guy."

Marc nodded. "I've gotten all the way up to the *H*'s, and Yoda and Emma are blowing through the data in the cloud. None of us sees a single red flag, and, like you, I doubt we will. My gut tells me this is a colossal waste of time."

"Yeah, but it still has to be done," Casey replied. "Because otherwise, I'm drawing a blank. Unless..." She paused. "I threw something out at the cops when they questioned me. It hit me out of the blue, and now I'm wondering if it could be true. Do you think Hillington could have been reaching out to me for help rather than accusation? I have no idea what help he'd be seeking, but is it worth looking into?"

Marc was already on board. "Definitely. It surely makes more sense than the alternative. We need to pursue that lead."

"I agree. We have to decide how. In the interim, I took another step. If you remember, Angela King said she wanted to meet me for a drink later to talk. We have to find some common ground to put even the most basic pieces together. I have to try to acquire more details on Hillington's alleged crime and imminent arrest. I think that my meeting her in a public place is a bad idea. If we're seen together, it'll raise all kinds of questions. So I invited her to the brownstone at five p.m. That should give her enough time to free herself up."

Marc pursed his lips and nodded. "I think that's wise. Was she amenable?"

"Very. Frankly, she sounded pretty frazzled. This is an unusual set of circumstances for us all. We're treading in unchartered waters."

As she spoke, Patrick rapped his knuckles on the open door and walked in. "I finished a basic personal rundown on Christopher Hillington. Is it a good time to go over it?"

Casey signaled for Patrick to take a seat. "Never better. What have you got?"

"I'll skip over his history—his childhood, his inheritance, how he made his additional millions, etc. etc. We'll circle back to that later, along with all the enemies I'm sure he made along the way, and the details attached to the hit-and-run, most of which I'm assuming you've already accessed. Right now, here are the important personal essentials. For starters, Hillington was five foot ten and weighed one hundred eighty-two pounds. We can use that data later to narrow down the identity of his killer. He left behind his wife of twenty-eight years, Charlotte, and their three grown children: Ashley, Brighton, and Lily—twenty-six, twenty-five, and twenty-two, respectively. The best education and subsequent lifestyles expected. Charlotte is spearheading the fundraising for four major charities."

Marc arched an irked brow. "Of course she is. The perfect role for the wife of a high-profile, rolling-in-money husband. What do the kids do?"

"Actually, not what you'd expect," Patrick replied. "Ashley is an assistant director and project manager at a small start-up company, Brighton writes music and has put together a band that seems to be taking off, and Lily is a nanny for a local Manhattan family."

Casey took that in with a thoughtful expression. "That doesn't sound like Daddy handed over wads of cash to subsidize them. Maybe he actually instilled in them a work ethic."

"Maybe," Marc said. "That doesn't mean any or all of them wouldn't love to get a piece of Hillington's fortune—ahead of time."

Patrick nodded his agreement. "Which, of course, points first to Charlotte—assuming her husband's will gives the majority of the estate to her."

"You never know the inner workings of a marriage," Casey answered dryly. "I wouldn't assume anything. What we *can* assume is that they're all at the top of the NYPD's questioning list." She gave a sarcastic laugh. "Although I'm willing to bet the cops grilled me before they did any of them."

"I've just touched the tip of the iceberg," Patrick said. "I wanted to give us a foundation to start with."

"Casey has another theory we need to discuss," Marc added. He filled Patrick in.

Patrick cocked his head as he considered what Marc was saying. "That's a solid thought. If it's true, it changes the entire focus of our investigation. Let me start looking into it."

"Thanks." Casey drank the rest of her muddied coffee and took a lackluster bite of her turkey sandwich. "I'm going to keep at what I'm doing for as long as I can stand it. Although I'd much rather be analyzing Christopher Hillington. It's the only way to determine the real reason he wrote my name as he died. Hopefully, Angela King will be willing to part with some info. After that, it'll all be on us."

A corner of Marc's mouth lifted. "Which one of us is going to be the hacker? Because I volunteer. I've hung out enough with Ryan. I'm pretty good at this."

Patrick looked relieved. He hated to blatantly break the law. "I think that's a good idea."

"So do I." Casey gave Patrick an understanding nod. "This definitely isn't in your comfort zone. It also isn't up my alley. And it certainly isn't Emma's forte."

"That's why I volunteered," Marc replied. He was clearly enjoying his new role. "Ryan introduced me to the dark web and showed me a few of his hacking tricks. Let's see what I can do—after Casey speaks with Angela. I might as well have as many facts as I can before I do my damage."

\*\*\*

*Fordham University*
*Gabelli School of Business, Rose Hill Campus*
*Bronx, New York*
*Monday, 4:15 p.m.*

Morgan Evans slid behind the wheel of her Jeep Wrangler and pulled her phone out of her backpack. She'd barely had a minute to breathe. Finals were right around the corner, and her courses this year were tough. She'd coasted through her freshman year, but as a sophomore, the courses were harder and the expectations were higher. So she'd spent most of her time either studying in the school library or locked in her room at home, buried behind her computer. That left precious little talk time with her mom, and, corny or not, she was still Morgan's best friend.

On that thought, Morgan tapped her mom's name in her iPhone favorites and waited.

Natalie Evans answered on the second ring.

"Hi, honey. Everything okay?"

"Fine," Morgan assured her. "I'm on my way home. I was hoping we could grab a pizza together. I could pick it up on my way home. It's been ages since we've had a good old-fashioned talk-and-eat evening. I miss you."

Natalie's voice got watery. "I miss you, too. And, yes, tonight would be perfect. It'll be healthy to put aside our respective workloads for one night. You've been going at it nonstop, and I'm bleary-eyed from reading my eighth graders' projects."

Morgan frowned. "You sound stuffy and exhausted. Are you getting sick?"

"Nope." Natalie's tone brightened. "Just overworked and worn out from grading. Now, hurry home with that pizza."

"On my way."

*★★

*Evans residence*
*210 Alameda Avenue*
*Douglaston, Queens, New York*
*Monday, 4:25 p.m.*

Natalie ended her call with Morgan and returned to what she'd been doing—looking at the last photo of her and Jonathan together. He'd been a wealthy orthopedic surgeon, and they'd lived in an opulent home in Great Neck. His death three years ago had come out of nowhere—a fatal heart attack from a man who'd never been sick a day in his life. Natalie had been numb, and Morgan had been a wreck. Only now were they slowly putting back together the pieces of their lives.

Jonathan had left Natalie very well off, and, given that it was now just her and Morgan, she'd chosen to sell the mansion and moved to a costly but definitely less opulent brick and clapboard house in Douglaston.

With tears sliding down her cheeks, Natalie put down the framed picture and reopened the photo album on her lap. It was very slim, and she went slowly through it, her heart tightening more with each passing page.

Finally, she shut the album and returned it to the locked drawer in her dresser.

She knelt down beside it, and her shoulders quaked as she sobbed her heart out.

Everything she'd hoped for and planned for was gone. And, other than Morgan, she was completely alone.

***

*Offices of Forensic Instincts*
*Small Conference Room, First Floor*
*Tribeca, New York*
*Monday, 5:10 p.m.*

Casey and Angela sat across from one another, sipping at their cups of coffee. The tray of small sandwiches sat, uneaten, on the glass coffee table. Each woman was determined to meet her agenda, and each had already formulated a strategy to do so.

Casey went for the element of surprise.

"Shall I go first?" she asked, setting down her cup and saucer.

Angela's brows rose, and she did the same. She looked surprised, but wary. "Go ahead."

"I think we've already established that, in this matter, we're not adversaries. You're stymied, I'm stymied, and we're both in search of information."

"I'd have to agree with that."

"Good." Casey nodded. "Because we have to figure out what's going on here. You and your firm's reputation are on the line. Your client, who was about to be charged with a serious crime, has now been murdered. The police—and the media—are dying to know if there's a connection between the two. Which puts your firm, and primarily you, under the microscope—in the worst possible way."

"True. But your entire life is on the line," Angela shot back. "You're looking at a potential prison sentence and the end of Forensic Instincts."

Casey didn't argue. "So our goals are the same. Figure out who killed Christopher Hillington and if the murder was connected to his imminent arrest. One-upping each other would only slow down the process."

"Agreed."

"Let me start by thanking you for showing me the crime scene in advance. It prepared me for what was to come. As you saw, I was stunned. Let me assure you that I never met Christopher Hillington before. Never had a case that involved him, even peripherally. I don't have the slightest idea of why he wrote my name on that desk."

She held up her palm to silence what she knew Angela was about to claim: that Casey had, in fact, told her nothing.

"That said, I'll also tell you that the police were here. They did a thorough job of grilling me. I had to contact my attorneys to shut them down. Clearly, they're suspicious of me, and I can't blame them, given the circumstances. As a result, there was no wriggling out of being a suspect." Casey spread her hands wide. "I'm literally clueless. Anything you can share with me would be greatly appreciated."

"Nothing you just said comes as a surprise. I assume you have your team investigating to the best of their ability?"

"You assume correctly."

Angela sighed. "There's very little I can share with you since my attorney-client privilege survives death."

Casey pursed her lips. She couldn't argue that point. "You're a defense attorney, yet I get the feeling that your professional relationship with Christopher Hillington was longstanding."

"Harris, Porter, & Donnelly represents all of Christopher's interests. We have for many years."

"And his wife's and children's?"

Angela looked Casey directly in the eyes. "As I said, my firm handles all of Christopher's legal matters."

Casey got the message. Charlotte's personal attorney was not employed by Harris, Porter, & Donnelly. Was the marriage estranged? Or had the Hillingtons always kept their legal counsel separate from one another's? And if the former were true, did Charlotte have a motive to kill her husband? For money, perhaps? That was something FI would have to dig deeply into—even more thoroughly than the police, who had undoubtedly questioned Charlotte Hillington as well as the three children.

Instead, Casey chose a different subject.

"Other than the news blips and blog suppositions I've read on my own, is there anything you can share with me about the vehicular homicide case your client is suspect in—suspect enough to be on the verge of arrest?" Again, Casey held up a palm. "Not the evidence the prosecutor has, or your defense strategy. Something personal—such as your opinion of your client's guilt? Normally, that's something a defense attorney never asks, not even of their client. Obviously, Mr. Hillington—Christopher—claimed to be innocent. What did you think? And you have my word that anything you say will remain between us."

Angela arched a brow. "Between us, or between me and the entire FI team?"

"Does it matter?"

"Yes. You're a suspect with her life on the line. They're not."

"Very well." Casey nodded. "Between you and me, then."

Angela slowly sipped her coffee, then set down the cup. "Christopher was a shrewd and brilliant businessman. He'd do whatever it took to protect his empire. But killing a man and fleeing from the scene? I don't believe he would do that."

"Even if he were speeding and intent on getting away from an area in Queens he'd have no reason to frequent?"

Angela's lips twisted in annoyance. "Now you're fishing."

"Touché," Casey returned, registering the fact that Angela knew very well why Hillington was in such a hurry and why he was in Queens to begin with.

"There's nothing more I can say," Angela concluded.

"I have something to say: Hire us."

Angela's chin shot up. "What?"

"Hire us," Casey repeated. "It's not a reach. Law firms the size of yours have quality investigators they turn to for help. Not only regular hires, but outside ones, as well. We're the best there is. So bring us in and we can pool our resources—legally and ethically."

Angela's lips twitched. "That's not only a lofty idea but a big surprise. Congratulations. I'm not often surprised."

Casey didn't answer, waiting for Angela to consider her option.

"Pooling our resources is a reach. Our investigators are required to turn over all their findings to us. That doesn't apply reciprocally," she reminded Casey.

"I'm aware of that. But I'm sure you'll see that it's in your firm's best interest to bend that rule as things unfold. If not, that's FI's problem, not yours."

Angela tipped her head in acknowledgment. "You're convinced you can solve this crime without our confidential input."

"I am," Casey replied. "Not only this crime, but Christopher's murder, as well. We'll provide you with all you need, plus exonerate me in the process."

Angela's wheels were turning. "The police have already questioned me and my firm exhaustively. Theoretically, there's no reason for us to reveal that we've hired you."

"None at all."

Slowly, Angela rose from her seat. "You drive a hard and an intriguing bargain, Casey Woods. Let me bring it to the partners at my firm. I'll get back to you as soon as we've discussed this and come to a decision."

"Do it quickly," Casey said, rising as well. "The clock is ticking."

# 5

*Offices of Harris, Porter, & Donnelly*
*Sixth Avenue, Fourteenth Floor*
*Midtown Manhattan*
*Tuesday, 9:30 a.m.*

Kristine Barrow was taking her turn manning the mahogany reception desk just inside the glass doors. It was all part of paying her dues if she wanted to walk in here one day with the title "Esquire" alongside her name. She'd been employed at the firm as a part-time paralegal for a little over a year now. Finally, she was finishing up her senior year at NYU, and studying furiously for her LSATs. She was determined to be a lawyer—and a great one—right here at Harris, Porter, & Donnelly.

Now, she was bent over her work, thinking that Contracts Law was definitely meant to kill her.

She looked up as the front door opened.

A tall, striking woman in her early- to midfifties stepped in, glanced around, and then approached the desk. She looked distinctly familiar to Kristine, although she couldn't quite place her. Expensively dressed, she was, no doubt, one of their clients.

The woman looked around hesitantly, and Kristine could see her eyes were puffy from crying, and that, beneath her expertly applied makeup, she had deep circles under her eyes.

"May I help you?" Kristine asked.

The woman wet her lips with the tip of her tongue. "I hope so. My name is Charlotte Hillington. My husband is…was…Christopher Hillington. I need to speak to whichever of our attorneys handles our trusts and estates, but I see your firm has three floors, and I'm not sure if I'm on the right one."

Kristine came to her feet as soon as she realized who she was speaking to.

"Mrs. Hillington, I'm so terribly sorry for your loss," she said with sincere compassion. "My name is Kristine Barrow, and, yes, you're in the right place. Trusts and estates are handled on this floor in the rear offices over there." She pointed. "Which attorney would you like to speak with?"

A rueful expression. "Truthfully? I'm not sure. Christopher handled all our legal matters. I did try to reach Angela King, both for her defense counsel and so she could steer me in the right direction for the attorney who handles our wills, but she was in a meeting and couldn't be disturbed. So I'm relying on you to help me."

"Of course." Kristine gestured at the large empty conference room to her left—all carved mahogany, with a dozen cushioned chairs situated around the table. She led Mrs. Hillington inside.

"Please have a seat," she said. "Can I get you some coffee or tea? I'll take care of it right away, and then look into the information you need."

Charlotte waved away her offer. "Thank you, but I'm fine. I'd like to meet with our attorney as soon as possible."

"I'll make that happen right away." After ensuring Mrs. Hillington was comfortable, she hurried down the long corridor, stopping at the cluster of offices with the gold plate over them that read: *Trusts and Estates*. Without pause, she walked up to the door of the largest office—the one belonging to William Donnelly, the named partner who handled this branch of legal work for their most prominent clients.

She knocked.

There was a quiet moment, after which he called, "Come in."

Kristine stepped inside and shut the door behind her. Mr. Donnelly had clearly been researching something important, because he'd been buried behind his computer and looked less than pleased about being interrupted. But Kristine had found him to be a decent man—one who wouldn't bark at her to go away without knowing the reason for her appearance.

He simply studied her from behind tortoiseshell glasses, his eyebrows raised. "Yes, Ms. Barrow? What can I do for you?"

She swallowed hard. "I apologize for interrupting," she began, "but we have a visitor who wants to speak to her trusts and estates attorney. She wasn't sure who that was, and I wasn't sure how to handle the situation without offending her, given that she's Charlotte Hillington."

Mr. Donnelly was clearly surprised. "Charlotte Hillington is here? I don't understand. She's not a client of the firm."

"She thinks she is. She wants to speak to both Angela King and her trusts and estates attorney. Will you speak to her?"

He gave a resigned sigh. "Of course. Please show her down."

With a murmured thank you, Kristine retraced her steps, returning a few moments later with their client's widow.

"Mrs. Hillington." Mr. Donnelly extended his hand and shook hers. "I'm William Donnelly. It's a pleasure to meet you. Won't you please have a seat?" As he spoke, he glanced at Kristine. "Thank you, Ms. Barrow. I'll take it from here."

He didn't have to tell Kristine twice. She was leaving the room, quietly shutting the door behind her as she heard Charlotte Hillington return the greeting and invite Mr. Donnelly to call her by her given name.

It was a good thing she didn't succumb to office gossip, because this was as juicy as it got.

\*\*\*

Inside the office, Charlotte eased into a leather chair, crossed one slim leg over the other, and waited.

William sidestepped his desk, seating himself in an adjacent chair so as not to make this meeting more formal and uncomfortable than it had to be.

"Let me begin by offering my deepest sympathies," he said.

"I appreciate that. Thank you." Even though she was visibly shaken, Charlotte pushed on to broach the subject she'd come here to address.

"Mr. Donnelly, I'll be frank. The police have questioned me. It's no surprise that the wife is always the first suspect when her wealthy husband is killed. I reached out to Angela King separately to discuss my representation, should I require it. She has yet to return my call. But, in the interim, I'd like to schedule a reading of Christopher's will. Not because I'm in desperate need of money, since Christopher and I also have a joint savings account, which he fed so I had more than enough money to take care of myself and run the household, but because I want this resolved. I know he provided well for me and our children, as well as other family members and charities—extensively, given that he was already a very rich man before he and I even met, thanks to the large inheritance left to him by his grandfather.

"Obviously, that wealth has grown in leaps and bounds," she continued. "His assets have increased and become more complex over the years, so he must have updated his will. The sooner we take this step, the sooner I'll stop looking like a money-hungry murderess."

Donnelly's brows knit. While he admired Charlotte's bravado and logical argument, he was totally confused as to where it was coming from.

Had Christopher kept her so much in the dark?

Evidently, the answer was yes.

The attorney cleared his throat. Unpleasant as this was about to become, he had no choice but to provide her with a portion of the truth.

"Mrs. Hillington—Charlotte—you're correct about Christopher making changes. One of those changes was to transfer all his legal matters, both personal and professional, to our firm—including his will."

"He told me as much. That's why I'm here. And why I'm reaching out to Angela King."

Again, Donnelly cleared his throat. Christopher might have told her a partial truth, but she was about to be hit with a bombshell.

"Apparently, there's an unfortunate misunderstanding here," he said. "Your husband transferred only *his* legal matters to us. As a result, you're not a client of the firm."

Charlotte did a double take. "Excuse me?"

"I apologize for having to tell you this, although I am surprised you haven't been informed. An oversight, I'm sure."

Indignation and embarrassment reddened Charlotte's cheeks and made her spine stiffen. "You must be mistaken."

"Sadly, I'm not."

"You're telling me that my will is still with the small law firm on the Lower East Side where we originally executed it? Salick and Wesson?"

"I'm assuming as much, since that's the law firm that forwarded Christopher's last will and testament to us." Donnelly was beginning to wish he were anywhere other than here, having this conversation.

"But Christopher told me—" Charlotte broke off, clearly thinking back over the conversation she'd had with her husband and what precisely he had said. "Naturally I assumed he meant…" Again, she stopped, then rose, stiff-backed, to her feet. "I apologize for troubling you. It's obvious I need to talk to our—*my*—attorney. Then he can arrange the will reading with you."

This was going to be the most difficult part.

Again, Donnelly swallowed and said what had to be said. "You should also know that recently Christopher signed a letter stipulating that his will not be read until specific criteria has been met. So the reading will be delayed."

Now, Charlotte's eyes blazed. "What letter? When did this happen?"

"I'm not at liberty to discuss specifics, but it is indeed the case. I myself handled all the details related to it."

"Enough!" Charlotte held up a restraining palm. "You'll be hearing from my attorney today."

Donnelly nodded. If Charlotte Hillington were unaware of this much, she clearly had no idea that her husband had executed a new last will and testament—one she would definitely *not* be happy with.

# 6

Casey had been pacing the floors all morning. When the phone finally rang with the message "caller blocked," she knew who it was. She hid her relief, and answered calmly. The news from Angela was good. Casey had the go-ahead to set things in motion—with the reminder that the whole FI team would be closely monitored and that daily updates were to be supplied.

Casey acknowledged that, hung up, and immediately called a team meeting.

"I just heard back from Angela King," she said as the team gathered around the table. Her lips twisted in annoyance. "Of course she took her sweet time getting back to me, even though I'm sure her firm jumped right on this, but making me wait was her chance to make me sweat. Which, frankly, I was starting to do."

"She said yes." Marc's comment was more a statement than a question.

Casey nodded. "We're officially on their payroll—although we'll be watched like hawks and expected to give them daily reports."

"We'll take that with a grain of salt and skew it as we need to," Marc said with an offhanded shrug.

"Yup," Casey agreed.

Patrick bent one leg and crossed it over the other. "I realize we've got to concentrate on solving the whole hit-and-run and determining whether or not Hillington was guilty, but, most important, we've got to figure out if Hillington truly was reaching out to Casey for help and, if so, why? Because I believe that's the thing that's going to exonerate her."

Marc pursed his lips. "The two things could be related—or not. We'll be doing comprehensive research on everything to do with Hillington—in all facets of his life—jumping on anything that so much as smells. You're on this, too, Yoda."

"Naturally." Yoda's response was purely matter-of-fact.

"I appreciate that," Casey said with a frown. "But we can't all be part of that techno-hunt. I'll lose my mind. I need to be *doing* something."

"Agreed," Marc replied. "Leave the online research to Yoda and me, with Patrick following up on our leads. Case, you and Emma need to be boots on the ground, starting with the obvious suspects."

"Hillington's wife and kids," Emma murmured.

"Yes." Casey's wheels were spinning. "The problem is we can't let them know who we are. We have to approach them from a different and unrelated angle."

She snapped her fingers and whipped open her laptop. "Let's probe the four charities that Charlotte Hillington spearheads. Maybe we can find a significant event coming up for one of them—something she simply can't wiggle out of attending, despite the fact that she's in mourning."

"Or one that she doesn't want to wiggle out of." Marc was typing as fast as Casey was. "It's possible that she picked these charities for a reason other than just being a highly visible showcase. She might feel passionately about one or more of them. And if any of those is holding a major event in the immediate future—that's our way in."

Emma was beginning to grin. "And once inside, Casey and I will approach Charlotte under false pretenses and establish a rapport with her. Not sure what yet, but false pretense is my middle name."

"You can't raise any flags at this first meeting," Marc warned, taking the wind out of Emma's sails. "It's way too soon. Charlotte is either really or seemingly in mourning. It would be too telling, and too disrespectful to approach her aggressively. That can come later."

"Agreed," Patrick said.

Casey was still typing, her brow furrowed. "We need to flesh out more about Charlotte, not just her favorite charities. After which, Emma and I will be on."

"Yes!" Emma punched the air.

"There's a significant chunk of info showing up here," Casey murmured. "Marc, you continue with the research into Charlotte's charities. I'm concentrating on Charlotte herself."

"Done." Marc began digging deeper into the four charities on his list.

Time passed. Marc had long since finished his task.

At last, Casey sat back, scanning the full amount of data she'd just dug up. "Wow, I've got a lot here—more than enough for Emma and me to act on. Marc, what have you got?"

"All the charities she heads involve women's causes. One in particular must be close to home because it's called the Suzanne Allerman Foundation. And since that's not a name I've ever heard, I'm assuming it's someone who's a part of Charlotte's life."

"*Was* a part of her life," Casey corrected him. "Suzanne Allerman was Charlotte's best friend. She died many years ago."

"Go on," Marc urged.

Casey complied. "Prior to marrying Christopher, Charlotte was a young, beautiful, and successful model. She left her career when she and Christopher married, which was when she was twenty-two and he was twenty-five. Evidently, Suzanne was also a model. She died of a stroke five years after Charlotte's wedding. Her death was declared a methamphetamine overdose."

"To keep herself at a size zero," Emma muttered. "Modeling is a brutal profession. It was even worse decades ago before plus-size models even existed. You were stick-thin or your career was over."

Casey nodded. "As a result, Charlotte's most personally funded charity, the Suzanne Allerman Foundation, is dedicated to women's eating disorders."

"That fits our agenda perfectly," Marc said. "There's a large Manhattan fundraising dinner for that charity in two days at the Pierre's Regency Room."

Emma's eyes widened. "The Pierre? Wow, talk about extravagant."

"No surprise," Casey replied, then turned back to Marc. "I know that's only two days away, but can you get Emma's and my names on the guest list?"

"Fictitious names," Marc qualified. "And yeah, I think I can manage that."

"Excellent. Could you also get into the charity's monetary database and enter a healthy contribution, backdating it to, say, six months ago?"

Marc looked thoughtful. "You want to make it appear as if you've been supporters of Charlotte's charity all along."

"Exactly," Casey replied. "And we won't need to fabricate a company if Emma and I introduce ourselves as wealthy sisters who believe in Charlotte's cause, and who have donated to it in the past. We'll have some personal connection to it—I'll come up with what that is—but we need to insert at least one contribution that was made recently."

Marc blew out a breath. "I'm afraid all this is above my pay grade."

A pointed silence hung in the air.

"No," Casey said, slicing the air with her palm as she dispelled the notion they were all entertaining. "We're not calling Ryan. Forget it. We'll have to find another way."

"Like what?" Emma asked. "If Marc can't do it…"

"Let me call Aidan," Marc interrupted. "He'll put Terri on it. This will be child's play for her, and Aidan will make sure it's number-one priority when he hears the person we're doing this for is Casey."

Aidan Devereaux was Marc's older brother. A former Marine captain, Aidan was a genius who'd spent his overseas military career specializing in communications and intelligence. During that time, he'd been fortunate enough to meet and to work with three other uniquely talented, stand-out professionals, all of whom had later become his core team in the Zermatt Group—a covert, international investigative firm. Their combined skill set consisted of leadership, information technology skills, investigative abilities, even the assessment of human personalities and capabilities. They each had their day jobs, but Zermatt was their true passion.

Terri Underwood, Aidan's right hand, was a former NSA analyst and a sought-after computer security consultant. She could handle anything IT related. In fact, she and Ryan had worked together in the past, when FI and the Zermatt Group had joined forces, and there was almost nothing she couldn't do.

"Are Aidan and Terri home in the Big Apple?" Casey asked Marc.

"Yup. I talked to Aidan yesterday. He and his team all returned to their respective countries and homes last week, having completed their latest international venture."

Casey heaved a sigh of relief. "If you're sure that he and Terri won't mind."

"Only one way to find out." Marc rose from the table and walked off toward a corner of the room. The FI team understood that, given the secrecy under which the Zermatt Group operated, all calls between

Marc and Aidan were confidential. Even Marc was privy to only so much, most of which he'd learned when he and Aidan worked together on that same case as Ryan had—only far more intensively.

The FI team folded their hands and waited.

Marc whipped out his cell phone and made the call. Not five minutes later, he hung up and rejoined the group.

"Done," he said. "Aidan will need full details, but he's all in."

Casey heaved another sigh of relief. "Thank you so much. And thank Aidan, as well."

"You can thank him yourself," Marc replied. "He and Terri are swinging by here within the hour to be brought up to speed. I just gave him an overview. We'll all figure out every way they can help us to help you."

***

Forty-five minutes later, Aidan and Terri arrived.

They were announced by Yoda and led into the conference room by Emma, who still looked at Aidan with a kind of hero worship. She'd played a small part in that same joint investigation that Marc and Ryan had—enough to realize the enormity of Aidan's intelligence and his reach.

He and Marc looked enough alike for people to immediately guess they were brothers—tall, powerfully built, with a commanding presence. But Aidan's eyes were round and dark blue, while Marc's were brown and slightly narrowed at the edges, favoring his mother's side of the family. And as reserved and private as Marc was, Aidan came across like a closed book.

"Hey, leatherneck," Marc greeted his brother.

Aidan didn't change expression. "Still need my help, frogman?"

Marc grunted. "Only because Ryan is away. You're second choice."

The brothers were always ribbing each other—Marc being a former Navy SEAL, and Aidan being a former Marine captain.

"Not again," Terri Underwood muttered under her breath.

"Terri's right," Aidan said, shooting Marc a let's-cut-it-out look. "Sounds like we have a lot of work to do. Marc gave me a brief overview, but I'll need more. The situation sounds bad."

He paused to wave a hand, indicating each member of the Forensic Instincts team. "Let's get the introductions out of the way. Terri, meet the FI troops." He introduced them one by one, then turned to Terri. "And this is my right hand, Terri Underwood. She says she's smarter than I am. Sometimes I think she's right."

"I am right." Terri shook each person's hand in turn. "A pleasure to meet you all."

"The pleasure is ours," Casey said. "And I can't thank you enough." Terri was as almost as intimidating as Aidan. She was a formidable woman, almost six feet tall, with dark hair and skin, and an intense, serious expression. She looked a whole lot like Wonder Woman.

Both she and Aidan grabbed a cup of coffee and sat down at the conference room table, leaning forward as they listened to the full details of the current crisis.

Aidan's brows drew together. "We're talking about a serious murder investigation—one that suggests Casey is involved. We've got a lot of ground to cover to prove them wrong, and to solve both this case and, in the process, to determine whether or not Christopher Hillington was guilty of that hit-and-run."

Without pause, Aidan continued. "If Casey is right and Hillington wrote her name because he was asking for her help, could that help be to exonerate him from the crime he was about to be formally charged with—to clear his name for his family's sake?"

That was Aidan. Always keenly assessing, and always straight to the point.

"That's one of the possibilities we were considering," Patrick replied. "Either that or Hillington already feared for his life and wrote Casey's name as he died because he wanted FI to investigate."

"Both viable options," Aidan agreed. "We have our work cut out for us."

"Some of that groundwork will be computer-based and some of it will require face-to-face communication," Terri added.

Casey nodded. "Hacking isn't my thing. I'm all about the in-person angle, starting with talking to Charlotte Hillington at that charity event. I'm hoping to get a read on her and see if she is a viable suspect in killing her husband. Emma will come with me. She's excellent when it comes to impersonation."

"No need to elaborate on that," Aidan responded. "I've seen Emma do her thing firsthand. She's impressive."

Emma beamed at the rare compliment.

"I know where you're headed with step one," Terri said. "But making a natural introduction to Charlotte is going to require more than just creating fictitious names. You'll need identities to go with those names, and backdated contributions to her charity."

"We were just discussing that," Casey replied. "Any chance you can help us? This is usually Ryan's area of expertise."

As Terri nodded, Aidan asked, "Speaking of which, when are Romeo and Juliet returning from Maui?"

"They just left on Sunday. They won't be home for another thirteen days." Marc looked grim. "That's way too long to let this fester."

"Agreed," Aidan said. "We've got to divvy up jobs here and now. Without organization, we'll all be stepping on each other's toes."

Both teams spent the next half hour brainstorming, capitalizing on each person's strengths in order to work most expediently while maximizing results. In the end, they nailed down a game plan, one that had to be fluid depending on how each step went.

Terri's first task would be to create fictitious names and a solid backstory for Casey and Emma. At the same time, she'd get into the charity's database and insert a few past contributions.

Simultaneously, Aidan would check out Christopher's business after some solid hacking from Terri. He had "ins" with businesses that Christopher was either working with or had screwed over. The end goal was to extrapolate an enemies-made list.

Casey and Emma would be the in-person investigative team, talking to Charlotte and hopefully her kids.

"That's all phase one," Aidan concluded. "Phase two will be probing the hit-and-run."

"Leave that to Patrick and me," Marc said. "We'll do the necessary recon as well as the research."

"Give me a couple of days to work with Aidan," Terri replied. "Then I'll come back here and hack into the NYPD database for you. Once I'm in and I've made avenues into what you need, you'll be all set. As for the recon, that's all on you."

Marc and Patrick nodded.

"Then we're done here—for now," Aidan said. "We'll communicate and reconvene as necessary."

"How's Abby?" Emma asked as Aidan pushed back his chair and rose.

Aidan's expression softened in the way it only did when he spoke of his daughter. He'd had no idea of her conception or existence until Social Services had placed her in his arms when her mother died. And he hadn't had the first clue how to be a father.

He'd learned on the job. And he'd fallen more in love with his precocious little girl every day.

"She's great," he answered. "In kindergarten, believe it or not. Still a whirlwind of energy, and with a more active social life than all of ours combined. It's one birthday party after another, so Joyce is perpetually in toy stores or on Amazon buying gifts. She's a wonder."

Aidan was referring to Joyce Reynolds, Abby's middle-aged nanny, who took care of Abby when Aidan was traveling or working and missing his little tornado. Joyce cooked, straightened up the apartment, and accompanied Abby to school and to all her other activities and play dates. She also spent many an overnight or a late night in the guest room as needed. She had twenty years of experience, an enormously long fuse, and a genuine fondness for her little charge. She was a lifesaver.

Now, Aidan gave a totally fabricated scowl. "Of course, I'm the one who's coerced into dressing up like everything from a princess to a dinosaur."

"Did you take photos?" Marc asked, a flash of something crossing his face before amusement took over. "Because I'd pay a fortune to see them."

"Nope, although Abby's tried. But it wouldn't do much for my image."

Casey began to laugh, although she was puzzled by that brief expression that had flickered across Marc's face. She knew how much he adored his little niece, and he usually beamed when he spoke of her.

She tucked the observation away for later.

"I'd pay more than that," she teased Aidan, actually grateful for this brief moment of levity. "Captain Devereaux, ruler of the dino kingdom and princess extraordinaire. Do the outfits actually fit you?"

Aidan stared her down. "Not my size. I drape them over my head and to my shoulders. That's as good as it gets."

This time he sidestepped the chair, prepping to leave. Terri did the same.

"I miss Abby," Emma said in parting. Much of her assignment in the shared case was to babysit Abby in Disneyland. She was half-dead when the assignment came to an end, but had established a warm bond with her little charge. "I'd love to see her again."

"Be careful what you wish for," Aidan warned. "But I promise to bring her by soon."

"We'll batten down the hatches," Casey promised.

"Yeah, well, it won't be happening before we resolve things and get you out of trouble—or danger."

"Danger," Casey murmured.

It wasn't as if she hadn't entertained the thought that whoever had killed Hillington had seen the photos of her blood-smeared name on the desk, labeled her a threat, and put her on his victim list. Hutch had warned her of the same possibility. She'd just shoved it away, concentrating on the facts and not the suppositions.

But it was the first time that the reality had been bluntly voiced aloud. And somehow, coming from Aidan made it all the more chilling.

"Stop ostriching, Casey," Marc stated flatly, reading her expression. "It's a definite risk, and you know it. Keeping you safe will be high on our list. Accept it."

Casey shot him a dark look. "Yes, boss."

"I've already assigned John to be your security coverage," Patrick told Casey in a more respectful tone. Only Marc could get away with speaking to her the way he just had.

John Nickels, the security guard who'd promptly driven Casey to Hillington's murder scene, was a long-term part of the team, and as good as they came. He was well over six feet with the body of a linebacker. He'd served the NYPD in the homicide department for twenty-five years before retiring, at which point Patrick had snatched him up for FI.

"John's our best. Isn't that overkill?" Casey asked.

"Nope," Patrick replied. "And I'm working on assigning his backup. It'll all be in place by tomorrow."

"Good," Aidan said with an adamant nod. "Now let's get moving."

# 7

Emma readjusted the contours of her pale blue cocktail dress for the fifth time. She felt like a total fish out of water.

"It'll take a miracle to keep me from wiggling around in this dress," she muttered.

Casey slipped on her designer pumps and stood up. Her formal black suit jacket with a swirling chiffon skirt was a knockout. "That's why I had us get dressed early. Plenty of time to get comfortable."

Emma's gaze swept Casey and she frowned. "You don't need any time. You look amazing. This isn't new to you either. To me, this is like being dropped in a foreign country."

"You're the fastest learner I know," Casey replied, reapplying a touch of mascara. "I'm not the least bit worried about that part."

Emma heard the emphasis on "that part" loud and clear and rolled her eyes. "But after a whole day of playing Eliza Doolittle in *My Fair Lady*, you're still concerned about my pulling this off."

"Not concerned," Casey corrected her. "Just hopeful that we had enough time to prepare."

"Enough time?" Emma asked incredulously.

"Yup. This was more than just a physical makeover."

Casey had spent the entire day taking Emma under her wing and teaching her basic lessons in reading people, their body language, and their "tells."

"Remember, consider yourself my student and me your mentor," she'd said repeatedly. "You have a natural aptitude for some of this, but you've got to up your game. No exclamations or outbursts, no expressions of wonder. Just low-key conversation. Act pleased, not exuberant. Concentrate on what you see and hear, not on your reactions. Tamp that part down. You're allegedly in your element and you have to act like it, while at the same time focusing on the vibes you pick up on."

Emma had sighed. "Okay, Casey. I know I'm not Claire. But after six hours—with a fifteen-minute break to stuff a yogurt down my throat—I really get it." She saw the flicker of annoyance in Casey's eyes and backed off. "I appreciate all the instruction, honestly. I won't let you down."

Casey looked appeased. "I know you won't—Madison."

Terri had given them their fictitious names. Madison and Hannah Ellers. Each name was a popular one during the decades that the two women had been born—the later 1980s and the late 1990s, respectively.

Their Terri-generated father, George Ellers, had been both a widower and an affluent businessman who'd left them a sizable trust when he passed away. Ten months later, they'd lost their dear cousin Jessica, who was the only family they had left other than each other. Jessica's death was ruled an accidental overdose, which didn't shock them but it did devastate them. Jessica had spent all of her adult life desperately fighting to shrink her slightly-above-average weight to an unhealthy below-normal size through any means possible. More than aware of Jessica's downward spiral, Hannah and Madison had tried everything from dragging her to the doctor and then to a therapist, to force-feeding her. Jessica had disregarded the doctor's advice, skipped her therapy sessions, and continued to eat like a bird and then to vomit up the food. Nothing worked, and her body finally just gave out.

Hannah and Madison were still in mourning. So when they'd stumbled upon Charlotte's charity, they were eager to use their inheritance to support others who were enduring the same agony that Jessica had.

Their three sizable backdated contributions to the Suzanne Allerman Foundation, together with additional hacking by Marc and Terri, had easily gotten them invites to tonight's gala.

Now, Casey glanced at her watch. "It's showtime."

***

*Pierre Hotel*
*2 East Sixty-First Street at Fifth Avenue*
*Manhattan, New York*
*Thursday, 7:25 p.m.*

The invitation had called for seven p.m., so Hannah and Madison Ellers were fashionably late.

They rode up to the second floor of the lavish Pierre Hotel until they got to the Regency Room. Inside, a large number of elegant, affluent people glided around the room, mingling with others whom they obviously knew from inner circle events. Also attending was a handful of less affluent guests who were not decked out in designer dresses and suits, but who were talking fervently about charity events to the others. It wasn't hard for Casey to determine that they were the boots-on-the-ground contributors, rather than those who showed their support through sizable investments.

Casey, aka Hannah, approached the front table and the attractive blonde woman who was handling the list of attendees.

"Good evening," she said in a friendly but low-key tone. "We're Hannah and Madison Ellers." With that, she waited.

The woman's smile was as plastic as a recyclable. "Good evening. Give me a moment." She scanned her computer and nodded.

"Welcome," she said, handing them each a name badge. "Enjoy your evening."

"Thank you," Casey replied.

And just like that, she and Emma were inside.

They immediately scanned the crowd, getting a more in-depth feel for the attendees, then scoping the room until they found the person they were most interested in talking to—Charlotte Hillington.

She was quite easy to locate, given the number of guests seeking her attention. She looked just like her online photo—slim, strikingly attractive, her hair in a dark updo with wisps brushing her cheeks. She was "done," but despite her makeup and her obvious show of being a gracious hostess, there were deep circles under her overly bright eyes and fine lines of tension around her mouth.

She was either truly in mourning, or doing a hell of a job faking it.

Emma's gaze shifted, first to the left and then to the right. "Pay dirt," she muttered under her breath. "Charlotte's kids. Ashley, Brighton, and Lily—twenty-six, twenty-five, and twenty-two." She recited what Patrick had told them early on. "They're all here. I recognize them from their social media pics."

"Where?" Casey barely moved her lips.

"Ashley is standing about six feet away from her mother, chatting with another guest. Lily and Brighton are at the bar, looking pretty wasted."

Casey nodded, her gaze first focusing on Ashley. She was clearly the team leader, her practiced smile and gracious demeanor a mirror image of her mother's. Definitely a need-to-talk-to. As for the other two... Casey nonchalantly scanned the bar. Emma was right—Lily and Brighton looked a trifle unsteady, each sitting with a fresh drink in their hands and a couple of empty glasses in front of them. Despite their easy banter and subdued laughter, they definitely looked out of their element. Lily occasionally paused to check out what her mother and sister were doing, and Brighton, who didn't so much as acknowledge them, looked as if he wanted to get drunk as fast as possible and then find the nearest exit route.

Reading each of them would be a nice plus, Casey thought.

Before she could voice that to Emma, her alleged "student" was on the move. "I know you want to talk to Charlotte. Ashley would be a good add. Meanwhile, I'll go over to the bar and find a way to chat up the other two kids. I'm about their ages. I'll get a lot more out of them than you will."

***

*Offices of Forensic Instincts*
*Main Conference Room, Second Floor*
*Tribeca, New York*
*Thursday, 8:20 p.m.*

Marc looked across at Patrick, who was seated at the opposite end of the broad oval table, doing his part in the investigation. As per their strategic arrangement, Patrick would focus on the "aboveboard" research, while Marc would perform the clandestine work—texting Terri as she'd advised him to do when he hit a roadblock.

Even though Marc had soaked up everything Terri had taught him like a sponge—including penetrating the NYPD's firewall—the entirety of the process was new to him. It took him a while to follow her instructions and locate the exact case he needed: the hit-and-run that Christopher was about to be arrested for. True, he and Casey had assembled a thin file on this case, but they'd done so the legal way—reading snippets of news articles and canvassing reputable blog sites. Now, Marc needed to know exactly what the NYPD did.

"Got it," he muttered.

Patrick looked up. "I want to know what you've got—not how you got it."

"Agreed." Marc nodded. "I'll share the data with you."

"Print out the pages," Patrick requested. "I do better with pen and paper. Old school techniques. Just tell me what I need to know and I'll jot down notes."

Patrick had spent thirty-five years as an FBI Violent Crimes investigator, which explained his reluctance for rule-breaking and his more traditional ways of handling things.

Marc didn't argue. He just instructed Yoda to execute the printout, and then relayed the info, watching as Patrick took notes.

Scowling, Patrick shook his head.

"No matter how many times I go over the facts of the case, I don't see how the NYPD can be so certain that Hillington's the guilty party," he told Marc. "Only two digits of the license plate are on record, doubtless due to the rain and fog. When the police did check out Hillington's vehicle, there was no visible damage—an impossibility if the car had been in a full-on collision. So how is that enough evidence to arrest the guy for vehicular homicide?"

"No clue," Marc said with a shrug. "But if the cops kept summoning Hillington for repeated interrogations and yet never actually pressed charges, there has to be more."

Patrick was still studying his notes. "I don't see a viable list of other suspects either. Several drivers who were in the vicinity were questioned on the scene. Nothing they said amounted to anything, so the cops took their contact info and never brought them into the precinct for formal interviews. If I didn't know better, I'd wonder if the cops were out to get Hillington."

Marc frowned, still hunched over his computer. "I'm not finding a reason for that. There's nothing to suggest that there was bad blood between Hillington and the NYPD. In addition, I see no evidence that there was any kind of personal relationship between Frank Vicario and Hillington. Unless Aidan's research turns up something I'm missing."

He paused, studying something he'd just found. "The news leaks were right. The case file has traffic cam video footage showing Vicario's maroon Toyota Camry crunched into a pile of metal, seemingly by a luxury sedan that was speeding and attempting to pass the Camry on the left."

"Seemingly?"

"Let me find it. Maybe that'll supply us with some answers."

Marc poked around for long minutes.

"You're no Ryan," Patrick muttered, glancing at his watch.

"You're right, I'm not." Marc continued what he was doing, ignoring the half-kidding barb. "But I'm getting there… Yes!" He punched the air with his fist. "Got it! Just give me a second and I'll screen-share it with you."

A corner of Patrick's mouth lifted. "The self-congratulations, the air punch—maybe more of Ryan than I realized rubbed off on you."

"I'm not sure if that's an insult or a compliment."

Both men chuckled as they viewed the footage and studied it.

"Okay, so the traffic cam picked up the victim in his car, traveling westbound," Marc stated.

"Yeah, and there's the luxury sedan heading in the same direction and approaching on the left."

Marc expanded the image and peered more closely. "The sedan is a black BMW 760i. But wow, is it hard to make out anything else. A single occupant—the driver—but who can even tell if it's a man or a woman?"

Patrick's brows rose when Marc announced the car's make and model. "I see a black sedan, period," he said. "How can you… Ah, another car show?" The whole team knew about Marc's and his wife Madeleine's hobby of visiting car expos.

"Yup. That's a pretty distinctive-looking car. Hard-edged. Kidney grill. Split headlights. I can pick up on those details even in the dark. I'm assuming one of the police detectives did the same. That plus the two digits of the license plate are more than enough to question Hillington.

There can't be that many 760is with matching digits on the license plate. But to arrest him? No. I see the frame with the battered Toyota, but no frame that shows Hillington's car hitting the Toyota, much less killing the driver. As far as I'm concerned, this is all circumstantial."

"Which would explain why official charges were never filed against Hillington. Still, there's obviously more," Patrick said. "Something we're missing, either from the video or the case file. The NYPD isn't sloppy."

Marc grunted his agreement. "Then whatever they know, we'd better figure it out, and quick."

# 8

*Pierre Hotel*
*2 East Sixty-First Street at Fifth Avenue*
*Manhattan, New York*
*Thursday, 10:00 p.m.*

Casey was fuming as she sipped at her glass of wine and made her way through the room. So much for Emma having heard a word she said. Impulsive to the last, her protégée had taken off like a housedog who'd worked their way out of the leash. The whole roomful of guests, not to mention Charlotte and Ashley, was now Casey's responsibility to assess. Emma would hear about this later—loud and clear.

As luck would have it, Casey's job turned out to be less difficult than expected to carry out. The guests were liquored up and chatty, so conversation was easy. The bad, but unsurprising, part was that, after making the rounds a few times, Casey hadn't picked up the slightest insight into Charlotte. It wasn't out of loyalty; it was out of lack of knowledge. Clearly, Charlotte was a pretty closed book.

Scanning the room, Casey could see that the fundraiser was drawing to a close. The crowd had dwindled down to just a handful of lingering guests.

It was time for the big contact. Charlotte was now mere feet away, the throng of guests who had surrounded her having totally dissipated. She looked relieved to be alone, exhaustion lining her face as she took a sip of her wine. Ashley, who was graciously easing away from the last of the guests, didn't look much better.

Casey sent a quick glance Emma's way, but her supposed protégée was on her third glass of whatever she was drinking, enjoying herself with Brighton and Lily, the three of them tittering away, totally wasted.

Biting back her anger, Casey plastered a smile on her face and approached Charlotte.

"Mrs. Hillington, it's a pleasure to meet you at last." Casey extended her hand, which Charlotte shook, zero recognition in her eyes.

Casey didn't keep her in the dark.

"I'm Hannah Ellers," she said. "My sister, Madison, is at the bar. We're new but enthusiastic supporters of your charity." A shadow slid across Casey's face. "We've suffered a family loss that is painfully similar to the loss of your dear friend. We want to help others by aiding you in your funding. We must bring awareness to this illness, to its roots, and to its consequences."

Exhausted or not, Charlotte forced herself to regain her energy. "It's a pleasure to meet you, although I'm terribly sorry you had to endure the same kind of ordeal as I did. Your contributions are greatly appreciated."

A somewhat automated answer. Still, Casey could tell that Charlotte's wheels were turning, as she doubtless was making a mental note to check out the size of the Ellers sisters' contributions.

"Thank you." Casey gave the tiniest of pauses. "Before we chat, I want to offer our deepest sympathy on your husband's passing. This must be a terrible loss for you."

This time, Charlotte's expression altered to reflect the sadness of a grieving widow. But Casey saw her back stiffen a bit. An odd combination. Was she just erecting a barrier to avoid conversation that would cause her to break down? Or was there some culpability she was determined to hide?

"I appreciate your kind words," Charlotte said. "Christopher's death was both shocking and tragic."

"I'm sure." Casey deliberately avoided getting into details. That would raise a blazing red flag. "It's obvious this charity means a lot to you. To hold a fundraiser like this one must be overwhelmingly difficult at a time like this. You're a strong and admirable woman."

Charlotte sighed. "I feel like anything but. But, thank you."

"We'll be making another sizable donation to the Suzanne Allerman Foundation immediately after this fundraiser," Casey told her, purposely supplying the answers she knew Charlotte was seeking. "Having attended this event, both Madison and I are even more committed to your charity."

Charlotte's face brightened. "I'm very grateful."

As Casey had hoped, Charlotte was visibly warming up to her and viewing her as a cash cow.

Corroborating that theory, Charlotte turned to capture Ashley's eye and signaled her to come over.

Ashley didn't hesitate. She excused herself and walked over to her mother's side with that same practiced smile.

"Ashley, I'd like you to meet Hannah Ellers," Charlotte said. "She and her sister, Madison, are strong supporters of our foundation. Hannah, this is my daughter Ashley. She helps me run the charity. I don't know what I'd do without her."

The women exchanged handshakes. Subtly, Casey studied Ashley. Pretty, poised, and politically correct. Definitely her mother's right hand.

Charlotte went on to explain to Ashley about Hannah's and Madison's own personal loss and their enthusiastic support of the foundation.

Ashley balanced pleasure with sympathy. "I'm so pleased you believe in our charity. However, I'm sorry it came from the loss of a loved one."

"I appreciate that," Casey replied. "We also both extend our sincere condolences after your father's death. You must be in a great deal of pain."

Ashley's reaction was exactly the same as her mother's. Sad and strained. But also stiff and defensive. Was it the need to shield her mother? Or for reasons of her own?

"Having your daughter by your side must be a tremendous relief at this time," Casey said, treading very carefully. "Also a great support system for the charity."

"I'm a very lucky woman," Charlotte replied, proud but distinctly uneasy.

"Ashley, is it just you, or do you have any siblings?" Casey continued, asking a question she already had the answer to in order to steer the conversation in her intended direction.

Ashley's gaze flickered to the bar, a disapproving pucker forming between her brows. "I have a brother, Brighton, and a sister, Lily." Reluctantly, she gestured to the bar with a wave of her hand. "They're over there."

"Our family is very close-knit," Charlotte jumped in defensively.

Casey followed Ashley's gesture, seeing exactly what she'd expected, other than the fact that there was yet another empty glass in front of each of the threesome. "Ah, I see my sister has already met your siblings. They seem to be enjoying themselves."

A look of displeasure shot across Charlotte's face, one that quickly vanished. "Brighton and Lily are taking their father's death very hard. Please excuse their behavior. They're not normally so frivolous when they attend my charity events."

Casey waved away Charlotte's excuse. "No explanation or apology necessary. Clearly, my sister's behavior is no better—and for the same reason. She's still in mourning and looking for something to ease her pain. I'm grateful your children are with her."

Time to end this evening with at least one productive gesture.

Casey retrieved a pen and a small writing pad from her handbag and quickly scribbled down her fake email address.

"We'd like to help with more than just money," she said, handing the piece of paper to Charlotte. "Please stay in touch, and don't hesitate to ask us for anything you need. As soon as you're up for it, let's arrange a Zoom call, when it can just be the four of us. We can discuss the ways in which Madison and I can be of help."

"I think it's an excellent idea," Charlotte replied, glancing down at "Hannah's" information. "And it does me good to be productive. I'll be in touch and we can plan something."

"It's been lovely meeting you both," Casey said. "And good night. I'll be collecting my sister so we can be on our way."

With that, Casey headed for the bar, wondering how she was going to play this, other than to kill Emma when they returned to the brownstone.

\*\*\*

Emma looked up, heavy-lidded, as Casey walked over.

"Hey," she said, her voice slurred. "Did you finish your business? Because I'm just fine here. As things turned out, Brighton and Lily's mother is the head of this fundraiser. Which is cool, because they were doing their duty by being here, and saved me from a night of total boredom." She wiggled her hand in Casey's direction while looking at her companions. "This is my sister, Hannah. Hannah, meet Brighton and Lily Hillington."

"Nice to meet you," Casey managed. "I'm glad you all hit it off."

Brighton pulled himself together long enough to say: "Hi, Hannah." He was not only barely able to sit up, but clearly irritated by having to be here. He was nothing like Ashley, more like a sulky kid who was doing his mother's bidding—and not too well.

Lily, on the other hand, looked embarrassed to be in this inebriated state. Casey read her in a heartbeat—the baby of the family, awed by her mother and sister, and more comfortable with her brother. She probably was well aware of right and wrong, and her instincts told her this was wrong.

"It's good to meet you, Hannah," she said, glancing uneasily over her shoulder to see what her mother was up to. Her drunken flush deepened as she saw her chatting quietly with Ashley, looking wan and eager to go home.

Slowly, Lily slid off her barstool. "The fundraiser's over," she said unsteadily. "I want to check on my mother and help Ashley see her home. Are you coming, Brighton?"

Her brother looked torn. "I'll text you?" he asked Emma hopefully.

"Sure," she replied. "I already texted you my number, remember?" She giggled. "Of course, that was a long time ago. You probably forgot."

As if to confirm what Emma was saying, Brighton took out his phone and checked. "Yeah, I've got it. Sorry."

"No problem," Emma assured him with a sunny smile. "As long as you use it."

Brighton looked like a tail-wagging puppy. "Text you soon."

"Can't wait."

Emma stayed put until Brighton and Lily were with their mother.

"I assume you want to go home?" she asked Casey, whose anger was a palpable entity.

"You assume right."

"'Kay," Emma said, clumsily picking up her purse and then easing off her stool. "Let's go."

Casey waited until they'd left the building and had hopped into a cab. Then she shut the window dividing them from the driver and turned to her so-called protégée with carefully controlled fury.

"What the hell were you thinking—?" She broke off as Emma stared back at her, triumph dancing in her totally clear eyes.

Casey blinked. "You're completely sober, aren't you?"

Emma began to laugh. "Student bests mentor. Bam."

# 9

*Offices of Forensic Instincts*
*Small Conference Room, First Floor*
*Tribeca, New York*
*Thursday, 11:30 p.m.*

Casey sent a terse Slack message to Marc and Patrick, telling them that she and Emma were having a private conversation, and that she'd call them down as soon as they were finished.

Then, she seated herself on the tub chair at the head of the room and signaled for Emma to have a seat on the adjacent love seat. Folding her arms across her chest, Casey waited as Emma complied. The younger girl was visibly unnerved. Casey hadn't said a word to her since Emma's teasing comment in the taxi.

Casey plunged right in. "I have a few things to say to you before I call the rest of the team down and we get into all I learned from Charlotte and Ashley, and whatever you learned from Brighton and Lily."

Emma nodded.

"Despite the fact that we're all like a family, I'm still the president of FI and what I say goes. Is that clear?"

Once again, Emma nodded.

"I realize you had the best of intentions when you ignored me and took off for the bar. I'm sure you learned lots of great information. That doesn't excuse your actions. If you'd told me what you had planned, I'd have given you the green light. But you didn't. You disregarded my instructions and took matters into your own hands. That's unacceptable. You've pushed the boundaries more than once, and I let it go. But it stops here. I appreciate all you do and your unique style, but don't do it without my permission. Is that equally clear?"

"Yes," Emma said sheepishly. "I apologize for the way I handled things. It won't happen again."

Casey studied her for a moment, and then nodded. "Good. Then we're on the same page. None of this has to be mentioned to the rest of the team. I'll call them down now and we can fill them in on the other stuff."

"Thanks, Casey."

A hint of a smile curved Casey's lips. "That's what family is about."

\*\*\*

Marc and Patrick received Casey's message. They gathered up their papers, made sure that everything they had—including Patrick's handwritten notes—were on screen share. They then headed down the flight of stairs to the first floor and walked into the conference room. Their brows were knit in curiosity as they filed into the room.

Marc glanced from Casey to Emma and back, saw that their "talk" had been about more than just fact-sharing, but decided to refrain from asking. He shut the door and sat in another tub chair. Patrick followed suit.

Marc swiveled around to face Casey. "So how was the fundraiser? Any good results?"

Casey nodded. "We did some of this together, and then split up for maximum results. It paid off. I'll go first, and then Emma can tell us her findings. We didn't have a chance to compare notes and we wanted to discuss things when we were all together, but not near prying ears."

"Smart idea," Patrick said in approval. He, too, had opted out of asking questions about Casey and Emma's private discussion.

Casey proceeded to give them a detailed accounting of her chat with Charlotte, followed by her interaction with Ashley.

"So you think they're hiding something?" Marc asked.

"I do. I just can't be sure what that something is." Casey rubbed her forehead. "They're definitely both defensive and worried about the way they're perceived. I don't think it's strictly about protecting the family and their privacy. Something's off. Charlotte made fervent attempts to assure me how close she and her children are. That closeness applies to Ashley, who's a perfect replica of her mother, but not to Brighton and Lily. They spent the entire night at the bar, showing no support for Charlotte and getting as drunk as possible to avoid the crowd."

"How disrespectful," Patrick said. "Especially having just lost their father."

Marc's fingers were steepled beneath his chin as he contemplated Casey's description. "Unless one or both of them had something to do with their father's murder."

"True," Patrick responded with a nod.

"Emma was with them for a few hours," Casey continued. "She'll have a broader perspective on them. From my minimum encounter, I'd say Brighton is a rough-around-the-edges, sulky child who wants nothing to do with his mother's charity, possibly even with his mother herself. Lily is a gentle soul who's uncomfortable with her role in the family, and unsure how to handle herself."

"That's pretty much dead-on," Emma said. She shot Casey a look of sheer admiration. "Clearly, our boss figured out the same things I did, but from a three-minute encounter. I was with them, pretending to be drunk, for ages. Lily is really sweet. She just can't find her place in the family. She's different from them. She's nothing like the powerhouses her mother and sister are. She loves being a nanny, and she adores her charges. Her father's murder hit her hard. She's sensitive and emotional, unable to conceal her feelings the way her older sister can."

"And Brighton?" Marc inquired.

"He's another story. He's everything Casey said, but I can't figure out how deep his dislike of his parents runs."

That perked Casey's ears up. "Dislike or resentment? Did he touch on anything that might lead to a motive? Is he the type to let his anger boil over? Do you think he's capable of killing his father?"

Emma shrugged. "I can't answer any of that—yet. But I will. Brighton took my cell number. He plans on texting me for a 'real date' this weekend."

Casey's lips twitched. "I was there for that part. You flirted nicely, and the guy was practically drooling over you. I'd bet money that you'll hear from him by midday tomorrow—once he's slept it off. That'll give you a *real* chance to get the lowdown on the Hillington family, and where we'd best put our energies."

She turned to Marc and Patrick with a quizzical look. "Anything on your end?"

Both men nodded, and Marc went on to fill the rest of the team in on what they'd found—and hadn't found.

"Lots of holes to fill," he concluded. "But either Hillington is on the NYPD's shit list for some reason we don't know, or there's more info buried where we have yet to find it."

As he spoke, Casey's cell phone sounded, announcing she'd received a text. She glanced down, her brows rising.

"It's Aidan," she announced. She went into the text itself and said, "He's finished up his research on a business relationship hate-list for Hillington. He wants to come by now to discuss." Casey glanced around the room. "Anyone need to get home now?"

They all shook their heads.

"Good." Casey was already texting Aidan back. "I'll tell him that we're waiting."

\*\*\*

It was a little after one when Aidan arrived at the brownstone. He and the FI team settled themselves in the small first-floor conference room, the team ready to see and hear what Aidan had put together.

He didn't make them wait, opening his laptop, and connecting the video cable so he could project his screen for all to see.

Columns had been neatly laid out. Company names. Executives or employees in-house who had reason to strongly dislike Hillington. Documented incident reports, including names and dates, where a clash of personalities had occurred. And cryptic explanations for the conflict and, where appropriate, hyperlinks to a document containing more comprehensive notes.

"Wow," Casey said. "This is great. Thank you, Aidan."

"No problem," Aidan replied with a nod. "Now, as you can see, Christopher Hillington had a number of unpleasant business relationships. He wasn't known for his decency or his straight shooting. That explains why the list you're looking at is pretty expansive."

"You can say that," Marc muttered as he read. "A first-class scumbag."

"Yup," Aidan agreed. "Now comes the time-consuming part. We've got a two-part job. With regard to solving Hillington's murder, we have to dig deep to figure out if anyone on these pages is capable of murder, and if they hated Hillington enough to kill him. Motive and opportunity. Also, alibis. This amount of research is going to require all hands on deck. Terri and me included."

He turned to face Casey. "But more importantly, Casey, you have to go through all these pages and see if you recognize any of the names. Because you're our prime concern. Who would want to implicate you in a murder and, in the process, jeopardize your life?"

Casey nodded slowly, realizing this would mean scrolling through dozens of pages. "I'll get started right away."

"You'll obviously need a copy of this spreadsheet. How would you like me to make that happen?"

"Yoda," Casey said in response. "Please upload a copy of Aidan's spreadsheet to our server."

"Yes, Casey," Yoda replied. "Aidan, please accept my request to connect to your laptop."

Aidan did so at once. "Done."

"The spreadsheet is now uploaded. I'm detaching from Aidan's laptop."

Casey looked at Aidan. "Then I'm ready to go."

# 10

*Offices of the Zermatt Group*
*West Seventy-Fifth Street, Seventh Floor*
*Manhattan, New York*
*Friday, 2:15 a.m.*

Aidan went straight to his apartment after his meeting with FI. He punched in his security code, let himself in, and headed directly for the windowless room at the rear of the apartment. That room served as the strategic command center for the Zermatt Group, aka the home base of Aidan's "other life." He and Terri called this space "the Cage" because the entire room was a Faraday cage. It didn't allow electromagnetic waves to enter and thereby protected all the sensitive electronic devices within its walls from electronic surveillance. All communications to the outside world were hardwired, heavily monitored, and protected with multiple firewalls. When someone tried to reach either Aidan or Terri on their cell phone when inside the Cage, the call would be routed instead to the desk phone in the room.

He paused in front of the solid steel door and the Hirsh keypad that controlled access to it. Adjacent to the keypad was a small red light.

When it glowed, either Aidan or Terri were inside and not to be disturbed.

It was glowing now, which meant Terri was hard at work.

"I'm doing a deep search on Charlotte Hillington," she announced, not even glancing up as Aidan entered the room. "She and her husband had different attorneys."

Aidan's brows rose in interest. "Was that always the case, or was it recent?"

"Far from recent. Years ago. Interesting that the last piece of Hillington's legal interests transferred were his trusts and estates. All moved to Harris, Porter, & Donnelly. Just his legal affairs, not Charlotte's."

"Interesting," Aidan said thoughtfully. "So who are her attorneys?"

"The same attorneys who handled both her and her husband's legal interests since they married. Salick and Wesson. They're a small law firm on the Lower East Side. The Hillingtons' wills were executed there. No change of representation shows up for Charlotte Hillington."

"I wonder if she knew about Hillington's decision, or if it came out of left field."

"The latter," Terri replied. "I texted Casey while you were on your way back here, and she, in turn, contacted Angela King. Evidently, the woman keeps the same insane hours that we do, and was awake and ready to answer Casey's question. It seems that Charlotte made a trip to Harris, Porter, & Donnelly three days ago. She wanted to discuss her husband's estate. She also left a message for Angela King to strategize Charlotte's defense in the event she was arrested for her husband's murder."

"So she assumed she was also their client," Aidan responded. "Hillington never told her otherwise."

"Nope. Now the question is, will Salick and Wesson be willing to talk to FI?"

\*\*\*

*Offices of Forensic Instincts*
*Tribeca, New York*
*Friday, 2:40 a.m.*

"I put together the pieces of your conversation with Terri and Angela," Marc said after Casey hung up the phone.

Casey nodded. "Angela was uncharacteristically forthcoming. Then again, Charlotte Hillington was not her firm's client, so attorney-client privilege did not apply."

"Interesting that Christopher Hillington only transferred his accounts," Patrick added. "So all wasn't sunshine and roses in that marriage."

"We have to discuss the ramifications of this." Casey was studying the exhausted faces of her teammates. "But first we have to review Aidan's spreadsheet, and that falls primarily to me. Go home, all of you. Get some rest."

"And what about you?" Marc asked. "You look like you're about to keel over."

Casey smiled. "I'll go upstairs to my old bedroom and catch a few hours of sleep. Then I'll get to work. You guys don't have to get back here until eight."

"Yeah, right," Emma muttered. "We're going to leave everything to you while we get our z's. I'll be back by dawn."

"We all will," Marc agreed.

"Then get out of here," Casey ordered. "I'll see you later."

\*\*\*

Before curling up in bed, Casey called Hutch.

He answered on the first ring. "Are you okay? Coming home tonight?"

"Yes and no." She explained the situation to him, leaving out the unnecessary details.

Hutch whistled. "You've got your hands full. I'm headed over. I'll make sure that you sleep and then start reviewing the spreadsheet with you."

"That's an offer I can't refuse," Casey replied, knowing full well how Hutch would ensure that she slept. "I'm quite sure you can send me into dreamland. Will you also make sure I get up in a few hours?"

"Promise." Hutch was as punctual and disciplined as a soldier. Casey herself needed very little sleep, but Hutch needed almost none. He had an internal alarm clock that never failed.

"See you soon," he said.

"I'll be waiting."

\*\*\*

*Offices of Forensic Instincts*
*Tribeca, New York*
*Friday, 6:30 a.m.*

As expected, the team arrived early and pretty much simultaneously. They found Casey and Hutch in the third-floor kitchen nook, perched on stools and munching on bagels. Casey's laptop was open on the counter in front of them, and they were poring over the names and facts on Aidan's spreadsheet.

"Hey," Marc greeted them, looking wide awake and ready to work. "I see you're already in high gear, and that you summoned midnight help. Smart."

"Hey, Marc," Hutch greeted his friend.

"I won't ask what time you got here."

As always, Hutch pulled a perfect deadpan.

Marc chuckled. "Okay, well, now we're all here, too. So why don't we move this to the conference room, where we can all divide and conquer."

Casey was already on her feet. "Great. Hutch got a bag of bagels and a tub of cream cheese. I'll grab them and bring them downstairs, so no one dies of hunger while we plow through this endless list of names. The Jura is already awake and brewing."

"Thanks, Hutch," Patrick said. "Much-needed sustenance for the team."

With mutters of agreement, they all headed down one flight of stairs, helped themselves to bagels and coffee, and settled around the conference room table. They each flipped on their laptop, opened the spreadsheet, and glanced up to follow Casey's lead.

"Hutch and I have thoroughly researched the *A*'s through the *C*'s," she told them with a disgusted sigh. "No familiar names on the list, or companies I've had dealings with. A complete bust."

Marc nodded, unsurprised. "This is going to be a needle in a haystack, so we'll divvy up the entries. You continue to slowly read each and every one, details included. We'll be backup, but do a more cursory read." He glanced quizzically at Hutch. "Can you stay?"

Hutch wiggled his hand. "For a few hours, maybe. Then duty calls."

"Fine. We'll take what we can get. You keep reading with Casey until you have to leave. We'll just keep at it until we find something."

"You got it." Hutch turned to Casey's laptop and began reading over her shoulder as she paused on each line, and then deep-dived into the details Aidan had provided.

Marc delegated the alphabetical entries to the rest of the team, assigning five letters to each of them, himself included.

\*\*\*

Two hours later, Hutch looked up with a rueful expression. "I've got to get to my desk. We've got a few high-profile cases to investigate."

"Go," Casey said at once. "You've given us a ton of time you don't have."

Hutch rose, then leaned over to give Casey a quick kiss. "Keep me posted," he said. "I mean it. Anything you find, I want to know."

"Yes, sir," Casey replied with a mock salute.

Reluctantly, Hutch left and headed off to the Bureau's New York office.

Filling up their coffee cups, the team went back to work.

\*\*\*

It was nearly eleven o'clock when Marc picked up his head, his eyes glittering with satisfaction. "Casey, go to the *S*'s. Near the bottom. You'll see a name you recognize."

Not only Casey, but the whole team did as Marc said.

Casey's eyes widened. "Oliver Steadman," she said aloud, somewhat shocked. "That's a name I thought I'd never see again."

Oliver Steadman had been a prime suspect in their last case. He'd worked as the head of Research and Development in the now-defunct company CannaBD, once a flourishing start-up. It was the same company that had employed their client, Amy Bregman, who was being targeted by a serial killer. Steadman sent up enough red flags to suspect he was that killer.

He wasn't guilty—*then.*

But now?

As if reading Casey's mind, Marc said, "We dropped the ball on Steadman. He wasn't our guy in the CannaBD case, but he was a time bomb ready to go off." Marc was clearly annoyed at himself. "We should have developed a profile on him from the start and stayed on him in the aftermath. He had a ton of bottled-up anger and he ducked us at every turn."

Casey nodded, then double-clicked on Steadman's name, accessing the profile Aidan had pulled together and projecting it on the large wall across the room so that the entire team could see it.

They all read together.

Steadman had grown up, an only child, in a small town outside Albany and gotten his mechanical engineering degree from SUNY Polytechnic Institute in Utica, New York. Good school, modest tuition costs. Lived at home to keep costs down. Parents paid for his tuition, but were now both deceased. Steadman got his first job at a local engineering firm, after which he went to the Big Apple and scored his enviable job at CannaBD.

Right after CannaBD dissolved, Oliver had been hired by Christopher's private equity firm, YNE. He'd doctored his college résumé enough to be exceptional and improved on the references from his first place of employment. Omitting references from CannaBD was completely understandable, given the company had imploded with both its CEO and its key investor now in jail.

It had been enough.

Ostensibly embracing his new job, he'd demonstrated top-notch skills, although it was clear early on that he balked at being a team player. Strike one. By two months in, his rep was shaky. Office gossip spread that he approached women in a verbally inappropriate manner. No official complaints had been filed, only a general consensus that he came across as a real creeper. Strike two.

Strike three—and the straw that broke the camel's back—came three weeks ago, at a time when Steadman had become increasingly ornery and reclusive. Somehow, thanks to social media and blogs, word leaked out that he'd been a prime suspect as a serial killer in a recent, high-profile murder investigation at the now-defunct CannaBD. That did it. He was discharged immediately, despite his multitude of emails to Hillington defending himself. The emails had been ignored, and Steadman had been escorted out of the building by security.

After that, no one else would even consider hiring him.

Casey frowned, giving voice to a supposition that had just popped into her head. "Steadman was fired less than a week before the hit-and-run. Could he be guilty of that crime and somehow framed Hillington for it? Then, when Hillington wasn't immediately arrested, could he have taken it a gruesome step further and killed the man?"

"A definite and plausible theory," Marc replied. "The timing is too coincidental not to consider it. And following your theory, could Steadman have forced Hillington to write your name in blood? After our last case, FI would be high on his shit list, and you're the team's president. He'd be taking care of a two-for-one."

"Shit," Casey muttered. "This is bad."

"*Very* bad," Patrick agreed.

Marc's eyes were blazing. "We aren't going to make the same mistake twice. That bastard might not have been our serial killer, but he was a loose end who was scum. He managed to elude us through-out the entire investigation and fell off our radar entirely. Not this time. Patrick, we're hunting him down and questioning him. That's number-one priority now."

"Well, that's not going to be easy," Casey noted. "As you can see, Aidan found no recent location for Steadman, try though he did. The man literally vanished, leaving us with nothing but his previous address on Randall Avenue in the Throggs Neck section of the Bronx. Aidan couldn't find anything more—not where he's staying, not any friends or relatives. Nothing."

"He's hiding out," Patrick muttered, scanning the details projected on the wall. "Maybe with friends. Maybe even with a new identity." Patrick rose. "He's making it hard, but not hard enough. We'll start asking the right questions of the right people—starting today. We'll make this our mission, and we'll find him."

"One minor thing before you go," Casey said. "I was going to call Charlotte's attorneys, Salick and Wesson, to schedule a meeting, before I realized what a bad idea it was. They're never going to say a word about their client or give us anything at all, including physical tells. Violate attorney-client privilege, especially with such a high-profile client? Not a chance. And by opening the door, we'll be tipping our hand. They'll contact Charlotte ASAP, and tell her that FI is poking around in her legal affairs."

"I totally agree," Emma said. "So far, we've been completely off Charlotte's radar. She only knows us as Hannah and Madison. Let's not risk blowing that cover."

Both Marc and Patrick voiced their agreement.

Casey frowned, visibly frustrated. She was used to running the show, but it wasn't the case this time. And she was *not* happy.

"What am I going to do while you're hunting down Steadman?" she asked. "I *must* be part of this. This is such a weird case. I'm at the center of everything, yet I'm not leading the way. That doesn't work for me."

Marc nodded. He knew Casey better than anyone, and he knew what this passive role was doing to her.

"I have an idea," he said. "You're the pro where it comes to people. Why don't you contact YNE and get to the head of HR. Pose as their equivalent at another company—one who's considering hiring Steadman."

"And get as much info on his professional life there as I can," Casey finished for him. Her mind was already racing as she took charge again. "Aidan gave us the facts. I'll get everything in between."

"Yup. Nobody does it better."

"So we'll be working in parallel. Good. We have two crimes to solve. And clearing my name is crucial."

"This isn't only about clearing your name," Marc reminded her as he and Patrick rose. "It's about protecting you from danger."

"We still have no proof that I *am* in danger."

"Maybe not, but I have a bad feeling. And until that feeling goes away, we're going to assume the worst."

# 11

Casey leaned back in her chair, having finished her research into Christopher Hillington's company.

YNE was thriving. Employees were paid a king's ransom. Even though it was listed, just as its competitors, as a private equity firm, its managing partner, Christopher Hillington, was a truly shrewd and creative businessman who was brilliant at zeroing in on acquisitions targets that would yield YNE the highest returns on investment.

The question was, how did Oliver Steadman fit into that financial structure? The director of HR must have seen something in him that was impressive.

Time to find out what that something was.

Casey picked up her burner phone and called YNE's main number. When the recorded voice answered, she tapped in the direct extension of Anita Jacobs, director of Human Resources. With any luck, the woman wouldn't be at lunch. Top execs rarely worked on traditional nine-to-five schedules.

Sure enough, a professional voice answered on the second ring. "Anita Jacobs." She sounded harried. So did every other corporate employee.

"Hello, Anita. This is Margaret Kramer. I'm the director of HR at Cashman Financial in Bozeman, Montana. If you have a few minutes, I'd like to ask you a few professional questions about a former employee of yours who's now a potential applicant to our firm."

"YNE has strict rules with regard to confidential information. So, unfortunately, I can't supply you with those answers." Anita was clearly a by-the-book department head who was used to receiving calls such as these and nipping them in the bud. "So if there's nothing else…?"

Casey got in under the wire. "The employee's name is Oliver Steadman."

There was a heavy pause at the other end of the phone.

"Mr. Steadman no longer works here," Anita said. "Good day, Ms. Kramer."

*Click.*

The firmness of that click spoke volumes.

Oliver Steadman hadn't quit. He was fired—and fired with cause.

\*\*\*

*Fordham University*
*Gabelli School of Business, Rose Hill Campus*
*Bronx, New York*
*Friday, 12:35 p.m.*

Morgan shrugged into her parka, slung her backpack over her shoulder, and left the classroom where she took her Philosophy of Human Nature course—a class Morgan not only found fascinating but that fulfilled a requirement for her bachelor's degree in business administration. She didn't intend to stop with her BS. Her plan was to go on to acquire her

MBA, also from Fordham's Gabelli School of Business. Its reputation was stellar and would open up a world of doors for her.

She'd always felt a sense of wonder and pride in her natural proclivity for business and problem-solving. They certainly weren't inherited gifts. Her mom was a natural-born middle school teacher and her dad had been an acclaimed orthopedic surgeon.

But Morgan had always loved the idea of business consulting, either in her own company or as part of a larger one. Her dad used to say that she had an entrepreneurial spirit.

He was right.

She now had a ton of work to do to keep up. She planned on heading to the library, but before she dove into her coursework, she wanted to pay her spring tuition bill. She had a few weeks before it was due, but the reminder email had already arrived, and she always liked to get the task off her plate and in the rearview mirror.

Morgan settled herself in the corner of the library that felt like home to her and flipped open her laptop. She opened her email and searched for the university's form letter. She found and opened it, using the link provided to get to the name and password page. Quickly, she entered the necessary data to access her account.

She clicked on the "pay your bill" section and waited.

Her eyebrows drew together in puzzlement at what popped up. *Zero balance.*

That couldn't be right. Surely she'd remember if she'd paid next semester's tuition.

She retried the process three times before logging out. Maybe there was a systems problem?

Time to head over to the bursar's office and straighten this out. But first, she'd double-check from her end to make sure she wasn't losing her mind.

She logged into the website of Kelson Reed—the financial institution that held the 529 plan her dad had set up for her. Twice a year, like clockwork, she'd access her tuition money and pay the university for the upcoming semester. She didn't want to have the money automatically sent. She liked having control of her life.

Using the required two-factor authentication, she got into her account. As she'd expected, no amount had been withdrawn since last semester's payment.

So the miscommunication didn't start with her.

She packed up her laptop, grabbed her parka and backpack, and left the library.

\*\*\*

Forty minutes later, Morgan was still totally at sea. The bursar had checked and rechecked, only to advise her that what she'd seen online had been accurate. There was no balance due for the spring semester.

Morgan wanted to ask for information about where the payment had come from, but the office was packed with students, and the bursar was becoming increasingly impatient, with no more time to devote to this.

Morgan would have to pursue this elsewhere.

She left the office, sank down on an outdoor bench, and shot off a text to her mom. Natalie's sixth period lunch would begin soon. Hopefully, she'd be able to give Morgan the quick call she'd requested.

Rather than heading back to the library, Morgan made herself comfortable on the bench, zipping up her parka and taking in the beautiful view of the nearby botanical gardens, enhanced by the holiday decorations strung all across campus.

December was underway, and it was starting to get colder. Snowflakes were drifting around her—a lovely reminder that finals were about to begin and that school would soon be out for winter break. Students were walking across campus in groups, all laughing and chatting, their aura captivating and converging with her own special childlike feeling of impending freedom.

As she mused, her cell phone rang, registering "Mom."

"Hi," Morgan greeted her.

"Are you all right?" Natalie was obviously worried. It wasn't like Morgan to call her in the middle of her school day.

"Fine," Morgan reassured her. "Just confused." She explained what was going on.

There was a slight hesitation before Natalie responded.

"I guess I should have told you, but I wanted it to be a surprise. I've decided to start making payments toward your undergrad education."

"What?" Morgan was startled. "Thank you…but why?"

"Because the tuition at Fordham is exorbitant," Natalie replied. "I realize there's a substantial amount of money in the financial plan Dad set up for you, but I want that to cover your master's with a great deal left over to live your life. Remember, Dad left me very wealthy. I should have thought of this sooner, but it just occurred to me as I was going through our finances. So, happy start to the holidays!"

Morgan felt a surge of gratitude, combined by the heavy weight of guilt. Her mom had never been involved in the household finances. It simply wasn't her forte. And now Morgan had to burst her bubble.

"Mom, that's a wonderful gesture. I'm so lucky to have you. Unfortunately, this doesn't work. The 529 Dad set up for me specifically covers only my undergraduate education. Nothing else. So we have to use that money to pay my tuition. Otherwise, it will go to waste."

"Oh." Natalie sounded crushed. "I didn't realize."

Morgan was surprised by her mom's overreaction. Clearly, this meant a great deal more to her than Morgan had guessed.

Even as she mused, she could hear her mom typing furiously on her laptop.

"Please don't be upset," Morgan tried. "I love you very much, and I'm sorry about this whole mix-up."

"Don't apologize." Natalie had stopped typing, and now sounded much more herself. "It's on me that I never got specifics from your dad. I have another idea that will accomplish what I want. I'll cancel the tuition payment and have you go ahead and pay all your remaining college expenses from the plan Dad set up for you. I'll reallocate my funds to pay for your master's and a short time thereafter, until you're secure in your amazing new career. After that, you can handle all your own finances. Deal?"

Morgan was speechless. "Mom, you're awesome. But you're already helping me so much with day-to-day expenses. Remember, I could have slowed down my educational timeline and taken a part-time job. You adamantly refused. So I'm on the fast track to get where I need to go."

"Not without getting your MBA, you're not. I know you're going to say that you'll get an internship and spread out your course load. That means it'll take longer to graduate. It's not going to happen. I have the means. Now please just accept my offer and say thank you, because you won't change my mind."

Morgan felt tears sting her eyes. She swallowed hard before she answered. "Mom, I…thank you. I really don't know what else to say."

"Then say nothing. I'll go cancel my payment, and you follow up as you've been doing." There was a smile in Natalie's voice. "Besides, you've kept me long enough. Now I have to bolt my lunch and get back to my classroom."

Morgan laughed through her tears. "Sorry about that. I love you and I'll see you tonight."

\*\*\*

Natalie put down her cell phone, wrestling with a decision she should already have made. Not only because Morgan was too bright to be fooled, but because she had a right to know the truth.

There really was no decision to make. It was time.

With that, a sense of rightness flowed through her. "I know this is what you'd want, my love," she murmured. Two tears trickled down her cheeks. "I wish you were here to watch Morgan soar."

# 12

*Hillington Residence*
*200 East Eighty-Third Street, Twenty-First Floor*
*Upper East Side, Manhattan, New York*
*Friday, 1:45 p.m.*

Charlotte stood in the family room, martini in her hand, staring out the panoramic windows. She didn't turn around, not even when she heard Ashley walk in. Every time her gaze shifted to the spot where Christopher's dead body had fallen, she felt like throwing up.

It didn't matter. Everything about that day was permanently ingrained in her mind.

"Mom?" Ashley crossed over, pausing at the side table that held the martini pitcher and pouring herself a drink. "You sounded really bad on the phone. I left work and came straight here. Are you okay?"

Charlotte took another sip of her drink. "Everything is unraveling," she replied. "I spoke to my attorneys again. There's still a hold on the reading of your father's will and I have no idea why or how long it will last. I only have so much in our joint savings account. This wasn't what I had in mind."

Ashley squeezed her mother's arm. "Your joint account still has a substantial amount in it. Then, there's Brighton's, Lily's, and my trusts. You're the trustee. If need be, we'll use some of that money to tide us over. We didn't expect this delay, but we can bridge the gap. Whatever the holdup, it will be resolved. Remember that one of the reasons the three of us are still living here is to save exorbitant amounts on rentals. That benefits us all."

"I know." Charlotte squeezed her eyes shut. "But it's not just the money. I have appearances to keep up, and I'm not sure I can do it anymore. Plus, the police have already been here twice."

"Say nothing to them," Ashley stated emphatically. "That's why we made sure to hire a top-notch defense attorney. It'll be okay. I don't see any immediate arrest on the horizon."

"That could change at any time."

"Not without evidence."

"They've questioned you, and your brother and sister, too," Charlotte reminded her.

"Our alibis are solid," Ashley replied. "We know what we're doing. We're all in this together. I don't care how many times the police interview you. They've got nothing. So just keep your fears in check. And lean on me." Ashley's jaw clenched. "I won't let anything bad happen. I promise."

Down the hall in his room, Brighton heard only bits and pieces of the conversation. He rolled his eyes. This was getting old. He wanted what was his, and hearing his mother blubbering and Ashley being her usual savior made him want to puke. He needed what was rightfully his, not a bunch of bullshit soothing.

He needed a pick-me-up. And not his usual joint or two. Another kind of medicine.

Grabbing his phone, he accessed Madison's number and began to type.

*Hey, remember me? I want to take you out in style. Dinner? Tonight?*

He paused and typed his name at the end of the text. Just in case she'd been too drunk to remember.

***

*Offices of Forensic Instincts*
*Tribeca, New York*
*Friday, 2:10 p.m.*


Emma felt her "Madison" burner phone vibrate. This was what she'd been waiting for. Eagerly, she scanned the text, a satisfied smile spreading across her face.

She'd quickly report in to Casey, and they'd bandy ideas about. Then, she'd take the plunge—answer Brighton with alleged enthusiasm after waiting an hour or so, just to heighten his nerves. She'd get the where and when, pleased that, besides a shitload of knowledge, she'd be getting a great meal to savor. Tonight, she'd make sure to linger over dinner, determined to get as much information as she could, knowing exactly what path she'd be following.

She had just the dress for this occasion.

*** 


*Evans Residence*
*210 Alameda Avenue*
*Douglaston, Queens, New York*
*Friday, 4:45 p.m.*


Morgan walked up the brick stairs and opened the front door with her key. Her mom was probably home by now, but, as two women alone, they always kept the doors locked. It was the prudent thing to do.

After Morgan had turned the lock behind her and hung up her parka, she noted that the family room light was on.

It was their usual hangout spot.

"Mom, I'm home," she announced, flipping on the hall light and heading for the family room.

"Hi, honey," Natalie replied in an odd tone. "Come on in."

"Hey." Morgan gave her mother a quick peck on the cheek and a quizzical look before dropping into the comfy La-Z-Boy recliner across from the love seat where Natalie was sitting. Natalie's fingers were tightly interlaced on her lap, and her expression was strained.

"Are you okay?" Morgan asked at once.

Natalie didn't respond to the question, instead saying, "We need to talk."

Now, Morgan was starting to get anxious. "Is something wrong?"

"Not in the way you mean." Natalie leaned forward to meet her daughter's gaze. "It's nothing health related, but there's a lot I need to share with you. I should have done this right after your dad passed, but I was terrified of hurting you and hurting our relationship. That was both selfish and wrong. You're a grown woman and need to know everything about your life."

Morgan was still as a statue. "I'm listening."

Natalie wet her lips with the tip of her tongue. "I'm not forgiving myself. I was young. I made mistakes. I'm older now, but I still make mistakes. Just know how much I love you. And how much your dad loved you. He was an amazing, caring man. He was also unaware of anything I'm about to tell you. This is all on me."

By now, Morgan had gone sheet white, her instincts telling her that whatever she was about to hear would forever change her life. "Okay," she said in a small voice.

Natalie blew out a breath. She was shaking as she pushed on. But she'd promised herself she'd be direct and honest.

"I loved your father dearly, but before we met, there was someone else—someone who meant the world to me. He and I were together for a long time. Too late, I found out he was married, and I immediately ended things. I think I died a little bit inside, and if it weren't for Jonathan, I'm not sure I would have come back to myself. But I did. He and I had met a few years before that, when I injured my knee in a skiing accident. As luck would have it, we reconnected at a social event. It was kind of a whirlwind romance, and we married a month later."

A painful pause as Natalie dropped the bomb. "Shortly after that, I realized I was pregnant."

Morgan gasped, desperately trying to process what her mother was telling her. "Are you saying… Is Jonathan my father?"

Natalie squeezed her eyes shut. "Biologically, no."

"Oh my God." Morgan pressed her hands to her face. "Are you sure?"

"I had a DNA test done in the hospital. So, yes, I'm sure."

"Did you tell him? Did he know?"

"No and never. As far as he was concerned, you were his. You were just born a little early. He didn't doubt his paternity, and had no reason to. He and I raised you together—with all the love in our hearts. Morgan, he *was* your father."

Morgan didn't respond to that, but asked another question. "And my biological father, did he know?"

"Not then. Not until last year. He tracked me down and found out about you. He did the math and saw the resemblance. I was cornered and had no choice but to tell him the truth. I probably should have told him and Jonathan from the start. They both had the right to know. But I refused to break Jonathan's heart, and I was too angry and hurt to tell your biological father. He had a family he'd lied about. I wasn't about to give him the satisfaction—or the responsibility—of dealing with another child."

"Especially an illegitimate one." The tears were trickling down Morgan's cheeks, and she made no attempt to stem them. "Who is he? Where is he? You said he tracked you down. What does that mean?"

This part was the hardest for Natalie. "That means his marriage was virtually over. He planned to file for divorce. He wanted to be with me. In the process, he found out about you. He was stunned, so he came back—not only to recapture what we once had, but to meet and get to know you." Natalie's voice grew softer. "He wore me down, countered every attempt I made to push him away. He agreed to take it slow with you. But with us?" A heavy pause. "Morgan, I loved him."

"So you took him back," Morgan said, visibly numb. "You're having an affair with him."

"Not anymore." Emotion tightened Natalie's throat. "He died this past Monday."

"I'm sorry." For her mother's sake, Morgan meant it.

"So am I. As for who he was, that's complicated, too. He was a young, brilliant guy in his twenties when we met. Since then, he's built an empire."

"Do his other children know about me? Does his wife?"

"No. That was my choice. He wanted to tell them everything and claim you as his own. I begged him not to, at least not until you and he had established a relationship. There would be so much publicity, and I didn't want to expose you to that. He finally and unhappily agreed."

"He's that well-known?"

"In financial circles, yes." Natalie never averted her gaze. "But then came more. As of a month ago, he became a suspect in a hit-and-run. It's all over the news…" Natalie broke off, unable to continue.

Morgan's eyes widened. "Wait, are you talking about Christopher Hillington?" she demanded. "Is *that man* my biological father?"

Natalie nodded, tears sliding down her cheeks. "Morgan, I know he didn't do it. I saw how traumatized he was afterward. But he was stoic when he talked to the police and to the media. That's who he was. He had so many enemies, and one of them killed him. I have no idea who…"

"Oh my God." Clearly, Morgan wasn't listening anymore. She stood and started pacing around the room. "Oh my God."

Natalie rose and started to go to Morgan, then realized she had no right. "Honey, I'm so sorry."

Morgan shook her head. "I need to be alone." She headed for the hall.

Natalie caught her arm, desperate for her to understand. "Christopher was insistent about meeting you. I know he drove to your school, sat in his car, and watched you. The night of the…accident…he decided he wasn't listening to my pleas anymore. He came here, and I let him in, but you weren't home. We argued. He wasn't listening. He perched on a kitchen stool and waited for hours. At last he gave up—but not without my agreement that he could come back tomorrow morning. That didn't happen. The police were all over him by then."

"Stop." Morgan jerked her arm free. "I can't listen to this. Please. Leave me alone."

She flew up the stairs, separating herself from everything she'd just been told.

Natalie sank back down on the love seat, rocking back and forth as she covered her face, and wept her heart out.

If she lost Morgan, she couldn't go on.

# 13

*Off-the-Beaten-Path Alley*
*Throggs Neck, East Bronx, New York*
*Friday, 5:30 p.m.*

Patrick and Marc had spent a busy day tracking people down and asking a ton of questions.

Now they were back in the car, drinking coffee and discussing today's findings, which were just the tip of the iceberg. Even though they were frustrated, they weren't surprised. Steadman wanted to be gone, so he wasn't going to make it easy for them to find him.

"Okay, so we spoke to three of Steadman's neighbors," Marc began. "That's more than I expected, given it was the middle of a workday."

"They didn't know a hell of a lot," Patrick replied. "None of them had seen Steadman in weeks. They'd all said he was a loner, so they knew virtually nothing about him. The best lead we got was to talk to that Vivian Moss, the building's busybody. The tenants claimed she knew everything about everyone. She was also at work, but evidently she comes home every day at lunchtime to feed her cat. We'll have to catch her tomorrow sometime around noon."

Marc nodded, scanning the notes on his iPad. "We took care of the post office and found out the name of Steadman's mail carrier, plus the usual times of his routes. Which means we have to get to Randall

Avenue tomorrow by ten a.m." A corner of Marc's mouth lifted. "Good call telling them you're former FBI. It got them to tell you that Steadman filed no change of address and has weeks of mail backed up."

"Even though they wouldn't show us that mail. That would be crossing the line since we had no search warrant."

Marc looked up from his iPad. "We also hopped online and migrated to the NYPD's Forty-Fifth Precinct. Eventually, we found out which officer would be most qualified to give us information. Once he heard we were former FBI, he agreed to talk to us, but not until tomorrow afternoon."

Patrick nodded. "Did you contact Casey yet?"

Marc nodded. "Yup. A couple of hours ago, when you were talking to the post office manager. She's on it."

Marc and Patrick had gotten the phone numbers of some of Steadman's former business associates and references from his first place of employment. Casey was going to make the necessary calls and attempt to learn more about his professional relationships, and maybe even his personal ones if she got more than just references at job number one. Maybe Steadman had a childhood sweetheart—one who, after all these years, would be willing to talk.

As if on cue, Marc's cell phone rang.

"Hey, Case. What did you get at your end?" he answered.

"A whole lot of voice mail prompts," she said with a sigh. "But I left messages that were intriguing. I should be getting return calls soon. It's the start of the weekend, so hopefully on Monday."

Marc chuckled. "I can just imagine." He filled her in on anything new that had occurred since they'd last spoken.

"The police officer is a great idea," she said. "If there's law enforcement dirt about Steadman, they'll have it."

"Agreed. Anyway, we're on our way back. There's nothing else to accomplish today."

"Sounds good. And FYI, Emma has a dinner date with Brighton Hillington tonight at seven. She'll be in her glory."

\*\*\*

*Vicario Residence*
*South Bayside, Queens, New York*
*Friday, 6:15 p.m.*

Isabel had tried her best to cook dinner, but her hands were still unsteady, and her grief still consumed her. She could barely remember how to cook a pot roast, much less what ingredients she needed to season it. So all she had was a chunk of raw meat and tears in her eyes.

The doorbell sounded, and Isabel's shoulders sagged in relief. Reinforcements had arrived.

She left the kitchen, crossed over to the front door, and opened it.

"Hi, Mom." Mia Vicario used one arm to give her mother a hug. Her other hand was taken up by a large tray of food.

Isabel glanced at it. "You didn't have to do this."

"Yes I did. Dinner with you and Franklin is a rare opportunity. He's always got his head stuck under a car hood, and you're not up for company, which is completely understandable. Honestly, I needed a night to spend with my family." She marched past her mother and carried the tray into the kitchen, where she placed it on the counter.

"Chicken cacciatore and roasted potatoes—your favorites," she announced.

Isabel gave a faint smile. "I can't thank you enough. I have an uncooked pot roast you can take home in return. I'm not doing it much justice."

Mia didn't look happy. Her mother had lost far too much weight and looked gaunt and frail. The cancer was back again, coupled with her devastation and grief, and there was little Mia could do to make it better. Only small gestures like tonight. Thank God that Franklin had temporarily moved in with their mother. He worried about her as much as Mia did, and his commute was a hop, skip, and a jump from here. So he'd volunteered to temporarily move in and see to his mother's needs.

Not only was Mia grateful to her brother, she was also grateful that her mom had started to eat a little. It hadn't been that way until now—not since Mia's father had died. Franklin was clearly doing a good job of restoring her will to live.

Mia put her hand on the small of her mother's back and guided her into the living room. "I'll heat dinner up soon. For now, let's get settled on the sofa and talk." She glanced around. "Franklin's not home yet?"

Isabel gave an anxious shake of her head. "He's at the pharmacy, trying to fill my prescription. Its cost is exorbitant, especially without any insurance to cover it. I'm starting to panic."

"I know." Mia sounded grim. Without her father's health insurance, they were in dire straits. "But please don't. You know Franklin. He'll find a way, and I'll help him. You'll never be without."

As she spoke, the key turned in the front door and Franklin walked in.

Mia rose and walked over to see for herself that her mother's medicine had been filled.

"Hey, sis," Franklin greeted Mia, shaking the white bag at his side. He also held up a steaming box of pizza. "Dinner, hot and ready."

Mia chuckled, relief flooding her face.

He breezed by her, stopping to give his mother a quick kiss. "A cheese pizza, hot from the oven." He sniffed the air. "Although I think I was outdone."

"You're both wonderful." Isabel's gaze was also fixed on the bag her son held. "Is that...?"

"Your prescription," he replied. "A month's worth of pills. Your pharmacy just filled it."

"Thank God," she breathed, clasping her hands together. "But the money..."

Fear flashed in Franklin's eyes, then vanished as quickly as it had come. "We still have the death benefit payment from Dad's life insurance policy. Plus, I worked a lot of overtime, along with doing a chunk of body work jobs on the side. And I've been saving on my rent payments, since I'm subletting my apartment. We're in fine shape."

Isabel gazed lovingly at her children. "How can I thank you?"

"By staying well and by eating all our food." Franklin headed to the kitchen and placed the pizza box next to the tray of chicken. Yeah, he'd gotten the money together to pay for this round of meds, but soon there'd be the next round—along with the exorbitant bills that went with it. The pressure was crippling him.

He had to vent, at least a little. "Although I can't say I'm not ripping pissed. The pharmaceutical companies are getting richer and richer at the expense of poor people—"

"Franklin." Mia's tone told him not to go on a rant.

He heard her loud and clear and clamped down on his tongue.

"Anyway, who wants a glass of wine?" he asked. "We have to toast this rare treat of having a whole evening together."

\*\*\*

*Offices of Forensic Instincts*
*Tribeca, New York*
*Friday, 11:15 p.m.*

Emma let herself into the brownstone, leaned back against the closed door, and blew out a long breath.

"Good evening, Emma," Yoda greeted her politely. "You seem agitated. My sensors are picking up on an elevated heart rate."

"Hi, Yoda," she replied. "And, yes, your sensors are dead-on. After my dinner tonight, I feel like I need a shower."

Casey, who'd been descending the stairs to the entranceway, caught Emma's comment.

Concern flashed across her face. "Are you all right? What happened?"

Emma gave a half nod. "I keep forgetting that rich spoiled brats like Brighton think they can have anything they want. And, in this case, that prize is me."

"What did he—?" Casey started to ask.

Yoda interrupted. "The fireplace in the first-floor conference room is now on, and the Jura is brewing," he announced. "May I suggest you talk in there, where you can be comfortable?"

"Good idea." Casey was already leading Emma in that direction. "Thank you, Yoda."

"My pleasure."

\*\*\*

After pouring two mugs of coffee and handing one to Emma, Casey settled herself on her usual tub chair, eyeing Emma as she sat down in the adjacent chair.

"Tell me." Casey got right to the point.

Emma took a few sips of coffee before answering. "I'm really fine," she assured Casey. "You know how well I can take care of myself. The problem is I'm used to the direct approach, and that would have fallen flat if I ever want to see Brighton and pump him for information again."

That made Casey's lips twitch. "In other words, he'd now be a gelding."

"Exactly." Emma nodded. "So I had to take a modified approach."

"That must have been quite the challenge. How hard did he hit on you?"

"Hard. He wasn't planning on taking no for an answer—with or without my roommates home. When I shot down that idea, he said that we'd go to his family's place. Apparently, no one there cares what the others are doing. Obviously, I said no to that, too."

"And he didn't take that well." Casey was beginning to feel her blood boil.

"Nope." Emma rolled her eyes. "I took a break at that point and went to the ladies' room. When I got back, he was sulking, but not as pissed. That was my cue to go all simpery. I told him that I just needed time, and that I really liked him a lot. I felt like puking, but at least he wants to see me again. I think I became not only the prize, but the latest challenge."

Casey's anger abated and transformed to admiration. "That was a fine line to walk. Good for you."

Emma gave a self-satisfied smile. "Thanks, boss." She leaned forward. "As for what I learned tonight, it was pretty interesting. Mostly about the Hillington family dynamics, and a lot about the various household relationships. Given what an arrogant prick he is, he also regaled me with every step of his life and his accomplishments."

With that, Emma whipped out her phone. "I recorded some of the highlights, but after we talk, I'm going to type up extensive notes for our database and save them in the cloud. This way, I won't forget anything, and the team can have full access."

"Excellent." Casey set down her mug. "Now tell me everything and play me the highlights."

Emma did just as asked. "As you and I picked up on at the charity fundraiser, Ashley is the cold, shrewd, undisputable sibling leader. She's her mother's right hand—and that was true even when their father was alive. It sounds to me as if Christopher and Charlotte had a stiff, old-fashioned marriage. He was all about his career and raking in the cash, and she was all about her charities, her kids, and spending the cash."

"None of that surprises me," Casey said.

"Me either. Nor does the fact that both Brighton and Lily shied away from the whole Hillington regime limelight. Brighton spends most of his time on his band and on his ego. Lily is totally wrapped up with being a nanny and loving the kids she takes care of. If you listen to Brighton, who rolls his eyes when he talks about this, it sounds like she almost considers them her own."

"Given the personality traits I saw in Lily, that description fits." Casey's mind was racing even as she hung on to Emma's every word. "She's a young girl, just out of college, and she comes across as being gentle and nurturing."

"I agree," Emma replied. "And even though Brighton was all about putting his family down, I got the feeling he has a soft spot in his heart for his little sister. She's probably the only one who looks up to him and feeds his ego."

With that, Emma placed her phone on the side table, her finger poised on the play button. "Given that we're concentrating on Hillington's murder, listen to what Brighton has to say about each family member's interactions with their father."

A second later, Casey heard Emma's voice echoing from the iPhone:

*"You must be a wreck about your father's death. What a horrible loss. From what I've read about him, he sounds like some kind of financial giant."*

*Brighton made an irritated sound.* "He was," *he said.* "So much that I think I saw him one day a month. We all knew what he was about. We got used to it. Ashley had nothing to get used to—she was and always has been my mother's protégée and confidante. Her relationship with my father was pure formality. Me? I also walked my own path—being rich was great, and my father and I had nothing in common, so I did my thing. Still do. Lily is another story. She always sought my father's attention and rarely got it. That hurt her a lot, and since his murder, I can still hear her crying in her room when I walk by."*

*"How sad,"* Emma murmured. *"Well, at least you have each other. I'm sure you were tight to begin with, and a tragedy like this one can only bring you closer together."*

*Brighton made a dubious sound.* "We're grieving together, I guess, or maybe pretending to. I don't know what Ashley is feeling. I never had much of a relationship with her. She's like an alien species. Lily is too naïve* *for her own good, and so different from the rest of us. But she needs me, so I'm there. And my mother? She seems pretty broken up. Ashley spends a ton of time with her, but I have no clue what's going on in her head."*

*There was definitely a note of impatience in Brighton's tone. "Let's cut the therapy session. We have a lot more exciting things to talk about than my family."*

Emma clicked off the recording. "Weird family dynamics, even if I did expect them."

"Yes," Casey said. "But hearing them firsthand gives me a lot to work with. Tells don't always come in physical form. Audible ones work, too."

"I know. And I leave that in your capable hands. Meanwhile, I'm going to poke around on social media to see if I can find alibis for each member of the family. I doubt something will pop up, but I want to cover all the bases."

"Smart," Casey said. She then held up her index finger. "Before you go on, tell me the most important thing. When are you seeing Brighton again?"

Emma gave a Cheshire cat grin. "Sunday. At his recording studio. He wants me to hear his band, especially since he wrote the music and the lyrics they're performing."

"A go-slow technique that's meant to convince you what a catch he is," Casey said. "I'm sure you'll be hit on again after the band disperses."

"I'm sure I will. I'll get more creative in my evasions. Still, I can't wait to see what I might learn."

Casey looked concerned rather than enthused. "We have to move quickly. Your body and our anonymity are on the line. You can't put the little prince off forever, nor can we risk his finding out who we really are. So let me listen to the rest of the recordings, read all your notes, and then see what kind of rapid tactics I can come up with."

\*\*\*

*My mistake is coming back to haunt me.*

*Casey Woods. I had no clue why the bastard was writing her name in blood on the desk before dying. I figured it didn't matter. That she'd now be the key suspect in this murder investigation, and I'd be off the hook.*

*What a fucking idiot I was. I should have wiped down that desk before taking off.*

*After keeping a close eye on her, it's clear she isn't sitting back and doing nothing, or even just deflecting the accusations. She and her famous team are working twenty-four seven to clear her name—and to find the real killer in the process. How far have they gotten? Am I on their radar? Have they taken their theories to the cops, who are probably miles behind them in their investigation? If so, have the cops bought into all their theories? Are they about to show up at my door with an arrest warrant?*

*This can't happen. I've worked too hard.*

# 14

*Casey and Hutch's Apartment*
*Battery Park City, New York*
*Saturday, 5:45 a.m.*

Casey had long since stopped tossing and turning and had gotten out of bed. Hutch hadn't been able to come home last night—some big case he was working on. In a way, she was glad. She'd needed time alone to go through all of Emma's material and try to work out a plan.

Exhaustion had finally won out, and Casey had literally passed out from lack of sleep. She'd then jumped up at three a.m. and resumed her thinking. She came up with a skeleton of a plan and then tried to catch a couple of hours of additional sleep.

That hadn't happened.

So she'd showered, dressed, and headed back to the office.

She punched in the entry code, walked in, and nearly slipped on a sheet of paper that was sitting just inside the door.

Frowning, she bent and picked it up, instinctively holding it at its very edges in case fingerprints were required.

The page contained a series of squares, each one bearing a cut-out letter that looked as if it had come from a newspaper—all different fonts and sizes.

Together the letters read:

*Casey Woods. Back off or you'll join him.*

Casey reread the page a few times, looking for any clue where it had come from and who had composed it.

Nothing.

She carefully set it down, calling out, "Yoda, was there any suspicious activity at the brownstone last night?"

"No, Casey," Yoda responded instantly. "No intruders or disturbances. The only thing out of the ordinary was the arrival of the page you're now holding. It was slid under the door. No one accompanied it."

"Thank you." Casey trusted Yoda implicitly. Still, just to reassure herself, she unlocked a hidden drawer and removed her pistol. Slowly and silently, she searched the whole brownstone, floor by floor and room by room, making sure Yoda's infallible abilities hadn't been tested.

As he'd claimed, no one was there. And nothing had been disturbed.

Ever cautious, she grabbed her coat and stepped outside the building. She pulled the door shut and kept her pistol in her pocket. She didn't call the cops; she had another plan in mind.

She paused to glance across the street and to give a quick thumbs-up to John Nickels, her security detail, who was parked, ready and waiting to protect her as needed. She didn't want to complicate things by getting him involved. She could handle this on her own—well, almost on her own.

Whipping out her cell phone, she called her attorney, Shannon Grazier, on her cell. She lived closer to Tribeca than her partner, Robert Cateman, and Casey needed her attorney ASAP.

"Casey?" Shannon sounded deep in thought. Casey understood. She knew Shannon's schedule. She was an early riser; on weekends, she took a crack-of-dawn run, and then hunkered down in her home office.

"Guilty," Casey replied. "You're obviously working, and it's only seven fifteen. I apologize for bothering you so early on a Saturday, but something's happened, and I must get over to the First Precinct ASAP and talk to whichever detective is available. So I need you with me."

With that, she quickly explained the situation.

"You're right," Shannon said, rustling around as she donned business attire. "You *do* need me." A pause. "You do realize they're going to pass this along to the Nineteenth Precinct the minute you walk out the door? And that they're going to accuse you of conjuring this up on your own to throw suspicion off yourself?"

"I'm well aware of that, but they'll have at least a modicum of doubt. In which case, they'll note that I'm cooperating. They won't have a choice but to agree to periodically send a patrol car by FI headquarters. That's all I want from them anyway."

Casey was on a roll. "We both know that it would be glaringly illegal to keep this piece of physical evidence from them. Plus, it's to my benefit to share it. I want to look like a team player, not like I'm trying to undermine their investigation. And second, because they have to be aware of the fact that I'm in potential danger."

"Agreed," Shannon said. "I'll grab a cab and get there as fast as I can."

"Please meet me at the First Precinct. I don't think it's wise for me to stay at the brownstone."

"It isn't. I'll meet you *outside* the precinct."

"Understood. Thanks, Shannon."

Casey breathed a sigh of relief as she hung up.

She went back inside long enough to scan the threatening page and upload it to FI's system. She knew that handing over the original would mean losing the chance to dust it for fingerprints, but her gut told her it would be clean. The killer wasn't an idiot.

That done, she slid the original page in a Ziploc, returned her pistol to its drawer, and locked it.

She buttoned up her coat and left the brownstone. She'd stroll around a bit to kill time.

As she walked, she sent a text to Marc, alerting him to the situation, asking him to do another sweep of the building when he arrived, and asking him to fill the others in on the morning's events and on her whereabouts.

With time to spare, she stopped to buy herself a cup of coffee, which she drank as she headed to the precinct.

Caffeine had a way of bracing you for anything.

***

*Aidan's Apartment*
*West Seventy-Fifth Street, Seventh Floor*
*Manhattan, New York*
*Saturday, 7:35 a.m.*

"Hi, George," Marc greeted the doorman at Aidan's building. "I think he's expecting me."

George's fingers were already wrapped around the door handle. "He is indeed, sir. I'll let him know you're on your way up."

"Thank you." Marc strode through the entranceway and straight to the elevators, pressing the number seven. Exhausted though he was, he was also pumping with adreneline, and highly anticipating his upcoming discussion with his brother.

Aidan was already opening the door when Marc got there.

"Hey," he said, eyeing his brother speculatively. "You sounded very mysterious on the phone. Come on in and we'll talk."

Marc complied, his gaze flitting around as he did.

"Mrs. Reynolds took Abby out for an early-morning hot chocolate," Aidan supplied, shutting the door behind him. "So we're alone. There's coffee. Clearly, you need it. You look like hell."

Marc didn't answer until they were sitting at the counter in the kitchen nook, sipping their coffee.

At that point, he didn't mince words. "I wanted you to be the first to know. Maddy and I are having a baby."

Aidan whooped and grabbed Marc in a huge bear hug. "Way to go, frogman. That's wonderful news." He paused, studying Marc's rumpled state again. "Are Maddy and the baby both well?"

"Thankfully, yes." Marc sank back onto his stool. "It's been rough going. We've had painful disappointments and a lot of sleepless nights. We wanted this so much, for so long, that it was starting to feel as if it were an unattainable dream. But now…" Marc's whole face lit up. "It's finally happened. The pregnancy is real, and the baby is officially healthy. Maddy's on bed rest and has a visiting nurse with her, but we feel like we won the lottery."

"I remember that feeling as if it were yesterday," Aidan replied, nostalgia dampening his eyes. "The circumstances were a lot different for me, but having Abby…" He broke off, returning to Marc's news. "So when am I going to be an uncle?"

"In June." Marc was still beaming. "And I've saved the best part for last. Abby is going to flip. She's going to have a cohort in crime. It's a girl."

"Oh, yeah." Aidan slapped Marc's hand in a high five. "Girls are the best!"

\*\*\*

*Tribeca, New York*
*Saturday, 8:35 a.m.*

Casey was on the return trip to the office, hands shoved in the pockets of her winter coat and puffs of air coming from her mouth as she muttered aloud about the total waste of time that meeting had been.

She was just as irked and disgusted as she knew she'd be. As Shannon had warned, the detectives had pored over the letter, kept it to dust for fingerprints and to place it in their file, and, rather than entertaining the fact that Casey might be cooperating with them, they'd drawn the immediate conclusion that this evidence could have been fabricated to throw them off track. After all, wasn't it a coincidence that Casey was suddenly being so forthcoming when she and her team had shared nothing with law enforcement up to this point?

Shannon had shut down that line of questioning in a nanosecond. She got one of the detectives to grudgingly agree to send a patrol car by FI headquarters on occasion and then ended the meeting.

The whole thing had lasted a little over twenty minutes.

Casey had thanked Shannon for her time and waved away her kind offer of having the taxi drop Casey off. FI headquarters was just a few blocks from the precinct, and Casey needed the fresh air to calm her down before she got to the office. She'd expected the dubious reaction. She hadn't expected the ice-cold, almost accusatory tone.

The walk had only partially done its job when she reached the front door.

Before she could punch in the entry code, Emma flung open the door and stared at Casey with anxious blue eyes.

"Are you okay?" she demanded. "We've been half-crazed looking for you. We were about to call the FBI's New York field office and get Hutch involved."

Casey stepped inside and shut the door, her brows drawn together in puzzlement. "Why? You know where I was. I left a message for Marc explaining everything. Didn't he get it?"

"We haven't seen him yet," Patrick said, joining Emma and Casey in the foyer. "Which was beginning to concern me, as well. He and I should be on the road by now. We have another full day ahead to dig up something on Steadman." A frown. "Are you all right?"

"I'm pissed off, but fine. It's Marc I'm concerned about. Even if he didn't get my text, he's never this late without letting me know." She'd already pulled out her iPhone as she headed for the stairs. "Let's head up to the conference room. While I walk, I'll call him."

She pressed Marc's number as they ascended the stairs.

It rang a lot longer than usual.

Finally, he answered, sounding flustered and weird—nothing like his usual professional self.

"Hey, Casey. Sorry I'm not at the office yet. I know that Patrick and I have to get going. But I've got an issue at my end, and I'm just wrapping up."

That sounded more out of character than Casey could ignore. "Are you well? Is Maddy?"

"Yes. Fine," he reassured her in that same distracted tone.

"Did you get my text?" Casey demanded.

"What text?" A pause as Marc flipped through his messages. "Oh, I see it. I apologize. I haven't looked at my texts or emails all morning." Another pause as he read the message. "Shit. I'm on my way to the office."

Casey stared at the phone as she disconnected the call. She didn't care *what* Marc said, something significant was up, and she was determined to find out what that was before he and Patrick left the brownstone.

Settled in the conference room, the team listened as Casey filled them in on the morning's events and showed them the scanned image of the note.

"This is no longer a guessing game," Patrick said when she'd finished. He looked grim. "You're in danger—a lot more danger than we've entertained up until now. We have to up the game and find this person. *Now*."

Emma murmured her agreement. "Casey, did you check the video our cameras picked up?" she asked. "Maybe we'll make out something about who our killer is."

Casey looked up. "No, I was too focused on getting out of here. But you're right. Let's move on that. Yoda," she called, "can you project the camera footage from four a.m. to seven a.m. on the wall?"

"Pulling up that data already, Casey," he replied.

A few moments later, the camera footage appeared on the long wall across the room.

"Nothing yet," Emma muttered as four o'clock inched its way to five.

At five ten, they got what they wanted.

A faceless, shapeless person, clothed all in black complete with a black mask and a black hood, was looking quickly around before approaching the brownstone.

"A unisex walk," Casey determined aloud. "No way of determining if our perp is male or female."

As she spoke, the intruder reached the front door and swiftly shoved a piece of paper underneath. Just as quickly, they retraced their steps, turned away until the cameras lost range, and vanished into the night.

The team rewatched the video three times, and each time they came up empty.

Casey rubbed her temples and sighed. "We're no closer to figuring out who the killer is than we were before."

"Right." Patrick's lips were drawn into a tight, thin line. "But we do know that the killer is also after you."

"I have an idea," Casey said. "I'll take Hero out and let him sniff around. He'll memorize the intruder's scent, and he'll be able to match it to a person, once we've zeroed in on one."

She rose and gestured at the alert bloodhound, who always attended the team meetings. "Let's go, boy. We have a job to do."

\*\*\*

*Private Cottage*
*5,000 Miles from Manhattan*
*Maui, Hawaii*
*Saturday, 4:05 a.m. HST/Saturday, 9:05 a.m. EST*

Inside their private beachfront hideaway, Ryan and Claire collapsed in each other's arms on the bed, each of them panting and bathed in sweat.

"Six days and nights of this, with more than a week to go," Ryan managed. "You might kill me yet, but I can't think of a better way to die."

Claire gave a small, shaky laugh. "That sounds like heaven. Count me in."

Ryan propped himself on one elbow and trailed his fingers through Claire's long blond hair. "I love you. I can't get enough of you. Can't we extend our trip indefinitely?"

"Ummm—so tempting." Clearly, Claire liked the idea. "But I think the team would have something to say about that."

A corner of Ryan's mouth lifted. "Then how about we stay in bed until our flight leaves next Sunday—and then join the mile-high club as we wing our way home?"

Claire's brows shot up. "You'd really jump at the chance if I said yes, wouldn't you?"

"In a heartbeat."

"Well, you're out of luck. I don't like taking intimate risks, or being crammed in an airline bathroom while taking them. You'll just have to drown yourself in me for eight more days, and then be patient."

"It's a nine-and-a-half-hour flight," Ryan grumbled. "So far, we haven't lasted more than two hours since we got to Maui."

"We don't have to think about it for days and days," Claire murmured, snuggling closer to him. "It's only after we leave that we have to exercise some restraint."

Ryan scowled. "Yeah, I know. That doesn't mean I have to like it."

"Me either," Claire said ruefully. "But somehow we'll find ways to—" Abruptly, she broke off, trembling as she lurched into a sitting position. She went sheet white, a faraway look that Ryan knew only too well widening her eyes.

Ryan shoved himself up, gripping her shoulders as he did. "What is it?"

"It's Casey," she said, her breathing harsh. "She's in danger. Grave danger. We've got to get home." With that, she scrambled to her feet, grabbed the plush robe that had been her clothing for most of the vacation, and shrugged into it.

Ryan swung his legs over the side of the bed and stood in one fluid motion. He ignored his robe, headed straight to the closet where they'd left their cell phones when they first arrived, and snatched his up. He turned it on, and scanned the screen.

"No messages from the team," he announced with a frown.

"That's because Casey ordered them not to bother us." Claire reached under the bed and pulled out their travel bag.

"Yeah, well, that's not the way it's going to be." Ryan was already pulling up Casey's number.

"Hi." Casey sounded upset but not surprised to hear his voice. She knew Claire's claircognizant skills and had seen them in action time after time as they solved a case. No doubt the threatening letter had been enough to trigger her sensory awareness.

"What the hell is going on there?" Ryan demanded.

"You've barely started your vacation, Ryan," Casey tried. "This can wait."

"In your dreams." Ryan was furious. "Talk to me—*now*."

There was no getting out of this one. Plus, Casey was too shaken to try. In a tone filled with tension, she gave Ryan an overview of what had been happening since he and Claire had left.

"Son of a bitch," Ryan swore. "Your life is on the line, and you didn't think we should know *and* be there?"

He cut off whatever Casey was about to say. "I'm calling the airline now. We'll exchange next Sunday's nonstop tickets to today. We'll be on that flight if I have to bribe someone."

Claire had already thrown some clothes into the bag and was now heading for the shower. "We'll be landing tomorrow morning around seven thirty eastern time," she called out to Casey.

Casey blinked away tears. "Thanks."

"Don't thank us," Ryan responded. "I'm livid. You'll see how livid when we land." A pause. "Stay safe." He disconnected the call and punched in the phone number of Hawaiian Airlines.

They had no idea who they were about to deal with.

# 15

Both Casey and Patrick grabbed hold of Marc the instant he walked through the door.

"I'm sorry, guys," he said at once. "I screwed up big-time. Casey, are you okay?"

"Yes. And no. We need to talk," Casey replied in a tone that said it was an order, not a request.

Patrick interrupted her in a way he rarely did. "No. We need to leave. Marc and I are already running far too late. You're in danger. Talking can wait."

Casey hesitated, holding Marc's gaze. He looked exhausted, but he also looked relieved. There was a gleam in his eyes—none of which had anything to do with this case.

"Okay." Reluctantly, Casey backed off. "I'm worried enough to let you go. Plus, I have to contact Angela and arrange a meeting so I can bring her up to speed. But as soon as you get back…"

"We'll talk," Marc assured her.

"Fine."

\*\*\*

Angela actually answered her cell. Based on the blaring horns and chatting people moving in and out of earshot, Casey could tell she was walking either to or from her office.

"Hi, Casey," she said. "I haven't heard from you in a while. I was starting to get pissed at my newest employees."

"I had nothing to tell you. Now I do. When can we meet?"

"I've got a client meeting in a half hour. After that, I'll have tons of follow-up work, but I'll make myself free."

"How about I pick up sandwiches and come to your office at twelve thirty? Enough time for your meeting?"

"I'll be waiting."

Casey hung up, glad that she had enough time to plan out what she was going to say to Angela, and what she was going to extract in return. Regardless of what she'd originally told Angela, this was going to be a reciprocal relationship.

Casey would figure out how to make this "share time" productive.

***

*Randall Avenue*
*Throggs Neck, South Bronx, New York*
*Saturday, 9:55 a.m.*

Marc and Patrick pulled into a parking spot near the brick building where Steadman had lived and headed up to the street.

"Just on time," Patrick said, spying the mail truck moving slowly along. "Ten o'clock mail delivery."

Marc nodded. "What time do you want to call Officer Perkins back?"

"Probably around one. We have more than enough time to talk to the mail carrier and then chat with Mrs. Moss, the building gossip. She'll show up around noon to feed her cat, and we'll be waiting."

Marc's cell rang.

He glanced at the number, scowled, and answered. "Hey."

"Hello, Judas," Ryan greeted him. "I know what's going on. We'll be home tomorrow morning."

Marc rolled his eyes. "You're a far cry from Jesus, so cut the whole Judas thing. I followed my boss's orders. I didn't like them, I didn't agree with them, but I had no choice."

"Yeah, fine. Fortunately, Claire sensed what was going on so we called Casey, and she brought us up to speed. I also called Aidan—I can't believe you turned to him and Terri rather than to me."

"Again, Casey's call."

"So I heard. Anyway, I have time to kill, which means I can start working from here. Give me details of what you and Patrick are doing to find Oliver Steadman. I can lighten your load by using my tech skills to accelerate the process."

"Good." Marc sounded as relieved as he felt. "We have enough gumshoe work to do in person, but this hunt would go a lot faster with you doing your magic. This way, we divide and conquer."

"I'm listening."

Marc glanced, first at his watch, and then at Patrick, who'd clearly put together the pieces of the ongoing conversation.

"Let's split up and not waste time," Marc suggested to him. "You handle the mail carrier. I'll go back to the car and give whatever I can to Ryan. I'll be finished in time to talk to Mrs. Moss with you."

Patrick gave him a mock salute. "On my way."

\*\*\*

"Well?" Ryan demanded as soon as Marc was reseated in the car.

"Steadman's Hyundai Tucson is still parked outside the building," Marc said. "We're going to dig around and see if he bought another car under his real name. But, if he did, I'm sure he paid cash, so our hands will be tied. This afternoon, we'll head over to the local DMV with his license plate number and see what we can learn."

"Forget it. They won't tell you shit," Ryan said. "You just ask around his building to see if you can get a lead on a car purchase, and clue me in the instant you find something. In the meantime, I'll hack into the DMV's system and start out with Steadman's old driver's license, registration, and license plate number. After that, I'm probably going to come up empty without a new name, but I have a few ideas about a starting point that will hopefully expand into many more ideas, based on what you give me."

"Good," Marc replied. "Also more up your alley, Patrick and I had planned to try our luck with the US Passport site."

"Yeah, definitely up my alley. I'll get into their system and see what Steadman's passport status is, and maybe if he applied for a new one under a different name. It's another long shot, but I'm relentless."

"Last, we have no financial data on Steadman—checking accounts, credit cards, savings account. I'm just not that proficient a hacker to go that deep."

"Well, I am. So leave it to me. By the way, who's Mrs. Moss?"

"The building gossip at Steadman's old place," Marc replied. "Evidently, she's rife with information about everyone in the building. She comes home from work every day at noon to feed her cat. Patrick and I will make sure to talk to her then. We're also speaking to a local cop later today. He agreed to share what he felt comfortable with about Steadman. Our FBI creds helped."

"What about an alibi?" Ryan asked. "Have you established one for Steadman?"

"Nope. He's not on social media, and he's not on the NYPD's radar—I saw that when Terri got me into their system. So we've got nothing to go on."

"That means it's on me. No problem. And FYI, when you got into the NYPD system to see what they had on the hit-and-run, I'm sure you accessed the case file of the 111th Precinct in Bayside."

"Uh-huh," Marc replied.

"Well, just remember that they've now passed all their data on to the Nineteenth Precinct, which covers the Upper East Side, where

Hillington was killed. Now, the First Precinct in Tribeca is also involved, because our office is where that love letter was delivered. Everyone's plugged in now, but the Nineteenth is running the show."

"Gotcha."

Ryan paused, his mind clearly racing. "Marc, did you guys ever consider that Hillington might have been reaching out to Casey for help, rather than trying to implicate her?"

"Casey did, so yes. We haven't tackled that angle yet. There simply hasn't been time."

"I'll jump on it. The other consideration, given the pattern of events, is that Hillington was trying to warn Casey. If he knew his killer or their motivations, he might have realized that there was a connection between himself and Casey, and that her life was now in danger."

"That's a strong point we never delved into—other than to contemplate the fact that Steadman could be harboring rage against both Hillington and Casey," Marc said. "Unless he's not guilty. Then all that speculation goes to hell." He made a frustrated sound. "There are so many facets to this case, and so many urgent paths to follow in order to protect Casey and to exonerate her. And sorting out those paths and the order in which they need to be pursued has yet to be determined. Aidan took us just so far, but now, we need to sit down as a team and organize things."

"Yeah, I agree," Ryan replied. "I have a little more objectivity, since I just learned all the case details. It occurs to me we're putting all our efforts into finding Oliver Steadman. And Emma is checking out Hillington's son. But what if the killer is someone other than them? Shouldn't we be broadening our search?"

"Yes. We should."

"Then I say we all follow through on our designated assignments today, and then convene tomorrow morning as soon as I walk through the door. Casey's the one who will assimilate all the data and lay out our course of action."

"It's good to have you on board," Marc said in parting. "I don't suppose you got much sun."

"Nope. Just the few times we hit the beach. Best minivacation ever."

Marc chuckled. "Sorry for the deluge of cold water."

"Don't be. Casey is worth it."

# 16

Casey arrived spot on time. It was clear that Angela had given instructions to the receptionist, because the young woman immediately escorted Casey down to Angela's office.

The door was ajar, and the receptionist knocked lightly and said, "Ms. Woods is here."

Angela looked up, rising from behind her desk. "Thank you, Kelly." She beckoned to Casey to come in as her receptionist returned to the front desk.

"Hi," she said. "I hope that brown bag contains our sandwiches. I haven't eaten all day."

Casey nodded. "It does."

Her gaze swept the room. Unsurprisingly, it was enormous and as formidable as its occupant—its bookshelves, furniture, and floor all solid, expensive mahogany, its darkness brightened by the three large windows at its rear.

"Nice," Casey said.

"It should be considering how many billable hours I bring in." Angela pointed to the love seat and chairs at the far corner of the room wrapped around a complementary coffee table. "Sit."

Casey complied, lowering herself into a cushioned chair and placing the bag of sandwiches on the table. Simultaneously, Angela crossed over to the side table where there was a thermal coffee carafe and matching mugs.

"You're taking a crap shoot," Angela said with a frown. "Normally, you'd get a premier cup of coffee brewed at our impressive coffee station. But it's Saturday, so we're operating on a skeleton staff. We can't ask all our employees to put in a seven-day work week, even though our associates do. So your refreshment is on me, which means a basic cup of joe. That okay with you?"

Casey smiled. "I hear you and it's no problem." She indicated the large paper bag in front of her. "I hope you like a turkey club."

"I most definitely do." Angela held up one of the two steaming cups, then glanced at her minifridge. "Milk? Sugar?"

"Black is fine. Nothing like straight caffeine."

"Agreed." Angela carried both cups over, set them on the coffee table, and then settled herself across from Casey.

For the moment, she ignored their lunch in lieu of business. "So tell me what's happened."

Casey took a sip of her coffee, and then said, "Lucky me. There was a love letter slid under FI's door waiting for me early this morning. I found it when I walked in."

Interest flickered in Angela's eyes. "A threat?"

"You guessed it." Casey went on to tell Angela what the creepy letter had said and how the pieces of it had been cut and pasted.

"Sounds amateurish—like it's the work of a newbie," Angela said, opening up her turkey club and taking a healthy bite.

"Maybe. Or maybe it's the work of a shrewd person who knows there's no way that method could be traced."

"Good point. Go on."

Casey also took a bite of her sandwich. She didn't remember the last time she'd eaten—sometime yesterday. And the sandwich was a definite lifesaver.

"I took the letter to the First Precinct, like a good girl," she said. "My attorney, of course, was with me. The detectives seemed eager to suggest that *I* could have composed the letter myself."

"Did you?" Angela's question was quick and blunt, meant to catch Casey off guard.

"No" was Casey's equally quick and blunt reply.

Angela didn't look surprised. "I didn't think so. That really isn't your style." She paused. "I assume that the second you walked out the door the First Precinct sent this on to the Nineteenth."

"I'm sure they did. Right into the files of Detectives Burt Ogden and Lorraine Banks."

A hint of a grin. "These precincts really don't like you, do they?"

"Nope." Casey continued eating. "And frankly, I don't much care. I did the lawful thing. The letter is now in their possession. Let's hope the perp really is an amateur and left fingerprints. But I wouldn't count on it. More likely, this was a blatant way of getting me off this case by implying my life is on the line. And maybe it is. But it's not going to scare me away from doing my job."

"I never expected it would." Angela looked thoughtful. "So your connection to Christopher takes on a new meaning. Instead of being a threat to him, you're a threat to the killer."

"Sure looks that way. My team and I are working to figure out why. And who. This case—these two cases—have a lot of tentacles leading in different directions. We're following every single one."

Casey stopped, abruptly changing gears. "Anything new here? Further visits from the police? Or have you just been doing subtle poking around to make sure your firm is in the clear?"

This time, Angela gave Casey a cool smile. "Nice technique. But status quo at this end."

"Right." Casey pressed forward with her plan. "I thought of one avenue we can pursue together, without your breaking confidence."

"Which would be…?"

"Charlotte Hillington and her kids. They're not and have never been clients of yours. Yet, they have glaring red flags hanging over their heads. Let's join forces and figure out their agendas, and if any one or all of them could be the killer or killers."

Angela pursed her lips, considering that option. "We'll be limited. Anything that even remotely involves Christopher is off-limits."

"But there's a lot that *doesn't* involve him. Let's cover those bases."

"I can agree to that," Angela replied.

"Then let's set up a follow-up meeting—one where we both have a solid block of time in which to strategize. Such as tomorrow. It's Sunday—a lighter day, I hope. Does that work?"

"Late afternoon, like three?"

"Works for me. Let's meet for coffee."

Angela shot her a shrewd look. "You really don't want me near your troops. They must be doing very interesting work."

"Always. And I'll keep you apprised when we zero in on something real."

"Fine. Tomorrow at three. I'm working from home, so come to my place." Angela rattled off her Manhattan address.

"Great."

Both women rose, shaking hands and carefully assessing each other.

"You know," Angela concluded, "I think I'm starting to like you."

\*\*\*

*Randall Avenue*
*Throggs Neck, South Bronx, New York*
*Saturday, 12:55 p.m.*

Marc checked his Apple Watch, then changed his position for the tenth time in almost an hour. Every few minutes, he started texting furiously. The texts were going to Patrick, who was sitting in the car, but Marc's body language screamed that he was pissed at whoever had stood him up. And he was making sure to munch on a hot dog while he marched around. The last thing he needed was to be noticed and questioned about why he was hanging out there—especially by a patrol car making its rounds.

He and Patrick had decided not to descend on Mrs. Moss in tandem. That would intimidate the hell out of her, and any chance of gaining information would be shot to hell. So Marc was taking this one alone.

He hoped this conversation would be more productive than Patrick's with the mail carrier had been. That had yielded only the barest filament of a lead, which, for now, could take them nowhere.

The guy had repeated what they'd already learned from the post office clerk: that Steadman's mail was backed up and being held after sorting by the post office. When Patrick pressed him on Steadman's previous mail arrivals, he'd said that—while he wasn't in the habit of snooping—he recalled that Steadman had received nothing but junk mail and bills, plus what looked like a few personal letters. Patrick had pounced on that, but the carrier had balked, saying he didn't remember the name or return address on the letters.

Actually, Patrick had believed him. He'd handed the carrier his business card, and asked only if he'd contact him if he did remember who the letters had been from or what the return address had been.

And that had been that.

Until now, when Marc had stationed himself outside the building, in the frigid December air, waiting impatiently for Mrs. Moss to get around to coming home and feeding her cat.

***

Ten minutes later, a plain-looking woman matching the description the tenants had provided yesterday walked down the street and climbed the few steps to the building's entranceway.

As she put her key in the lock, Marc approached her.

"Mrs. Moss?" he asked with a friendly expression.

She turned, startled. "Yes. And you are…?"

"Marc Devereaux." He flashed her his business card so that she could see he was a PI. "May I please come in and ask you a few questions? Your neighbors all rave about how well you know everyone in the building."

The middle-aged woman beamed. "I pride myself on keeping on top of things. And, of course, on being hospitable. By all means, come in. I assume we can chat in the lobby?"

Marc had figured as much. He couldn't blame her for not welcoming a total stranger into her home.

"Of course," he replied, following her into the building and over to the small sitting area just inside.

They both took a seat, after which she asked, "What can I do for you? I don't have much time. I'm running late, and my poor cat must be famished. I'm also due back at my desk soon."

"This will only take a few minutes," Marc assured her. "I was wondering if you knew Oliver Steadman?"

Mrs. Moss's smile turned into a frown. "Why are you looking for him? Did he commit a crime?"

Marc didn't change expression. "I don't know. Why would you think so?"

"Because the man is a creep. He never speaks to any of us, just holes himself up in his apartment. I've heard arguments between him and a woman, and she usually ends up crying. Other than that, he just walks past all of us as if we're invisible. The other tenants don't notice, but I do. He's a very sketchy character."

Marc's antennae shot up. "So I've been told. Have you seen this woman you're referring to or heard Steadman say her name?"

"I've never seen her." Mrs. Moss shook her head. "But her name…" She looked thoughtful. "I heard him say it once, but it was muffled. I couldn't have heard it clearly unless I pressed my ear to the door. Which I never would. I'm not that kind of person."

Marc hid his smile. "Of course you're not. Do you recall even a syllable?"

Mrs. Moss pursed her lips. "It was a short name, like Barb or Bev…" She snapped her fingers. "Beth. It was Beth. I'm sure of it."

"That's great," Marc praised. "Anything else you could make out?"

"She had some kind of accent, like an inflection. I can't place it, but she's definitely not a metropolitan New Yorker. And, like I said, they argued whenever she was here."

"Recently?"

"Maybe a few weeks ago."

"Have you seen Steadman around lately?"

Mrs. Moss's brows drew together. "Now that you mention it, not for a while. About three weeks ago, I was walking past his apartment and I heard him on his phone, saying something about buying a car. I wish I'd listened more closely. I'm guessing he's running away from trouble. I hope he didn't hurt that poor girl."

"I hope not, too." Marc rose. "Thank you for your time. You've been very helpful."

"I wish I could tell you more." Mrs. Moss stood, as well, accepting Marc's proffered business card. This time she studied it closely. "Oh, I've heard of you. Forensic Instincts is pretty famous. I'll help you out whenever I can. If I think of anything I forgot, I'll call you right away."

"That would be great." Marc could sense that she was about to spill her guts to the immediate world about helping out the one and only Forensic Instincts. He had to nip this in the bud.

He met her gaze and pressed his forefinger to his lips. "Please keep this between us. If Steadman gets wind of the fact that we're keeping tabs on him, he'll take off again. We need to find him. Can you do that?"

"Of course." Mrs. Moss was clearly unhappy about keeping her enthralling news from the entire world. Still, the thrill of all this intrigue, and actually helping out FI, was enough to make her agree. "Mum's the word."

# 17

*Evans Residence*
*210 Alameda Avenue*
*Douglaston, Queens, New York*
*Saturday, 4:15 p.m.*

Natalie was sitting at the kitchen table, sipping a cup of coffee and trying to read her newsfeed. But her mind was numb and her eyes were swollen from crying and from lack of sleep. She was absorbing next to nothing of what she was reading.

With a heavy sigh, she placed her cup and iPhone on the table and pressed her fingers to her temples to rub away the throbbing headache that had plagued her all night and all day.

Morgan hadn't come out of her room since yesterday, and Natalie was anxious and heartbroken. What had she done to her daughter? What could she do to ease her pain and to help her accept the truth? Was that even possible? Oh, God, maybe she should never have told her. But was that fair to Morgan? She had Christopher's blood running through her veins. Shouldn't she know about him, his feelings for her, and what he'd done about those feelings?

As Natalie tortured herself with grief and guilt, there was a sound in the doorway. She looked up, new tears trickling down her face as she saw Morgan standing there.

"Hi," Morgan offered, looking like a lost little girl. "May I come in?"

"*May you?*" Natalie blurted out. "I've been praying you would. I'm so worried, so ridden with guilt, and so terrified I'd lost you forever."

Morgan crossed over and gave her mother a hug. "You'll never lose me. I just had so much to process. I needed time alone. But now—can we talk? I have so many questions."

"Of course." Natalie went to the fridge, made them each a fruit cup, grabbed two spoons, and placed it all on the table. At the same time, Morgan was pouring herself a cup of coffee.

"Thank you," Morgan said, settling herself beside her mother at the table and eating a spoonful of fruit. "Somewhere in my mind, I realize I need food."

"We both do," Natalie replied. "After we talk, we'll put together a real meal. Neither of us has eaten since yesterday, but talking comes first. Ask me anything, and I'll answer honestly."

"Please do. We both need this. It might not make it better, but it's the only chance I have of making peace with the truth and finding some sort of closure."

Natalie nodded and waited.

"What did you see in him that made you love him, and act so out of character to be with him?" Morgan asked. "He was married. Plus, from what I've been reading about him, he sounded cold and ruthless. And, from the press conference I found on YouTube, he looked remorseless about the hit-and-run. Even if he was innocent, that poor man died. Didn't Christopher Hillington have a shred of compassion?"

Natalie had anticipated those questions. They were valid.

"The private Christopher and the public Christopher were two entirely different people," she said. "With me, he was the real Christopher. Loving, generous, and kind. And not only when he was young, but when we got back together. I so wish you'd had the chance to meet him. You would have seen it, too. When we first became involved, did I find out he was married? Yes. Did I guess what kind of businessman he was? Of course. But, given how he was when we were together, it was easy for me to look away. To separate the two Christophers. I guess it's true that love is blind."

Morgan processed that and gave a dubious nod. "I've never experienced that depth of romantic love, so I can't condemn you. Maybe I'd be the same way, too."

Natalie gently shook her head. "No you wouldn't. You're much more level-headed and grounded than I was at your age. You'd probably have kicked him to the curb for good the instant you realized his deception and torn him out of your heart forever. But I couldn't."

She swallowed and continued. "As for the hit-and-run, you have no idea how devastated he was. He knew he was innocent, but that didn't stop him from pitying that poor man and his family. He was also very angry. The police had all but out-and-out accused and arrested him. There was not a solid bit of proof, but that didn't stop them. Especially given the fact that he wouldn't reveal why he'd been in South Bayside to begin with."

A light bulb went off in Morgan's head. "He was here that night. South Bayside is on the route from Douglaston to the city."

"Exactly. He was waiting to meet you, with or without my permission. He didn't give up until after dark. Then, he left, announcing to me that he'd be back in the morning to strike up a relationship with his daughter. His words, by the way. He was frustrated and upset, so I'm sure he was speeding on his way home. Still, he never struck that car, even though the police were convinced otherwise—especially when he wouldn't tell them where he'd been. He wasn't willing to bring us into the ugly investigation, so he refused to answer their questions, which only made him look guiltier than the police already thought he was."

"Wow." Morgan took a fortifying sip of coffee. "You certainly paint a different picture than the media does."

"And how often is the media wrong?" Natalie asked quietly.

"Pretty often," Morgan had to admit.

"I may be starry-eyed, but I'm not an idiot. If I thought for one moment that Christopher was guilty, I would have ended it on the spot. But I knew otherwise. Did your research mention that the very next day, the police came to his apartment building to check out his car, and it didn't have so much as a scratch on it? Does that sound feasible to you? Even a powerful man with connections couldn't get a body shop to fix a bashed-up car in a day."

Again, Morgan gave a thoughtful nod. "That's true." A pause. "Okay, I accept your belief that he was innocent of the crime. I even understand how your feelings for him kept you from pushing him away, especially once he knew I was his biological child. But what made you pick yesterday for the big reveal? Something must have prompted it."

This time it was Natalie who took a spoonful of fruit and quickly swallowed it. She hadn't realized her hands were shaking so badly.

"Other than the fact that I felt you had the right to know? It was the whole misunderstanding about your tuition. Christopher wanted to take care of that, to take care of you, even when I refused to let him meet you and tell you who he was. As soon as he realized you were his daughter, he set up a trust fund for you, making me the trustee. I foolishly knew nothing about Jonathan's restrictions in the use of his funds for you. So, right after Christopher was so brutally murdered, I made that payment from your trust. As I later promised you, I stopped the payment and restored the money to where it belonged."

"Which is why you said you'd take care of my graduate program and my getting set up in a career," Morgan deduced. "You loved him, I was biologically his, and he was gone."

"Precisely. I'm sorry I deceived you. That's a significant reason why I told you the truth."

"I understand." Morgan reached across the table and squeezed her mother's hand. "I'm sorry he was murdered. You must be shattered."

"I was…and I am" was the frank reply. "And I couldn't share that heartbreak with anyone. Not even you—not until you knew the whole truth. So I've been grieving alone." Natalie's voice quavered. "It's been hell."

"I'm here now. Let me in."

Natalie smiled through her tears. "Gladly. For starters, I have a thin album of photos. Just Christopher and me. Would you like to see it?"

Morgan nodded at once. "Yes."

\*\*\*

*Offices of Forensic Instincts*
*Tribeca, New York*
*Saturday, 5:30 p.m.*

Patrick and Marc walked into the brownstone, cold and exhausted.

They'd probed all they could about Steadman. They'd met with Officer Perkins for a half hour, and he'd corroborated what Mrs. Moss had said about Steadman's maltreatment of women. There'd actually been some domestic violence complaints about him, though no proof and no arrests. Still, Patrick and Marc had gotten three women's names from the officer, which meant they had something to go on. Unfortunately, none of the names was Beth or anything close to it.

Tracking down a recent car sale had been a dead end. Obviously it had been a cash deal, and who knew where Steadman had gone to make it. Marc had instructed Yoda to scan local social sites in Steadman's neighborhood for mentions of car sales. Hopefully, something relevant would soon turn up.

So many outstanding questions. So few answers.

Casey walked into the foyer as they were hanging up their coats. Seeing her, Marc glanced at his watch. "I have to get home soon."

"Not until we talk," she replied in a no-nonsense tone. "Patrick can fill me in on what you learned once you take off, but right now, we're going to your office and having a conversation."

Marc nodded. "I'm a man of my word."

Together, they climbed the stairs to Marc's third-floor office, went inside, and shut the door. Marc perched at the edge of his desk, and Casey leaned back against the door, her arms folded across her chest.

"Well?" she demanded. "What's going on with you? You've been so far out of character that I barely know you. I don't need to enumerate. Just tell me."

To Casey's surprise, a broad grin split Marc's face. "Maddy and I are pregnant. We're having a healthy baby girl."

Casey practically ran over to hug him. "Oh, Marc, I'm so thrilled for you both."

"We're over the moon," he replied, still grinning like he'd won the lottery. "It's been a tough go. Maddy is past thirty-five, with some physical issues, which makes this a high-risk pregnancy. We had a few scares. So we were waiting fourteen weeks until we could find out our baby was healthy before sharing the news. That she's a girl is a plus. Abby will be driving Aidan and me crazy with I-don't-want-to-wait excitement. Anyway, I planned to tell you this late last night, right after we got the news. But then, Maddy started not feeling well. It wasn't just the usual nausea and fatigue. By the middle of the night, she started cramping and I flipped out. I raced her to the ER. Thankfully, the cramps were just the result of all the probing and prodding. They stopped soon after we got there, but we stayed for a while, just in case. Early this morning, I stopped at Aidan's to tell him, which is why I never read your text and why I've been less than proficient at doing my job. I hope you understand."

"I more than understand," Casey said, her smile almost as wide as Marc's. "I've seen the way you and Maddy are with Abby, and I knew you were born to be parents. I'm sorry it's been a tough ride, but just seeing your face—it was more than worth it."

"Sure was." Marc paused. "I want to tell the team, but I'd rather wait for tomorrow when Ryan and Claire are back. That way, my whole work family can find out at once. Plus, I really do need to get home to Maddy. She's on bed rest and, in opposition to what a good nurse she is, she's a lousy patient. I finally called one of her friends who's a visiting nurse and she's spending the days at our place. Otherwise, I don't think I'd ever leave the house."

"Go," Casey urged. "Send congratulations to Maddy."

"I will. And I'll be here early tomorrow, ready to go."

"Good, because I'm Slacking the team to say we're having a meeting as soon as Ryan and Claire walk in."

# 18

Casey was in the hallway when the front door of the townhouse blew open and Ryan and Claire rushed in.

Ryan dropped their travel bag to the floor, and then spoke in terse, still-angry sentences. "Like I said in my text, turbulence slowed us down. We came straight here from the airport. Marc's been keeping me up-to-date. I also spoke to Aidan. I still can't believe you turned to him and Terri rather than to me."

Claire waved him off. "Ryan, stop." She didn't wait for a reply, just walked directly to Casey and gave her a big hug. "I'm so grateful you're okay," she said. "Ryan's been working since yesterday. I, unfortunately, had nothing to aid me. Now that I'm home, all that will change."

Ryan walked over and squeezed Casey's shoulders. "I'm still ripping pissed," he announced. "But my skills and I are back. Let's go to the conference room, grab a cup of coffee, and get this team meeting started."

"You go on ahead. I'll Slack the troops to give them a heads-up that we're ready."

"We'll be waiting." Ryan started for the stairs. "And I'll be pacing."

A hint of a smile touched Casey's lips. "Duly noted."

***

*Sunday, 9:25 a.m.*

The FI team gathered around the conference room table, this time at full capacity.

Ryan and Claire were welcomed back, and Marc made his announcement to the team. There were hugs, handshakes, and congratulations all around.

"Super cool," Ryan said, grinning. "I'll be her brilliant uncle Ryan who teaches her to be an IT whiz. And during her early years, she'll be trained by Abby in being a hellion."

"Yeah, that's what I'm afraid of," Marc said with an answering grin.

Just as quickly, he sobered. "We have a lot to catch up on, and we need to plan our next steps. So let's get started." He glanced at Patrick, then at Casey. "Should Patrick and I go first?"

She nodded her approval. "Go."

Quickly, the two men filled Casey and the team in on all they'd discovered about Steadman—and all they hadn't.

"The officer you met with and that Mrs. Moss gave us some useful clues," Casey responded. "Let's run with them."

"We intend to," Patrick agreed.

"Okay, me next," Ryan said. "I've been pounding away since yesterday. To begin with, Steadman has no alibi I can find. Based on his IP address, it looks like he was always online, alone in his apartment. The constant flow of his Internet traffic from there, plus his lack of personal interactions, suggests he had no friends. So that was a dead end. And he wasn't in the habit of working late, so I got nothing from there either. That doesn't mean I'm giving up—not on anything I'm telling you.

"From there I hacked into the DMV and the US Passport sites. All the old address and passport data was filed under Steadman's name. No change of ID on either site. His old passport hasn't been used in ages and expired. I haven't yet found an avenue where I can further track him, not until I know the new name he's using. But I will. Same problem with financial info on him—I ran his checking accounts, credit cards, and savings account. All the money was pulled three weeks ago. None of the credit cards have been used, and the money is in no way enough to live on for more than a month, especially if he's paying rent. I'll keep trying to trace the money and see if he uses his credit cards."

"Maybe he's not paying rent," Casey pointed out. "Maybe he's shacking up at someone else's place."

"Like his girlfriend's," Emma said. "A love-hate relationship. It's a strong possibility, but we're still hitting our heads against a brick wall, because we can't find his new ID."

"It'll happen," Ryan assured her. "I have channels still yet to explore. And now that I'm here and able to work with Yoda, the process will be accelerated."

He paused. "I want to hear what everyone else has to say, but first I want to suggest that we broaden our search. I told this to Marc yesterday, and I'm telling you all now. If it turns out that Steadman is not the criminal we're looking for, we've got next to nothing. We have to lay out all the players and all the facts we can't streamline yet and dig into them. I'm worried that our scope is too narrow."

Emma responded, "'Madison' is seeing Brighton Hillington again today. I'll push harder to get some answers about him, his mother, and his sisters. I've already read through all the kids' social media account postings, but I'm still going through them. Hopefully, I can establish some alibis."

"And I'll go up to my yoga room with the copy of that threatening letter and see if I can pick up anything from holding it," Claire said. "What I sense might not be as powerful as I'd like, since it's not the original letter, but maybe I'll get lucky."

"Good start," Ryan said. "But we have to do more and work faster. After this meeting, I'm getting deeper into the NYPD's system and both Hillington case files—his murder and the hit-and-run. Marc, you did a good job on the latter, but frankly, I can do better."

"No argument." Marc held up his hands. "I'm a novice. You're a pro. Dig as deep as you can."

"I will. We need all the details of that hit-and-run, and we need to combine it with what we learn about Hillington's murder."

"You think there's a connection?" Patrick asked.

Ryan shrugged. "Maybe, maybe not, but they both happened within weeks of each other. We have to consider every possible angle."

"Such as?" Casey could see there was something specific on Ryan's mind.

"Such as maybe Hillington *was* seeking your help. Or maybe he knew the killer and his MO, and was trying to warn you that your life is in danger. I know you don't want to hear that, but it's a distinct possibility."

"You're right, I don't want to hear it," Casey said flatly. "But I agree we should look into it. And, speaking of other angles, I met with Angela King yesterday and we made plans to meet again this afternoon. I told her about the threatening letter and the police. Then I suggested we pool our resources to investigate Hillington's family—they're not protected by privilege—and she agreed."

"Smart," Marc said. "In addition to Emma, we'll have an ally on that front."

Ryan was still frowning and thinking.

"What are we leaving out?" Casey asked.

"What Hillington was doing in South Bayside, Queens, where the hit-and-run took place. It's bugging the hell out of me. It wasn't a coincidence. I've got to figure this part out when I dive into the hit-and-run. The case file must have something on the subject, something deeper than Marc could go. I think the answer to that question is going to give us a solid lead—and I plan on finding it."

"So here's today's plan," Casey said. "I'm going to Angela's place to see if we can come up with anything on Charlotte Hillington and her kids. Marc and Patrick, review all the leads you got yesterday and run with what you can. Claire, you spend as much time as necessary in your yoga room to see what you can sense from the threatening letter or the camera footage from the morning it was shoved under our door. Emma, you keep your date with Brighton Hillington—but be careful. And Ryan, you've got the weight of the world on your shoulders. Do it all and succeed."

Ryan grinned. "No pressure there. But you know I will."

Casey nodded, then rose. "Let's get going."

\*\*\*

*Nineteenth Precinct*
*153 East Sixty-Seventh Street*
*Manhattan, New York*
*Sunday, 10:05 a.m.*

Detectives Lorraine Banks and Burt Ogden were both at their desks, each of them too bugged by the conflicting facts of the Hillington murder to hang out at home. And the letter Casey had delivered to the First Precinct yesterday was now added to their case file. Its existence, and all the details Casey had provided, further complicated their investigation into her.

Lorraine took a swallow of cold coffee and studied her partner's face. "Bottom line, do you think Casey Woods is on the up-and-up or lying through her teeth?"

Burt scowled. "The truth? I don't think any of this is her style. I'm not dismissing it, but do you really think Woods would commit that type of brutal murder and then try to fabricate her way out of an arrest?"

"We've bandied the first part around since we found her name in blood on Hillington's desk, and, so far, we've come up with nothing. Frankly, I think we're wasting our time going after her, unless we come up with a motive that's evading us. So, no, I don't think Casey Woods killed anyone, and I do think it's possible that she's more likely on the victim list. I hate the fact that Forensics Instincts is one step ahead of us in this investigation—which my gut tells me they are. It's the whole group of them we need to keep an eye on."

"Yeah." Burt was still scowling. "I'm sure they've got something up their sleeve that they haven't shared with us."

"Do you think they've talked to Leonard, the Hillington doorman?" Lorraine asked. "He'd willingly tell them about the restaurant delivery person. Not to mention, Casey can be quite persuasive."

"Tell them what?" Burt demanded. "The description Leonard provided of the delivery person was beyond minimal. And even if it was one of our suspects, who? Any one of them could have disguised themselves and come out as a blond-haired, gender-unknown employee, wearing a black parka, hood up, and a scarf and gloves. We don't even know the restaurant or café the food came from."

"I know." Lorraine was clearly irked, just as she had been since they'd started investigating this dud of a lead. "We've got nothing except for the fact that the person arrived on a bike with an insulated bag, allegedly carrying breakfast for Hillington. And, according to Leonard, Hillington didn't hesitate when Leonard announced his visitor. He simply asked Leonard to send them up. Delivery people are usually invisible—which is exemplified by the fact that none of the other residents we talked to remember a delivery person. Worse, no one saw them leave. Leonard was on break, and when he got back, the bike—and its owner—were gone."

Burt waved his hand dismissively. "We've discussed this ad nauseam, Lorraine. Right now, this is a dead end. I realize it's suspiciously coincidental, but Hillington's housekeeper was off that day. And no one else in his family was home. Angela King didn't show up at Hillington's apartment until it was time for their nine-thirty meeting, at which time she found the body. So it's plausible he ordered breakfast. We did find that crumpled, bacon-smelling bag in his kitchen trash. He was hungry. He didn't plan on being killed."

"I know." Lorraine blew out a breath. "But the timing—it still bugs me. Just like Forensic Instincts bugs you."

Burt grunted. "They're another matter entirely. If the chasm between us gets wider, I opt for a subpoena to go through their files. Unfortunately, we don't have grounds for that yet. Especially with Casey Woods coming forward with that letter. It suggests she and her team are cooperating with us, even if it's because Woods's life is in danger."

Lorraine took another sip of coffee and winced. "This stuff sucks. I'm going to make another pot. It'll still suck, but at least it'll be hot."

She started to get up, then paused. "They might be a step ahead of us, but they obviously have no idea who killed Hillington. They might not even have a solid number of suspects. If they did, Woods never would have come clean with us about the letter. She'd have dusted it for prints and tried to link whatever she found to her prime suspect."

"But there *were* no prints," Burt reminded her.

"She didn't know that. If Forensic Instincts had messed with the letter, our evidence team would have seen it."

Burt's jaw clenched. "You're right. So our job is to move even faster and, if need be, subpoena them. That'll scare the shit out of them, even if their data is deeply hidden."

"Nothing scares the shit out of them. And don't sell Ryan McKay short. He'll make it near impossible for us to access what they have."

"Then we'd better have it first."

*** 

*Offices of Forensic Instincts*
*Claire's Yoga Room*
*Tribeca, New York*
*Sunday, 11:30 a.m.*

Claire sat on her yoga mat in lotus position, photos and news clippings spread out around her, the threatening letter right in front of her. She paused to lean back on her hands and roll her shoulders in order to get rid of the headache the past few hours had brought on.

It wasn't a surprise that this was a difficult one. She had only secondhand material to go on.

She'd gotten a few flashes of insight while lightly running her fingers over the letter, but no bursts of awareness that always accompanied her major realizations. Still, she wasn't leaving this room until she channeled something.

She resumed her position, settling herself and clearing her mind. She concentrated on her memory of the video footage outside the brownstone that she'd viewed before coming in here. There was a strong connection between the visuals and the letter. Obviously, they were tied to the same person, but she had no clear vision who that person was, including Oliver Steadman. So that tactic had fallen flat.

She wished she had something real of Steadman's to handle. That would definitely jolt her into something. Marc had promised her that he'd find a way—whether legal or illegal—to get into Steadman's apartment and grab some personal items for her. Hopefully, that would open doors for her.

For now, her mind kept centering on the Hillington family.

Something there wasn't right. Deception. Power struggles. Disastrous alliances. Was it Charlotte? Any or all of her kids? The entire family? Was it all tied to business subterfuge and clawing their way to Hillington's money? Or was it more? Did any of these dark connections include murder?

Claire gave a frustrated sigh. There was so much more beneath this surface, but she was behind the eight ball. She'd stepped into this case late. She'd never met any of the Hillingtons, so she had nothing to go on. She needed firsthand connections.

She had to find a way to get them.

# 19

Whatever Emma had expected Brighton's studio to be, it certainly wasn't this.

Her mental picture had been of a modest loft with two equally modest rooms—a control room and a recording room. What she and Brighton walked into was an enormous, oak-floored, multiroomed state-of-the-art audio recording studio, as aesthetically beautiful as it was functional.

Emma took in the tech-savvy control room, the two large recording rooms, and a breakout room containing four gaming stations and a semicircle of leather couches surrounding a high-end TV—not to mention an adjoining kitchenette and bathroom. The place looked more like the extravagant studio of a famous rock group than it did like a budding artist's workspace.

Brighton was watching "Madison's" face, and he grinned as he saw her reaction. "Not bad, huh?"

"Bad?" she managed. "I never expected…"

"My father was filthy rich. Like I told you before, this haven was a birthday present to me. He was good at presents. Not so good at the father stuff, but, hey, I'll take it. Money makes the world go round, like the song says." Brighton's jaw tightened. "At least it did until the end."

Before Emma could probe that final comment, Brighton had guided her inside. "Let me show you around."

He took her through the entire place, pointing out all the jaw-dropping highlights—everything from the control room with the elaborate sound board, to the audio equipment, to the two large recording rooms, both soundproofed so that all noise was kept to a minimum.

"Nothing for the neighbors to hear," Brighton said in his most seductive voice. "We'll spend time alone in here later."

Emma was barely listening, much less responding, her mind focused on how she was going to get more information out of him.

"Madison?"

"Oh…yes," she replied with a sunny smile. "I guess I'm a little overwhelmed by everything."

He grinned his understanding. "Come meet the rest of my four-part rock band. I'm the lead guitarist *and* the lead singer. That alone should impress you. Then again, I intend to impress you all afternoon—and not only with my musical genius."

Emma managed a breathy sound and a nod.

She then shook hands with the other three members of Brighton's band—his rhythm guitarist, his bass guitarist, and his drummer. Last came Todd Denny, the live sound-mix engineer now in Brighton's employ.

Todd returned her handshake. "Why doesn't Madison watch from inside the control room?" he asked Brighton. "It's the best seat in the house. And she can hear everything."

Brighton nodded his agreement. "Good idea. We'll do a little of my old stuff, but mostly my new stuff." He winked at Emma. "Feel free to look elated and to even dance. This music will make you move."

Emma's eyes lit up. "I will."

As soon as Brighton had left the control room, Emma swiveled a leather chair around to face the larger recording room. The band had finished setting up and she grinned at Brighton, giving him a thumbs-up.

The recording session started, and Emma's brows rose.

Her mind might have been elsewhere, but she had to admit the band was good. Really good. So were the songs—the music and the lyrics. Brighton had talent, and he also had a great voice. With enough money to back him, his band would go far.

With enough money... Her thoughts returned to the odd comment Brighton had made earlier. *Money makes the world go round—at least it did until the end.* What did that mean? Did he and his father have a falling out, which made Hillington cut off his investment in Brighton? And if so, and it was at the end of his life, how would Brighton have reacted? Now he was being glib about it, but had he been furious—furious enough to do something violent?

Emma had to snuff out the questions—for now. She'd bide her time. And, when the opportunity presented itself, she'd be all over it.

***

The opportunity didn't present itself for hours.

First came the entire rehearsal session, complete with some cool jamming by the band. Then came the dismantling of mikes and equipment, accompanied by Emma's enthusiastic praise and excitement. And finally came the second round of handshakes as the band members grabbed their instruments, said their goodbyes, and left, closely followed by Todd.

Leaving Brighton and Emma alone.

Brighton perched at the edge of the leather chair next to Emma's, clearly revved up by the session, and equally revved up by this time with "Madison."

"Want something to drink?" he asked her. "I've got everything, from hard to soft. What's your pleasure?"

Emma weighed her options. She wanted to keep her head as clear as possible. On the other hand, asking for a Diet Coke sounded decidedly unromantic. She opted for in between.

"Maybe a glass of wine?" she asked.

"Sure." Brighton jumped up. "White or red?"

Emma's brows rose quizzically. "That depends—is there food to go along with this?"

Brighton chuckled. "There's a pizza en route. I knew I'd be famished after performing, and I hoped you would be, too. I got plain cheese, since I didn't know your toppings of choice, and I want to please you. In fact..." He shot her a seductive look. "I plan on pleasing you for as many hours as I can coax you to stay."

*Boy, he really has his technique down pat*, Emma thought.

"Wonderful!" she said aloud. "Then I'll have a glass of white wine while I wait for the pizza to arrive." Her eyes sparkled. "And maybe another while I eat."

"Done." Brighton went to the kitchenette, pulled open the fridge, and paused to pop open a can of beer. After setting it down on the table, he reached inside for a bottle of white wine. He poured Emma a glass, and then brought both drinks back to the control room.

"So, you really liked the performance?" he asked, reseating himself and taking a swallow of brew.

"Loved it." This part, Emma didn't have to fake. "You were amazing—I mean, the whole band, but mostly you. Between your writing, your guitar playing, and your singing—wow. Your success is a done deal."

Brighton beamed, reaching over with his free hand to link his fingers with hers. "Just what I needed to hear. Thanks."

"It's the truth."

The pizza would be here soon. There'd be time for eating and talking—and drinking. Emma would have to sip slowly. She'd also have the chance to get some answers before the sex dance began, and she had a great solution for that, too. But, first, she had to get all the answers she could, because there'd be no further chances, not unless she was okay with sleeping with Brighton. Which wasn't about to happen, now or ever.

"Hey, drink up," Brighton urged. "I'm almost ready for another beer."

Emma raised her glass. "Congratulations to a budding superstar," she said, taking a sip of wine.

Brighton squeezed her fingers tightly, then traced her palm with his thumb.

Luckily, the sound of the door buzzer interrupted.

He blew out an irritated breath, releasing Emma's hand and coming to his feet. "Lousy timing. But it's food first, dessert after. I'll get our pizza, and then you can keep telling me how awesome I am."

Emma nearly rolled her eyes at his arrogance. "Sounds great," she managed.

Brighton was back three minutes later, waving the pizza box in the air and gesturing toward the recording room.

"Let's eat in here," he called out, going in and placing the box on the floor.

Emma nodded, not the least bit surprised. One room. Food then sex. An all-purpose venue.

She took her wine and Brighton's beer and went to join him in what was now a dimly lit, noise-free den of intimacy, rather than an electrically charged concert.

Given the gleam in Brighton's eyes, she'd better chew slowly.

"Have a seat." He lowered himself to the floor, stretching his long legs out in front of him and patting the spot beside him. "The pizza's getting cold."

Emma laughed, sitting down cross-legged beside him. "Doubtful. It just got here piping hot. I can see the steam rising." She placed down the drinks and distributed paper plates and napkins.

"True." Brighton opened the pizza box and placed two generous slices on each plate. "Let's start with that. There's a slice left for each of us."

"Not for me." Emma puffed out her cheeks. "I might only manage one slice, maybe a slice and a half. Each piece is monstrous."

Chuckling, Brighton took a big bite. "Umm. Don't make promises you can't keep. This stuff's amazing."

Emma followed suit, making sure she took two bites before having more wine. "I'm so psyched about your band," she said. "Obviously, your father also knew you were going places. I'm sure that's why he bought you this place."

A harsh laugh. "Hardly. He never even heard me play. My father was all about work. Buying things for us filled his role as a parent, and he even ditched that part before he died." Brighton took another bite of pizza, this time tearing it with his teeth.

He was furious. Time for Emma to know why.

"I don't understand," she asked in total puzzlement. "You said something about that earlier. Did his business start failing? Was he unable to support you guys as much as he had been doing?"

"Failing?" Brighton snapped. "No, Madison, it was thriving. He had more money than he knew what to do with. He was just a selfish prick. I was kept on a short leash, other than my allocated gifts. Stuff like his over-the-top tech equipment, his top-shelf liquor collection, and, oh, his precious BMW—those were off-limits. And, even though I obeyed all his rules, at the end, he screwed me over big-time. It sucked. *He* sucked."

Emma heard the scary-angry tone of his voice and lowered her gaze. "I'm sorry. I didn't mean to pry."

"You didn't." Brighton forcibly took it down a notch. "I didn't mean to bite your head off. This is just a sore point—one I don't even understand. It seems the bastard made provisions not to have his will read until certain conditions were met. No idea what those conditions are, but until they're met, I'm not getting a penny of my inheritance. Neither are my mother or my siblings. Mother has plenty of assets of her own. Ashley has a great job. Lily is secure and well paid, too. Me? I'm pretty much broke."

"Oh, Brighton, I'm so sorry." Emma covered his hand with her own. "I'm sure things will work out. Besides, you'll be making a ton of money soon enough. Just book your first performance."

"Easier said than done." Brighton was back in fuming mode, and, seeing his livid expression, Emma knew she had pushed this as far as she could.

She rose, taking her empty glass with her. "I'm getting more wine. Want another beer?"

He blinked and looked up, abruptly realizing the turn their conversation had taken and how off course it was from what he had in mind.

"Yeah," he replied. "Let's drop this subject anyway. I have plans for the rest of this day, and it doesn't include a discussion of my father."

Emma heard him loud and clear. She had to stop. Not only to keep from arousing his suspicions, but because he was a different guy when he talked about his father. Dark. Angry. Chilling. Possibly over the edge if he were driven to it. Emma had no desire to be with him if and when that happened.

For the first time, she felt a sliver of worry about what she'd planned next—*and* his reaction to it.

She'd better make this good.

With a bit of a wince, she headed to the kitchenette. "Consider drinks on the way and the subject changed."

By the time Emma returned with their drinks and settled down beside him, Brighton's anger had visibly dissipated, and the charming and seductive Brighton was back.

He took a few deep swallows of beer, waiting while Emma took a few sips of her wine. Then, he took away her glass and placed both their drinks to a side.

"Meal over. Dessert time."

No more preliminaries.

Brighton slid over until he was against Emma. He nuzzled her neck, then used his forefinger to turn her head to meet his kiss. It wasn't a prelude. It was hot and deep and demanding.

Emma forced herself to respond, fighting the urge to yank herself away and then take off. This was fast getting out of hand.

She reached around him and deliberately picked up her slice of pizza. "Another bite?" she teased softly, holding up the slice to bite. "And another taste of me."

Brighton turned his head to comply. "Delicious," he murmured. "But doesn't come close to the real thing."

He pushed the plate aside and reached for Emma again. As he kissed her this time, his fingers slid under the neckline of her sweater, and he urged her down to lie against him. "So many clothes," he muttered, pressing deeper. "Way too many. Time to take care of that."

Supposedly caught up in the magic, Emma slid down onto the floor, wriggling around to get into a comfortable position. As she did, her arm whacked her pizza plate, and what was left of her slice flew up and into her face.

"Ugh!" She jerked into a sitting position, automatically swatting at her face to get rid of the mess.

"Hang on." Brighton grabbed some napkins and stilled her motions, dabbing at the tomato sauce and stifling a laugh.

"Not funny," Emma said, also biting back a smile.

"Of course not." Brighton finished up his task—almost. He then put down the napkin and leaned forward, slowly licking the last bits of sauce and cheese off of her chin. "Better?" he muttered.

"Much better," Emma assured him. "Thanks for turning embarrassment into something far more sensual."

"My pleasure." Brighton kissed each corner of her mouth, his fingers tracing the lacy edge of her bra.

Emma shivered, hard, indicating it was as much from the chill in the room as it was from passion.

Brighton lifted his head at once. "You're cold," he said. "This room gets that way. Not to mention that this floor is rock hard. I'm getting a couple of blankets." He rose. "We can't have you uncomfortable in any way."

"I really appreciate it." Emma sat up, wincing again and shifting her weight in discomfort. "While you're getting the blankets, may I use the bathroom?"

"Of course." Brighton pointed toward it. "I'll meet you back here." He noted her distress, but chose to ignore it. Instead, he gave her a suggestive wink—one that was returned with a wan smile.

Emma rose, glancing back anxiously as she made her way to the bathroom. Inside, she shut and locked the door.

Nice onset, she praised herself. Even the creepy man-baby had noticed.

She turned to look at herself in the mirror, taking a deep, settling breath. Then, she got down to business. She washed her face, ridding herself of all her makeup, all the pizza, and all traces of his touch.

That done, she turned the faucet down to a trickle, and used the narrow stream to put droplets of water on her cheeks and eyelashes. Tears. Fake, but good. And, if necessary, she'd force some real ones. She was a hell of a good actress.

Another glance at the mirror. This had better do the trick. If not, she knew she was screwed.

Emma left the bathroom and returned to the recording room. As she got there, she noted that Brighton had worked fast. Their pizza and drinks had vanished. He'd kicked off his shoes and gotten rid of his sweater, after which he'd stretched out on the blanket, propped himself up on one elbow, and was gazing, heavy-lidded and hungrily, at the door.

He started when he saw Emma's face, tear-streaked and miserable.

"What's wrong?" he asked, bewildered. "Are you okay?"

Emma shook her head, biting her lip as fresh tears came. "I'm so sorry. I screwed everything up." With that, she grabbed hold of the doorjamb, gripping it as if to keep herself from collapsing.

By now, Brighton was on his feet, walking over and studying her pale, tear-streaked face. "I don't understand. You were fine a few minutes ago."

"Not really." She winced, doubling up and pressing her hand to her abdomen. "I just kept hoping my body would wait. But it didn't. I got my period," she said as if it were the most embarrassing of admissions. "It's bad. And I've got low blood pressure, so I'll faint if I let go of this doorjamb." She gazed up at him through miserable, wet eyes.

Brighton's expression went from shock to fury to forced acceptance.

"You've got lousy timing," he muttered. Realizing he sounded like a bastard, he walked over and slipped an arm around her waist. "How long will this set us back?"

"Five, maybe six days," Emma replied, keeping the miserable, guilt-ridden expression on her face. "I'm so sorry. I wanted this as much as you did."

That seemed to placate Brighton a little.

"That part's good," he said. "Because the minute it's possible, we're continuing this—and finishing it. I've been patient, but it's wearing thin." He didn't wait for an answer. "I'll get an Uber to take you home."

"I'll do it." Emma worked her phone out of her pocket, opened the Uber app, and entered her order. "They'll be here in ten minutes," she said.

Brighton nodded and led her to a chair. "Sit here until they come." He walked over and got her the glass of wine he'd whisked away. "I assume this will make you feel better?"

She nodded. "Yes. I really appreciate it." Her eyes squeezed shut, then reopened as she battled the alleged cramps.

Brighton ignored her display of pain. "Here, then." He thrust it at her, still looking sulky and pent up with sexual frustration.

Emma drank the whole glass this time, not caring if she got dizzy. It would only support everything she'd said.

The minutes ticked by slowly.

At last, the Uber arrived.

Wordlessly, Brighton pulled her to her feet, stuffed her in her jacket, and whisked her out the door and down the elevator. He then waited while she climbed into the Uber, turning to leave the instant he could. "Call me when you're better," he said over his shoulder.

*Yeah, right*, Emma thought to herself. *Don't hold your breath.*

# 20

*Offices of Forensic Instincts*
*Tribeca, New York*
*Sunday, 4:50 p.m.*

The brownstone was quiet when Emma let herself him.

"Anyone here?" she called out, squirming out of her jacket and hanging it on the coat rack.

"Good afternoon, Emma," Yoda greeted her. "The only team members here at the moment are Claire and Ryan. Actually, only Ryan, since Claire took Hero out to relieve himself. But they should be back soon."

Emma blew out a breath. "Thanks, Yoda. Is Ryan in his lair? Or is he too busy to get an update?"

"I believe you should go downstairs and speak with him," Yoda replied. "Your accelerated heart rate and elevated temperature tell me so."

Emma smiled. "You really are omniscient, aren't you?"

"I do my best."

Emma followed Yoda's instructions and headed down to the basement and to Ryan's lair. The door was slightly ajar, so she knocked and then poked her head around the corner.

"Do you have a few minutes for me?" she asked, seeing that Ryan was leaning over his laptop, staring at the monitor, his fingers poised over the keyboard. He looked deep in thought.

"Hmm?" he murmured absently.

"It's okay," Emma said, turning away. "I'll wait for Claire."

The odd tone of her voice sank in, and Ryan swiveled around, frowning as he saw how out of sorts she was.

"You okay?" he asked, his forehead creasing. He had a big-brother, little-sister relationship with Emma. She was plucky, bright, and accomplished. She hadn't had an easy life—a life that had left its scars. But she'd risen to the challenge, and he admired her gutsy, winner-takes-all approach to life.

Now, she looked too depleted to suit him.

"Hey." He rose and pulled over a chair for her. "Sit. Tell me what's going on."

"Thanks." Emma took him up on it, pouring herself a cup of Ryan's lousy coffee and settling herself in the chair. "It's been a long afternoon of cat and mouse. I pried some good info out of Brighton, but I barely pried my way out of there."

Thunderclouds erupted in Ryan's eyes. "Did that little prick—"

"No." Emma waved away the question. "Not for lack of trying. I'm just better at this game than he is. Pretty much better than him, period. Still, he's a persistent, creepy guy. I'm not sure what he's capable of. And unless I parade in front of him naked next time, I've definitely worn out my welcome."

Before Ryan could respond, she went on to tell him what Brighton had revealed about his father's selfishness, his postponed will reading, along with how livid and broke Brighton was.

Ryan's lips narrowed into a thin line. "Interesting turn of events. I'll dig into this and get answers. Now tell me what you had to do to get this info."

Emma rolled her eyes in disgust. "I did a tender, emotional dance with him, then worked my magic and got the hell out." She went on to fill Ryan in on the details, culminating with a dramatic sigh.

"Alas, even though he ordered me to contact him the instant my body was available, I think our romance is over."

"Ya think?" Now that Ryan knew all the facts, he clearly felt a lot better.

"I *know*." Emma turned her palms up. "Where is everyone?"

"Well, I've been in my lair since the meeting ended this morning," Ryan replied. "But Casey came down before she left for Angela's to fill me in. Seems Yoda turned over a lead to Marc and Patrick: a post in Steadman's local Next Door warning others to look out for a scammer who buys cars and shortchanges the seller. They're following up on it now."

Claire walked through the door, Hero at her heels. "They're also breaking into Oliver Steadman's apartment to get me some personal items to work with."

She handed Ryan a power bar, but her gaze was fixed on Emma.

"Something's wrong," she stated.

"Not anymore," Emma assured her. She went on to retell the story she'd shared with Ryan. "So that's it. I've officially broken up with Brighton," she concluded.

Claire wasn't laughing. "You took a huge risk, Emma. If Brighton is dangerous, he could have hurt you." She paused. "I get a bad feeling when we talk about him."

"How bad?" Ryan demanded.

Claire's shoulders lifted, then fell. "I'm not getting a solid read. I've never even met the man. Everything I'm picking up on is from Emma."

"I'll tell you every detail I can remember," Emma told her. "He also touched my sweater, so maybe holding that would be helpful."

"That's a good idea. We can go to my yoga room and work on it right now."

"Good." Ryan's gaze had shifted back to his computer. "I'll add your update about Hillington's will to my to-do list, but I'm in the middle of researching a bunch of loose threads."

Claire gestured at Emma. "We're on our way. We'll have plenty of time to reconvene when the team returns. You look exhausted—and with good cause."

Emma rose. "I am pretty beat. Thanks for listening, Ryan. You can go back to work. I'm in good hands." She snapped her fingers. "Let's go, Hero. You don't want to be locked in here without food or attention, and Claire and I will offer you both."

Clearly, Hero agreed, because he bounded after them.

***

The instant the door shut behind them, Ryan went back to work.

He'd already hacked into all of Hillington's email accounts and come up empty. That wasn't a surprise. Someone like Hillington wouldn't put incriminating things in writing.

Next came the NYPD's system, which Ryan had hacked so many times, it was child's play. There were two separate files: the hit-and-run and the murder itself, all of which was now combined at the Nineteenth Precinct. He started with the hit-and-run, getting deeper into that case file than Marc had been able to, poring over written reports to get a sense of where the detectives' heads were.

Clearly, they were bugged by the same thing Ryan was: the location of the accident. Why had Hillington been in that neck of the woods—and speeding away from it—to begin with? And why hadn't he provided a reason, especially since that reason could help exonerate him?

Ryan folded his hands behind his head and streamlined his thinking. The cops might be coming up empty, but he didn't intend to do the same.

To his way of thinking, there were just a few reasons for Hillington to refuse to cooperate. One, he was involved in something criminal that would convict him even before the hit-and-run had occurred. That possibility seemed underwhelming. It was rare that high-level millionaires drove around to conduct illegal business activities themselves. They got others to do that kind of dirty work for them. Still, it was a possibility that couldn't be dismissed. The other option was that Hillington's motive for silence was something personal, something he didn't want made public. An equally viable possibility.

Both avenues led to the same intersection of points: *where* had Hillington been, and *who* had he been meeting with. If Ryan knew how long he'd been driving before he got to South Bayside, he could draw a circumference around the area and narrow things down.

Abruptly, his head came up as something Emma had said, together with something he'd read, popped into his mind. *His precious BMW was off-limits.* That didn't sound spiteful. It sounded like someone who treasured their vehicle. And people like that took great care and caution to make sure their "baby" was safe and driven by no one but them.

There was a great way to ensure that. And if Ryan was right, he'd just hit pay dirt.

His fingers were back on the keyboard, and, once again, he called up Hillington's personal email account. He remembered something he'd read before—something that, at the time, hadn't made his antennae go up. His bad. He also remembered when that email was sent, which was the day after the car's purchase date.

A minute later, Ryan found what he was looking for: an email from DriveCheck, welcoming Hillington to their family and issuing him a new account number and instructions about how to set a new password and to download their app onto his cell phone. The software would be forthcoming.

Not only did DriveCheck have GPS functions, it also had a history function—one that tracked all trips taken over the course of months, both starting and ending points. And since the only person who had access to this particular DriveCheck account was Hillington, he'd want the software in place at all times.

Ryan's mind was still racing. Hillington had been dead for only a week. Doubtful that someone would have thought to terminate the account in that short time. But Ryan wasn't counting on probabilities. What he wanted were certainties.

He didn't have Hillington's password, and he had no time to do a hunt-and-peck to figure it out. It was far easier to hack into Drive-Check's database and extract the data he needed.

He switched screens to recheck the police file. The hit-and-run had occurred on November seventeenth at approximately nine fifteen p.m. So reason would have it that the entire route would be documented and mapped out.

With a broad grin, Ryan began his task.

It was great to be a genius.

*\*\**

*Offices of Forensic Instincts*
*Tribeca, New York*
*Sunday, 6:50 p.m.*

Ryan was pacing around the entranceway when Casey, Marc, and Patrick all arrived within seconds of each other.

"What took you so long?" he demanded, nearly accosting them before they'd taken off their coats. "Didn't you see that my message said urgent?"

Casey bit back a smile at Ryan's typical outspoken impatience. "We were each in different directions, none of them around the corner," she replied. "Marc and Patrick were in the Bronx, and I hit a ton of traffic on my way from Angela's place. So cut us some slack. We were on our way as soon as we got your message."

Ryan looked somewhat appeased, although he did mutter, "I didn't expect traffic on a Sunday."

"The city never sleeps," Marc reminded him. "Besides, we're here now. We won't even take off our jackets. Especially Patrick. He needs his. We'll explain upstairs, but let's not waste time arguing." He looked around. "Where are Claire and Emma?"

"Here we are," Emma announced as they hurried down the stairs. "We were working until the rest of you guys got back. Neither of us could stand being around Ryan."

"You were acting like a caged lion," Claire agreed. "So we got some work done in my studio, rather than standing around listening to you bellow."

Ryan glared at her, but she met his stare with her own calm, unyielding one.

"Fine," he conceded. "I guess I was a little on edge, but I have big things to tell you all. Let's go to the conference room."

They all filed up to the second floor and into the main conference room.

"There's coffee," Ryan told them. "The Jura is more complicated than hacking a database, but it's done."

"With or without Yoda's help?" Emma teased.

"I merely called out some settings," Yoda replied. "Ryan did do the rest on his own."

Ryan rolled his eyes as the rest of the team got their coffee and gathered around the table, having a good laugh as they did.

"Settings are subjective, Yoda," Ryan reminded him. "Engineering is not."

"Customarily true," Yoda sort of agreed. "I'll leave you to your meeting. I'm on standby in case my services are needed."

"Thanks, Yoda," Casey responded. She took her filled mug and seated herself in her usual spot at the head of the table.

Glancing around, she said, "I'm assuming we all have updates to share, but since Ryan's is clearly urgent, he'll go first."

Ryan didn't even pause to take a swallow of coffee. "I put all research into Steadman on hold for today. Ditto on the Hillington murder investigation, although who knows if what I found will tie into it. But what I found was huge."

He went on to outline what he'd done, and to tell them what his search had led him to.

"So now we have two names and an address," he concluded. "Natalie and Morgan Evans, mother and daughter, living at 210 Alameda Avenue, Douglaston, Queens." He looked up, pride splashed across his face.

"Wow," Casey said. "So he was going to meet with one or both of them."

"Not just that night," Ryan added. "But the next night, as well. I also went back farther in the tracking data. He visited that location a bunch of times over the past six months, so I dug deeper. Natalie is a middle school teacher. Morgan is a sophomore at Fordham University's Gabelli School of Business. Her grades are stellar. She's really going places. But it's Natalie I focused on. She's widowed, and sold her house in Great Neck right after her husband died. He was a sought-after orthopedic surgeon, so Natalie isn't poor. I checked to see if there were any media-type references to their marriage. Nothing. But the date they got married—now that intrigued me. They were only married for seven and a half months when Morgan arrived."

The entire team was riveted at this point.

Then Claire said, "I don't know where you're going with this, but Morgan could have come early."

"Yeah," Ryan replied. "That seemed logical to me—at first."

"At first?" Marc's brows rose. "Did you check her birth certificate?"

"Of course. Natalie's husband was listed as Morgan's father. That means shit and you know it."

Casey interlaced her fingers in front of her. "Are you jumping ahead and suggesting that Christopher Hillington might have been Morgan's father? If so, that's quite a reach."

"I'm not suggesting it. I'm stating it. I checked out Natalie's and Morgan's financials. Morgan has a trust fund that was set up for her a few years ago and that named Natalie as the trustee. And guess who set up that trust fund?"

Emma's eyes were wide. "Hillington?"

"Yup," Ryan confirmed. "In addition, I dug up the fact that Natalie Evans arranged for a DNA test right after Morgan was born. I called Aidan and together we got the results of the test. Morgan and Hillington were a match. So what do you say? A pretty good icebreaker to start your conversation when you meet with them, huh?"

Dead silence.

"Shit." Marc broke the silence. "Hillington had an illegitimate child. No wonder he kept his mouth shut with the police. His family probably has no idea that either a child or a mistress exists. And he wasn't about to start a scandal *and* a family feud."

"Wait. Think about this," Casey said, holding up her palms in excitement. "This answers two *huge* question marks for us. One, the reason why Hillington put a hold on his will reading. And, two, why he wanted my help badly enough to write my name with his own blood before he died."

"He wanted you to discover all this and to protect Morgan." Marc's eyes glittered with satisfaction. "Once Hillington knew about her, he must have had his attorney draw up a new will—one that provided for her, as well, maybe even cutting back on other recipients' initial allocations. Until he could meet his newly discovered daughter and make things right, he put a hold on the new will reading, to protect Morgan in the event of his death, not only from the media, but from the backlash that would come from Charlotte and their kids. With things still so up in the air, he was reaching out to you to ensure her well-being."

"Which also brings up the question of how well Hillington knew his killer," Ryan added, thoroughly pumped. "*And* how well his killer knew him."

"You're wondering if the killer also knew about Natalie and Morgan," Claire said.

"Damn right I am."

"Let's slow down," Patrick suggested. "Take this whole revelation one step at a time. I don't want to jump on any one suspect like a bucking bronco."

"Patrick's right," Casey said. "Let's get back to the basics of what Ryan just told us. On the night of the hit-and-run *and* the night after, Hillington was meeting with either Natalie or Morgan or both. Which means they might know details about the vehicular homicide that no one else does."

"I'd go with that assumption," Emma said.

Marc nodded. "So would I."

Claire had grown quiet, her gaze faraway. "It feels right," she said softly. "My senses are telling me so."

"Well, between you and Ryan, that's good enough for me," Casey said. Her eyes narrowed as she thought. "I'll make a phone call to the Evanses, let them know who we are and that we're investigating Christopher Hillington's murder. If they care about him at all, they'll want to find his killer and see them prosecuted." She glanced over at Claire. "Come with me. I'll need your insights."

"Of course," Claire replied.

"Ryan, this is a major, major breakthrough," Casey praised him. "Exceptional work on your part."

A corner of his mouth lifted. "Aw, shucks. Thanks, boss."

Grinning, Casey turned to Emma. "While we're on the subject of the Hillingtons, I want to hear from you next. What happened at Brighton's music studio?"

Emma chewed her lip, knowing Casey wouldn't be happy with how far things had gone. Still, she went on to repeat what Ryan and Claire already knew.

Casey's eyes were flashing with anger, but at the same time, she was biting back laughter. "I don't know whether to sing your praises or lecture you about your customary recklessness."

"Claire and I have already done both," Ryan informed her.

"I did get some good info," Emma replied, immediately defending herself.

"Yeah," Ryan concurred. "The part about the BMW led to my epiphany about the car tracking."

"And I had the chance to touch Emma's sweater," Claire added. "There's some dark energy coming from Brighton Hillington."

"Not a surprise," Casey said. "Also, I got Angela to discuss the delayed will reading today—only as it came to the family. Evidently, all of them have been bugging her law firm to accelerate the process. Except for Lily. She seems more broken up about the loss of her father than she does about getting her inheritance. Charlotte and Ashley are angry and persistent. Brighton is up in arms. He's clearly the same guy Emma is describing—a nasty, pampered son of a bitch. Angela thinks very little of him."

"Interesting," Patrick commented. "And surprising. Since when has Angela King become the talkative type?"

"Since now," Casey replied. "She wasn't uncomfortable because we got to all this without bringing Christopher Hillington into the conversation. But I have a hunch that she's starting to trust me—and to like me." Casey's eyes began to twinkle. "She sure seems to be having a good time bandying ideas around. I guess it's a whole lot more creative than being a defense attorney."

With that, she turned to Marc and Patrick. "It's now your turn to fill us in."

"It was a busy day," Marc replied. "We met with the guy who put up that Next Door post. His name's Dan Rivers, and he lives in a lousy section of the Bronx. He was ripping pissed about being screwed over. Two-plus weeks ago, he sold his 2005 gray Ford Escape to a guy matching Steadman's description. The price was a thousand dollars. Steadman only had eight hundred. He promised to return the next day with the remaining two hundred."

"Of course he was a no-show," Casey surmised.

"Yup. As for the sale, he provided no name and neither guy wanted a sales receipt. But Rivers did add that the guy who bought the car was really on edge and kept looking around as if he was being followed."

"All that fits," Ryan said.

"Yeah. Anyway, we got the license plate number, although I'm sure those plates are long gone. And, to ensure his cooperation should we need it, we gave him the extra two hundred dollars plus some." Marc sent a glance Ryan's way. "I uploaded all the data to the cloud. Maybe you can turn up something."

Ryan nodded. "That's shit money for a pretty good car," he said. "It must have been in lousy condition."

"Yup," Marc agreed. "But pushing the guy wouldn't have been smart. We didn't want to make an enemy."

Again, Ryan nodded.

Patrick spoke up, looking uncomfortable but resigned to what the job had required. "After that, we did our work at Steadman's old apartment," he said. "I kept watch. Marc picked the lock and was in and out in five minutes with Steadman's hairbrush, T-shirt, and an abandoned iPhone that Steadman was probably terrified would be traceable." Patrick dug into his jacket pockets and handed the first two bagged items over to Claire, and the bagged cell phone over to Ryan. "I hope these help."

Claire gave a sigh of relief as she took the brush and T-shirt. "These are perfect. I'll get to them as soon as this meeting breaks up. Thanks so much, guys."

"Thanks from me, too," Ryan added as he turned the bagged iPhone over in his hands. "Steadman's not the brightest crayon in the box. Maybe he left something on here that will help us find him."

Casey nodded. "I agree."

"But your head is somewhere else—like on the phone call you're about to make," Marc noted.

"Yes," Casey responded. "It's still dinnertime, not too late to call. You guys take our new leads from here. I'm contacting Natalie and Morgan Evans so we can see them first thing tomorrow morning."

# 21

*Evans Residence*
*210 Alameda Avenue*
*Douglaston, Queens*
*Monday, 6:30 a.m.*

Casey steered the FI van into the circular driveway. Even in the predawn hour, she could see that the grounds were well-kept, despite being drizzled with snow. The house was a charming brick and clapboard split-level, and it exuded a kind of warmth and welcome.

"How lovely," Claire murmured, gazing around. "It must be beautiful in the daylight."

Casey nodded. "Natalie Evans was clear that she had to be at work before eight, and that Morgan was also heading out early to take a final. They chose the time, and I was happy to accommodate them."

"They were obviously shocked to hear from you," Claire said, referring to the recap that Casey had given her during the ride.

"Stunned. I thought Natalie was going to drop the phone. But, as I said, she recovered and sounded almost eager to talk to us. As if a great weight had been lifted from her shoulders. So, in we go. We don't want to waste a minute."

Casey turned off the car and the two women hopped out.

"So much loving energy," Claire murmured. "This is a happy house. Mingled with tinges of sadness and loss, but filled with love."

Casey locked the car and blew out a frosty breath. "That fits. Let's find out about those tinges of sadness and loss."

After climbing the front steps, Casey rang the bell, Claire at her side.

Immediately, the door opened and a pretty woman in her midforties, wearing gray slacks and a black and gray sweater, stood nervously before them.

"Natalie?" Casey asked. "We're Casey Woods and Claire Hedgleigh from Forensic Instincts. You and I spoke last night." The two women flashed their credentials.

"Of course. Come in." Natalie stepped aside and waited until both women had complied. "Please, let's have a seat in the living room. I made coffee. Morgan will be down in a minute."

"Thank you," Casey said. She shot a quick look at Claire, who was clearly overwhelmed by the anxiety and pain that exuded from Natalie Evans.

As she spoke, a young woman with long dark hair and a solemn expression descended the stairs. She wore jeans and a hoodie and looked like a typical college kid.

"I'm Morgan," she introduced herself. "I've read up on your investigative firm. You're very impressive." She put her hand on her mother's arm. "You okay?"

"Just fine," Natalie assured her. It was obvious that mother and daughter were close, and that Morgan was very protective of her mom.

Casey set the record straight before they even moved to the living room.

"As I told your mother on the phone last night, we're here to help. We have no desire to hurt or upset either of you. So please relax."

Natalie gave her a half smile, and then led them into the living room, where they all made themselves comfortable—Casey and Claire in wing-backed chairs, and Natalie and Morgan side by side on the sofa. Before they began talking, Natalie poured them each a cup of coffee. Her hands were shaking.

"Thank you for coming so early," she managed, reseating herself.

"Of course," Claire said. "We appreciate your seeing us."

"I'd do anything to put Christopher's killer behind bars."

Based on the fervor of Natalie's tone, it was clear she meant every word. Still, Casey couldn't help but notice her choice of pronouns. *I*, not *we*. Natalie cared deeply about Hillington. But Morgan? Were her feelings equally as strong? Casey had to get a better read on her.

With that, she turned to face Morgan. "I'm sure this is extremely difficult for you, as well."

Morgan tucked a strand of hair behind her ear. "Not nearly as difficult as it is for my mom," she said frankly. "I never knew my biological father. Evidently, that would have changed had he lived, but his killer made that impossible. So I'm very upset, yes. But the bond he and my mom shared…" She broke off, unwilling to say any more than she already had.

"We understand," Claire said in that gentle, soothing way of hers. "Losing someone you feel deeply about is very, very painful."

"Thank you," Natalie replied.

Morgan lowered her gaze. "Honestly, I don't know how I feel about him. I only just learned of his existence. My mom's description is a far cry from what I'm reading and hearing about him now, but I trust my mother. And he was my biological father, so I want information and I want justice. Most of all, I want my mother to have a measure of peace and some closure."

She paused, lifting her gaze to meet Casey's. "Can you tell us who hired you?"

"I think you already know that that information is confidential. But believe me when I stress that our client will do whatever it takes to get exactly what you just described: answers and justice."

Morgan nodded, but pressed on. "How did you find us? My mom said something about technology and route tracing."

Casey explained, supplying only the basics of what Ryan had done. Then, she turned back to Natalie, who was still pale and shaky.

"Christopher Hillington visited here on numerous occasions, not just once," she segued. "I don't mean to be intrusive, but I'm assuming you and he had a longstanding relationship?"

Not even the slightest hesitation. "We loved each other," Natalie replied, as frank as her daughter. "We met years ago, but life intervened and we couldn't stay together. Later, Christopher found out about Morgan, and that changed everything. But he had a family who knew nothing about me or Morgan, so we kept things discreet."

"But you planned on introducing Morgan to him. Why didn't that happen?"

"That was my fault," Natalie said sadly. "He was hell-bent on meeting and striking up a relationship with his daughter. I kept waiting for the right time—a time when Morgan wouldn't be caught up in a scandal."

Claire's gaze was clear, her words more of a calming statement than a question. "And now was that time," she said. "Christopher was planning on asking Charlotte for a divorce. He wanted to be with you and Morgan."

Natalie's brows rose in surprise. "That's true, although I'm not sure how you knew it."

Casey explained quickly so they wouldn't get off track. "Claire is a claircognizant. She intuitively knows things. It's a wonderful asset for us." A brief pause. "What was prompting Christopher to ask for a divorce at this particular time?"

"His kids were grown," Natalie replied. "His relationship with Charlotte was strained to breaking. He was waiting for me to give him the go-ahead to meet Morgan, after which he planned on telling his family—his *other* family—the truth and file for divorce." Tears filled her eyes. "Two and a half weeks ago was supposed to be that time."

Casey nodded. "And then came the hit-and-run." She paused. "Is it possible that Charlotte already knew about you and about Christopher's plans to leave her?"

Natalie spread her hands, palms up. "I don't think so, but anything is possible. Why? Do you think…?"

Casey shrugged. "Just wondering. But as for the hit-and-run…"

"Christopher didn't kill that poor man." Natalie defended him at once.

"The police seemed to think so. They questioned him several times."

Natalie's eyes blazed. "I don't care how many times they questioned him. He didn't do it. I begged him to tell the police where he was that night so they'd put that unanswered question to rest, but he wouldn't reveal his relationship with me or his ties to Morgan. Not until we were official. He was adamant about that."

She dashed tears from her eyes. "You didn't see him after Frank Vicario was killed. I did. He came back the next night, and he was completely broken up. I've never seen him like that. He was always so strong. Not this time. He wept like a baby when he swore to me he didn't do it. I knew he was innocent even before that. I know— knew—Christopher. He was a hard, sometimes ruthless businessman, but he was a good human being. He wasn't even as upset about being a suspect as he was about the man's death. You're welcome to think I'm a biased lover, but that doesn't play into this. He simply did *not* do it."

"I don't think he did," Claire murmured. "Did he tell you anything else?"

Casey's jaw dropped, but Natalie only looked utterly grateful.

"Yes, as a matter of fact, he did," she said. "He was racing to get home. He barely saw the Camry and sped by it with another car squeezing between him and Mr. Vicario, trying to get by. Christopher heard the crash as he passed. He was blocked both ways, so he couldn't turn back."

Casey's mind was still reeling. "You're saying he missed Frank Vicario's car, but heard the impact of the crash an instant later? Did he say what kind of car struck the Camry? Make? Model? Was the driver male or female?"

"The driver was wearing a hoodie that covered his entire head and face, so he couldn't tell. Driving a small SUV that was either gray or silver." Natalie's eyes welled up with tears again. "It was rainy and foggy, and, of course, pitch dark. He had no idea how bad the accident was. All he could make out was the damaged Toyota and the other car swerving away."

"Why didn't he tell all this to the police?"

"He did. They didn't believe him. Their video didn't show the other car. It must have gotten by before it was caught on traffic cameras. Or the angle of their surveillance was off." Natalie turned her palms up. "That's all I know."

"Which explains why Christopher's car wasn't damaged," Claire said. She inclined her head. "Do you think it's possible that the two crimes—the hit-and-run and the murder—could be related?"

Natalie's eyes widened. "I never... Is that what you think?"

Claire looked troubled. "I'm not sure. It's just that the two tragedies occurred within several weeks of each other. Something about that just doesn't feel right." She gave Natalie a quizzical look. "Do you have anything personal of Christopher's that you'd be willing to lend me? Of course, I'd return it as soon as possible. I just need to make a solid connection with him."

Natalie was about to rise when Morgan stayed her with her hand. "Are you going to share this with the police? Not only whatever my mom is giving you, but the entirety of what we spoke about? Should we be expecting an official visit from law enforcement?"

Casey wasn't about to lie. "No, because you're going to go to them first. The Nineteenth Precinct. I'll text you the address, and I'll give you an hour head start before I follow. You'll be in an interviewing room, and I'll be waiting to talk to them. That way, you'll avoid obstruction of justice charges, and so will I. Tell them you didn't know where to turn, and you knew of our reputation, so you contacted us. Then, tell them your story and why you kept quiet—and why you realized you'd have to come forward. Do you have an attorney?"

"Yes." Natalie nodded. "But I don't know if she handles criminal cases."

"We have several independent and impartial defense attorneys we work with. I think one in particular would be a good match—Randy Braum. I'll call him as soon as we wrap up here, explain the situation, and put him in touch with you. He'll be on standby while you're at the precinct. If the detectives make you feel in any way interrogated or as if you're suspects of any kind, stop talking. That's the time to bring Randy in."

"Are we in real trouble?" Natalie asked.

Casey pursed her lips. "Not where it comes to the hit-and-run. There's no motive. The police won't be happy that all you have is each other as alibis, but it's a reach to think you'd take off with Christopher and run a car off the road. So that's not my real concern."

"What is?"

"That the detectives might view you as suspects in Christopher's murder. You'll both have alibis—Natalie, teaching at your middle school, and Morgan, attending class. Still, you'll probably become persons of interest."

Natalie started. "That never occurred to me. What possible reason would we have to murder Christopher?"

"They could decide I held a grudge because he never acknowledged me," Morgan said. "Or that you, Mom, were a spurned lover because Christopher would never leave his *real* family."

"Exactly." Casey shot Morgan an admiring look. "I truly doubt this will amount to much. Just the cops doing their jobs. From what I understand, there's a long line of people who'd want Christopher dead. Law enforcement will be putting their efforts into finding alibis for all of them."

She glanced at her watch. "I don't want to make either of you late. So, Natalie, if you could just give Claire an item or two of Christopher's things, we'll be on our way."

Natalie hurried up the stairs and into her bedroom, returning minutes later with a comfy sweater and a photo album.

She offered both to Claire. "The sweater was always a joke between Christopher and me. No matter what the season, I was always chilly inside the house. He gave me his sweater to keep me warm. And the photo album…" Natalie swallowed hard. "The pictures in it are every memory I have of us together, both when we were very young and recently. I go through it every night."

Gently, Claire took the items, and Casey could sense an immediate stillness come over her. "I'll take excellent care of them," Claire said, hiding whatever she'd been sensing. "And I'll return them as soon as possible. I know you'll miss them, but you're doing everything you can to bring Christopher's killer to justice."

Natalie nodded, tears in her eyes. "Please make that happen. Please."

Casey didn't hesitate. "We will. I'll set things up with Randy right away. What's your cell number?"

Natalie provided it, and Casey texted her the address she needed. "Go to the police precinct right after you both finish up with school. I'll be close behind. The sooner we do this, the more likely your explanation will sound, and the less likely any of us will be brought up on charges."

# 22

Casey and Claire had arrived at the brownstone fifteen minutes ago, and the team now gathered around the kitchen nook, drinking coffee and eating the muffins that Emma had picked up. No one had been able to concentrate on their work during Casey and Claire's visit to the Evanses', other than Ryan, who'd gotten some info on the three women who'd allegedly been harassed by Oliver Steadman. Obviously, nothing he'd found had been too impressive, because he'd waved away the idea of him going first in favor of hearing from Casey and Claire.

Casey told everyone the full conversation they'd had, from the truths to the nuances.

"That's quite a story," Marc said when she'd finished. "It paints a very different picture of Christopher Hillington. And it sure fills in a lot of blanks. The question is, how much of it is fact and how much is fabrication?"

Claire didn't hesitate. "No fabrication. All fact. I realize emotions are running high with Natalie, and that she isn't objective. But, in this case, she's right. Hillington did *not* collide with Frank Vicario's car. I don't know what the cameras recorded, but they were misleading.

Another driver did this." She looked at Ryan. "It's your job to figure out the details."

A corner of Ryan's mouth lifted. "Tall orders. I'll get on it as soon as this meeting breaks up. Do I have anything to go on?"

"Hillington described the car as a small SUV, either silver or gray," Claire replied. "And the driver was wearing a hoodie pulled over his head and face."

Patrick nodded. "That matches the description of the SUV that guy who sold the car to Steadman gave us."

Emma frowned. "Who keeps their hoodie up when they're driving? Even if it's freezing, which it wasn't that night, people drop their hoods as soon as they're behind the wheel. Otherwise, their field of vision is narrowed. So why did the driver of the other car leave their hood up?"

"To make sure recognition wouldn't be possible." Patrick provided the perfunctory answer to begin the team's process of picking the situation apart. "Which means that this was no accident. Someone meant to kill Vicario and cast blame elsewhere."

Ryan's brows drew together. "Maybe. Maybe not. Maybe Frank Vicario wasn't the intended victim. Maybe Christopher Hillington was. That would certainly link the hit-and-run to his murder."

Casey nodded. "It's a good theory. But following it through, that means that Christopher Hillington had no idea anyone was gunning for him. If he had, he would have confided that to Natalie. And, trust me, Natalie bared her soul to us. If she had even an inkling that Hillington was the intended victim of that car crash, she would have told us immediately."

Ryan shoved back his chair and rose. "I've got to get back to my lair, and to find our answers."

Casey held up a wait-a-minute hand. "Before you go, what did you find out about the three women Steadman harassed?"

Pausing in the doorway, Ryan said, "Their full names and contact info, and the nature of their complaints. All of which mimicked the incidents at YNE, and all of which added up to smoke, but no fire."

"I'll reach out to the women themselves," Casey said. "They'll be much more likely to discuss this delicate a matter with another woman." She tapped one fingernail on the countertop. "I've also got to give Angela a call. Time to clue her in to the fact that I know what she knows—at least where it comes to Hillington's reason for driving through South Bayside that night. And I have to wrap up in time to follow Natalie and Morgan to the cops. I called Randy from the car. He's in."

Claire had grown thoughtful, her lips pursed as she grappled with something that was clearly bothering her.

"Ryan," she said. "I spent a good part of last night handling Oliver Steadman's personal items. I picked up on some dark and consistent auras. Don't put him on the back burner."

Ryan studied Claire's face. "Do you think he's our killer?"

Claire turned her palms up. "I don't know, but he is significant. Go back to the beginning. And find that woman who was in his apartment—Beth."

***

*Ryan's Lair*
*Monday, 10:25 a.m.*

Ryan was sequestered in his man cave and back at his computer.

He had to rereview the video footage on the hit-and-run, but this time he'd review it on his latest and greatest app. That app would magnify images and expand the viewing field—showing up to a three-hundred-sixty-degree sweep. It was all the more important that he use it, given all Casey and Claire had learned during their visit today.

Despite the urgency of his task, he was bugged by what Claire had said about Steadman.

She'd sensed that Ryan was moving his focus away from the scumbag, and she was right. He *had* pushed Steadman to the back burner, and that had been a sloppy thing to do. He'd been so convinced that the obnoxious weasel was just a loose thread getting in the way of the crux of the investigation.

Evidently, he'd let the pendulum swing too far the other way.

This was a complex case. He couldn't allow himself to be myopic, nor to ignore Claire's insights. So, he'd do the deep dive into the video footage—one that would surpass the NYPD's analysis, given his new app's sophisticated capabilities. Once he'd located and enhanced what he hoped to find, he'd switch gears and get back to Oliver Steadman.

"Can I be of assistance, Ryan?" Yoda inquired.

"Maybe. Probably. There's got to be something here," Ryan muttered with a frown. He had to focus on his initial task first. "I'm going to be exploring for a while, so please be on standby."

"Of course."

Ryan got into the hit-and-run case file and opened the video footage. Evidence or not, it was just stagnating there, with no progress made on its relevance. Clearly, the detectives were stuck.

Ryan didn't intend to be.

He dragged the video file onto his app's icon and waited for it to respond.

As he'd already seen, one camera angle had picked up the victim's car and Hillington's BMW speeding up to it. The other angle showed Frank Vicario's mangled car, with the BMW beside it, seemingly shoving it into the line of parked cars and to the curb beside them.

Something about that series of images bugged Ryan. He understood why the cops, as well as Marc and Patrick, had interpreted what was happening the way they had. It was the natural conclusion to draw.

But now, beginning with the assumption that Hillington was innocent, and combining it with the fact that his BMW had sustained not even a scratch, it was easier for Ryan to be objective. In truth, there was no footage showing the actual point of impact. No full-on view of the BMW sustaining damage as it slammed Vicario to his death. No solid evidence that the BMW had done this at all. Just logical suppositions.

Ryan enhanced the second video clip. As he stared at the footage, he could make out a flash of light reflected off a lamp post on the street.

A headlight. Belonging to another car.

He sat up straighter. The outline of the other car was subtle, cast in shadows. It was coming up behind Hillington's. More isolation and enhancement using the app's tools revealed it to be a small grayish SUV that was plowing down a nonexistent lane between the BMW and the Camry.

Quickly, Ryan employed the other cutting-edge feature of his app. He changed the perspective, rendering a nonexistent view so he could see between the cars, rather than just a side view where the SUV was blocked by the length of the BMW. The "phantom" car was swerving side to side, veering toward the BMW, before it abruptly skidded on the wet road and crashed full-on into the driver's side of the Camry.

Vicario's Camry was demolished. No one could have survived that collision.

Hillington's BMW continued on its way.

"Shit!" Ryan exclaimed, jumping to his feet.

Hillington was telling the truth. He hadn't been guilty. It was another car, an SUV whose driver was targeting not Frank Vicario's vehicle, but Hillington's.

On that thought, something else struck Ryan—something that might explain a hell of a lot.

He bolted to his feet, dashed out the door, and up the stairs to the third floor, texting Marc and Patrick as he did:

*Where are you?*

Patrick opened the door to the War Room where he and Marc had been brainstorming and motioned for Ryan to come in.

Ryan wasn't waiting. He blew into the room.

Marc's head came up at the same time as Patrick shut the door behind them—standard protocol when any team members were in the War Room.

"What did you find?" Marc asked.

Ryan held up one finger. "First, remind me about the car that guy sold to Steadman. What were the specifics?"

Patrick gave Ryan the answer he suspected he already knew. "A 2005 gray Ford Escape, which matches the description Hillington allegedly gave Natalie. It's the same info Claire reported back to us."

"Yesss," Ryan replied, punching the air.

"Care to fill us in on your discovery?" Marc asked.

Ryan nodded. "I think that was the car—and the driver—that totaled Frank Vicario's Camry and killed him. And Steadman wasn't gunning for Vicario. He was gunning for Hillington."

"Damn," Marc hissed through his teeth, not even bothering to ask Ryan if he was sure. Ryan didn't act this way unless he was. "So Steadman is our guy—at least for part one of this investigation."

"Details," Patrick said, wanting to hear all the steps that had led Ryan to this conclusion.

Ryan complied, explaining his app's capabilities and the conclusion it had allowed him to draw. "By the way, I could make out a J and a 2 on the plates. That gives me even more to go on. I know I haven't handed you hardcore proof. I'll get it. But, in the meantime, this is way too much of a coincidence to be bullshit."

Marc nodded. "I agree."

"What kind of shape was the SUV in after the collision?" Patrick asked. "And did its owner even slow down to check out the damage he'd done?"

"No answers to either of those questions" was Ryan's reply. "The footage stopped there. But we have to assume the driver didn't pause, and that his SUV is in bad shape."

"I wonder if the driver is, too," Marc murmured. "He could have had injuries requiring treatment, which means hospitalization, maybe even the ER. Plus a body shop for his car—one he'd have to pay some serious cash to in order to make the car drivable. This gives us a lot of new possibilities to look into."

"I'm all over it," Ryan assured him.

"So are we. And we'll fill Casey and Emma in, as well."

\*\*\*

*Offices of Harris, Porter, & Donnelly*
*Fourteenth Floor*
*Midtown Manhattan*
*Monday, 12:50 p.m.*

Angela was banging out something on the computer when the receptionist showed Casey into her office.

"I'm swamped," Angela announced. "I've got about fifteen minutes.
Thirty, if you brought lunch again."

Casey's lips curved, and she held up the steaming bag in her
hands. "Best chicken parm subs around. Enough to buy me those
thirty minutes?"

"Oh, yeah." Angela was on her feet, sniffing appreciatively as she
headed to the sitting area. "You just saved me from passing out in
court, not to mention saving me time from scrounging up food before
I left. The half hour is yours."

Casey settled herself at the table and handed out foil-wrapped
sandwiches. "Actually, the half hour is not just mine—it's ours."

Angela's ears perked up even as she took an appreciative bite of
the steaming-hot sandwich. "What does that mean?"

Casey joined her, munching on her sub, as well. She hadn't eaten
a thing since she'd spent the rest of the morning mulling over Ryan's
revelation and leaving compassionate voice mails on Steadman's
victims' cell phones.

She swallowed and replied. "It means I can now pass along info
to you that you already have, but will be happy that I have, as well. It's
one less thing we have to dance around."

Angela chewed slowly. "I'm listening."

Putting down her food, Casey supplied Angela with the straight-forward facts: They knew why Hillington had been in South Bayside that night. They knew who he was seeing and why. They'd be moving forward with this new information.

Angela's lips curved slightly. "I've pored over reviews of your team's success stories. Yet, I still find myself impressed. How did you get this information?"

Silence.

"Okay, I'll try an easier one. Have you talked to the Evanses?"

Casey nodded. "Early this morning. I'm sure you interviewed them, as well. Wanna compare notes?"

This time, Angela chuckled. "You are a piece of work, Casey Woods. I'd like to hear whatever you have to say, but this conversation is going to be very one-sided."

"I doubt that," Casey said, deadpan. "Not once I tell you we have data that suggests Christopher was not only innocent but the intended victim in that hit-and-run."

Angela nearly dropped her sandwich. "What?" This time she made no move to hide her astonishment. "You're telling me the collision was intentional and that Frank Vicario was the collateral damage of an attempt on Christopher's life?"

Casey nodded. "That's what I'm telling you."

"You have proof of this?"

"Not enough to share with the police, but enough to convince me and my team, and to pass along to you."

"So you're not going to the police yet?"

"I am, but not with that info. I'm following Natalie and Morgan Evans—and their attorney—there in a few hours. The game plan is that they'll say they were too terrified to call the police and, instead, had reached out to us for advice. I'll show up a half hour after them, allegedly having no idea they're already there. It's the only way that both they and I won't be charged with obstruction. I know they might become suspects in Hillington's murder, but they have strong alibis, so hopefully they'll just get a warning to stay local."

Angela gave a hard nod. "Agreed. I would have advised them similarly, had I been allowed to speak with them."

"Christopher asked you not to." Casey stated a truth that had just occurred to her. "He was all about protecting them."

Angela gave Casey a one-word answer. "Yes."

"And you didn't approach them after Christopher was killed?"

"As I said, my client's privilege survives death. I was given specific parameters. My hands were tied." A pause. "I'm glad yours aren't."

"This also explains what Christopher wanted of me and why he wrote my name on that desk. He wanted me to protect Morgan until his new will was read." Casey studied Angela's face. "But you knew that. Which means you let me run with the fact that I was a suspect even though you knew very well why Christopher had done what he did."

Angela blew out a sigh. "Your help has been invaluable."

"Nice to be used," Casey replied. "But flattering, as well. Not to mention that FI's involvement is key to eliminating me as a prime suspect. So I forgive you."

A hint of a smile. "I appreciate that. As I said, my firm's hands are tied in a way that yours aren't."

"Yours aren't either—not with what I need your help on."

"Murder suspects."

Casey nodded. "Yes. We've already covered the other Hillingtons, but I need the rest of the suspects you've been checking out. My team is going through a deep digging process. But if you and I can jump ahead of any of their efforts, it would certainly speed up the process."

Angela frowned. "I'm walking an ethical tightrope here."

"Yes, I know," Casey replied, mentally assessing her own approach. There was no way she was mentioning Oliver Steadman. That was FI's secret to keep and to investigate. "But you owe me," she pressed on.

"Plus, we both want Christopher's name cleared of the manslaughter charge, and his killer found and convicted. So let's get to who's on your suspect list. One by one, who do you think hated him enough to go after him, not once but twice."

A long pause. "You're going to get me fired, Casey Woods."

"Not likely. You're not telling anyone. I'm not telling anyone. And if we figure out who the killer is, you'll probably make partner."

# 23

*Queens Medical Associates Oncology Center*
*176-60 Union Turnpike*
*Fresh Meadows, Queens, New York*
*Monday, 2:20 p.m.*

Franklin sat down across the desk from the oncologist, waiting for an update on his mother's condition. He was already having a full-blown panic attack. His mother, everything, was spiraling out of control. Isabel had given him full permission to act as her proxy. Her pain was worsening, and she was too tired and overwhelmed to run this show. She knew he'd take good care of her.

Mia was still in the examination room, helping their mother get dressed. Both she and Franklin were consumed with worry about Isabel's physical state. Her increasing fatigue and frailty, and her sharp onsets of pain—those couldn't mean anything good.

Now, Franklin wasted no time. "Tell me what the lab results are and what your exam today determined, Dr. Maywood."

The doctor sat back in his armchair, meeting Franklin's anxious gaze.

"Nothing we didn't expect," he replied. "The cancer is taking its toll, but the chemo medication and the fentanyl patches are doing their jobs. Even with the fentanyl, there are breakthroughs of pain. Continue applying them religiously."

"Is the cancer getting worse? Because my mother can't survive another round of hardcore chemo and radiation treatment. She's much too weak."

Dr. Maywood pursed his lips. "I agree. So I've adjusted the number of pills she has to take a week. We have to count on the medication to do its job. It's our best course of action. Frankly, I'm growingly more and more concerned about her state of mind. Since your father's passing, she's given up. There's no more fight left in her, and that can be detrimental to her illness."

Franklin propped his elbows on his knees and pressed his fingertips to his eyelids. "I know. Mia and I are doing everything in our power to give her a reason to live. And the medication is a godsend. It's just draining us. Is there any new program to help mitigate the cost?" *Please let him say yes.*

A deep sigh dashed any hope Franklin had. "None that I'm aware of. I know you told me you have resources. Dwindling or not, use them. Hopefully, monetary assistance or at least a generic form of the drug will become available sooner rather than later."

Franklin swore under his breath. *Resources—yeah.* "My family is bleeding money," he said. "I'll contact Medicare again—or the pharma company if I have to. Someone has to have a shred of compassion." Even as he spoke, he gave a harsh laugh. "Who am I kidding? It's all about profit. Everything is about profit. The rich get richer and middle-class people like us are always screwed." He came to his feet. "I appreciate all you're doing, Doctor, and I won't burden you with our money problems. When do you want to see my mother next? We'll make ourselves available whenever that is."

The doctor rose, as well. "I'll have my nurse schedule an appointment for eight weeks from now. As always, if your mother takes a turn for the worse, contact me immediately."

"Thank you." Franklin was speaking on autopilot. He was drowning and fighting for air. And he wouldn't be able to breathe again until he fixed things.

He had to be here to take care of his family.

\*\*\*

*Nineteenth Precinct*
*153 East Sixty-Seventh Street*
*Manhattan, New York*
*Monday, 4:25 p.m.*

Natalie and Morgan arrived at the Nineteenth Precinct, having braced themselves for what lay ahead. They walked through the door and up to the front desk, where Natalie introduced herself and Morgan, and then asked to speak to whichever detectives were in charge of the Christopher Hillington cases.

Immediately, they were shown into a shabby, institutional-looking room, small and gloomy. The chairs were hard, the table was harder, and the atmosphere was tense—even before the two detectives walked in.

It got tenser when they did.

One female, one male. Both with deadpan expressions, and both with take-charge attitudes that made the hair on Natalie's nape stand up.

"Mrs. Evans, Ms. Evans," the female detective said, joining her partner in pulling out a chair and sitting down. "I'm Detective Banks and this is Detective Ogden. We're handling the Christopher Hillington murder. I understand you have some information for us?"

Natalie didn't hedge. "Yes we do. Not on his murder, but on Christopher himself. And on the hit-and-run you were about to wrongly accuse him of."

Banks and Ogden exchanged glances.

"I'm guessing, given the fact that you refer to him by his first name, that you knew Christopher Hillington?" Banks asked, brows raised.

Again, Natalie answered directly. "I not only knew him, I loved him. Had he not been killed, we would have started a new life together as a family—him, me, and our daughter, Morgan." She gestured in Morgan's direction.

This time, Banks's jaw dropped, and Ogden began scribbling on a pad.

"You'd better explain," Banks said, recovering herself.

"I will, but first let me fill in what might be a question mark for you. Morgan and I live in Douglaston, Queens. South Bayside is on the way from our house to Manhattan. We're the reason Christopher was where he was on the night of the hit-and-run."

"I see." Banks wasn't letting down her composure again. "And you're first telling us this because...?"

Natalie let out a deep sigh. "Because Christopher was intent on keeping us safe and out of the picture. I wanted to go to our local police precinct and fill in the blanks, but he insisted he had things under control. So I did as he asked. But then he was killed and everything changed." Her voice broke. "I was, I am, shattered and in shock. I didn't know where to turn. Plus, now there were two precincts—the 111th and you—involved."

Ogden spoke up. "We've combined resources. We're the detectives of record, working both cases. Still, you could have gone to the 111th and they would have plugged us in. So why didn't you?"

Natalie's lips trembled. "All I could focus on was that the man I'd loved forever had been brutally murdered. He was gone. After all we'd been through, we were finally—" She broke off. "Morgan didn't even know of her father's existence until a few days ago. Once she did, she took over where I couldn't. She called an investigative firm called Forensic Instincts, who has an exemplary reputation, and turned to them for guidance. Their president told us to come straight to you."

A pulse was now beating at Burt Ogden's temple. "You called Forensic Instincts? Why?"

"Because I know nothing about police procedure. Because I was frozen in place. I'm a middle school teacher. All I know about law enforcement is what I've seen on TV. So Morgan took over. She has a much more level head. She sought professional advice." Tears were now trickling down Natalie's cheeks. "I apologize if that was the wrong thing to do."

Morgan spoke up for the first time. "My mother has nothing to apologize for. The reason I contacted Forensic Instincts is because I'd heard they'd been seen around our neighborhood, asking questions. I didn't have a clue how much they knew, but I knew they were investigating. And, yes, their reputation is stellar, so I called Casey Woods for advice."

Ogden opened his mouth, ready to deliver a scathing reply, but Banks stepped in ahead of him.

"Okay, let's take it down a notch. Start at the beginning. Your relationship, which you're implying was long-term, with Hillington. Your daughter and why Hillington didn't bring her into the picture until the end of his life. And what he might have told you about what could amount to a manslaughter charge."

Natalie was only partway through the details when the officer who'd been manning the front desk knocked and then popped his head into the room. He gave the detectives a meaningful stare.

Detective Banks rose at once. "Excuse me," she said to Natalie. "Hold off for a sec."

She approached the police officer with a this-better-be-good expression on her face. "Yes?"

"Sorry for the interruption," he said. "But I thought you'd want to know right away. Casey Woods is waiting to speak to you."

Banks's brows rose. "Is she now? Well, by all means, send her in."

A few moments later, Casey walked through the door, looking distinctly puzzled. "I thought you were with someone. I was prepared to wait." Her mouth snapped shut when she saw Natalie and Morgan sitting there.

"You got here just in time," Banks responded. "How coincidental."

Casey bristled. "I came to report the phone call I received from Morgan Evans. I did advise them to seek you out, but I had no idea we'd all arrive together. Shall I leave?"

"No," Ogden stated flatly. "Let's hear this whole story at once."

Casey joined them at the table, and stayed silent as Natalie told the detectives everything she could.

"So you're trying to convince us that Hillington was so over-wrought about Frank Vicario's death that he couldn't possibly have been the one who killed him," Ogden stated.

Now, Natalie was starting to get angry. "I'm not trying to convince you of anything. I'm telling you that I knew Christopher better than anyone. And, based on his emotional state the next night, I'm certain of his innocence."

"This man who lied to you about his marital status, and who relegated you to an insignificant piece of his past?" Banks shot at her.

"I won't dignify that with an answer."

"And who, coincidentally, was just about to leave his family for you and a child he'd never met?"

"It wasn't a coincidence," Natalie replied. "It was the right time. The fact that he was murdered doesn't change that." She leaned forward, gripping her handbag. "Look, Detectives, I came here with Morgan to provide necessary information. Not to be interrogated."

*Good for you, Natalie*, Casey thought. *Good the hell for you.*

"Okay, let's say that everything you told us is true, and that you were heartbroken when Hillington was killed," Burt said, his lips drawn so tight that Casey thought they might vanish into his face. "Let's even say you were as much in shock as you claimed. That doesn't change the fact that the man you claim to love was murdered in cold blood. Didn't you want his killer caught?"

"Of course I did. I still do." Natalie's eyes were flashing. "But I have no suspects or thoughts that could help you on that front. And, frankly, I'm not sure I trust you. Christopher told me he passed along relevant information to the 111th Precinct—information I'm sure is now in your possession. It suggested there was another car on the scene that might have been the one that struck Frank Vicario's vehicle. The police dismissed the whole idea and were still convinced of Christopher's guilt. Of course I was ambivalent about coming to you. And even when I got past that and realized I'd have to come forward, I was nervous. I'm a middle school teacher, not someone who's dealt with law enforcement. And, as Morgan told you, she'd gotten word that Forensic Instincts was around our neighborhood, asking questions. So she contacted them in the hopes that they could lay out the necessary steps for us to come forward."

"Or was it more to protect you from possible prosecution? There's a little something called obstruction of justice."

"Detective Ogden," Casey interrupted, having reached the end of her rope. "These two women have been traumatized. If you continue to interrogate them like criminals, I think a lawyer would be in order. Say the word and one will arrive."

"One you have on standby, I assume," Burt snapped.

"We have two separate crimes we're dealing with here," Casey replied, sidestepping the question. "Mrs. and Ms. Evans are here providing you with information on the hit-and-run. They have no knowledge of the facts surrounding Hillington's murder."

"Very well," Lorraine said, realizing it was time to call a halt to this line of questioning. "I'll accept that—for now. Give us your contact information. And tell your attorney…" A glaring stare at Casey. "That you're not to be leaving town for any reason, and that you should be available for further questioning."

"We're actually suspects?" Natalie's brows rose.

"Not suspects," Lorraine amended. "Let's just call it contacts of the deceased." She avoided the phrase "persons of interest." "Possibly having information even you're not aware of. This is a homicide we're investigating. And you knew the victim intimately."

"Fine." Natalie couldn't dispute that fact. "We have no travel plans at all. If there's a way we can help…" She swallowed hard. "I'll do anything to find the animal who killed Christopher."

"Good," Burt said. He turned to Casey. "You stay behind once the Evanses leave. Detective Banks and I have a few more things to review with you."

*I'm sure you do*, Casey thought with a nod. *I can hardly wait.*

***

The door had barely closed behind Natalie and Morgan when both detectives turned their full attention on Casey.

"How much of that was bullshit?" Burt demanded.

"I doubt any of it," Casey replied. "But all I can confirm is that they told you exactly what they told me."

"And you sent them straight to us," Lorraine said.

"Yes I did. You're the ones investigating the Hillington murder."

"Are we?" Burt's voice dripped with sarcasm. "And you and your team aren't conducting your own investigation—one that you're keeping close to the vest?"

Casey bit back a smile. Part of Burt's anger was because the FI team was sharing only isolated pieces of their investigation to find Hillington's killer. The other part was that they were succeeding in their efforts.

"I never denied that Forensic Instincts was digging to find answers," she said. "I've passed along our findings to you. And may I remind you that it was my name that the victim wrote in blood on his desk? You can hardly blame me for working to clear my name."

"That's not what we're blaming you for," Lorraine replied. "We're blaming you for telling us what you choose to. We're not stupid, Casey.

How much more info has your team amassed that you've conveniently chosen to keep to yourselves?"

"We're cooperating just as we said we would," Casey answered carefully.

Burt propped his elbows on the table and glared at her. "That had better be the case. Because, if need be, we'll subpoena your case file and find out how forthright you've been."

"Thanks for the notice." Casey rose. "I'll have my attorney at the ready. But make sure you have enough evidence for a subpoena. It's always possible that the evidence FI collects might not be admissible. It wouldn't help your cause if a judge shot you down." She buttoned her coat. "Is there anything else we need to discuss?"

Burt was fighting back his temper. Lorraine saw it, too, because she spoke up before he could answer.

"Not at this time," she said. "Unless you have anything else to share?"

"Nope." Casey shook her head. "But as soon as I do, you'll be the first to know."

# 24

Ryan was on his third cup of coffee since an hour ago when Marc and Patrick had taken off. He'd fully briefed them, and they were on a mission to succeed. Since the door had shut behind them, he'd been pacing around his man cave, wondering how long it would be before he heard from them.

His entire focus today had been on Oliver Steadman. He'd started with an area-wide search around South Bayside, Queens, looking for the auto body shop where Steadman had left his car to be fixed, as well as a nearby medical facility where he could have had his injuries treated. The neighborhood had to be close, given the severity of the car crash, and the places had to be cheap, with owners who were all too happy to accept cash. Steadman hadn't even tried to use his credit cards, so somehow cash was it. *Where* he got the cash was Ryan's task to figure out.

Yoda had run coordinates for him and compiled a list of possibilities. Ryan had made the phone calls.

Dead end after dead end.

Finally, pay-dirt.

An off-the-beaten-path auto shop in Crotona Park East, where a scratchy-voiced man answered the phone: "George's Auto Body."

"Is this George?" Ryan asked.

"Yeah. Who's this?"

Ryan bypassed the question, hurriedly relaying the details of the gray Ford Escape and asking if the mechanic had seen it and its driver.

George had practically hung up on Ryan.

"I don't know you," he said. "And I don't want any trouble."

"There won't be any," Ryan said quickly, realizing he'd found the right guy. "In fact, there'll be a five-hundred-dollar cash reward for anyone who helps me find the owner of the car. His family is worried sick about him."

An indecisive silence. "Why? Is he running from the cops?"

Ryan didn't miss a beat. "No. He just lost his job, took off, and got into a car accident. He's ashamed to face his family."

The mechanic grunted. "Yeah, he was here. I worked on his car. When do I get the reward?"

"After you convince me you're telling the truth—and after you give me information that'll help me find him."

"What do you want to know? The guy was in bad shape. Doubled-up and bleeding from the car accident he was in. I sent him to the urgent care place down the block. It's a dump, but they have a real doctor there. He patched him up. The guy who owned the car said they had to make sure he didn't have a concussion, so they kept him overnight. Took me just as long to make that car drivable. But he was in a crazy hurry and didn't want to wait for me to do a real good job. He could barely walk, but he just stuffed cash in my hand, grabbed his keys, and drove away like a bat out of hell."

"What direction did he take?"

"I don't know. Maybe north."

"Did he tell you his name?"

"Didn't ask."

"And what did he look like?"

George made a frustrated sound. "He was just some guy. Thirties. Kind of weird. Tall. Wearing jeans and a sweater that were shredded from the crash. Came back wearing different clothes. He was wincing and wrapping his arms around his middle. He lifted his sweater to check some bandages. There were sure a lot of them. That's about it."

"Did he say anything? Anything at all?"

Ryan could actually hear George scratching his head.

"Just that he'd had to get the cash from someone. That she'd brought it when she came down. That's it. Maybe he's cheating on his wife and that's why he doesn't want to go back."

Ryan ignored the comment, focusing on the fact that the "someone" was a woman and that she'd "come down" from somewhere. "Did he say anything else about the woman who'd brought the cash?"

"Nope. Is that enough to get the five hundred? In cash?"

Ryan's mind was already racing ahead. "Give me your address and I'll have someone drop it off."

"Sure." George sounded pleased as punch as he relayed his information to Ryan. "Also, I'd talk to the doctor if I was you. Don't know his name, but the place is called Urgent Health. Maybe he knows something, too. But I'm not splitting my money with him," he added quickly.

"Of course not. You'll get the full five hundred. I'll get it to you tomorrow."

\*\*\*

Next up was Urgent Health. It might be a dump but it was still sophisticated enough for Ryan to have to press a bunch of buttons to get through to the front desk.

Finally, a girl with a youngish voice answered. "Urgent Health."

"Hi," Ryan said. "I understand you treated my cousin a few weeks ago. He'd been in a car accident and was in bad shape. I'm trying everything I can to find him."

The girl paused. "I'm not supposed to give out information like that."

"I'm family. Surely that makes a difference?"

"I guess." Frankly, she didn't sound like she gave a damn. "What's his name?"

Ryan blew out a breath. "That's the problem. He lost his job right before the accident. He was so freaked out and ashamed that he took off. I'm sure he didn't use his real name, but I can describe him." Ryan went on to do just that, being careful to match the words that George the auto mechanic had used. Then, he elaborated, providing eye and hair color, approximate height and weight, and build.

"From what I understand from the auto mechanic who worked on his car, he had cuts, bruises, and likely some broken ribs. Also, a possible concussion," Ryan continued. "You kept him there overnight for observation."

"Yeah, that was Charlie Olson," the girl confirmed. "He was a mess when he got here. But, don't worry. We fixed him up. And his girlfriend was here to cheer him up and give him the money to pay his bill."

"Which girlfriend?" Ryan was treading carefully. "He's got a few. What did she look like?"

"Brown wavy hair. Big eyes. Tall and thin. She wasn't from around here. Her voice was kind of twangy."

The big leap. "Oh, that sounds like Beth."

"Yes," the girl responded. "That's what he called her. He was very relieved when she showed up. I got the feeling he couldn't pay us on his own."

Ryan made a sympathetic sound. "Thank goodness. At least he's safe. But I do want to check up on him. Any idea if they were headed back to her place?"

"I don't know. Does she live in Catskill? Because that's where I heard him say he was headed."

"She does." *Upstate New York. That explained the twang.* Ryan was having trouble not punching the air and shouting out "Yesss."

"You've been such an amazing help. I'll get in touch with him right away to make sure he's okay and his wounds have healed. Then I'll find a way to get him to come home. My aunt and uncle will be weak with relief."

"No problem." She sounded a lot less nervous now. "Glad I could help."

\*\*\*

It hadn't taken long for Ryan to find the right Beth in Catskill, New York. As he'd already discovered, Steadman's phone was a dead end. The snake had wiped the entire thing clean before disappearing, so that wasn't a starting point. Instead, Ryan had instructed Yoda to find every Beth in the Catskill vicinity. There were three. One was way too old and lived on the outskirts of Catskill.

The second didn't match the physical description that the girl at Urgent Health had provided.

Number three was the winner. Beth Landow. Right description, right age, and address solidly in Catskill.

While Yoda produced all her contact information, Ryan hopped on social media to check her out. Sure enough, she had a full Facebook profile, rife with supporting evidence.

She was thirty-three and worked as a consultant for an online pharma company. That paid nicely enough for her to financially support Steadman, especially if he was shacking up with her and paying zero rent. She had a bunch of friends and a lineup of photos to match.

Over a dozen of those photos showed her with Steadman—both recent and dating back to SUNY Polytechnic Institute in Utica, and, before that, to Lincoln High School in a small town just outside of Albany.

Judging from the coziness of the photos and the comments beneath them, it was clear that the two of them had been childhood sweethearts and were still together after seventeen years.

That's what Claire had meant about finding Beth and going back to the beginning. She'd meant Steadman's youth and with whom he was hiding out.

Brilliant woman.

"Ryan, I can provide you with both an address and phone number," Yoda announced.

Ryan was already out of his seat. "Thanks, Yoda. Slack them to me, along with directions. There's no way I'm calling and giving Beth—and Steadman—a heads-up. I want Marc and Patrick to speed up there and grab this guy."

It had taken two minutes for Ryan to get upstairs to the War Room, five minutes to explain, and five more for Marc and Patrick to review the directions, lock and load, and leave the brownstone.

That had been an hour ago. Another hour and change and they'd be there.

*** 

*Offices of Forensic Instincts*
*Small Conference Room, First Floor*
*Tribeca, New York*
*Monday, 6:10 p.m.*

The FI team, sans Marc and Patrick, were all seated in various chairs and love seats, all staring at Ryan. They'd received his urgent Slack message, and, since Casey was now back from the precinct, they'd all been in-house when it arrived. He'd just finished giving them the lowdown on the Oliver Steadman situation.

"Wow." Emma spoke up first. "I can't believe it. We're finally going to get the scumbag."

Casey was still typing notes into her iPad. "I agree. Ryan, you did another seamless job," she praised. "This will wrap up the hit-and-run chapter of this investigation."

"But not the murder," Claire said grimly, the sweater and photo album Natalie had given her lying on her lap. "I'm more certain than ever that Oliver Steadman did *not* kill Hillington."

Casey looked up. "Do you have any idea who did?"

Claire made a frustrated sound. "When I hold these items, I get strong senses of rage and desperation that aren't linked to either Natalie or Morgan. They're all about Hillington. They're coming from somewhere or something closer to home than Steadman—very powerful and very personal."

"Brighton?" Emma piped up. "He certainly fits that description."

"It's possible. I'm not sure." Claire wet her lips with the tip of her tongue. "These emotions are escalating, and a frightening threat is building. Casey, we *must* solve Hillington's murder."

As her words sank in, Ryan's iPhone rang. He glanced down, saw it was Marc, and immediately put him on speaker. "You've got the whole team."

"We're here," Marc replied. "And we're going in."

# 25

*Secluded Log Cabin*
*Catskill, New York*
*Monday, 6:45 p.m.*

Marc and Patrick had driven slowly past the broken-down log cabin twice before heading down the rutted road to hide their car behind a line of snow-covered pine trees.

They'd studied the house. No visible activity, but logic told them that Steadman and his girlfriend were inside. It was dinnertime, she worked from home, and Steadman wouldn't venture out too often. New ID or not, he'd be cautious enough to stay inside his safe house.

Marc and Patrick were pros. They both knew the time was right. If, by some chance, Steadman and Beth weren't home, the two men would go back to the car and wait until they were.

Staying low, they crept toward the house, using the woods for cover. The ground was snow-covered, but not so much that walking in hiking boots was difficult. And it was nighttime dark, which gave them the ability to stay hidden as they moved.

They slowed down as they reached their destination, each of them set to spring forward, each of them with their Glock at the ready.

By the time they eased up to the front door, they could hear two voices from within—one man and one woman.

That's all they needed.

Patrick kicked in the front door, and both he and Marc rushed in, weapons raised as they went straight to the kitchen, where the voices were coming from.

The woman—Beth Landow as per the images Ryan had provided—screamed and dropped the casserole dish she'd been carrying. The glass shattered into dozens of fragments, sending stew splashing in all directions. Steadman—whose images Marc and Patrick had long since memorized—hoisted himself up from the table, his injuries causing him to slip and slide on the food as he frantically attempted to get to the counter to grab a kitchen knife.

"I wouldn't." Marc cocked his pistol, which was aimed at Steadman's head. "You'll be dead before you touch the handle," he successfully bluffed.

Steadman's arm fell to his side, and he turned with terrified eyes to face his captors.

"Who are you?" he demanded.

"That cuts me to the quick, Oliver," Patrick replied, talking to Steadman, but keeping his gun aimed at Beth in case she tried to run. "After two investigations, you don't recognize us?"

"We never officially met," Marc pointed out. "But I assumed you checked all of us out on the Internet. Guess it was just Casey. Casey Woods—does that name ring a bell?"

Steadman went sheet white. "You're...you're..."

"Forensic Instincts," Patrick supplied. "Gotcha, Steadman."

Steadman made an instinctive move toward the door.

Marc stepped in front of him and shoved Steadman back into his chair, ignoring his wincing and whimpering. That done, he grabbed some thick zip ties and pulled Steadman's arms through the chair rungs, locking them behind his back. He used another set to bind his ankles together.

Patrick was doing the same to Beth, who was openly sobbing. "I didn't do anything..."

"Shut up," Steadman demanded. "They don't know anything."

Marc gave a bark of laughter. "You're not even a good liar. We know everything—about you and Ms. Landow." He pulled another chair across from Steadman and straddled it, his hand still gripping his pistol.

"We have a lot to talk about." Patrick was perched against the table, adjacent to Beth. "Let's start with the hit-and-run in South Bayside."

Steadman tried not to react, keeping his expression nondescript. "I don't know what you're talking about."

"You've got a very short memory, then," Marc said, emanating a scary Special Ops kind of anger. "So I'll refresh it. On November 17 at approximately nine fifteen in the evening, your just-purchased gray Ford Escape struck Frank Vicario's Camry, shoved it into the sidewalk and a row of parked cars, and killed him. Ring a bell?"

Steadman stared at his shoes and said nothing.

"Not enough?" Marc continued, leaning forward to grab a handful of Steadman's sweater in a vise grip and shoving his Glock into Stead-man's ribs until he winced and cried out. "Then how about this." Marc's voice was cold steel. "Vicario wasn't your target. Christopher Hillington was. You were trying to mow him down, and instead your car skidded the other way. Pretty careless of a guy who thinks he's brilliant."

Steadman's head came up, and his eyes were now blazing. "I am brilliant. Too brilliant to do what you're suggesting. You've got a gun, but no evidence and no motive."

Marc met his blazing stare with his own. "I have both. Hillington fired you for numerous complaints of sexual harassment. Being the dick you are, you couldn't get another job anywhere. Pretty good motive, huh? As for physical evidence, there's video footage showing your vehicle tearing down a nonexistent lane between the other two cars, aiming at Hillington's BMW, and then losing control, smashing full force into Vicario's Camry instead. That's not a hit-and-run. That's attempted murder *and* manslaughter."

Those words, together with Marc's overwhelming presence and his gun shoved into Steadman's chest, snapped the bravado.

"Fuck you!" Steadman bellowed, visibly terrified. "That son of a bitch took away my life. There was no way I was letting him keep his. So, yeah, I tried to mow down his car—and him. I'd do it again if I had the chance."

"You could and you did." Patrick took over Marc's lead. "The following week, you went to Hillington's apartment, beat him over the head with a sledgehammer, and brutally killed him."

"I did *what*?" Steadman was totally unraveling. "What the fuck are you talking about? I never spoke to Hillington or saw his apartment. And I sure as hell never beat him to death. That's murder one, and you're not pinning it on me."

Both Marc and Patrick watched his reaction and recognized it as genuine. But Steadman didn't need to know that.

"You're saying you didn't know that Hillington had been murdered?" Marc fired at him.

"Yeah, I knew." Sweat was dotted all over Steadman's face. "The whole world knows."

"But the whole world didn't want him dead. You did."

"Me and about a hundred other people."

"Got an alibi?" Patrick kept the pressure on.

Steadman moaned again as a hard jab of Marc's pistol reminded him what was at stake. "Beth's my alibi." His breath was coming fast and uneven. "I've been here with her since I took off."

"That's true." Beth gave a fierce nod.

"Since you took off—meaning right after you killed Frank Vicario in the hit-and-run?"

"Yes, okay?" Steadman practically shrieked. "Since then. And I haven't been back. Are you happy?"

"Not until you tell us the details of the hit-and-run."

Steadman sucked in his breath. "Fine." He didn't see Marc press the record button on his iPhone. Instead, he poured out all the details they already knew. His clothes were plastered to his body when he finished. "I knew the other guy was dead. I veered down another narrow side street. No one saw me. I got myself and my car fixed up. Then I didn't stop driving until I got to Beth's." He gazed fearfully from Marc's pistol to Patrick's. "Are you going to shoot us? I swear I didn't kill Hillington."

"Not for want of trying." Marc spoke carefully, knowing that his voice would be on tape from this point on. "But no, shooting you isn't in the cards. Locking you up is."

He stood up, clicked his pistol into neutral mode, and pocketed it. At the same time, he signaled for Patrick to aim his Glock at Steadman. Beth was still bound to the chair. She wasn't going anywhere.

"We're taking you to the cops," he told Steadman as he released the zip ties behind his back long enough for the scumbag to wobble to a standing position, then relocking them around his wrists. "They'll take it from here. But know that you'll be going to jail for a long, long time."

***

Once both Steadman and his accomplice-girlfriend were safely contained in the car with Patrick babysitting them, Marc stepped away and called Casey.

"Got him," he told her. "Got them both."

"Good job," Casey replied.

"How do you want to handle this?"

"You drive directly to the Nineteenth Precinct," she replied. "I have to give the detectives a heads-up and some kind of explanation before you walk in. We've got to look as cooperative as possible, and dispel strong suspicions that we've been keeping a major investigation from them."

"That's going to be tough," Marc said. "They'll never believe we just fell into this."

"I'll be convincing. Some truth, some omission. Like Aidan and his background work. That's taboo." A thoughtful pause. "I'll tell them we've been suspicious of Steadman since the CannaBD case, and when we realized—very recently—that he worked at and was fired from Hillington's company, we tracked him down. I'll leave out everything Ryan did. Let them think what they want. They're going to anyway."

"Not even a doubt," Marc agreed.

Casey paused. "How bad did it get?"

"Not too. A little roughing up and intimidation. Two unfired pistols and four sets of zip ties. Oh, and I have a present for the cops that I'm sure they'll like. I recorded Steadman's confession to the hit-and-run. It's not enough to take to court, but it's sure enough for the detectives to play for Steadman. He's so about to implode that he'll blurt the whole thing out again and sign a written confession to avoid being accused of murder one. Personally, I don't think he killed Hillington, but let them make that call. We'll pursue other avenues."

"Anything we'd want them not to hear on that recording?"

"Nope," Marc assured her. "It's only Steadman's confession. Whatever else that happened in that cabin never made it to audio."

"Okay. Then I'm off to make that phone call."

"And we're off to the Nineteenth Precinct."

***

*Offices of Forensic Instincts*
*Main Conference Room, Second Floor*
*Tribeca, New York*
*Monday, 8:20 p.m.*

Alone in the room, Casey digested all Marc had told her, organized her plan, and called the Nineteenth Precinct. Both Lorraine and Burt had gone home for the night, but the desk clerk told Casey he'd try to contact each of them to see if they could make themselves available.

Casey had to stifle a laugh. Oh, they'd make themselves available. As soon as they heard Casey's name and that she had additional information for them, they'd battle it out for the chance to call her back.

It would be Lorraine, Casey deduced without much effort. Burt just couldn't hide his abrasiveness, and they needed a pleasant conversation to achieve the maximum update.

Casey glanced at her watch. She could squeeze in a quick but important call. And if Lorraine returned her call in the meantime, she'd just have Emma put her on hold. Building tension was a good thing.

She punched in Angela King's number.

"Yes?" Angela answered on the second ring. She always sounded as if she was ready for a brawl.

"It's Casey. I've got news."

"Shoot."

Casey filled her in on what had happened and where things stood right now. "So you've got your hit-and-run guy."

Angela let out a long whistle. "You certainly move fast. Did this Steadman guy also murder Christopher?"

"Not sure," Casey replied. "I'm going to let the police run with this for a while."

"Which means you don't think he's guilty, and you're spreading out in different directions."

"No comment. I can't share yet. I've got nothing concrete."

"And when you do?"

"You'll hear about it right away."

Angela gave a heartbeat of a pause. "Has our firm's name come up, especially in joining forces with FI?"

"Nope. And I don't intend for it to. Banks and Ogden will have no reason to suspect our alliance. I'll keep it that way, but I need you to keep me posted. We talked about suspects. Let's get on them. Especially the Hillington family, Brighton in particular. He meets the profile."

"I'll do what I can."

"And share it with me?" Casey reminded her.

"Yes," Angela answered without hesitation. "You've kept your part of the bargain—at least so far. I'll reward it with what I can find."

"Good. Gotta go," Casey said, seeing Emma's signal from the doorway. "I'll be in touch."

She disconnected the call and switched to the other line.

"Casey Woods."

"Detective Banks," Lorraine replied, her voice as taut as a tightrope wire. "What've you got for us?"

Cautiously, watching her every word, Casey told Lorraine what was going on.

"Shit," Lorraine responded. "This Oliver Steadman—you just put all the pieces together and found him?"

"Pretty much," Casey replied.

"And got him to spill his guts?"

"Uh-huh."

"I'm not stupid enough to believe that or that you're telling me the whole truth. When did this capture actually occur?"

"Ten minutes before I called you. Marc and Patrick are driving straight to your precinct with Steadman and his girlfriend."

Lorraine gave a resigned sigh. "Should I say thanks?"

"That would be nice."

"Don't hold your breath."

"I didn't plan to."

Lorraine was clearly irked. "As you well know, I can't prove you're lying and I have no grounds for a subpoena. I suspect I wouldn't find anything anyway."

Silence.

"Fine. I didn't expect an answer."

"Then you're not disappointed." Casey was enjoying this cat-and-mouse game.

Lorraine wasn't. "I'll text Burt. It'll take a few hours for your team to get here. But we'll be waiting. And Casey—keep yourself available."

***

*Fuck Casey Woods. She's peeling back all the pieces. She knows about the son of a bitch's mistress and his illegitimate kid. She went to their house. What did they tell her? Worse, she's been visiting that defense attorney. Why? How much has she learned? How close is she? I have to stop her—now.*

# 26

*Casey and Hutch's Apartment*
*Battery Park City, New York*
*Tuesday, 6:00 a.m.*

Casey stopped pressing the sleep button and made herself get out of bed. Normally, she was awake before her alarm went off. Not today. She'd been in full work mode all night. And, after all the demands of this case, she was exhausted.

"You okay?" Hutch asked, standing at the foot of the bed and tying his tie.

"Barely." Casey stretched her arms over her head. "I'm always amazed that you can go on zero sleep. I only need a few hours, but I didn't even get one. My phone rang with texts and calls all night."

"Yeah, well, from what you told me, it was a productive evening. And from what I tried not to overhear, it was a productive night."

"Productive, but a pain in the ass. I'll be happy when I'm rid of obnoxious detectives who never believe a word I say."

Hutch threw back his head and laughed. "And when was the last time you told them the full truth? Or let them do their jobs without being outdone?"

"Point taken." A smile curved Casey's lips. "Still, I'm pretty convincing where it comes to law enforcement."

Hutch arched a brow.

"Okay, fine, I hear you. I'm convincing, but there are lots of holes I can't—and won't—plug up. But, I did get away with it last night. Marc and Patrick delivered Oliver Steadman and his girlfriend to Banks and Ogden, along with Marc's recording. They're pleased, even if their feathers are ruffled."

She stood up, running her fingers through her tousled hair. "The best news is that they believe Steadman also bludgeoned Hillington to death. So they'll be focused on him and off my back—at least somewhat."

"You don't think he did it?"

"Nope. And don't ask me why."

Hutch frowned. "I'm not going to ask you anything. I'm going to remind you how worried I am. If your instincts are right—and they always are—a killer is still out there. And that killer has their sights on you."

"We don't know that I'm their priority."

"I do." Hutch walked over and wrapped his arms around Casey. "Please be careful."

"I promise." Casey reached up and gave Hutch a tender kiss. "Any chance you can wait for me to shower and dress, and maybe we could grab a breakfast sandwich before heading off to our separate workplaces?"

Hutch deepened the kiss. "I'd like that offer better if I could shower with you and do what I wanted to do last night." A sigh. "Sadly, I'll have to accept your offer as is. I've got to be in by eight."

"Rain check?"

"Only till tonight. We're both coming home at a normal hour, stripping, and hitting the sheets. Phones off."

"Yes, sir." Casey snapped off a mock salute. "No time for dinner?"

"Nope. We'll eat later. We'll be hungrier—much hungrier."

Casey fought the urge to take the kiss further. But, if she did, they'd never get out of the apartment.

Seeing her feelings reflected in Hutch's gaze, she moved away and headed toward the bathroom. "I'll shower fast. I need coffee." She gave him a teasing glance over her shoulder. "And I need you."

Hutch's gaze darkened. "Stop. Now. Or there'll be no work today."

Casey scooted into the bathroom.

***

Forty minutes later, they left the apartment building, strolling hand in hand down the paving-stoned pathway, banked on either side by lush gardens and private parks.

"I'll never stop marveling at how beautiful this place is," Casey said, looking around. The trees glistened with snow, the sun was just starting its rise, and a number of residents were hurrying off to work, chatting with others as they did. It was like a minisuburb in the middle of a bustling city.

Hutch nodded, following her gaze. "It is beautiful. You're more beautiful."

He was rewarded with a dazzling smile. "Keep saying things like that, and tonight will be…"

Time stopped. The world stopped.

It was like a nightmare playing out in slow motion. One moment Casey was talking, her hand in Hutch's, and the next, her hand jerked free, her body lurched forward, and she was lying facedown on the ground, blood pouring from her body.

Hutch reacted in a heartbeat, sucking in his breath and forcing his professional self to take over. He dropped to the ground on his knees next to Casey, tore off his jacket, and applied direct pressure to the wound. Simultaneously, he yanked out his cell phone, called 911, and provided the dispatcher with their address and their location on the property. Somewhere on the outskirts of his mind, he heard a woman scream and sensed people stopping nearby to stare. A few of them approached, offering help.

Hutch shook his head, checking for a pulse. Faint, erratic, but there. Casey was breathing, so rather than moving to CPR, he pulled out his Individual First Aid Kit, a trauma kit carried by all FBI agents in order to save themselves, if need be. In addition, he was trained in how to control hemorrhage.

To that end, he was about to grab a tourniquet and some combat gauze when he heard the ambulance siren. Shoving his equipment aside, he concentrated fully on keeping his jacket on Casey's wound, applying direct pressure until he heard pounding footsteps, and two paramedics rushed on the scene, rolling a gurney. By this time, the blood flow had worsened, soaking Casey, Hutch, and everything around them.

The paramedics didn't wait. Casey was on the gurney in seconds, and inside the ambulance minutes later. Hutch put on his face mask and jumped in behind them. The doors were slammed, and the ambulance took off, siren blaring.

Hutch hunched down in a corner, staring from his bloody hands to the paramedics, who'd instantly begun doing their jobs. He had to stay out of the way, no matter what he was feeling.

The paramedics were moving lightning fast. An IV hookup. Oxygen. IV fluid lines inserted to give Casey life-sustaining fluid. Continuous monitoring of her vitals. Valiant attempts to stop the hemorrhaging. And enough of an examination to call out to the EMT, "Level One Trauma Center."

Hutch knew what that meant. A Level One Trauma Center was a hospital within a hospital. It had twenty-four-seven trauma coverage and trauma physicians available. It was the highest level of treatment center for life-threatening conditions.

The EMT responded, contacting New York-Presbyterian Lower Manhattan Hospital, the closest Level One Trauma Center to Battery

Park City. "Female. Midthirties. Gunshot wound to the torso. Copious blood loss."

"We'll be ready" was the reply.

Hutch could visualize every surgeon and specialist in the Trauma Center snapping into action.

The hospital was just seven minutes away—the longest seven minutes of Hutch's life.

\*\*\*

*Offices of Forensic Instincts*
*Main Conference Room, Second Floor*
*Tribeca, New York*
*Tuesday, 7:20 a.m., moments after the shooting*

The team had all trickled in and were getting cups of coffee, ready to gather around the conference room table for a full update from Marc and Patrick on the Oliver Steadman situation.

Patrick glanced at his Apple Watch and frowned. "Where's Casey?" he wondered aloud. "It's not like her to be late to—"

Claire's cup of herbal tea clattered to the floor. Her hands flew to her cheeks, and she let out a high, thin cry. "No! Please, no!"

Emma jumped in first. "Claire? What is it? What's happened?"

"Casey," Claire said in a terrified whisper, her gaze faraway, and her body shaking uncontrollably. "She's hurt. Worse than hurt. Oh, God."

Marc acted first. He grabbed his phone and first tried Casey.

"No answer," he said. "I'm trying Hutch."

Scowling, Marc hung up. "He's not answering either."

"First Precinct," Claire said.

"The police?" Emma turned sheet-white. "Oh, no."

Marc immediately did just that. "This is Marc Devereaux of Forensic Instincts. Has there been a recent report of violence in Tribeca or Battery Park City? We have reason to believe the president of our company, Casey Woods, has been hurt." A pause. "I don't know any specifics. I'm not calling in to provide information. I have none. Just tell me whether or not you received notification." A longer pause, and Marc paled. "Yes, I'll be available. You know where we are."

He ended the call and turned to the group. "There was a shooting inside Casey and Hutch's apartment complex minutes ago. No word of how bad it was. Victim is being taken by ambulance to the hospital. That's all I could get out of them."

Ryan was pacing. "That, at least, means the victim is alive. Where do we go? Which hospital?"

"Level One Trauma Center," Claire managed.

Marc looked ill. "New York-Presbyterian Lower Manhattan Hospital. It's the Level One Trauma Center that services Battery Park City and Tribeca."

Not another word was uttered.

The team all grabbed their coats and dashed out.

***

*New York-Presbyterian Lower Manhattan Hospital*
*Level One Trauma Center*
*New York, New York*
*Tuesday, 7:27 a.m.*

The ambulance pulled up to the dedicated Trauma Center entrance. The entire medical team was in motion the moment the wide doors activated and slid open. Hutch watched as Casey was rushed to the emergency department. He stared after her long after she disappeared behind the double doors.

He then hurried up to the front desk.

"I'm FBI Supervisory Special Agent Kyle Hutchinson," he iden-tified himself to a woman at the desk. As he spoke, he showed her his ID, knowing that the ED was about to go into lockdown. That was the procedure any time a shooting occurred, to avoid information leaking out, nosy people or the media getting in, and most of all, to avoid retaliation from the offender or offenders. Law enforcement was already arriving on the scene, security was screening everyone who came in, and it was good for the Trauma Center to know that there was an additional professional on hand.

"I appreciate you telling me that," the woman replied.

"I'm also the appointed agent on Ms. Woods's health care proxy," Hutch continued, providing this all-important information. He pulled out his cell phone, got into the appropriate folder, and scrolled to the page he needed. He then displayed the document. "Please give me the center's direct email address and I'll send this to you now."

That done, he continued. "I need to be where the patient is and also to be kept apprised of everything that goes on. I'll fill out whatever paperwork you have right now, so I can be free to do that."

She reached over the counter and handed Hutch a clipboard. "Here it is, sir."

Hutch took the clipboard and a pen. "In addition, I'd appreciate it if you'd notify the trauma doctors and surgeons that my blood type is O negative." He was well aware that blood type O negative was the universal donor. "I'll be going to the lab to provide blood for a transfusion."

She was typing into the computer. "This information is now available to everyone in the Trauma Center."

"Thank you. One last thing. Casey's work team will be arriving as soon as I call them. I'll give you their names." He dictated them to her. "They're more like family than coworkers. Please allow them into the waiting room."

"The ED waiting room is no problem. I'll get permission if Ms. Woods needs to be taken into surgery."

Hutch nodded, then walked over to a chair, sat down, and blasted through the paperwork. He returned to the desk, handed over the clipboard, and began pacing.

Minutes ticked by. He had no idea how many.

Finally, an ED doctor, garbed in medical scrubs, stepped out, his gaze darting around.

Hutch didn't wait to be located. He strode over to the doctor.

"I'm Kyle Hutchinson," he identified himself. "How's Casey?"

The doctor looked grim. "Not good. We did a CT scan and an ultrasound of her belly. We took labs to see if we're missing something and to crossmatch her blood type. You're type O negative?"

"Yes. I'll donate as much blood as possible."

The doctor nodded. "Do that ASAP."

Hutch's gut clenched. "What did the scan and the ultrasound show?"

"Extensive internal bleeding that requires emergency surgery. The surgical team will have to open her up, clean out the blood, and see the extent of the damage. Her abdomen is swelling with blood accumulation—and it's getting worse. Her vital signs are dropping. I need your immediate permission for the surgery."

"You have it. I'll sign whatever's necessary."

An attendant handed him a clipboard with a surgical consent form. He read it and signed his name ASAP.

As he handed the clipboard back, he saw Casey being wheeled out.

"Surgery—stat," the doctor ordered the attendants. "The surgical team is waiting."

Organized chaos erupted as Casey was moved directly to an operating room.

Hutch stared after the woman he loved. She had IV lines in, plus a transfusion line through the IV to get restoring blood into her. She was intubated to help her breathe. She lay there, very still, white-faced and unconscious.

Pain lanced through him.

His Casey. His strong, unyielding Casey.

This couldn't be happening, not to her.

The ER doctor spoke up. "After you donate blood, you can go to the surgical department and sit in the waiting area. That way, you can get updates as soon as possible."

"How long do you expect the surgery to take?"

"That depends on whether or not there are complications. I can't give you a definitive answer. The SD will be providing that as the surgery progresses."

"Thank you, Doctor." Hutch paused for just a moment, trying to clear his head. He had phone calls to make, responsibilities that were his and his alone. Casey's parents, who'd moved to Arizona. They'd inform other family members. But, ahead of that came the FI team—after the blood donation.

He determined the location of the lab and walked briskly in that direction.

He changed his mind as he walked. He needed support, and FI needed to know. They were her real family. He could talk and give blood at the same time.

He called Marc.

# 27

Hutch heard the echoing ring of Marc's cell, not through his own phone, but right there in the Trauma Center, about thirty feet away.

"Hutch!" Marc called out. "We're here."

Hutch came to a standstill. "How did you know?"

"Claire," Ryan replied. "She sensed it. She got us here." He took in the blood covering Hutch's hands and clothes and swallowed hard.

"Tell us as much as you can," Marc said.

"I'm on my way to donate blood. Marc, you walk with me. I'll fill you in and you'll do the same with the rest of the team. The Trauma Center has strict rules." Hutch's voice broke. "One of you check in at the front desk. They're trying to get the okay to allow you into the surgical department's waiting area. I'll meet you there."

"We'll be there," Emma said fiercely. Her eyes were brimming with tears.

"What's Casey's blood type?" Patrick asked.

"A positive" was the reply.

"That's me," Ryan said. "I'll go with you, Hutch."

"Thanks." Hutch was desperately trying to keep it together.

During the quick walk to the Trauma Center's lab, he told Marc and Ryan all he could. "I don't know what the weapon was—not until CSI turns up the gun, the bullet, or the casing."

"I'd bet on the bullet or casing," Marc replied. "The shooter probably took the weapon with him and either tossed it or destroyed it."

"Yeah," Hutch agreed. "I'm sure CSI is combing the grounds of our complex by now. We'll see what they find." He gave another hard swallow, his mind racing back to Casey.

Marc put his hand on Hutch's shoulder. "She'll make it, Hutch. Casey is the strongest fighter I know."

Hutch gave a shaky nod. "She *has* to make it. I won't accept anything less." He headed into the lab with Ryan. "Go fill in the rest of the team," he called over his shoulder. "We'll join you soon."

\*\*\*

*Surgical Department Waiting Area*
*Tuesday, 11:15 a.m.*

The room was dead silent.

The entire FI team sat rigidly in chairs, each one afraid to speak their fears aloud. Claire was openly weeping, continually dashing tears from her cheeks in an effort to curb her reaction. Emma was even worse, her hands covering her face, and her shoulders shaking with silent sobs.

The men weren't faring much better. Ryan had his head turned away from the group, clearly trying to regain control. Patrick and Marc looked grim, exchanging glances as they maintained their composure—barely.

Hutch was out of his mind.

He stood just outside the inner doors, peering through the small window panes for the umpteenth time, as if willing someone to emerge. Then, he turned and stalked back to the team.

"Why doesn't that trauma resident come back out?" he demanded, his voice hoarse. "Casey's been in the OR for three hours, and all we know is that it's touch and go, that she's lost a tremendous amount of blood—which we already knew—and that they can't produce a bullet because it was a through-and-through."

Marc was perched at the edge of a chair. "It's obviously a complicated surgery," he said as gently as he could. "We'd rather have the trauma resident, Doctor Rawlings, in the OR working to save Casey's life than out here talking to us. They know how anxious we are. We'll hear something soon."

"It's bad. Really bad." Hutch was speaking half to himself, almost as if he hadn't heard Marc's words. "If I'd only lunged over, moved a split second sooner, it would have been me. Why couldn't it have been me?"

He completely broke down, openly weeping and muttering the same words over and over.

Marc went to him and put both hands on Hutch's shoulders. "Stop," he said, his voice pained and low. "There's no way you could have known, much less prevented it. You can't blame yourself."

"Yes I can." Hutch leveled his tortured gaze at Marc. "It happened on my watch. We all knew Casey was in danger. And the only reason John Nickels wasn't close by is because I was with her. I didn't protect her. And now, she's…"

"She's fighting," Ryan said, turning to face him. "That's why this is taking so long. She won't give up, Hutch. We all know Casey. She's going to pull through this." He looked helplessly at Claire. "Do you sense anything?" he asked. "Anything at all?"

She wiped the tears from her cheeks. "She's still with us," she managed. "She wants to live. For Hutch. For all of us."

Ryan nodded and swallowed deeply. Claire's words were like manna from heaven. "Listen to Claire, Hutch. Casey has a will of iron. She'll come back to us."

"When are we going to get another update?" Hutch demanded again.

"Not for a while," Claire replied. "But I pray the news will be good."

***

The news came three hours later.

The doors slid open and Dr. Rawlings strode out.

"We've closed up the patient," she reported. "Her spleen was ruptured and had to be removed. We managed to stop the bleeding, but there's still so much internal blood, it remains touch and go. She's been moved to the trauma surgical ICU."

Hutch froze in place. "What about other organs and blood vessels?"

"Fortunately, the bullet passed straight through and didn't nick anything else in the abdominal cavity. That was the best possible scenario."

"You can live without a spleen, right?" Emma asked.

Dr. Rawlings frowned. "Yes, if the body can reabsorb all the lost blood."

Hutch ran a shaky hand through his hair. "I don't understand. If it was only her spleen…"

"The spleen holds twenty-five to thirty percent of the body's blood," Dr. Rawlings explained. "She's lost a great deal of that."

"Oh, God." Hutch sank down in a chair. "How long until you'll know?"

"Ms. Woods's body will tell us. She's receiving transfusions to restore blood to the rest of her body. She's on a ventilator, and she's being given her fluids intravenously. We need her to wake up a little and to breathe on her own. That means off the ventilator within twenty-four hours."

"And if that doesn't happen?" Hutch's voice was tortured.

"Let's not get ahead of ourselves," the doctor replied. "She made it through the surgery. We're taking it from there."

"When can I see her?"

"Let the ICU attending staff get her settled in. It shouldn't be long—maybe a half hour. And visitation will be limited only to you, Mr. Hutchinson. The rest of you can go back to the main waiting area."

Hutch nodded. "Thank you."

Dr. Rawlings cleared her throat. "I understand that you're with the FBI. We'll be letting the police department know that the surgical team did an excellent job of not disturbing bullet holes and clothes so that law enforcement can collect gunshot residue or whatever other physical evidence they need."

Hutch looked blankly at her, as if he didn't so much as understand.

"We appreciate that, Dr. Rawlings," Marc said, stepping in. "I'm sure the First Precinct will be relieved to hear that you made their jobs a little easier."

She nodded and retreated back into the OR.

Once she'd gone, Marc gave Hutch's shoulder another squeeze. "This is all good news. Casey is on her way back to us. We'll be waiting for you once you've had your visit." A pause. "Do you need me to call anyone?"

Hutch shook his head. "I don't think so. I called Casey's parents. They'll be flying in tomorrow. They're calling everyone else, family and friends, who need to know. If you think of someone I'm missing, please go ahead and contact them. My entire focus is going to be on Casey."

"Of course." Marc's mind moved quickly. "I think I'll call Angela King so she doesn't wonder why Casey will be going radio silent for a while. And I'll give Detectives Ogden and Banks a heads-up. I'm sure they're all over this by now, but I can update them with more details, and get whatever I can out of them. Hopefully, my calling will soothe their ruffled feathers over the fact that we got Oliver Steadman, and he wasn't even on their radar. More important, I want to remind them that Oliver Steadman is in custody and can't possibly have shot Casey. Whoever did that is still at large, and is also the one who bludgeoned Hillington to death. Casey is now officially off their suspect list and on their victim list."

A terse nod. "Good idea. Thanks, Marc."

"No thanks necessary. I saw that the trauma surgical ICU is adjacent to where we are." Marc tipped his head in that direction. "Go visit our girl."

"Hutch?" Claire interrupted. "Talk to her. She'll feel your presence, even though she's still unconscious. Tell her you love her, and that you're right beside her. Tell her the whole team is out here waiting for her to come home. It will help tip the scales in our favor."

"She'll live?" Hutch asked quickly.

"I'm not certain, but I do feel optimistic. You have to feel that way, too. It matters. I know that much."

"I will."

# 28

The access doors slid open, and Hutch walked through them and into the intensive care unit. Like the rest of the Level One Trauma Center, it was a huge open area. As had been explained to him, it was staffed with professionals of all kinds, all of whom bustled about—everyone from trauma surgeons, critical care associates, trauma registered nurses, trauma nurse practitioners, to respiratory therapists and trauma patient care associates. They were all in the hospital twenty-four hours a day. Multiple surgical procedures could be performed right at the patient's bedside. And the access doors to the unit were secured at all times to maintain patient privacy and security.

In other words, Hutch had certain parameters that had to be stayed within. That was fine. He'd do whatever was asked of him. All he wanted was to see Casey and for her to live.

It took him a split second to skim the dozen and a half beds and to find her.

She was in a semireclining position in the bed. She looked small and helpless, white as a ghost, with a major apparatus breathing for her and tubes connected everywhere. The heart monitor beeped rhythmically. She'd been cleaned up, but there were still traces of blood in her hair and on her face. There might be more, but the blankets and hospital gown hid them from view. Her eyes were shut as she remained in an unconscious state.

Hutch stood very still, dealing with his emotional reaction on the spot. He had no intention of transferring it to her.

When he felt in control, he walked over to the bed, and sank down into the chair beside it.

"Hi, sweetheart," he greeted her softly. "You gave me quite a scare. But I know you, and I knew you'd come through this like the trouper you are." Hutch cleared his throat. "You're a very popular woman. The entire FI team is outside, your parents are flying in, and I plan on staying twenty-four seven, if I'm allowed. You came through the surgery with an A+, and I'm sure in a day or two I'll be pinning you to the bed to keep you still."

The ventilator slid up and down, and the continuous beeps of the heart monitor reassured him that Casey was alive.

*Was she hearing him? Could he will her to regain consciousness?*

"I love you, beautiful," he continued. "I still intend to collect on the all-nighter you promised me. So get well fast. On that front, I'm not a patient man, and you know it." He leaned over, lifted her hand ever so slightly, and kissed her cold fingertips.

He kept talking, telling Casey the wonderful things they would do once she was back to herself. He intermingled them with love words, and gentle caresses of her hand, even touching her cheek a few times just so she felt his presence.

She *had* to wake up.

***

Some unknown time later, one of the critical care associates approached him.

"Mr. Hutchinson? The trauma surgeon is on his way in to examine Ms. Woods. If you could step outside for a few minutes?"

"Of course." Hutch rose. "Rest," he told Casey. "I'll be back before you can miss me."

He took the opportunity to go back down to the ED waiting room and to fill in the FI team.

They all jumped up when they saw him, their eyes pleading for good news.

Hutch explained what was going on.

"You took my advice," Claire murmured. "Good. She heard you, Hutch. I can sense it."

"I pray you're right." For the first time in ages, Hutch glanced at his Apple Watch, stunned to find that it was inching past four fifty. Over two hours had passed since he'd stepped into the ICU. "They closed her up more than three hours ago," he said, a fine tension in his voice. "When is she going to wake up? When is she going to start breathing on her own?"

Claire answered in that soothing voice of hers. "Dr. Rawlings said within twenty-four hours, Hutch. It's nowhere near that."

Emma stood up, eyeing Hutch with concern. "You look like you're about to collapse. You haven't eaten all day." A pause. "Actually none of us has eaten all day." She scooped up her handbag. "I'm finding a cafeteria and getting us some sandwiches."

"I'm not hungry..." Hutch began.

"Oh, yes you are." Emma sounded like a drill sergeant. "You just don't know it. But Casey needs your strength, and I'm making sure you have it."

With that, she marched off.

Hutch's jaw dropped, and he stared after her.

Ryan's lips twitched. "That's Emma in true protective mode. Feel honored, Hutch. She doesn't get that way too often."

"I guess." Hutch let out a long sigh. "Sorry if I've been a bear, guys. I'm just...shattered. And I'm not used to feeling this way, or being so helpless."

"No explanation needed," Patrick replied, back to being the father of the team. "We're all pretty shattered. But I do believe that Casey is going to come through this, fast and furious. That's just who she is."

"Amen," Claire agreed quietly. She was fidgeting in her seat, her eyes going from dazed to clear.

"What is it?" Ryan demanded.

"Everything's changed since Casey's shooting. I was blocked. Now my sensory awareness has opened up and is running rampant. I've haven't gotten a firm handle on any of the images that keep darting through my mind. But I'm surer than ever that the killer is tightly tied to Christopher Hillington. Nothing like Steadman. Deeply emotional and deeply personal."

"Family?" Ryan asked quickly.

"Family—yes."

"Then as soon as the surgeon gives us the thumbs-up on Casey and we're able to go back to the office, I'm starting with a deeper dive into Hillington's wife and kids. We're clearly missing something. I'll find it."

*\*\**

*Nineteenth Precinct*
*153 East Sixty-Seventh Street*
*Manhattan, New York*
*Tuesday, 5:50 p.m.*

Lorraine Banks hung up her phone, frowning at CSI's update. "No weapon has been found on the scene," she reported to Burt Ogden, who was hunched over his computer, rereading the full report the First Precinct had provided for them. "Even worse, no bullet or casing has been found. Apparently, the shooting happened on a section of the path that has sewer drains on either side. Crime Scene is still combing the grounds, but the slope of the ground there is against us. They suspect the bullet and casing fell into one of those drains. Dammit!" Her fist struck her desk in frustration.

"Yeah, well, we seem to be thwarted at every turn," Burt replied with a scowl.

"This truly sucks," Lorraine added. "And, regardless of how much we clash with Forensic Instincts, I feel terrible about Casey Woods."

Burt gave a tight nod. "It's a shitty way of proving her innocence." His scowl deepened. "On another note, I'm still pissed as hell about Oliver Steadman. We never heard of him, and all of a sudden Forensic Instincts waltzes him in and advises us that he was guilty of the hit-and-run—and that Hillington was his intended victim."

"I hear you, but we can't wage a war with Forensic Instincts. Because, of course, the evidence and Steadman's written confession confirm their claims." Lorraine waved that away for a moment. "What's most important is exactly what Marc Devereaux said when he called. Steadman couldn't have shot Casey. The real killer is still out there."

Burt rubbed the back of his neck. "We've exhausted most of our leads."

"We could go back to the doorman at Hillington's apartment building and see if he remembers anything more about the delivery person who showed up around the time Hillington was killed."

"And what is he going to tell us? We grilled the hell out of him. We also watched the video footage a dozen times. There was nothing there." Burt shook his head. "I know you think that's how our killer got in, but it's a weak link."

Lorraine's shoulders lifted, then fell. "Okay, then what if our killer didn't have to get in. What if he or she was already in the building—or in the apartment, waiting."

"Which brings us back to Charlotte Hillington and her kids," Burt stated. "We already agreed that every detail they shared seemed rehearsed. And their alibis all checked out perfectly—maybe too perfectly. They didn't know about Hillington's will being on hold, but they did know that Hillington was greedy about sharing his fortune. Plus, we have no guarantee that Charlotte Hillington didn't know about Natalie and Morgan Evans. You know what they say about a woman scorned."

Lorraine was nodding even as Burt spoke. "Sometimes the most obvious candidate really is the guilty one. So what do you say we pay the Hillingtons another visit?" She reached for her cell. "I'll say enough to shake them up a little and to set up a time for the four of them to be together. *Tomorrow*."

\*\*\*

*Trauma Center ICU*
*Tuesday, 6:20 p.m.*

"Mr. Hutchinson."

The words were accompanied by a slight shake, although none was needed. Hutch snapped out of his light doze in an instant, jerking up to a rigid sitting position. Something was going on.

"What's happened?" he demanded, recognizing the trauma RN as Nurse Yates, whom he'd met at some unknown point in the ICU.

"Don't panic. The news is good," she replied. "Ms. Woods's vital signs are improving, and she's waking up. I'll be removing the endotracheal tube now so she can breathe on her own. I'll temporarily switch her over to nasal cannulas to give her oxygen. That will help make the transition to normal breathing easier. The nasal cannulas are more convenient than masks, because they'll allow the patient to eat, drink, and talk."

Hutch's heart was pounding as he looked over at Casey. Her eyelashes were fluttering, and she was fidgeting a bit, clearly in protest of the invasive tube positioned way down her throat.

"Oh, thank God," Hutch managed. He was literally shaking with relief.

"I'm going to ask you to step outside during the extubation process," the nurse continued. "It won't take long. Then you can come back and encourage her to fully awaken."

Hutch half rose, but he couldn't seem to tear his gaze away from Casey's face.

"Mr. Hutchinson?" the nurse prodded.

"I'm sorry. Of course." Hutch pulled himself together, stood up, and left the room. The sooner he did, the sooner he'd be back at Casey's side, saying everything she wanted and needed to hear.

***

The nurse acted quickly. She removed the air from the inflated gasket on the tube and released the tape that was holding the tube in place. Casey's eyes were open now, glazed from the painkillers. Still, her gaze was anxious and questioning.

The nurse gave her a reassuring smile. "I'm Nurse Yates, Ms. Woods. I'm removing the endotracheal tube so you can breathe easily and independently. It will feel unpleasant for a moment, but then you'll feel much better. Please relax."

Casey gave a small nod of her head and tried to do just that.

Nurse Yates gently pulled the tube from Casey's mouth.

Casey immediately began coughing, her breath coming in sharp rasps.

"Extubation often causes coughing and a sore throat," the nurse soothed her. She then inserted the nasal cannulas into Casey's nostrils and adjusted the strap around her neck. "These will help the transition to normal breathing."

Casey drank in the oxygen gratefully, her breathing evening out right away. Her gaze was darting around as she tried to orient herself.

"The surgeon will be in shortly to check on you," Nurse Yates answered Casey's unspoken question. "I'd say to make sure to have another person with you to listen to the update, since you still won't have your full faculties for a while. But that's not an issue, since there's a certain FBI agent outside who's been perched at your bedside all day. He wants very much to see you awake."

Another smile as she checked the elevation of the bed and made sure Casey's knees were raised. "I assume it's okay if I send him in?"

"Yes…please…" Casey replied.

\*\*\*

Thirty seconds later, Hutch came striding into the room, his gaze fixed on Casey as he made his way over to her. He couldn't believe how much better she looked, her beautiful features unimpeded by the apparatus that had kept her alive, a small smile lighting up her face.

"Morning, beautiful," Hutch said, bypassing the nasal cannulas and giving her a soft kiss. His own breath broke a little. "Thank you for coming back to me."

She gripped his hand. "Please sit… I need to know…"

Hutch knew that meant that Casey wanted every detail, asking him to spare her nothing.

Before he did just that, he asked, "Are you in much pain?"

"Yes…but the drugs…are helping."

Hutch nodded, squeezing her fingers. "If you need more…"

"Nurse…will adjust." Pain or not, Casey looked impatient. "Tell me."

Hutch felt his chest tighten with gratitude. His Casey was back.

"Do you remember being shot?" he asked.

Her eyes narrowed. "No. Maybe. Pain…then nothing."

"The pain was the bullet." Hutch swallowed hard. "The injury was bad. You're at the Level One Trauma Center at New York-Presbyterian Lower Manhattan Hospital. You just had over six hours of surgery, followed by five post-op hours in the ICU. The surgeons removed your spleen. You lost massive amounts of blood, but, thankfully, no other organs or blood vessels were nicked. It's going to be okay now that you're awake and your vital signs are getting stronger."

"What time…and day…is it?"

"It's still Tuesday. And it's past six thirty p.m. You were shot between seven and seven thirty this morning, so it's been a long day."

Casey accepted that with a dazed nod. "Okay." Even though she was still somewhat out of it, her wheels were trying to turn. "Shooter… is our killer… Did you catch them?"

"No one, including me, even saw them. The shot must have come from behind the trees at our apartment complex. I didn't take time to search for them, and I don't know details. All that mattered to me was you. I've been here since we arrived by ambulance. Marc spoke to the detectives, but I didn't—not yet."

"FI has to find…murderer." She paused, drank in some air. "Marc…in the office?"

"No, Marc is here. The entire team has been here since before I called them. Apparently, Claire just knew and led the way."

Another smile. "I'm glad…"

"You'll be able to see them only one at a time," Hutch informed her. "Maybe two, if you win over the doctors. The rules here are very strict."

"Yes…sir."

This time it was Hutch who smiled. "Oh, and your parents are flying in tomorrow. Needless to say, they were shocked and frightened. I'll let them know right away that you're awake." His brows drew together. "They're calling other members of your family and family friends. Marc called Angela King and Detectives Banks and Ogden. Is there anyone else you want me to contact?"

Casey's brow furrowed. "Don't think so. Need my head…to clear." Her eyelids drooped.

Hutch pressed his forefinger to her lips. "Shhh, it's okay. We have time." *All the time in the world, thank heavens.* "You've been through hell and are only first coming back. So let your body heal. We can talk or not talk. I'm not going anywhere."

Two tears slid down Casey's cheeks. "I…love you."

Hutch caressed her face, wiping her tears away. "And I love you. More than you could ever know. More than *I* ever knew."

# 29

*Emergency Department Waiting Area*
*Tuesday, 7:15 p.m.*

After Hutch got a full report from Casey's surgeon and she started to doze, he left long enough to call Casey's parents and to fill in the FI team.

Marc was just hanging up the phone with Madeleine's visiting nurse and had reassured himself that his wife was okay. Maddy had called out that she was fine and that Marc should stay where he was until he had good news to share.

The instant he saw Hutch, he—and everyone else on the team— jumped to their feet, staring at Hutch with worried but hopeful gazes. Their expressions brightened as they saw the smile on his face.

"She's awake," he announced. "She's also breathing on her own, and her vital signs have improved tremendously. Oh, and she's talking. Even on major painkillers and with her voice weak and raspy, she ordered me to tell her everything."

Everyone wept with joy, hugging Hutch and each other as they drank in this miraculous and wonderful news.

Claire wiped away her tears. "Did you fill her in, or was it too much?"

Hutch's smile turned into a full grin. "Oh, I filled her in. She pretty much ordered you to find the shooter, who she clearly stated was also Hillington's killer."

Marc threw back his head in laughter. "The formidable president of FI, back in business."

"Is that a surprise?" Ryan asked, his voice still a bit unsteady.

"Did you get an update from the surgeon?" Emma piped up.

Hutch nodded. "No complications, and all signs are good. She needs rest—she was dozing when I left the ICU. If all continues to go well, which the surgeon believes it will, Casey will be moved out of the ICU and into a regular trauma floor bed in a day or two. Tonight, when she wakes up, the nurse is going to give her sips of water to see if she tolerates liquids. If she does—which she will—she'll be on a liquid diet tonight, and she'll be reevaluated tomorrow. Also tomorrow, she has to start walking a little, with help, of course."

"In other words," Patrick said cheerfully, "you'll be battling with the nurse to be Casey's aide."

"Probably." Hutch was equally upbeat, not at all offended by Patrick's comment. He sucked in his breath, able, for the first time, to think beyond Casey's life. "What did the detectives have to say?" he asked Marc.

Marc snorted. "What do they ever have to say to us? All I know is that the shooter hasn't been apprehended, and that CSI was on the scene looking for a weapon and ammunition."

Ryan looked at him, the haze in his head also clearing. "I'll get into the NYPD system and check out the file. Maybe there's been an update since then. That'll precede my deep dive into the Hillingtons."

Claire gave Hutch a hopeful look. "Any chance that we can visit Casey, or is that an outright no."

Hutch grinned at her. "Actually, that's a yes. The surgeon said that, starting tomorrow morning, two of you at a time can go in and see her. Only for you guys would I relinquish my spot, even for a little while. I'm going back in there now and sitting with her until she's awake.

Once she is, I'll let you know. Then, I'll perch on my makeshift bed in the ICU. The rest of you should all go home and get dinner and some sleep."

"Sleep? No way," Ryan said. "I'm going back to the office to start looking for more information. We've solved the hit-and-run. Now comes the crucial part—solving Hillington's murder. We'll catch that fucking killer and, finally, Casey will be well and truly safe."

Hutch gave an emphatic nod. "Amen. But Ryan, work at home," he advised. "You'll get more done and you can conk out when you run out of gas. I want that animal caught more than you do, but we need to be firing on all cylinders to make it happen."

"Hutch is right," Marc said. "And not just about me, since, in my case, I need to get home to Maddy. We're all wiped and have zero reserves. Let's recoup and get here early to see Casey. Ryan, tonight work only as you're able. Tomorrow we'll all go at it, full force."

The team reluctantly nodded.

"In the meantime, you can battle it out as to who goes in to see Casey first," Hutch suggested.

They were already doing just that as Hutch turned around to retrace his steps.

\*\*\*

*Hillington Residence*
*200 East Eighty-Third Street, Twenty-First Floor*
*Upper East Side, Manhattan, New York*
*Tuesday, 7:30 p.m.*

Charlotte and her three children were gathered together in their sunken living room, each one of them freaked out by the detectives' phone call.

Ashley's arm was looped around her mother's shoulders as she tried to reassure Charlotte and herself. Brighton was on his second drink and eyeing a third. And Lily was sitting on the sofa like a frightened doe, her eyes huge and her face sheet white.

"Why is this happening?" she asked. "We were all interviewed. We had alibis. The detectives were satisfied. What changed their minds? And, as I keep saying, why would they think one of us killed Daddy?"

Brighton set down his tumbler with a thud. "Because of money, my naïve little sister. None of us has any without him supplying it, even now after he's dead. We need that will to be read."

"And there are other reasons, as well," Charlotte said bitterly.

"Such as?" Brighton prodded.

"Shut up, Brighton." Ashley turned around and shot him a dark look. "This isn't the time to interrogate each other. This is the time to lock in our stories and make sure they haven't deviated from our original ones. Innocent people go to jail, too, so we'd better be as convincing as possible."

"Fine." Brighton picked up his drink again. "You and Mother were working on a charity event and having coffee right down the way at Madame Eloise's Café. Naomi, who served your coffee and scones, vouched for that. Lily was on her way to work, and she arrived right on time. That was confirmed by the family she works for. And I was at my studio. My whole band was on board with that. Good enough?"

Ashley's lips thinned. "Stop being so flippant. The detectives are coming here for a reason, and it can't be a good one. We have to be as flawless—and accommodating"—a purposeful glare at Brighton—"as possible. Understood?"

"Yeah. Understood." Brighton sank down on the sofa, looking like a petulant child. He pulled out his phone and started scrolling through it. "Time to take a break and see what's going on in the world."

Charlotte turned to snap, "Now, at this crisis moment for our family, you've suddenly become interested in current events?"

Brighton ignored her, continuing to look irked as he skimmed his newsfeed. But he couldn't keep his gaze averted forever.

"I'm trying to distract myself, Mother," he replied at last. "There's nothing we can do about the detectives' visit. We'll handle them. We did last time—with the help of what's-his-name, the attorney."

"What's-his-name is Raymond Tudor," Charlotte said in an icy voice. "He's a renowned and successful attorney. Angela King recommended him, since her firm can't represent us. As I told you, representing us would be a conflict of interest, because they represent your father and his estate."

"Yeah, right. So we're in good hands," Brighton replied. "I think we should keep our mouths shut as long as possible and let Raymond Tudor do his job. Isn't that pretty much what he told us to do last time?"

"Yes, and we will," Ashley said. "My biggest concern is what new information they have. I doubt they're just revisiting our alibis. If they'd returned to badger any of the people who vouched for us, one of them would have let us know."

"Leonard?" Lily asked, eyebrows raised in question. "Could he have remembered something?"

"Nope." Brighton shook his head. "He's loyal to our family. If he had something to say, he would have first said it to us. He wouldn't just contact the police." He polished off his drink, set it down on the end table, and rose. "I've had enough of this guessing game. I've got a practice session to get to. We'll have our answers at ten o'clock tomorrow morning."

"Raymond will be here at nine thirty, Brighton," Charlotte stated. "Be here at nine fifteen. Is that understood?"

"Understood. Don't sweat it. I'll be here."

\*\*\*

*Ryan's Loft Apartment*
*Fifth Avenue*
*Park Slope, New York*
*Tuesday, 11:20 p.m.*

Ryan had been at his desk in his all-purpose room since he and Claire had gotten here hours ago.

He rubbed his temples, then peered at his computer through glazed eyes. He'd compiled a shitload of data on the Hillingtons and had been battling to review it. But his brain had started to rebel an hour ago and was refusing to let anything more in. Plus his head was throbbing, both from fatigue and from the emotional roller coaster of the day.

He swore under his breath. He had to get this done. He had to then hack back into the NYPD's system to see what updates they had on the Hillington murder and cross-check it with whatever he'd collected on the Hillingtons. The attempt on Casey's life must, obviously, have been added to the file by now. He wanted to try to get a read on where Banks's and Ogden's heads were, to see if there were hints as to where they were next headed.

Things from all sides were bugging him, but he couldn't seem to focus.

"You're not going to get any further tonight," Claire said from his bedroom doorway. "You're just out of energy. Ryan, get some sleep. We'll visit Casey in the morning, see for ourselves that she's okay, and then you'll be back to yourself, exporting tons of information."

With a sigh, Ryan rubbed his eye sockets. "This sucks."

"It doesn't have to." Claire had a tone in her voice that Ryan recognized very well. He heard a rustle of clothing and spun his chair around to face her.

Claire had shimmied out of Ryan's T-shirt and dropped it to the floor. "I'll bet I can lull you into a dreamless sleep."

"Without a doubt." Even as Ryan's gaze devoured her naked body, he yanked off his sweats and headed toward her. He steered her straight to the bed and dropped down beside her.

"Sorry," Claire murmured as she wrapped her arms around his neck. "I used blackmail."

"Uh-uh. You offered incentive," he replied, threading his fingers through her hair. "I promise we'll both get a great night's sleep—starting in about two hours."

# 30

Casey sank back in her hospital bed, feeling totally wiped, emotionally drained, and more physically taxed than she could ever remember. And the pain was excruciating.

She winced as Nurse Reynolds—one of her morning nurses—settled her in. The nurse upped the morphine drip and gave Casey a cup of water, which she downed greedily. She'd already managed some broth and a bit of toast.

Hutch stood by, looking drawn and concerned.

"You did too much," he said once the nurse had left. "Two laps around the ICU and three sets of visitors—first Claire and Ryan, next Patrick and Emma, and last Marc, who you talked to for way too long. Are you okay?" He caressed her cheek.

Casey forced a small smile. "You're just peeved because Nurse Reynolds wouldn't let you assist me in my walks. She's trained, Hutch. You're not—at least not in this."

Hutch didn't laugh. "You've been talking for hours and doing physical therapy in between. You're not ready for so much in such a short period of time."

Casey looked as if she wanted to agree, but didn't. Instead, she said, "The surgeon seems to feel that I am. The walks were short and were spaced two hours apart. Plus, I'd hardly call what I was doing walking; I was leaning heavily on Nurse Reynolds and a cane, and still barely hobbling. And I wasn't talking for hours. The team stayed only fifteen minutes a pair. They gave me breaks in between."

Casey shut her eyes and gave a long sigh. "I hate this," she whispered.

Hutch linked his fingers with hers. "I know, sweetheart. But you're alive. You're here with me, and you're getting stronger by the hour. I just don't want you to overdo."

Casey nodded and opened her eyes. "The team was so devastated," she murmured. "And Emma lost it completely. I don't know how to help them."

"Now that they've seen for themselves that you're alive and healing, they'll start channeling their energy into finding Hillington's killer."

"While I sit here and veg," Casey said in utter frustration.

"Veg? Casey, for God's sake, you were just shot—almost fatally. You've got to give yourself time to recover."

Casey arched a brow at him. "Would you be happy with such sage advice?"

"No," Hutch stated flatly. "But I'm not in love with me. I'm in love with you."

Casey tried hard not to laugh. It aggravated the pain beyond bearing. "Honest to a fault, SSA Kyle Hutchinson. Okay, I see where you're coming from. I'll be a good girl and listen to the ICU team's instructions. But as soon as I can manage to make work-related phone calls without needing oxygen as a result, I'm back in the game."

Hutch looked relieved. "Good. In the meantime I brought you some personal items you'll need, like a toothbrush. When it comes to discharging you, I'll bring you some clothes."

"Thanks." Casey frowned. "I doubt yesterday's blood-soaked outfit is still here. The NYPD must have it." Her frown deepened. "Has the media run with this story yet?"

"Nope." Hutch shook his head. "Both the NYPD and FI have managed to keep the news under wraps, but I wouldn't hold my breath. I doubt we can contain it much longer. By tonight, some obnoxious, well-connected citizen journalist will have gotten the information and will be showcasing it for all to see."

Casey was starting to fade. "I need to sleep," she said. "But please ask Marc to call Lorraine or Burt. Ask them to schedule a news conference for this afternoon. It's important that the initial report comes from them." Her eyelids drooped. "And maybe it will upset the shooter into doing something."

"Like coming after you again?"

"No. Like giving him or herself away."

"You know this will tell the killer that you're still alive and still a threat. I don't like it."

"Please, Hutch. The Trauma Center is like a fortress. Nobody's getting to me."

"Fine," Hutch replied. Casey's point was the only reason he was agreeing. With luck, the killer would be in custody before Casey was discharged. "I'll call Marc right after you fall asleep."

Casey was asleep a minute later.

\*\*\*

*Hillington Residence*
*200 East Eighty-Third Street, Twenty-First Floor*
*Upper East Side, Manhattan, New York*
*Wednesday, 10:00 a.m.*


Charlotte had opened the door herself and led Detectives Banks and Ogden into the living room. All of her children were gathered there, seated on the long, circular sofa. They'd left the center cushion for their mother. Raymond Tudor was seated in a matching chair, sipping a cup of coffee. He was tall, with salt-and-pepper hair and sharp blue eyes—eyes that were now fixed on their adversaries.

"Good morning," he said to Lorraine and Burt. "I'm surprised to be having another gathering, but I'm sure you'll tell us why we're all here."

"We intend to." Lorraine's voice had a bite to it. Tudor was just too smooth and calculating to suit her. Then again, did she expect anything less from the Hillingtons?

Charlotte gestured toward two other chairs. "Please sit," she told the detectives with a polite, if strained, smile. "Can I offer you anything?"

Lorraine shook her head. "Nothing but answers."

The tension in the room shot up several notches.

"I'll have a cup of coffee," Burt said. "Just black." He glanced around. "Is your housekeeper here? Or is she off—like she was on the morning your husband was killed?"

"Careful, Detective," Tudor said. "That sounds suspiciously like an implication."

Charlotte's smile faltered. "She's coming in later today. I thought this talk of ours should be conducted in private." She turned toward the kitchen. "I'll get your coffee."

Once Charlotte had left the room, Lorraine glanced around, studying each of the three kids. They presented a united front, all straight-backed and wary, ready to provide carefully rehearsed answers.

"You look like soldiers about to march into battle," she said.

"Isn't that what we are?" Brighton retorted.

Ashley shot him a look. "My brother doesn't mean to be rude," she explained. "We're all just a little thrown by this meeting. We provided you with everything we know. It's disconcerting that you felt compelled to return."

Tears had gathered in Lily's eyes. "All we want is for you to find our father's murderer. Does your visit mean you have some news?"

"I was about to ask the same." Charlotte reentered the room and handed Burt a cup of black coffee. He and Lorraine had sat down on two adjacent chairs and were looking very stern and official. "You didn't say much when you called. You made it obvious that you had additional questions, but do you also have answers?"

Lorraine folded her arms across her chest. "We have a new occurrence to bring to the table—one that ties to your father's murder. It answers some questions and raises new ones. You'll hear about it soon enough. We'll be giving a news conference at one o'clock this afternoon. In the interim, do any of you have something to share with us? Because we'll need all your alibis for yesterday morning between seven and seven thirty."

"Stop the games, Detective," Tudor intervened. "What are you talking about and why do you need additional alibis from my clients?"

Burt set down his cup of coffee. "Another violent attack relating to Hillington's murder has occurred. Now answer Detectives Banks's question. We need alibis for you all."

Charlotte was starting to tremble. "I was asleep in my bed—alone. I have no one to vouch for that."

"I was brewing a pot of coffee when you came into the kitchen, Mother," Ashley reminded her. "That was around seven forty. We were both in our nightgowns and were barely awake. So we're each other's alibi."

"Very convenient," Burt muttered.

"The question has been asked and answered," Tudor stated. "Move on."

Lily licked her lips. "I was on my way to work. I stopped to pick up a bagel and a coffee at our local Starbucks. I'm not sure who'd remember me, maybe Leonard, our doorman, or the Starbucks barista who made my drink? Either way, that's where I was."

Lorraine Banks studied Lily for a moment, and then turned her attention to Brighton. "And you?"

"I woke up early," he said. "I took a long run and then went to my studio to write some music. I'm not certain of the exact time, nor do I know if anyone saw me. I don't think Leonard was at his post. In any case, it had to be around seven thirty."

"Well," Burt Ogden said. "That's a whole lot of nothing."

"It's all my clients have to offer," Tudor said. He half rose. "So if there's nothing further…"

Lorraine's mouth thinned into a grim line as she took the questioning a step further. "Are any of you familiar with Forensic Instincts? Particularly with their president, Casey Woods."

Charlotte's brows rose. "I know they're a successful private investigation firm, but I don't know them personally. Why? Are they working for you to find Christopher's killer?"

Burt sidestepped the question. "The Forensic Instincts team has made the headlines many times over." He pulled out his cell phone and went into his web browser, finding and opening the FI website. Then, he rose, went over to the sofa, and scanned through the photos attached to their bios, one by one. "Recognize any of them?" he asked.

Brighton and Lily were caught completely off guard.

"That's…?" Lily sucked in a breath. "But we know them as—"

Raymond Tudor shut her down in a heartbeat. "My clients are finished answering questions. Direct anything else at me."

The damage had been done.

Lily looked shocked, and Brighton's face was beet red. Even Charlotte and Ashley looked shaken.

Burt took it all in, then turned to Tudor. "I take it your clients know the Forensic Instincts team under different names. Please supply them."

"It's okay," Charlotte said, waving away her attorney's protest. "We have nothing to hide. Those two"—she pointed at Casey and Emma—"attended one of my fundraisers. They masqueraded as two sisters, Hannah and Madison Ellers, who were eager to contribute a large sum of money to my cause. I have no idea why they'd go to such lengths to do so."

"Holy shit," Brighton muttered. "It was all a façade?"

"What was?" Lorraine asked quickly.

"Brighton, enough," Tudor commanded in a no-nonsense tone.

Brighton pressed his lips together and shut his mouth.

Lorraine and Burt exchanged glances. They were livid—as much at FI as they were at the Hillingtons, albeit for different reasons.

Tudor stood up straight and tall. "This meeting is officially at an end. Badgering my clients into telling you things that have no bearing on Christopher's murder is crossing the line. They've told you everything they know. Check out their alibis, if need be. But unless you have something new and significant to offer, please leave."

Both detectives rose. "Check out the one-o'clock news conference," Lorraine said, glancing at her watch. "And stay available. We might just have more to discuss with you at that time."

# 31

Ryan rubbed his eyes. He'd been holed up within these four walls since before seven a.m.

He couldn't do everything at once, so he and the rest of the team had divvied up assignments so as to maximize productivity. Marc and Patrick were deepening their investigation into the Hillingtons, seeing if there was a single thing they'd missed. Emma was back on social media, checking out every new or caption-edited item that any of the Hillington kids had posted. And Claire, who was even more out of sorts than usual, was trying to channel her restless energy into something productive. She had the feeling that she should be contacting Natalie Evans and telling her about Casey. And she would—after the news conference. There was some reason she felt compelled to call. She just couldn't grab hold of what it was.

Ryan's role was to do what he did best. The instant he flipped on his computer and instructed Yoda to stay on alert, he'd hacked immediately into the NYPD system and gone straight to the Hillington murder file. He'd gone over it with a fine-tooth comb, seeing what he might have missed when he'd been buried in the hit-and-run case. For the first time, he saw the entry about Leonard the doorman and the mysterious "food deliverer" who'd showed up around the time of the murder. The police had tied the footage to no one and had found a discarded paper bag in Hillington's apartment that smelled like bacon. So they'd considered that a loose end not worth their time or efforts to pursue.

Not Ryan. He didn't believe in coincidences.

He exported the video footage captured by the apartment cameras and engaged his app to zoom in on every angle of the delivery person that was visible. While the average camera showed a bundled-up person on a bike—signifying nothing other than the fact that it was a cold winter day—Ryan's app said otherwise.

This person wasn't just bundled up. He or she was literally an amorphous blob, someone who wanted to remain as invisible as possible. Every feature was hidden, and every part of the body was concealed, either by a parka, its hood, or by a scarf and gloves. A small shock of blond hair peeped out from the hood, but that said nothing. It could just as easily have been a wig. In fact, it actually looked as if it were purposely displayed by a person who wanted it to be perceived as a vital identification clue.

Bullshit this was just a restaurant delivery person. No one went to such great lengths to cover up because they were cold.

Ryan moved on to the next segment of footage and froze it there. The delivery person was about to climb off the bike and approach Leonard.

Ryan used his app to turn the visual ninety degrees so he could get a side view. Hiking boots, ones that could be found in any sporting goods store, were large, oversized for the foot. Could it be a woman pretending to be a man? Possibly. But, Ryan just couldn't picture Charlotte, Ashley, or Lily Hillington as the person he was viewing. He believed, as he had from the start, that if any of the women were guilty, they would have hired someone to do the job, especially since the weapon was a heavy sledgehammer that had been swung several times to crush Hillington's skull. They weren't tall or muscular enough to have done this themselves.

No, more likely, it was someone trying to disguise the size of their foot the same way they were disguising everything else.

Something caught Ryan's eye—a tiny spot of color in all that black.

He fine-tuned his view still more and zoomed in close. In this segment of the footage, the person was collecting an insulated bag, allegedly containing Hillington's breakfast. The flash of color was a tiny spot of Caucasian skin showing at the wrist. But on that skin was a brown shadow, one that Ryan's app revealed to be either a skin mole or a birthmark. Not round. Slightly triangular. No other distinguishing characteristics. But a solid clue, nonetheless.

Ryan put aside the video footage in order to read Banks's and Ogden's additional notes. They had a point. Hillington had obviously expected this delivery person, since he'd told Leonard to send them right up. Which means he either knew them or at least knew they were coming with his food. If he hadn't ordered breakfast, why would he tell his doorman to allow them up?

That was an interesting question. To Ryan's way of thinking, either Hillington was familiar with this person or he was expecting someone else and instead gotten a killer. The Upper East Side was an affluent part of Manhattan, one that boasted any number of upscale cafés. That offered no avenue of investigation. If a delivery person had been hijacked or worse, it would have been reported to the police. Since Banks and Ogden had nothing of the kind on record, it was doubtful that would be a fruitful path to follow.

Rubbing his forehead, Ryan saw that there were two very recent reports added to the Hillington case file. The first was about CSI's thus-far empty sweep to find the weapon used to shoot Casey, as well as the bullet that had passed through her, and its casing. He hunched forward, reading every detail. The weapon had disappeared, and divers were searching the nearby part of the Hudson River in the hopes of recovering it.

Doubtful, Ryan thought. The law enforcement divers had too high a success ratio in situations such as these. And this was taking too long. More likely, the killer had taken the handgun with him and tossed it in a dumpster far away, or had even destroyed it.

Next came the part about the location of the sewer drains right near where Casey had gotten shot. If the bullet and casing had yet to be located, it was very likely they'd rolled into one of the drains. Which left the detectives—and Forensic Instincts—with another big, fat goose egg.

Ryan went on to read the second case entry, which had become part of the file just twenty minutes ago, and it was about a meeting the detectives had conducted with the Hillingtons this morning. The discussion, held with the Hillingtons' attorney present, had been about providing alibis for when Casey was shot.

Ryan leaned forward, very interested in seeing their replies. All their alibis, with the possible exception of Lily's, pretty much sucked. Banks and Ogden could poke a dozen holes in them. It was clear from the tone of the report that the two detectives were rankled. And only part of that was due to the less-than-inspiring alibis of the family.

When Ryan read the rest of it, he knew FI was in trouble. He'd better move fast and advise the team to come up with a milquetoast version of what Casey and Emma had in mind when they'd approached the Hillingtons as fictitious contributors to their charity. And Banks and Ogden had heard only the tip of the iceberg. When they figured out that Emma had been dating Brighton as an information-gathering tool, their heads would explode.

He glanced at his Apple Watch. Twelve thirty. That gave him a half hour to brief the team before they all watched the news conference.

He sent a Slack message to everyone and rose.

"Yoda, the news conference is at one," he said, fully aware that Yoda needed no reminders.

"Yes, Ryan," Yoda replied. "I'll broadcast it on the long wall of the main conference room, so everyone can watch simultaneously. And I'll remain on standby."

***

*Offices of Forensic Instincts*
*Main Conference Room, Second Floor*
*Tribeca, New York*
*Wednesday, 12:30 p.m.*

The team filed in and took seats facing Ryan's monster screen on the far wall of the room. This way, they could hear Ryan's update, and then, without rearranging the chairs, be ready to turn their attention right over to the news conference.

Ryan perched at the edge of the oval table.

"I want to combine all our updates," he said. "I've got a lot to tell you. But before any of that, there's an immediate fire we've got to put out, so we must get into it now. Because I have a feeling that we only have a brief interlude—which is however long this news conference takes—before Banks and Ogden are all over us."

Marc sighed and folded his hands behind his head. "For what this time?"

"The detectives interviewed the Hillingtons this morning. They were fishing to see if any of them knew or wanted to hurt Casey. Alibis—pretty shitty ones—were provided, but, more important, photos were shown. Hannah and Madison Ellers are now out in the open."

"Yeah, I know that only too well," Emma muttered. "I've been getting nasty texts from Brighton since the detectives left their place. Most of them start with 'You bitch.'"

Patrick leaned forward in his chair, his jaw tight with concern. "I've been worried about this one since Terri got started. False identities. Interviewing witnesses. Emma's dating fiasco with Brighton. And not sharing any of this with the NYPD. The detectives are going to see this for exactly what it is: major interference with their investigation."

"At least we made good on those charity contributions," Ryan pointed out. "So we can't be accused of fraud."

"That's little comfort," Marc muttered. "The meeting at the charity event and Emma's get-togethers with Brighton are enough."

Claire looked thoughtful. "The only way we can mitigate their reaction is to tell them that we learned absolutely nothing. Our methods might deserve a slap on the wrist, but all our attempts to information-gather amounted to a total dead end."

Marc shook his head. "I agree with your approach. But, a slap on the wrist? We're well past that. Given how high on their shit list we already are, this might push them over the edge. And we all knew that was a possibility going in. I'll give our attorneys a call."

"How much did Brighton tell them?" Emma asked Ryan. "He was in terrifying mode in his texts to me. And my leading him on was the most prolonged aspect of what we did."

"He started to say something," Ryan replied. "But their attorney shut him down in a nanosecond. That doesn't mean they won't be back to demand a full explanation."

Without hesitation, Emma said, "When they break down our door, we'll all meet with them. But where it comes to the subject of Brighton, let me talk. I can placate them." She waved away Ryan's dubious look. "You've all seen me in action before. Trust me on this one."

"Okay," Ryan conceded. Emma was right. She'd more than earned their trust.

Marc glanced at his Apple Watch. "Eight minutes till showtime."

Ryan turned to Emma. "Just one more thing. Do you remember if Brighton had a triangular birthmark on his wrist?"

Emma thought long and hard. "I'm not sure. Truthfully, it wasn't his wrists I was worried about. Why?"

"Keep thinking, because whichever one of our suspects has that birthmark—that's our killer."

\*\*\*

*New York-Presbyterian Lower Manhattan Hospital*
*Casey's Hospital Room, Trauma Floor*
*New York, New York*
*Wednesday, 12:53 p.m.*

Hutch sat down in the chair beside Casey's bed and took her hand in his. As sober as he was regarding the news conference that was about to begin, he was thrilled that Casey had been moved out of the ICU and into a regular trauma floor room. It was still the Trauma Center, with specialized nurses and staff that were separate and apart from the rest of the hospital. Nonetheless, it was one step closer to recovery.

Casey gave a heavy sigh. She looked wiped out from her longer walks up and down the hall, while leaning heavily on her cane, not to mention all the activity that had accompanied the room change. In the middle of all this, she'd visited with her parents, who were frantic with worry, yet wise enough to see how exhausted Casey was. They'd kept the visit short and planned to come back later in the day.

Now, Hutch turned his head to glance over at Casey. "You okay?"

"Tired," she replied, eyeing the commercial that was still being shown on TV. "But I'm very curious to see how Lorraine and Burt handle this—how forthright they'll be, and whether or not they'll imply the possible link between my shooting and Christopher Hillington's murder."

"I wouldn't hold my breath on that last part. They don't have tangible proof, and they won't want to have to backpedal or have egg on their faces later on."

A disgusted grunt. "You're right."

Casey broke off as one o'clock arrived and the screen switched to Lorraine and Burt walking up to a podium.

She turned her entire attention to the TV. "Let's see how they decide to play this."

*** 

The entire news conference lasted fifteen minutes, since Burt and Lorraine made it clear that no questions would be taken. Lorraine did the talking, informing the viewing audience that Casey Woods, president of Forensic Instincts, had been shot in broad daylight the previous morning, had undergone major surgery, and was now in the ICU fighting for her life. Intelligently, she made no mention of which hospital Casey was in, nor did she touch on the subject of the Trauma Center. But she did convey how grave the injuries were and how close Casey had come to death. And she went on to ask the public to call a direct hotline—the phone number simultaneously flashing across the bottom of the screen—if they had any information at all about this crime.

"Smart," Casey muttered as Lorraine added that they'd interviewed on-the-scene witnesses, and that Crime Scene was tirelessly working the investigation. "The implication is that I haven't been able to tell them anything yet. Let the killer stew, worrying what I might say *if* I come to."

The news conference wrapped up, and the screen went back to its regular programming.

*** 

After getting a quick take from Hutch, Casey picked up her cell phone and called Marc.

"That was fast," he answered dryly. "We're all on speakerphone."

"What did you think?" Casey asked.

"Actually, all things considered, I thought it was a solid news conference," Marc replied. "Of course, we would have liked for them to bring up a possible link to the Hillington murder, but we all knew that wasn't going to happen."

"The killer probably wet himself," Ryan added. "Banks and Ogden were smart enough to leave your current health status out of the report, so anyone listening wouldn't know if incriminating evidence was in the cards."

Claire frowned. "Are you sure you're up for this conversation, Casey?"

Casey jumped on that one. "In other words, we have a lot more to get into besides the news conference. In which case, yes, I'm fine."

"Fifteen minutes," Hutch ordered the team. "Then I'm taking Casey's phone away."

They all murmured their assent.

Patrick cleared his throat. "You might want to leave the room for this, Hutch. I wish I could."

Instantly, Hutch rose. "Thanks for the warning. I'll be back in fifteen."

As soon as the door shut behind him, Casey said, "Let's get into it now. Hutch isn't kidding."

"Nor should he be," Claire replied.

"Patrick and I found nothing new that's damning on the Hillingtons," Marc said. "Emma?"

"Some social media posts. Nothing consequential. But Ryan got a lot. We don't even know how much. He saved it until after the news conference."

"Go, Ryan," Casey said.

First, Ryan filled everyone in on his solid suspicions of the delivery person, followed by his discovery of the triangular birthmark on the person's wrist.

"Good find," Casey praised. "Emma, did Brighton have that birthmark?"

Emma blew out her breath. "Ryan asked me the same question. The truth is, I just don't remember. If I'd known ahead of time, I obviously would have studied his wrists. But, given the circumstances, all I was focused on was getting as much info as possible before I became a sexual prize."

Nobody laughed.

"I won't let this lead drop," Ryan said. "I'll find photos of all the Hillingtons and use my app to do the rest. But frankly, if one of the women is guilty, I think we're screwed. Given all we have, I'm willing to bet money that they'd hire an assassin. And that would make things tougher. But I won't give up. You know me—I'm like a dog with a bone."

Casey made a frustrated sound. "What worries me is that all we've got left for suspects are the Hillingtons. We've exhausted Aidan's list of Hillington's enemies and gotten nowhere. Steadman is innocent—at least of this—and besides, he's in jail. What if we strike out with Charlotte and her kids? Are we back to square one?"

"The police are worrying about the same," Ryan said. "From what I can see in their files, they've exhausted all other avenues. They visited the Hillingtons' apartment again this morning. The only damning information they got out of that meeting is about us—your and Emma's little masquerade at the charity event and Emma's misleading Brighton. I'm sure they're fuming, but it doesn't change the fact that they're counting on the killer being a Hillington. Then again, so are we." Ryan paused. "Oh, and by the way, CSI has come up with nothing. The gun is gone and they're surmising the bullet and casing fell down the sewer by the benches. So we're really running on empty."

The team fell silent.

Claire was still focused on the Hillingtons and their guilt. "My instincts are still telling me that everything relates to family," she said in frustration. "But I'm not at peace. Something is wrong."

"What?" Ryan demanded. "Claire, you're going to have to do better than that."

"I would if I could," she shot back. "Don't you think it's driving me crazy, too? I've been in my yoga room all day, holding personal items and trying to force answers. They're just not coming yet."

"Well, that had better change fast. Otherwise, we're SOL," Ryan responded, clearly irked.

Now Claire was getting pissed. "Since when do you wait for me to solve cases with the metaphysical, when you've got all the science in your corner?"

Casey interceded. "Both of you, stop. We're all doing the best we can. We'll get there."

"Hopefully soon," Ryan muttered. "Sorry, Claire-voyant. I didn't mean to bite your head off."

"We're all on edge," she replied. "But I'm still convinced I'm missing just one crucial piece. It's close. It will crystalize soon."

Marc cleared his throat. "Meanwhile, our fifteen minutes are about up. Besides I'm expecting an unannounced visit from the detectives within the hour. We'd better prep. Our lawyers will be on standby unless this gets really ugly."

"I'll handle the first round by phone," Casey said without pause. "Maybe I can placate them."

"The hell you will." Hutch's voice came from the open doorway. "I don't want to know what the police want from you, but whatever it is, your team is more than capable of dealing with it. You're not having a knock-down-drag-out fight with the detectives. You look sheet white and drained. It's rest time."

"We'll do just fine, Case," Marc assured her. "We're pros, too. Get some sleep. We'll bring you up to speed later."

# 32

Emma had just finished arranging the most recent bouquet of flowers that had arrived for Casey. There'd been a steady flow of deliveries, phone calls, and emails from previous clients to friends, wishing her well and praying for a speedy recovery.

The conference room table looked like a combination of a toy store and a flower shop. Emma grinned at the variety of teddy bears and balloons that had come with some of the flowers. They were so *not* Casey. Her reaction would be priceless.

"Detectives Banks and Ogden have arrived," Yoda announced.

Emma glanced at the grandfather clock, noting that the detectives were spot on time. Surprisingly, they'd been courteous enough to schedule this meeting, rather than just barging in the door.

Emma wasn't sure if that was a positive or a negative sign. There was something about a prearranged appearance that made it all the more official. And that hinted at ugly possibilities.

She crossed her fingers. "Thanks, Yoda," she said. "We're prepped and ready. I'll show them into the first-floor interviewing room."

"Coffee is prepared," he responded.

"Great. I'll let you know if we need our attorneys."

"I'll be ready."

"Wish me luck."

"You don't need luck," Yoda replied. "You have skill. Like me, you've evolved nicely."

Emma smothered a smile. She still couldn't get used to this new, humanlike Yoda that Ryan had updated.

\*\*\*

After climbing down the stairs, Emma disarmed the Hirsch pad and opened the door to see the same sober-faced detectives she'd shown in to interview Casey at the onset of this case—which seemed like a lifetime ago.

"Good afternoon, Detectives," she greeted them, indicating that they should enter. "The team is waiting for you."

Lorraine and Burt stepped in, hung up their coats, and followed Emma into the meeting room in which they'd first interviewed Casey.

The FI team was seated around the rectangular table, mugs of coffee in their hands, nondescript expressions on their faces.

"Have a seat," Marc said, gesturing at the two empty chairs at the table.

The detectives did just that.

"Coffee?" Emma asked.

"Yes. Both black, please," Lorraine replied.

A minute later, they all faced each other. The FI team waited, since the detectives had been the ones to request this meeting.

Burt wasted no time. "Detective Banks and I acquired some unpleasant news about your conduct during this case. It's not the first time, but it is the most egregious."

Marc's brows rose. "Which is?"

Burt went on to bluntly tell them what they already knew—that Casey and Emma had used fictitious names to meet and speak with the Hillingtons, and that the NYPD sources reveal that their suspicious activities had extended beyond that.

As planned, the group let Marc be the spokesperson—for now.

"Your information is accurate," he said, knowing the detectives would be thrown off by his flat-out admission. "Charlotte Hillington was holding a charity function. We saw that as a perfect opportunity to make contact with her and her family. The fictitious names were simply to avoid any obvious recognition of those belonging to Forensic Instincts team members."

"Your faces aren't exactly a secret either," Lorraine noted.

"No, they're not, but we've had no past interaction with the Hillingtons. We took the risk that, even though they'd most likely know our names, they wouldn't know our faces. If we were wrong, our plan would obviously have failed. We took that chance."

Burt bristled. "Your plan," he repeated sarcastically. "Why were you bypassing us to make contact at all? And, since that's always what you do anyway, why weren't we given a heads-up?"

Marc didn't bat an eye. "We've made it clear to you from the beginning that we were investigating this case with Casey as our client. So I think the answer to your questions are self-explanatory. We had no intention of keeping you in the dark."

"I'll ignore that absurd statement for the time being," Lorraine said. "Instead, tell us now. What did you learn from this interaction? Because more than just a chat between you and the Hillingtons took place."

Emma knew that was her cue to step in.

"It did," she replied. "While Casey spoke to Charlotte and Ashley Hillington about their charity, I sat at the bar with Brighton and Lily Hillington. We talked. They were pretty drunk, so not much was said. But Brighton made it clear he wanted to go out with me. That's what eventually happened—which I assume is the additional suspicious behavior you're referring to."

Burt's eyes looked like they were about to pop out of his head, and Emma realized she'd just supplied them with this piece of the puzzle. Good. It made her look all the more forthcoming.

"You dated Brighton Hillington?" Burt was visibly stunned.

"Three times," Emma supplied helpfully.

"Giving you three opportunities to pump him for information—all without keeping us in the loop."

Emma's expression was the essence of honesty. "I'd planned to tell you everything I learned. Unfortunately, that amounted to zero. Brighton wasn't interested in talking. He was interested in getting into my pants."

An uncomfortable silence.

"I can tell you everything that was said," Emma added. "But it gets pretty graphic. Do you still want me to fill you in on the details?"

Lorraine's eyes narrowed. "And you learned nothing else?"

"Not really." Emma shook her head. "I learned that his family is very wealthy, which I already knew. I can supply you with the names and numbers of the two restaurants we went to, and the address of his music studio. Other than that, all I can say is that he's a pig."

Ryan was biting back a grin. *Good for you, Emma.*

"The only other thing I can fill you in on is Charlotte Hillington's charity," Emma said, wrapping up her performance. "It was named after Suzanne Allerman, a close friend of hers when they were both young models. Ms. Allerman died of a stroke caused by an overdose—not an uncommon occurrence among models who are desperate to stay thin. It's a passionate cause of Mrs. Hillington's." Emma spread her hands. "That's all I found out."

Clearly, Emma had taken the wind out of the detectives' sails. There'd be no need for lawyers today.

The whole team was having a hard time keeping straight faces.

"When you first told us you planned to investigate on your own, we agreed, stressing that you immediately tell us anything you learned," Burt said—clearly the onset of a lecture. "That was then. This is now. Now we're closing in on a killer. And you're not getting in our way. So back off and let us do our jobs. Can I make that any clearer?"

"We understand, Detective," Emma said demurely. "I'm sorry for the steps I took. I just thought I could gather information and bring it directly to you. I was wrong."

Burt looked mollified. "Will Casey's interview concur with yours?" he asked.

"Yes it will."

"Before or after you prep her on this interview?"

"There's no reason to prep her," Emma replied. "We compared notes after the charity event. I've told you everything."

Lorraine frowned and made a try. "Even so, I'd feel better if we heard all this from her. Can we give her a call?"

"Absolutely not," Patrick inserted quickly. "It's been a day and a half since she was shot. She's not up for talking."

"Yet you've visited her."

"To check on our *friend*," Claire said, angry color in her cheeks.

"We're not cruel, Ms. Hedgleigh." There was actually some compassion in Lorraine's voice. "We don't want to jeopardize Casey's recovery. But we do need to talk to her as soon as she's able, and not just about this. About anything she recalls from the shooting."

The team couldn't argue that.

"What would you like us to do?" Marc asked, sensing that Lorraine had something in mind.

"I'd like you to call SSA Hutchinson now and have him speak to Casey's doctors. Get a timetable as to when we can speak to her."

"On the phone or in person?" Ryan demanded. "A short phone call is much less taxing than a lengthy visit. We've only been permitted to stay for fifteen minutes at a time, and that was pushing it."

"Duly noted," Lorraine said. "We'll take what we can get." She gave Marc a questioning look. "Will you make that call?"

"All right," Marc replied, knowing full well that, if Casey had her way, she'd be talking to them right now. "But the ultimate decision will come from Casey's doctors."

"Understood." Lorraine nodded. "We'll wait while you get your answer."

Marc played their game. He didn't even step away. He just picked up his phone and called Hutch.

"Hi, Marc," Hutch answered. "Any update on the shooter?"

"I think not," Marc replied. "But Detectives Banks and Ogden are here. They want to know when Casey will be up for a brief phone call, or possibly a ten-minute meeting. They need to question her about the shooting, to gather any information they can to help with their investigation. Can you check with her doctors and see when they think that would be possible?"

"She's very weak." Hutch was clearly controlling his temper. He was also dealing with Casey, who was tugging at his arm and saying "Tomorrow" at the same time.

"Fine," Hutch finally acquiesced. "I'll go ask. Hold on."

It took a full five minutes before he returned.

"Sorry," he said. "I had to track down one of Casey's doctors. She understands the situation. If Casey's recovery continues on its present course, Dr. Jackson thinks she can meet with either Detective Banks or Detective Ogden tomorrow afternoon at three fifteen—for ten minutes. *Just one of them,*" he emphasized. "The doctor doesn't want Casey upset or overtaxed. And, if for any reason, she's being examined or having a PT session when they arrive, they'll have to wait."

Marc repeated Hutch's words to the detectives.

"Much appreciated," Lorraine said. "One of us will be there promptly and stay only the allotted ten minutes."

With that, she and Burt rose to leave.

"Stay out of our way," Burt ordered again. "And, if you should come upon a clue, tell us. Otherwise, you won't like the consequences."

\*\*\*

The minute Emma returned from showing the detectives out, the entire team clapped and high-fived her.

"What a performance," Claire said with a broad smile. "Casey will be bursting with pride."

"*I'm* bursting with pride," Ryan added. "And I don't get impressed easily."

Marc was already pressing Casey's number and placing his cell down, speakerphone engaged.

"Talk to me," Casey answered.

"Emma deserves an Oscar," Patrick told her. "She said precisely what you would have—and what you'll be expected to corroborate."

"Yeah, they were placated and we're not in jail," Marc added dryly.

"Great job, Emma," Casey said without even hearing the details. "Now fill me in."

\*\*\*

*Casey's Hospital Room*
*Wednesday, 8:05 p.m.*

Casey was tremendously relieved to be back in bed, with no one in the room but Hutch.

The rest of the day had been a hectic blur. She'd had two lengthier PT sessions, and had briefly let go of her cane—even if she did have to snatch it right back, while feeling like a bent-over tree. Not to mention that her leg strength and her strength in general just plain sucked. She wasn't stupid. This recoup was going to take a long time, but she was thoroughly committed to it. She *was* going to be herself again, and soon.

She'd also been allowed to check her iPad, which, no surprise, had reports on the police's news conference, and bloggers wildly speculating over who could have done this. Given they knew nothing about her ties to the Hillington murder, their guesses were absurd and all over the place, right down to disgruntled clients who'd overpaid for their services.

If it hadn't hurt so much, she would have burst out laughing.

Her parents had paid her another visit, this time arguing that they should come home with her when she was released and stay through the holidays to take care of her. It was Hutch who had convinced them that she'd be well cared for and that she'd be having at-home rehab and PT sessions. He would be with her most of the time, and when he wasn't, the finest health care professionals would be at her beck and call. As for the holidays, he'd suggested that they all celebrate together in a few months, when Casey was whole.

Thank heavens her parents adored Hutch and trusted in him. The last thing Casey needed was for one or both of her parents to overexert themselves and get ill. Plus, love them though she did, she really needed time alone to focus inward and get better. The rest of her energy would be consumed with helping the team solve this case.

Minutes ago, Hutch had asked the hospital staff to hold all visitors. He then walked over and sat down in the chair beside Casey.

Casey studied his face. He'd been exceptionally quiet and introspective the past few hours, making her wonder if the past two days had really been too much for him.

"You okay?" she asked.

A corner of Hutch's mouth lifted. "I think that's my line. This place has been a madhouse. You must be wiped."

"Actually, I'm not," she replied. "I feel as if the worst is behind me. But I am concerned about you. You're not yourself. Is something wrong? Do you need to be at work? Because I have an entire hospital staff to care for—"

"I'm fine and it's not work," he interrupted her.

"Well, something major is on your mind."

Silence.

"Please talk to me." This time it was Casey who took Hutch's hand.

"Are you up for it?"

"Definitely."

Hutch sat forward in his chair and stared straight into her eyes. "Good. Because this has been a long time coming."

He pressed on in his customary direct manner.

"Casey, you almost died a few days ago. Thank God you pulled through and will soon be whole. But a trauma like that changes people. I know it will profoundly change you, and it has already changed me. Things that were assurances of life are no longer givens, and things that could wait are suddenly urgent."

"You're right," Casey said softly. "I'm dealing with a lot of that right now, as well. Reliving those moments, reliving the past two days, feeling the vulnerability of life—I know that, even if I'm lucky enough to be one hundred percent physically, emotionally I'll never be the same."

"Then maybe you'll understand when I ask you this next question. I know it's coming out of the blue, and for that, I apologize. But I have to ask, and I want you to be totally honest with me, as I will be with you."

"Okay." Casey's gaze widened, but she kept it fixed on his. She felt the weight of what was to come, even without knowing the question.

Hutch didn't make her wait. "How do you feel about having children?"

Casey sucked in her breath. She'd been expecting something big, but not this. She should have. It was something couples talked about, made decisions about. She and Hutch had a loving, committed relationship. This was a natural point to come to.

Maybe she'd been pushing it away because she was afraid that if she spoke the truth, it would change everything—the very essence of their relationship.

Nevertheless, she owed him the honesty he sought. So she gave it to him.

"My whole life has been about becoming who I am," she said. "I've been single-minded about it, driven since I was young. And, as an adult, I haven't changed. I'm not a loner, but I do walk my own path. I never even expected to find someone like you, someone I could truly share my life with. Fortunately, I was wrong."

Casey paused, only to study Hutch's expression. It was unchanging as he waited for her response.

She took the plunge. "But, as for children, I already have one—Forensic Instincts. It's the baby I created and will always be nurturing. I want to give it everything and more. There's no halfway. Not with me. So, while I'm sure I'll spoil Marc and Maddy's baby shamelessly, that's not my path." There were tears in her eyes now as she prayed she hadn't broken his heart or fractured what they had together beyond repair.

Hutch released a breath. "You forgot to add that there's no way you could live such a dangerous life, not with a child depending on you. That applies to me, as well. My life is equally dangerous, and I could never live with myself knowing a child's very existence depended on my survival."

This time, Hutch did move, covering their intertwined fingers with his other hand. "I love you," he said with a fervor that wrapped itself around Casey's heart. "I never knew that love this deep was possible, at least not for me."

"Nor for me," Casey added in a trembling voice.

"So we're in agreement on the life-altering decision of not having kids. However, that doesn't mean I'm content with keeping things the way they are."

Casey's brows drew together in question.

"No more living together," Hutch said in reply. "I want to marry you. I'm as all-or-nothing as you are. As soon as that sick killer is behind bars, and the minute you're well enough, I want to put a ring on your finger. I want you to be my wife. Is that too old-fashioned?"

Now Casey was openly weeping. "It's not too old-fashioned. It's what I want, too. As long as I get to put a ring on your finger, too."

Hutch's smile reached his eyes. "I wouldn't have it any other way." He leaned forward to kiss her, tenderly and meaningfully. "I know I said I'm not a patient man. Well, I really will be patient about waiting until you feel well enough."

"Well, I won't be. I'm getting out of here by Sunday. The surgeon said it's possible, and I say that it's happening. I'll need a few more weeks of hardcore physical therapy, and a couple of months before I can consummate our marriage the way I want to."

"The consummation can wait." Hutch sounded like a man condemned.

"Oh no it can't. This wedding isn't happening until my surgeon gives me the okay. It will be sooner rather than later. I'm motivated."

Hutch's lips twitched. "Then we'll do everything in our power to make your surgeon happy ASAP."

That settled, Casey's mind worked at a lightning pace. "Let me call Fiona tonight," she said, referring to Fiona McKay, Ryan's younger sister, a one-time client of FI's and a brilliant goldsmith and jewelry designer who lived right there in SoHo. "She can come and meet with us tomorrow. I know, I know. We'll keep it short. But we'll bandy around ideas, and come up with a pretty solid concept of what we're looking for. The rest we'll leave to her creativity. That should give her enough time to design our ideal wedding bands, so they'll be ready when I am."

Casey paused only to draw in a much-needed breath. "Meanwhile, I'll call The Club at our apartment complex and see how far ahead we have to book the room. Is that okay? I'm sure they'll accommodate us."

By now, Hutch was laughing. "I never thought of you as a giddy bride. But, boy, am I loving every minute of it. Go ahead. Call The Club. And I'd suggest you bring Emma into the fray. She'll have the decorating, catering, flowers, and music all arranged by the time you check out of here. This is going to make her day."

"Are you kidding?" Casey laughed back. "It's going to make the whole team's day. Can we tell them right after Fiona leaves tomorrow?"

"Can we swear her to secrecy until then?" Hutch teased.

"Absolutely. Yes, she's Ryan's sister. But she's the whole team's friend, too. She'll give us our moment. Although she'll probably insist on staying to watch their faces when they hear the news."

Even though Hutch thought it was a great idea, he probably would have said yes to just about anything Casey asked at that moment. "Then it will be just that way. I want you to have everything you want."

"Too late," she said softly. "I already do."

# 33

Casey was sitting up in a chair, with Hutch perched beside her, when Fiona McKay arrived, practically vibrating with excitement.

With a warm wave at Hutch, she rushed straight to Casey, hesitated for a moment, and then decided that hugging would be a bad idea. Instead she grabbed both of Casey's hands, her own eyes filled with tears.

"Thank God you're okay," she said between sniffles. "I've been a wreck, calling Ryan every few hours to check up on you. I prayed so hard. And now..." She assessed Casey through her dark blue eyes and smiled. "You look radiant."

Casey shot her a rueful look. "Passable, maybe. Radiant? That's only because of this amazing man beside me. I'm very, very grateful to be alive. I'm sorry I worried you all so much."

"You're forgiven—especially after you shared your news with me last night. I'm so thrilled—congratulations!"

"Thank you," Casey and Hutch said in unison. They were both still oozing joy and excitement.

Fiona was already opening up her sketch pad. She pulled up another chair and sat down beside them. "I've been told to make this visit short, so let's not waste time."

A grin tugged at Casey's lips. In so many ways, Fiona was just like Ryan. Independent. Straight to the point. Utterly committed to her work. Even physically, the resemblance was striking. Both tall, with thick black hair—Fiona's long and wavy as opposed to Ryan's short cut—midnight blue eyes, and compelling features, Fiona was a female replica of her brother. Slim and fine-boned as he was solid and muscular, she was a beautiful woman, and he was a drop-dead gorgeous guy. They were both in heavy demand. Hearts had broken everywhere when Ryan committed himself to Claire. He didn't give a damn.

Neither Ryan nor Fiona focused on their looks. Family, friends, and work were what mattered. The rest was an accident of nature.

Now, Fiona's brow was furrowed as she glanced from her blank sketch pad to her friends.

"First, let's hear your thoughts," she said. "That way I can make some preliminary sketches right away."

"Don't rush your process," Hutch told her. He was just as eager as Casey to see what Fiona came up with. But he was more eager to give Casey something to look forward to—something that would take her mind off the investigation.

That idea fell flat. Hutch didn't know who looked more crestfallen, Fiona or Casey.

Fiona studied Casey's expression, then perked right up. "Sorry, Hutch, but that's not happening. My juices are already flowing. When I'm tossed out of here, I'll stay in the waiting room and play with some sketches. I'll have something to show you just before your team arrives." Her face lit up. "I can't wait to see their reactions to your news."

"Nor can I," Casey admitted. "I can't believe how exuberant I am about all this. It's so unlike me."

Fiona's smile reached her eyes. "You're getting married. With you and Hutch, this will be a one-time, forever event. Savor every minute of it. Now tell me what you had in mind."

Casey and Hutch had discussed this, so Casey was ready with an answer.

"Nothing flashy or outlandish. No huge gemstones. Simple, symbolic, but unique. Very 'us.'"

"And nothing flowery for me," Hutch added. "And zero gemstones. Something solid that complements Casey's."

Fiona nodded, her mind racing. "I've already got some ideas, based on who you are and what you want." She stood up. "What time is the team coming?"

"At noon," Casey replied.

"That gives me an hour and a half." She squeezed both their hands this time. "Talk about a labor of love. Let's see what I can do."

***

*Casey's Hospital Room*
*Thursday, 11:55 a.m.*

Fiona showed up five minutes early so she could show Casey and Hutch the ideas she'd sketched.

Casey was a little tired from her longer walk around the Trauma Center's wider loop, but she'd eaten a light lunch and was still sitting in the chair, eager and waiting to see Fiona's sketches and then to break the news to the team.

"I had a brain explosion," Fiona announced as she flew through the door. "I love these. I hope you do, too."

Once again, she sat down beside Casey and Hutch, this time flourishing the sketches she'd drawn.

"Filigree," Casey murmured. "I love that."

"Me, too." Switching into professional mode, Fiona used her pencil to point and explained, "The rings will be hand-rolled solid twenty-two karat gold. Without boring you with details, I make this practically pure gold alloy in my studio using heat and a rolling mill in order to create that open scroll design. Each ring will have an S scroll between two thicker wires with tiny granules as accents. Casey, your ring will have twenty very tiny sparkly diamonds inside the curve of each scroll. Hutch, your ring will have no diamonds, but it will be a thicker, heavier version of Casey's. The way I'll handcraft the rings, the design will be ancient and modern at the same time."

Fiona glanced from one of them to the other, looking like a hopeful puppy. "What do you think?"

"I think they're going to be exquisite," Casey breathed, tracing the pencil lines of the ring with her forefinger. "Hutch?"

"They're magnificent," Hutch replied, peering at the sketch with a thoroughly impressed expression. "I'm beginning to think you're more of a genius than Ryan is."

"In her dreams," Ryan rebutted as he walked in with the rest of the team. "What's this about? Why is Fee a genius, and why is she here?"

"Hello to you, too," Fiona said to her brother. "I was just born that way. And I'm here to see Casey—and Hutch." She quickly tucked her sketch pad away.

"Why Hutch?" Ryan was still openly peeved.

"Oh, Ryan, cut it out," Claire said, her gaze on Casey. "Look at you." She walked over and squeezed Casey's hands. "In your own room and sitting up in a chair." There was something more in her eyes, and Casey realized that she knew.

"She still looks wiped," Ryan said, glaring at his sister. "How long have you been here talking her ear off?"

"Fiona isn't talking my ear off," Casey said. "She's making Hutch and me very happy. That's why I wanted you all here at once."

"You're sure you're up to whatever this is, Case?" Marc asked. "Ryan's not wrong. You look pretty depleted. And one of the detectives is going to be here in three hours to question you. You need to be at full strength."

"I have to agree with Marc," Patrick said. "Are you sure you're not overdoing it? Maybe this should wait."

"I'm sure. And, no, it's not waiting."

"Well, I'm dying of curiosity," Emma said. "Why did you ask all of us to come together? Do you have a better idea of when you're going to be discharged?"

"If I work hard and if my doctor continues to be amenable, I'll be out of here on Sunday, probably late afternoon," Casey replied. "And I can't wait." She waved away whatever Emma was going to say next. "We'll talk about my discharge date tomorrow. Right now, Hutch and I have something amazing to share with you."

Claire's eyes were positively glowing. "Go on."

Hutch linked his fingers with Casey's as she made her announcement. "We're getting married," she said, her entire face lit up. "As soon as I'm healed enough, we'll become Mr. and Mrs. Kyle and Casey Hutchinson."

The explosion of excitement in the room made a nurse poke her head in and admonish them. "There are too many of you in here," she said. "And making way too much noise. Please keep it short and quiet." She looked at Casey and Hutch and smiled. "Congratulations to you both."

"Thank you," Casey replied. "And I'll keep these well-wishers under control."

"Oh, Casey." Emma and Claire hurried around and gave Casey the gentlest of hugs, making sure they made contact only with her neck. They moved on to Hutch, giving him full-blown hugs.

"You and Hutch—married," Claire breathed. "Nothing could be more perfect."

Emma gave an emphatic nod, her mind already on a roll. "What can I do to help?"

"We already have a list for you," Hutch replied with a grin. "We'll keep you busy planning this momentous day."

Emma's eyes widened with joy. "Thank you! When is it? Do you have a date picked out? A venue? What colors do you want? What kind of flowers? Music? Food? Cake?"

Ryan rolled his eyes good-naturedly as he kissed Casey's cheek and clapped a firm hand on Hutch's shoulder. "Slow down, Emma. The man just proposed."

Emma ignored him, turning to Fiona. "Are you designing the rings? Is that why you came before us? Did you already make sketches?"

Fiona had always loved Emma's exuberance. "Sure did. But don't ask to see them. They're a wedding day surprise for all of you."

Ryan looked sheepish. "Sorry to jump down your throat, Fee. You're a world-class goldsmith and jewelry designer, even if I'm still more of a genius."

The rest of the team laughed, both Marc and Patrick pumping Hutch's hand and gently kissing Casey's cheek.

Marc was lit up like a Christmas tree. "Remember that I introduced you two. What a brilliant move on my part!"

Casey gave him a soft smile. "We'll be forever grateful."

Emma waved everyone away. "Are either of you going to answer my questions?"

"Sorry, Emma," Hutch said. "Actually, we're going to leave most of the planning to you. You have a few months, since we're waiting for Casey to be back to herself again. So figure sometime in March." He gazed quizzically at Casey, looking for corroboration.

She wiggled her hand. "Maybe the end of February if I heal fast. We'll have it at The Club in our apartment complex. The rest Hutch and I will talk over, and Emma, I'd be so grateful if you could make all the arrangements."

"I'm on it—with pleasure." Emma looked like the Cheshire cat. "And Claire, Fiona, and I will all go dress shopping with you. You need the perfect gown. We'll find it. When will you be up to trying things on?"

Casey sighed. "Another question for my surgeon. But with both your help, maybe soon into the new year." She shifted in the chair and yawned.

"That's it," Hutch said, coming to his feet. "Announcement over. My bride-to-be needs to sleep before she deals with law enforcement."

Even Casey didn't argue. She was pretty spent.

The whole team and Fiona reiterated their congratulations and were out of the room in the amount of time it took Hutch to help Casey back into bed.

"Sleep," Hutch ordered.

Casey was already leaning back on the pillows, her eyes half-closed.

"You'd better not be one of those bossy husbands," she murmured, a smile in her voice.

"I wouldn't dare," Hutch replied. "I know who I'm up against."

# 34

Casey was bodily tired, but her mind was alert and racing. Lorraine Banks had left forty-five minutes ago. The team would be waiting for an update, and Casey was eager to supply it.

She'd walked two laps around the hospital floor, gone through some leg-strengthening exercises, and was back in bed with a snack and a large cup of orange juice. A few minutes ago, Hutch had literally passed out in the chair. The poor man needed to sleep.

Casey picked up her cell phone and called Marc.

"Hey," he answered. "How did it go?"

"Exactly as you'd expect. I was a good girl, echoed Emma's story, and apologized for leapfrogging Lorraine and Burt's investigation. I'm sure Lorraine didn't believe a word of the apology. She did buy my conversation with Charlotte, which I expanded on, since nothing came of it."

"So it was Lorraine who came."

"Did you doubt it?" Casey asked. "She has a shred of empathy and it's evident when she speaks. Burt is like an angry bear. Right now, he's totally focused on the facts of the case, on the fact that he's ripping pissed at us, and on the fact that he'd love to subpoena our files and get enough on us to lock us up. If he'd been the one to come, it would have been an interrogation and I'd have shut the door in his face."

"I see your point," Marc said.

"I did imply my distrust for Brighton Hillington. I told Lorraine how drunk and rude he was at the charity event, and how appalled I was at the way he'd come on to Emma. Since I know that Lorraine and Burt are focusing on the Hillingtons, this might send them in a helpful direction. Of course, I kept it at that. Nothing on Ryan's suspicions of the delivery person, or on the birthmark."

Marc grunted his approval. "What about the discussion on your shooting? Did anything come of that?"

Casey sighed. "In this case, I wish I had more to tell them so they could find the bastard. Lorraine bluntly admitted they're linking the attempt on my life to the Hillington murder. Finally. But all I recall of the shooting is the sting of the bullet. I racked my brain, but I've got nothing else. I asked Hutch to come in and add whatever he could, but he never saw the shooter or even sensed his presence. After that, his total focus was on me. So we both pretty much drew blanks. And CSI hasn't found the weapon, the bullet, or the casing, so they're coming up empty, too."

Casey paused. "Marc, I can't just lie here anymore. You're all hard at work and I'm on the periphery. I've got to participate. I know I'm usually the in-person team member, and that I can't do any of that for the time being. But please, you and the team come up with something I can do."

Marc understood only too well. He knew Casey. And he knew this inactivity was killing her.

"Let me talk to the team. Everything we've been doing is in the cloud, so you can catch up by reviewing it. In the meantime, let us think. Either you or we will come up with some meaningful thing you can do."

"Immediately," Casey stressed.

"Immediately," Marc reiterated. "Call us later this evening when you can. We'll have a full team meeting and get you involved. Fair enough?"

"Fair enough—unless I come up with something first."

***

*Casey's Hospital Room*
*Thursday, 7:15 p.m.*

By the time the team meeting took place, Casey had already gone through everything in the cloud three times and made a list of things she had questions about.

"Hey, Case," Marc answered, instructing Yoda to put the call on speaker.

It was done immediately.

"How're you feeling?" Marc asked. "Is Hutch still out for the count?"

"I'm healing, and no, Hutch is up and elsewhere in the Trauma Center catching up on his work. As soon as he heard the topic of our conversation, he made himself scarce."

"A wise choice," Patrick said. "He shouldn't hear anything we're about to say."

"Or about any plans we make," Ryan added.

"Let me start, because I have some amusing news," Emma said. "Out of the blue, I got an uberpolite, apologetic email from Brighton. Addressed to Emma, not Madison. He said he's grateful that FI is working hard to find his father's killer, and that he fully understands why I had to be 'Madison' in order to accomplish that. He assured me that he's immensely sorry for anything he did that was out of line, and that he's available to me and the team if there's anything he can do to help. I almost puked."

Casey whistled. "You've got to admit, the Hillington lawyer is smart. When Brighton first learned the truth about us, he lashed out. His lawyer got word of that and shut it down. Suddenly, Brighton is making nice rather than blasting us. It makes him look like a sensitive, great guy."

"And, he hopes, like less of a suspect," Ryan muttered.

Emma made a disgusted sound. "Does he really think we're that stupid? Or that I didn't keep those texts?"

"No," Casey said, ever the behaviorist. "He really thinks he's that smart. He's convinced he mollified you and, as a result, that you mollified us. Quite the ego on display."

"I'm working hard on figuring out the owner of the birthmark," Ryan said. "I'm actually hoping it belongs to Prince Brighton."

"Don't let your dislike for Brighton sway you," Casey warned him. "We want to catch the real killer. If it happens to be Brighton, it'll appease our anger at him for his despicable treatment of Emma. But let's keep our eyes on the prize—with open minds."

"Yes, boss," Ryan replied.

"Let's get back to what I can do to help in this investigation," Casey said. "Before you all shut me down, I realize my hands are pretty much tied until I get out of here on Sunday and the world finds out I'm alive and doing well."

"At which point, you're vulnerable," Patrick reminded her. "Unless the killer is caught before then. If not, he'll be out there, either hiding out or planning ways to finish what he started."

Casey sighed. "Yes, I know. I hear it ten times a day from Hutch. Still, between now and then, I can do behind-the-scenes stuff. For example, Ryan has to focus on the Hillingtons. But what if they're not guilty? It's time for me to pull up Aidan's hate-list for Christopher. We only concentrated on it until we zeroed in on Steadman. It's time to consult it again. I assume Aidan and Terri know I'm alive?"

"Of course," Marc replied. "I notified them right away."

"Good. Then I have contacts I can turn to if need be."

"Don't go down this path, Casey," Claire said, shaking her head. "Whoever killed Hillington and shot you are not obscure enemies

Christopher Hillington made in business. They're close to home. Family."

Casey paused for a second. "You're sure?"

"Yes."

"Then let's move on, this time using a looser translation of the word *family*." Casey glanced at what else she'd jotted down. "Natalie and Morgan—has anyone spoken to them since the shooting? I don't see any notes about it in the files."

"That's my bad," Claire said. "I did call them after the news conference. I felt compelled to, although I'm not sure why. I told them only that you were in the ICU fighting for your life. They both sent wishes for a speedy recovery. Natalie was particularly freaked out. She was afraid that she and Morgan were next on the killer's list."

"I really don't blame them," Casey replied. "Patrick, can you assign security to keep an eye on them? Just in case."

"Consider it done," he replied.

"Claire, then you can call them and put their minds at ease."

"Yes." Claire heaved a sigh of relief. "That's why they were on my radar. They might need protection."

"Well, now they'll get it—needed or not." It was Casey's turn to sigh. "This investigation is driving us all a little crazy. We not only need to find the killer, we need to establish motive. Once we figure out the 'why,' we can figure out the 'who.' Claire, getting back to your instinct to call Natalie and Morgan, I think their safety was just one part of what was bothering you."

"What else?" Claire asked, feeling a tingle of affirmation.

"My guess is that they still factor into this equation. So, using that as a starting point, who besides Charlotte Hillington and her kids would be screwed if news about Christopher having another family got out? Hillington wanted me to protect Natalie and Morgan, and to ultimately proclaim them as his. Someone else didn't want that to happen. That could well be our motive."

"Who besides the Hillingtons would kill to keep the status quo?" Emma asked.

"We're not sure of that—yet." Casey was typing into her iPad as she spoke. "But Ryan is all over that angle. I've got to get at it from another one. Anything that comes to mind, feed it directly to me. I'm broadening our search."

"Done." Marc was clearly pleased by these results.

Casey scowled at the phone. "Don't sound so relieved. Once I get home, I'll be right back in the field."

"With John Nickels glued to your side," Patrick stipulated. "I've already arranged things with him. He and I are going to bring in another one of our security pros. You'll be watched twenty-four seven. No one is getting to you. That you can take to the bank."

Despite her customary independence, Casey felt a surge of gratitude. Getting shot had changed her. She recognized how precious life was.

"Thank you, Patrick," she said. "And Hutch has appointed himself to be my official guard dog. Between him and your guys, I feel very safe."

"Then don't be reckless. Follow the rules."

"I will," she said softly. "Count on it."

# 35

*Ryan's Loft Apartment*
*Fifth Avenue*
*Park Slope, New York*
*Friday, 1:35 a.m.*

Ryan and Claire lay, intertwined on the bed, their breathing slowly returning to normal.

"Better?" Ryan murmured, running his fingers through Claire's damp hair.

"Much," she replied, draping her arm across Ryan's naked chest. "You?"

"Less stressed. More wiped." He kissed her bare shoulder. "You wrecked me. You always do."

"You do the same to me," Claire returned. "I can hardly move." She gave a wide yawn.

Ryan grinned. "That was the point. Your mind is flying like the wind. I know something major is bugging you, but you need to unwind and rest."

"Family," Claire muttered.

"Shhh," Ryan said. "I know. Now, sleep."

"Yes, sir." She was already half-asleep.

\*\*\*

*Ryan's Loft Apartment*
*Friday, 2:50 a.m.*

Claire jolted up in the bed, sweat trickling down her back. Her breath was coming fast, and she pulled up her knees and wrapped her arms around them to still her shaking.

Ryan was already sitting up, rubbing slow, soothing circles on Claire's back. He waited a few minutes for her to come back to him.

"Can you talk yet?" he then asked.

Claire didn't answer right away. She was still trembling, her gaze focused on something intangible and faraway.

Finally, she nodded. "I can talk," she replied in a weak voice. "And I have to. Right away. Before it evaporates and I lose it."

Ryan pressed a soft kiss to her neck. "Go on."

"Two visions," she said. "One wrapped around the other. An overwhelming sense of evil crushing my chest. The ultimate danger closing in on Casey. The killer is desperate. Beyond reason and into recklessness." Claire squeezed her eyes shut. "All these emotions compressed into a small building. Old. Cracked brick exterior. Tiny parking lot. A sign outside." A pause, as Claire grasped at the last filaments of her vision. "Zenith Pharmacy. The image is fading. I can't see any more."

She opened her eyes, her gaze now clear and in the present. Two tears trickled down her cheeks. "I'm sorry, Ryan. It's gone."

Ryan was ready to race to his computer, but first he had to make sure Claire was okay.

"Don't be sorry," he said, giving her a gentle hug. "You just gave me enough information to run with. You're amazing."

Claire sensed his urgency and wriggled away. "Go. See what you can find. We have to move fast to save Casey. And I'm still..." She shivered. "I need to lie down and come back to myself."

Ryan hesitated. "What can I do?"

"You can go do what you do best." She gave him a half smile. "Maybe what you do second best. It's a tie."

Ryan grinned. "Hold that thought. As soon as I find something, I'll be back to tip the scales."

***

*Ryan's Loft Apartment*
*Friday, 4:05 a.m.*

Claire was curled up, sleeping, when Ryan slid back into bed, his open laptop in his hands.

Instantly, Claire sensed his presence, rolled over, and sat up. "You found something. Tell me."

Ryan was wired. "A lot, thanks to you. If you hadn't envisioned that sign, I would have assumed the building was someone's home."

"But it's not," she said. "It's a drug store."

"Yup. And fortunately, there are only a few Zenith Pharmacy locations nationwide, each privately owned. Take a guess where the closest one to us is."

"I give up. Just tell me."

"South Bayside, Queens."

Claire's eyes widened, and she gasped. "That's where the hit-and-run took place. It's also near where Natalie and Morgan live."

"And precisely where Isabel Vicario lives."

"Yes." It was as if some cobwebs in Claire's mind cleared. "Casey was right about widening the search. And that's what's been bothering me. When I said the darkness is all about family, we all assumed we were talking about the Hillingtons. Maybe that's true. Maybe it's not. Christopher Hillington had another family—Natalie and Morgan. And the Vicarios are a family, as well. Frank Vicario lost his life in that car crash."

"Both additional families have reason for motives of anger and revenge," Ryan said. "Although you and Casey met with Natalie and

Morgan, and were with them at the police precinct. I'm pretty sure one of you—especially you—would have picked up on some negative vibes during those prolonged meetings."

Claire nodded. "I agree. Plus, I've been holding the photo album and the sweater that Natalie gave me. I sense nothing but love, pain, and loss. We should dig deeper, just in case I'm wrong, but I'm not feeling it. Plus, why would either of the Evans women shoot Casey? She's no threat to them—unless one of them killed Hillington." Claire's tone was dubious. "This feels to me like a square peg in a round hole."

"Unless the Evanses are potential victims." Ryan watched Claire carefully. "You said they were terrified. Revealing their identities could blow things up for the killer—especially if that killer is one of the Hillingtons. Being part of a major scandal, plus losing their stature and maybe even part of Christopher's estate, wouldn't that light a fire under one of his legitimate family members' asses?"

"You think they know about Natalie and Morgan?" Claire asked.

"More importantly, do you?"

Claire sighed. "I don't know. But your point is well-taken."

Ryan blew out a breath. "The central part of your vision was Zenith Pharmacy. When we get back to work, I'm going to hack into their database. Maybe that will give us a name."

"Good," Claire agreed. She rubbed her temples. "I'm worried about the Evanses. If you're right, they could be in danger. Maybe that's why I felt compelled to contact them after Casey was shot. I'm glad Patrick assigned someone to them. And we haven't even touched on the Vicarios. You said the detectives did their due diligence and decided they were a dead end. Why? And should we ignore their decision and initiate our own investigation?"

Ryan sighed. "You're more revved than you were before."

"So are you," she countered. "You can't wait to get to the office, alert Yoda, and get started."

"You're right. So let's grab a couple of hours' sleep. After that, our work resumes."

***

*Offices of Forensic Instincts*
*Main Conference Room, Second Floor*
*Tribeca, New York*
*Friday, 6:55 a.m.*

The team was gathered around the table five minutes early. All of them were eager to hear the basis for Ryan's urgent Slack.

"Should we get Casey on speakerphone, or is it too early?" Emma asked.

"It's way too early," Marc replied. "However, if we don't at least try, she'll be livid."

"I say go for it," Ryan said. "This is crucial stuff. Casey needs to know about it, and not secondhand. Especially since she's the one who came up with the idea of expanding our search."

"Agreed," Patrick said.

"Hey, Yoda," Ryan said. "Call Casey's cell and put the call on speaker."

"Certainly, Ryan," Yoda responded at once.

Casey answered on the first ring, clearly wide awake and at the ready. "Hi, what's up?"

"I sent an urgent Slack out to the team before dawn," Ryan told her. "This meeting has to happen *now*. I was afraid I'd wake you up if I included you in the Slack."

"I expect to be included in everything." Casey sounded royally pissed.

"Well, you are," Marc said. "We just gathered around the conference room table. Ryan's about to tell us what's going on. You haven't missed a word."

"Good. Go on, Ryan."

"I'll let Claire start," he replied. "She lit the match on this one."

Claire nodded and told the group everything about her vision. Ryan followed up with what he'd dug up on the Zenith Pharmacy and its location.

"Great new jumping point," Casey said, choosing to ignore the part of Claire's vision that dealt with the imminent danger surrounding her.

"Wow, talk about a shocker," Emma said. "This Zenith Pharmacy makes us ask a whole new set of questions."

Patrick was processing this. "I really don't see the Evanses as killers. Their motives are weak, their actions are those of love and loss, and Claire picked up nothing negative from them when they met."

"Neither do Ryan nor I," Claire replied. "If anything, I see them more as victims. As Casey pointed out, they're probably terrified that they're on the killer's hit list. I could hear it in Natalie's voice when I spoke to her. As for Casey, they view her as their savior. She's helped them every step of the way."

"You did feel compelled to call them," Casey reminded Claire. "We explored that angle. But did you truly sense they're in danger?"

Claire shrugged. "I'm not sure."

"I don't want to throw a monkey wrench into all this," Marc said. "But we keep talking about the Evanses as a unit. They're not. Natalie's feelings for Hillington and her desire to find his killer are solid. But are Morgan's? She allegedly never knew about her father. Could she have found out the truth before Natalie told her? Could her anger for the man who'd fathered her and walked away and had hurt her mother so deeply be powerful enough to propel her to kill?"

Ryan whistled. "Good point. I never thought of it from that angle."

"Me either," Casey said. "But I'm not sure I buy the theory. For one, Morgan isn't an irrational person who'd hire an assassin to kill someone, no matter how livid she was. And two, Morgan is supertight with her mother. If she knew everything you just said, Marc, then she'd also know how deeply Natalie loved Christopher Hillington. She wouldn't hurt her like that. If anything, she'd confront her and have it out."

"I agree," Claire said in a quiet tone that told them she was inside her own head. "Casey and I spent a fair amount of time with Natalie and Morgan. Morgan is a straightforward, grounded person. She was blunt about her thoughts and her feelings. And her aura—she didn't know about her biological father before Natalie told her. I think we're hitting the wall on this premise."

"I have to agree," Casey said. "Which leads us somewhere we haven't yet gone—to the Vicarios. Ryan, what made you decide not to do a deep dive into them?"

"I did do a preliminary search on them," Ryan replied. "Then I got to the police report. The detectives had checked out the whole family's alibis and found nothing. I did the same. It seemed like a dead end." He paused. "Maybe it wasn't. Maybe I didn't delve deep enough into their alibis. The cops have been wrong before, and the Zenith Pharmacy is right in their town. Shit, I'm pissed at myself."

"Don't be pissed. Be proactive," Casey said. "Was there anything about that pharmacy mentioned in the police report?"

"No. That was all Claire."

"Then get into their database. Find out who their customers are and even the medications they're buying. Is that possible?"

"Not only possible, but on my agenda the moment we hang up." Ryan still sounded angry at his own omission. He rarely made mistakes, but when he did, he beat the hell out of himself.

"Ryan, stop," Casey commanded. "Channel your anger into your work. You'll recover whatever ground you lost in hours." She paused thoughtfully. "I'm going to give Angela a call. Maybe she'll know something about the Vicarios that would help us. She'll have no problem talking about this subject. It doesn't involve Christopher Hillington, so no attorney-client privilege is being compromised."

"At least wait until a decent hour," Marc teased.

"Angela works twenty-four seven. I'll call her after I eat the breakfast that was just delivered to my room, and after I've done my second walk of the morning."

"What time do they get you up?" Emma asked in surprise.

Casey sighed. "Walk number one is just after five. I'm usually awake anyway, and happy to get out of this bed. I'm losing my mind. Sunday can't come fast enough for me."

No one answered. Much as they were thrilled that Casey was hopefully being released in two days, they were worried about the killer's accessibility to her. No matter how much security detail Patrick assigned to her, she'd still be vulnerable.

"Yes, the doctor is optimistic that Sunday will be the day, and yes, I'll be fine," she answered their silence. "I'll follow every one of Patrick's instructions and take zero risks." She paused. "I'm not the same woman I was before. Life is precious. Speaking of which, Marc, how is Maddy feeling?"

Marc's expression softened. "She's a trouper. No matter how frustrated she is about the inactivity, she knows it's necessary. And, thank heavens, she and the baby are both great. Thanks for asking."

"That's wonderful news," Casey replied. "Soon enough, I'll be able to visit her."

"Casey…"

"I'm off to savor my breakfast." Casey clearly did not want to be warned about the danger at her door again. "After I talk to Angela, and after Ryan's done a chunk of research, we'll reconnect. Bye."

# 36

*Casey's Hospital Room*
*Friday, 8:10 a.m.*

Casey settled herself in the armchair that had become her solace after endless hours in bed. Hutch was getting himself a cup of coffee and a muffin in the cafeteria, giving her privacy to talk to Angela. After that, he'd sit with her for an hour or so before heading off to work.

She knew he hated leaving her, but she also knew that he'd been out of the office for days. The Bureau needed him.

Picking up her cell phone, Casey pressed Angela's number.

Angela answered on the first ring. "Casey?"

"It's me," Casey confirmed.

"Thank goodness," the usually ball-breaking attorney replied. "How are you?"

Quickly, Casey filled Angela in on where she was, the state of her health, and her hopeful Sunday release day.

Angela blew out a breath. "You've really gone through hell. And, no surprise, you're fighting your way back."

"Damn right I am. By the way, you're one of the few people privy to this information. I'm laying low. Let the shooter think I'm at death's door."

"That's just what I would have advised," Angela replied. "Consider it done. Your health status stays with me."

"Thanks. I'm calling to tap your brain about something, or rather, someones."

"Back to working." There was a smile in Angela's voice. "Whatever you need. As long as it doesn't touch on—"

"It doesn't," Casey reassured her. "I don't even need to mention Hillington's name."

"Then go for it."

Casey got right to the point. "What do you know about the Vicarios?"

Somehow, Angela didn't sound surprised. "Not much."

"Come on, Angela. There was every chance that Frank Vicario's family would file a law suit against your client, if Christopher were found to be guilty of the hit-and-run. You're way too smart not to do your due diligence. You and your in-house investigators would find out anything and everything about the family as you could—just in case."

"You're right," Angela stated flatly. "We did. But, as I recall, we didn't turn up much. Just the same superficial facts you probably already know. And I only laid eyes on the Vicarios once. They were leaving the police precinct when Christopher and I were arriving. Isabel Vicario looked broken and beaten. From what I gathered, she was totally devastated by the loss of her husband."

"Nothing deeper or more personal?" Casey asked.

"Nothing that comes readily to mind." Angela sounded cautiously interested. "Why all the questions? Do you suspect any or all of them of being guilty of Christopher's murder and the attempt on your life?"

Casey answered honestly. "We're not sure. But, as you know, we're leaving no stone unturned. So, while we're dissecting the Hillington crew, plus any other suspects we have, we're doing the same thing with the Vicarios."

"That's logical," Angela agreed. "I'll go back and reread everything I have on them, then pass it on to you. Am I allowed to call your cell?"

"Not allowed, invited," Casey said. "I'm losing my mind from all this inactivity. I'm always on the go. This whole invalid thing doesn't jive with my personality."

Angela burst out laughing. "You're a force to be reckoned with, Casey Woods. I respect you. And I don't say that often. Frankly, I think I'm smarter, shrewder, and more intuitive than pretty much everyone I face. You're the exception. Get better fast. The world needs you."

\*\*\*

*Offices of Forensic Instincts*
*Ryan's Lair*
*Tribeca, New York*
*Friday, 10:10 a.m.*

Ryan sat back in his chair, having finished scanning the Zenith Pharmacy database, and then focusing on what he needed to know.

Isabel Vicario was a long-term customer at the pharmacy and had a house account. Her pharmaceutical purchases ranged from NSAIDs, to energy-boosting drinks, to high-dose sedatives that had first been prescribed right after the date that her husband was killed. Most recently, two new entries had been added on a regular basis—fentanyl transdermal patches and a drug Ryan couldn't even pronounce, much less recognize. One that cost thousands each month.

He passed that information on to Yoda and asked him to follow up on the medication details.

Ryan, in the interim, checked into the frequency and the specifics of the pickup. While Isabel was the one with a house account at the pharmacy, it seemed that most of her meds, at least those obtained after her husband's death, had been signed for by one of her children. Particularly Franklin. Not a shocker, since he lived closer to his mother than Mia did. Still, it was interesting that, before that point, Isabel was more likely to pick up her own medications.

She was doubtless reeling from her husband's death. Later, Ryan would check more thoroughly into her behavior, but he'd be willing to bet that she'd become a virtual recluse.

"Ryan, I have the answers you've requested," Yoda announced. "The drug you're inquiring about is a new and powerful oral chemo-therapy medication. It treats a variety of different cancers—pancreatic, intestinal, and lung, to name a few. The medication is accessible, but very expensive. Insurance companies, particularly Medicare, have been reluctant to cover it."

Ryan was quiet. *Cancer. Shit.*

"Do you need something more, or should I stay on standby?" Yoda asked.

Ryan swallowed, knowing that his next step would have to be checking out Frank Vicario's life insurance amount. But first, he needed to talk to Claire. "Stay on standby, Yoda."

\*\*\*

*Claire's Yoga Room*
*Friday, 10:35 a.m.*

Ryan stopped outside Claire's door, which was slightly ajar, and knocked. "It's me."

"Come in." Claire was sitting cross-legged on her yoga mat, frowning as she contemplated some thought that was bothering her.

"Bad time?" Ryan asked, stepping inside.

She shook her head. "I'm at an impasse anyway." She paused, studied Ryan's face, and said, "I'll tell you about it afterward. You're upset. What is it?"

Ryan shut the door behind him, walked over, and lowered himself to the opposite side of the mat, stretching out on his side and propping up his elbow so he could rest the side of his head on his fist.

"I got into Zenith Pharmacy's database," he told Claire. "Isabel Vicario is a regular customer there. Since her husband's death, she's stopped picking up her own medications. Her son, Franklin, does it. I thought it was because she was so deeply affected by the loss of her husband that she wasn't leaving her house."

"But it's more." Tears were starting to gather in Claire's eyes.

Ryan nodded. "She has cancer. She's taking an oral chemotherapy drug, along with fentanyl patches." A pause. "I guess it got to me, all that poor woman has had to endure. And I feel like a bastard pressing on. I just needed to talk to you and have you settle me so I can go on with this pitiful angle of the investigation." He paused again, this time to shake his head. "Do you believe this is me—this emotional man?"

Claire dashed the tears off her cheeks. "Yes, I believe this is you. It's always been you. You just never tapped into it before."

"Before you," Ryan amended.

Claire nodded. "Before me." She reached over to take Ryan's hand. "This is a heartbreaking development," she said with her customary quiet compassion. "The poor woman's entire life is shattering around her."

"And I can't drop my investigation into her the way I want to," Ryan said, clearly filled with guilt. "I have to look into Frank Vicario's life insurance policy. This drug is new and expensive. Medicare is balking at covering it, but Isabel is getting the money to pay for it somewhere. And then there are her kids. I haven't even started a deep probe into them, their lives, and their financial statuses. Are they helping pay for the meds? This part of my job sucks."

Claire intertwined their fingers. "I know. You're a fine and wonderful man, but you have to pursue these leads so we can find out who's after Casey. The Vicarios might be a total dead end. Then again, they might not be. So think of this as ensuring Casey's well-being, not as solving Hillington's murder."

"The two are linked anyway," Ryan agreed. "That's a good way of thinking about it. Thank you." He kissed her fingertips. "Now tell me what's got you so perplexed."

"I'm still at that same damned impasse. I just can't break through that barrier. The Hillingtons, the Evanses, and the Vicarios—there's a thread I'm missing." She paused and shook her head in frustration. "I need something tangible of the Vicarios' to hold, to connect with. How do I get that?"

Ryan blew out a breath. "That's a tough one. Maybe we should talk it out with Casey? She's the best at coming up with creative ideas."

"Plus, she probably talked to Angela by now. Maybe she can pass along something Angela said that would help us both."

Ryan clearly agreed because he called out, "Yoda, Claire and I are in her yoga studio. It's just us, so an all-team meeting won't be necessary. Could you get Casey on her cell and hook her into here?"

"Of course, Ryan," Yoda replied.

***

*Casey's Hospital Room*
*Friday, 10:50 a.m.*

It took a bunch of rings before Casey answered the phone. And when she did, she sounded breathless.

"Hi, guys," she managed.

"Are you okay?" Claire asked at once.

"Fine. Just finished my longest walk yet." She paused to take a few swallows of water. "What's up?"

"Maybe we should call back…" Claire began.

"No way." Casey was adamant in her reply. "If you're calling, there's a reason. Is everyone on the line?"

"No," Ryan answered. "It's just Claire and me. We're stuck and we're hoping you can help."

"Go for it."

Ryan went on to tell Casey everything he'd dug up on Isabel Vicario and what he planned to do next.

"This is difficult for me," he concluded.

"*Very* difficult," Casey replied. "You've got a lot of painful work to do. I'm sorry." She never asked Ryan if he wanted to back off. She knew what the answer would be.

"Ryan's bind feeds into mine," Claire continued. "I'm still spinning in neutral. We already know the Hillingtons and, on a separate level, the Evanses are crucial pieces of the puzzle. I need to know if the same applies to the Vicarios. And the only way I can get a full picture of what we're dealing with is to have something of theirs to hold, to try to pick up the right energy from."

They could actually hear Casey frowning.

"We've got to tread very carefully," she said. "Ogden and Banks have put us on notice. One more proactive step without notifying them first, and we're toast. We've pushed this as far as it can go. So we have to come up with a seemingly innocuous way to approach the Vicarios."

"Exactly." Claire nodded. "Did you learn anything from Angela that might flesh the family out for us?"

"Only what Ryan already knows from his initial alibi check. That Isabel has two kids, Franklin and Mia, both in their midtwenties. Mia is an office manager and Franklin's an auto mechanic. My opinion? They're way too young and unestablished to help pay for a drug as expensive as the oral chemo drug you just described. It's good that you're checking out Frank Vicario's life insurance. It's the only possible way I can think of to offset the cost. Although, frankly, I don't think even that amount will come close to being enough for the long-term. I've seen my hospital bills. Without my insurance, I'd be screwed."

Ryan's antennae went up. "You're right. Frank Vicario worked as a store associate at a Home Depot. How much could his life insurance be worth? We're discussing a chemo med that costs thousands upon thousands, every month. And the idea is for Isabel to live as many years as possible. So how are her kids making this work?" A pause. "I'll see what I can dig up."

"I'm hoping I'll be able to offer you more to go on," Casey said. "Angela and her in-house investigator did a documented search into the Vicarios. She's revisiting it now and then sharing the findings with me."

"That's all great," Claire said. "And Emma is checking out social media, since, even though Isabel won't have accounts, her kids will. However, that still leaves me stuck in no-man's land."

"Wait." Abruptly, Casey's tone changed. She'd clearly thought of something. "Everything you have in play is good. But, Claire, you're right—more waiting is a no-go. I have a thought that might help solve your impasse."

"What?" Now Claire was all ears.

"You don't have something of the Vicarios to interact with—yet. In the meantime, Ryan has a great deal of material. Ryan, do you have any printouts? Specifically about Isabel, not just Zenith Pharmacy?"

"No, but I can easily make that happen," Ryan assured her.

"Do that. Add whatever you uncover about Frank's life insurance policy. Give all those printouts to Claire. Include whatever Emma comes up with from social media, including photos. In fact, Claire, you sit with Emma so you can see what she's doing firsthand, and then decide if you need a printout. It's not as good as the real thing, but it might trigger a reaction. It's happened in the past."

"You're right." Now Claire sounded as stoked as Casey did.

"Ryan, I want Marc in the loop about all this. Especially once you've figured out how the Vicario kids are paying for their mother's medication. I'll need him to take the in-person investigative lead if a visit to the Vicarios' becomes necessary. And, guys? I want to hear every detail as it occurs. I'm back and running this show."

# 37

*Casey's Hospital Room*
*Friday, 12:40 p.m.*

Hutch eyed Casey as she fidgeted in her chair. The fidgeting wasn't from pain. It was from something about her case. As was the expectant look in her eyes. None of it was making him happy.

"What's got you poised to take off like a racehorse?" he asked.

Casey gave him an honest answer. "You don't want to know."

"I'm sure I don't, but you're not rushing into the fray—not even from your hospital room. You're concentrating on recovering—" Hutch broke off. "Oh, who am I talking to? You're not going to listen to a word I say."

"I always listen to what you say," she told him sweetly. "I just don't always comply."

Hutch's lips twitched. "You're impossible."

"I aim to please. And, by the way, you're impossible, too."

"Touché." Hutch rose from his chair, bent down, and kissed her. "I have to get back to work. I'm telling the nurse to keep an eye on you, and to make sure you don't overtax yourself. And I'll be back tonight as soon as I can get away."

As soon as Hutch left, Casey called Ryan.

"You've got something?" Ryan asked in greeting. They'd already talked an hour ago after he'd reviewed the death benefit payment from Frank Vicario's life insurance policy. Isabel's medical bills were definitely being drawn from it, but, as they'd suspected, it wasn't a huge sum. It wouldn't cover even a fraction of the cost, and certainly not for months or years. Not to mention that Frank was the sole breadwinner and the death benefit would have to cover Isabel's living expenses, as well. So where was this money coming from?

They'd also discussed the fact that nothing had clicked with Claire yet, and that she was now sitting with Emma, physically viewing all of Mia's and Franklin's social media posts.

"I heard back from Angela," Casey said now. "She filled me in on all of her in-house investigator's notes on the Vicarios. Mostly stuff you already turned up in your initial alibi check. Isabel has a son, Franklin, and a daughter, Mia. Franklin is the elder. Both of them are in their midtwenties, but here's something new. Franklin has not only moved into his mother's house, he's sublet his apartment, so he obviously plans to be with her for a long time."

"He's staying close," Ryan replied. "That could be simply to care for his mother. Or it could be to stay where he'd have a better chance of being in charge of everything, including her finances."

"Maybe. Also, Angela's investigator wasn't sold on Franklin's or Mia's alibis. There was no disproving them. But there was no absolute way of proving them either. As you already ascertained, Mia's alibi is a customer in the hardware store whose office she manages, and Franklin's alibi is another mechanic in the auto shop he works in. Either one of those alibis could have loopholes."

"Yeah," Ryan muttered, his thoughts racing. "Let's start with Mia. She could have manipulated the customer into remembering things wrong. But I'm sticking to my guns, which means it wouldn't be necessary."

"You're convinced that a woman isn't the killer," Casey said.

"Not firsthand, no. So if Mia hired someone, she could easily have kept her regular work hours at the hardware store."

"Okay, I think I'm on board with that—although I don't know where Mia would find the money to pay off an assassin."

"We're not talking about a renowned military sniper," Ryan said in reminder. "The hitman could have come cheap."

"And Franklin's alibi?"

"Maybe he simply asked a pal to do him a favor and lie for him. He could have made up a believable excuse for needing him to do that. Like he was scoring drugs on the street."

Casey paused, then added, "Isabel was alone at home, but do you honestly believe she hired someone to kill Hillington?"

"No, but it's not out of the realm of possibility." Ryan swore. "I really dropped the ball on all but the basics. When we hang up, I'm digging into all alibis—and associations. Not to mention bank accounts and credit card balances. This time, I'm covering everything."

\*\*\*

*Offices of Forensic Instincts*
*Small Conference Room, First Floor*
*Tribeca, New York*
*Friday, 1:35 p.m.*

Claire was sitting beside Emma, peering at her laptop screen.

Emma had found tons of social media posts on both Franklin's and Mia's accounts. She'd also found comments on those posts, as well as lots of photos. Both of them had active social lives, although those social lives had stopped dead in their tracks the day Frank Vicario had been killed.

Mia's had just begun again, only at a trickle rather than a flow.

Franklin's had not.

Printouts would have been time-wasters. Claire much preferred viewing everything on the computer screen. It made her feel closer to the process. Plus, it was easier for Emma to switch platforms in an instant, as Claire requested. Some thoughts tied to other thoughts and had to be explored simultaneously. If there was anything that made Claire's antennae go up, Emma would print it out and give it to Claire to hold.

So far, nothing.

Claire leaned back in her chair and frowned. "This has been a total zero. I don't plan on giving up, but the photos are driving me crazy. None of them is focused specifically on Mia or Franklin. Even their home page photos are not head shots. And the rest are all group photos of them with friends. Plus, there's nothing at all on Isabel. Not a post, not a photo. Not even a birthday or anniversary picture."

Emma nodded, equally as disgusted as Claire. She'd been at this all day and had found tons of items, but nothing productive.

"That's not a big surprise," she said. "People my age are usually independent, and maybe even living in another state or another country than their parents. Family ties are not as strong as they once were."

"I know." Claire did know—very well. She'd been estranged from her own parents for over a decade. "But words alone are not enough. I need clear photos to work with. Otherwise, I can't establish a connection."

"Then let's keep going."

\*\*\*

*Ryan's Lair*
*Friday, 2:10 p.m.*

Ryan was occupied with digging into Mia and Franklin Vicario's finances.

He'd checked out their bank accounts and credit card statements, then weighed them against their incomes and lifestyles. Nothing about Mia raised any red flags. She was living within her means, and everything seemed to be aboveboard—although she clearly couldn't make any contributions to her mother's medical expenses.

Franklin was another story entirely.

Every month, the guy made substantial withdrawals—withdrawals that might suggest he was the one paying for his mother's meds. Still, his withdrawals plus his salary didn't come close to being enough.

Something was off. There wasn't time to methodically conduct this part of the investigation. So Ryan went for fast and furious.

With Yoda's help, he downloaded the surveillance video of the building across the street from the auto repair shop where Franklin worked. Most of what he saw were normal day-to-day operations. Cars in, cars out. Boring.

Abruptly, he struck gold. Two meetings, both of which screamed something illegal.

Each meeting took place at the end of a workday, when darkness was falling. On each occasion, a different guy had walked up to the shop and met Franklin outside. They'd each handed him a wad of cash, after which Franklin handed them the keys to a vehicle. Minutes later, an expensive car was driven away from the shop.

Ryan caught the makes, models, and license plates of both vehicles. When he reviewed the auto shop's business records, neither of the cars in question appeared in the service records. It sure as hell smelled like Franklin was doing side jobs without the owner's knowledge.

Ryan took out his phone and called Casey.

"This is great work, Ryan," she said when he'd finished. "I want Marc to drive out to South Bayside and question Franklin in whatever manner he deems necessary. My problem is, Banks and Ogden. If we take the lead on this, they'll come after us—hard."

Ryan made a disgusted sound, then racked his brain for a way to bypass the detectives.

Finally, his lips curved. "I have an idea."

"Go on."

"I checked in with Claire and Emma a little while ago. They were still stuck, and Claire is starting to freak out." Ryan went on to explain Claire's ongoing frustration and what it would take to snap it. "What if I could get her the photos she needs to unblock her? I might have a way. In fact, I'm pissed at myself for not having thought of this sooner."

"I'm not going to ask you for details," Casey said. "I don't want to waste time. I have full confidence you'll get what you're looking for. Then what?"

"Then I pass on what I find to Claire and let nature take its course."

Now it was Casey who was smiling. "We tell Ogden and Banks the lead was Claire's. They'd never be caught dead pursuing a lead generated by a 'psychic.'"

"Bingo."

"That'll cover our asses. Marc and Claire will both drive out to Queens, Marc to pressure Franklin, and Claire to use her instincts. If 'Claire's lead' gathers steam, Marc knows how to reach me. I'll get in touch with the detectives so it's their ball game and they'll be able to take full credit."

"I'm loving this more every minute," Ryan responded cheerfully.

"Okay, I'll call Marc and bring him up to speed."

\*\*\*

Ryan jumped right on his part. He was still annoyed at himself for not having gone this path sooner. But, in his defense, the source he was about to delve into was sketchy, and FI was always way ahead of them, so it wasn't one of Ryan's go-tos.

Urgent times called for urgent measures.

He logged into the dark web.

There was a specific blogger he knew of who was fascinated with violent crime cases in New York City—especially high-profile ones. This blogger posted all kinds of eerily accurate pieces of information and photos that hit too close to home to be fiction. They must have some high-level source feeding all this to them and getting kickbacks in exchange. Ryan would pay money to find out who that source was. Someone in law enforcement and handling these high-profile cases? That would be Ryan's guess.

In any case, Christopher Hillington definitely fell into the high-profile category.

Ryan did a quick search of the current subject matter and, sure enough, found a subject entitled: *Christopher Hillington*. He clicked into it and found a wealth of information on the man himself, on his murder investigation, and, lastly, on the hit-and-run he'd been the key suspect in prior to his death.

Ryan read every single entry and looked at every single one of the photos. It was scary how close to reality this blogger had come, including details on Casey's shooting and classified pieces of the NYPD's investigation. The most relieving thing was that the blogger didn't mention Casey's whereabouts or the status of her injuries, which meant they didn't know them.

What they did know was everything about the hit-and-run, including the fact that Hillington had been the targeted victim, while, due to an ugly twist of fate, Frank Vicario had been killed. They'd even stated that a scumbag named Oliver Steadman, who held a major grudge against Hillington, was the driver who'd plowed into Vicario's Camry and turned it into an accordion.

Ryan would have probed deeper just to figure out this blogger's identity, but there wasn't time. He was on a mission, and he wasn't giving up until he found what he needed.

The name *Frank Vicario* was linkified, so Ryan immediately clicked on that link.

Gruesome photos of the manslaughter scene appeared, with captions to go with them.

Ryan skipped past those, scrolling down a little at a time.

Pay dirt.

A clear photo of Frank's funeral, followed by one of his burial. The funeral was a decent-sized crowd of people, all of them too far away to zero in on. But the burial photo was just of the family surrounding the coffin, weeping, and holding on to each other's hands.

The *whole* family.

An older woman who had to be Isabel Vicario was standing with her palm pressed against the coffin, tears running down her face. She, Mia, and Franklin were all prominently displayed, all of their faces etched with grief.

"Yoda," Ryan called. "I need you to zoom all the way in on this photo, and then enhance it using every tool I've got. I need the people in it to be as close-up and crystal clear as possible."

"Already initiated, Ryan."

"Good. I'll wait and pace."

***

Not ten minutes later, Ryan had what he needed.

"Yesss." He punched the air. "Great work, Yoda. Now please send the photo directly to Claire via Emma's laptop. I'll follow up with a printout." He was already on his feet.

"The photo should now be available for Claire to view on Emma's laptop," Yoda reported. "You'll find the printout all ready for you on the color printer."

Ryan grinned. "Have I praised you for your genius often enough?"

"No," Yoda answered frankly. "But let me remind you that you created me."

"Then the praise belongs to us both."

\*\*\*

Ryan burst into the first-floor conference room to find Claire staring at the screen, wide-eyed, and Emma sitting up triumphantly beside her.

"Your photo just arrived," Emma told him. "It seems to have sparked a reaction."

"Something's wrong," Claire murmured. "Very wrong."

Ryan leaned over her shoulder. "Here." He slid the actual photo into her hands. "See if this clarifies things."

The instant the photo came in contact with Claire's fingers, she let out a cry and bolted to her feet. "Pain," she said. "Excruciating pain."

"Who?" Ryan demanded. "Who's in excruciating pain?"

Claire's hands were shaking. "Isabel. At home. The cancer. And so much dark energy. I can barely withstand it."

Ryan reached over and gripped Claire's trembling fingers. "Claire, think. Is Franklin with his mother?"

"I don't have to think. Both Mia and Franklin are there. Besides the pain, there's anguish. And anger. Both revolving around the pain." She gave a hard, dazed shake of her head. "The agony is worsening, and the darkness is growing. I need to be there, to bring comfort—and something more. I'm not sure what."

"Well, I am," Ryan replied gently. He studied Claire's tormented, faraway expression and knew he wouldn't get through to her—not fast enough. But there was one person who could.

Still gripping Claire's fingers, Ryan pressed their boss's name on his cell phone, simultaneously putting his cell on speaker.

"Talk to me," Casey answered.

Ryan didn't waste time. "Claire is sensing Isabel at home in horrible pain," he said. "She's also sensing growing darkness. And anger. She wants to rush over to the Vicario house."

Casey didn't miss a beat.

"Claire," she said quietly. "I know you're freaking out, and with good reason. I'm not going to stop you from going, but you don't know what you're walking into. It might not be just a sick woman needing assistance. The darkness might be more—things you're not prepared to contend with, especially not in this state of mind. You need support and protection. I want Marc to go with you. Remember, you not only want to help Isabel, you want to gather information. You'll be able to concentrate on the metaphysical and the emotional while Marc will be able to focus on the various Vicarios' culpability."

Claire went still, letting Casey's words sink in. "There's more to this, isn't there?"

"Yes." Now that Claire was calmer, Casey proceeded to tell her what she and Ryan had conjured up. "Not only will you be able to use your gift, but you'll save us from Banks's and Ogden's wrath. And Marc can cross whatever lines are necessary. It's a win-win."

Slowly, Claire nodded. "I assume you have Marc at the ready?"

"I do. He's just waiting for word from me."

"Give it to him, please. I want to leave as soon as possible."

"Consider it done," Casey replied. "And hang in there. It's a forty-five-minute drive."

Ryan shook his head. "Not when Marc's at the wheel, it isn't."

# 38

Marc and Claire turned onto the quiet street where Isabel Vicario lived.

The houses were small and close together, but they were also well cared for and emanated a kind of warmth and charm.

Much like the others, Isabel's house was brick, with a tiny garage and a green overhang. Marc parked on the driveway pad, cut the engine, and angled himself to face Claire.

"You okay?" he asked.

Claire had become more and more agitated as they'd neared their destination. Her eyes were wide and focused on something her mind was seeing but Marc was not. And her hands were shaking so badly that the photo she held was fluttering up and down.

Marc had to get things under control. Despite Claire's unique gift, this was his show to run. He had to guide Claire in her efforts. Their arrival had to stay low-key and explicable. They couldn't rush in like some overwrought SWAT team, nor could they actively oversee anything that became a criminal investigation. He knew his job and Claire knew hers. Marc had only to get Claire grounded.

"Hey," he said gently, putting his hand on her forearm. "It's going to be okay. Can you listen to me?"

Claire nodded, forcing common sense to overcome emotion. "Isabel is still weeping. The darkness is growing stronger. The anger is boiling into rage." She drew in a calming breath, then released it. "I'll be okay. I've accessed my serenity. I'll do my job and not walk in there like a wild woman."

Marc sighed with relief. That was just what he wanted to hear.

"We've got to take this slow," he told her. "No rushing into the house. Just like I said on the drive here. We'll ring the bell, tell them who we are and why we're allegedly in the neighborhood. After that, you handle the compassion and concern. I'll handle any investigating that needs to be done. If there's something to be found, we'll find it."

"And then get Casey to call the police." Claire stilled her hands and forcibly calmed down. She lay the photo, upside down, on her seat. "I'm ready."

***

*Vicario Residence*
*South Bayside, Queens, New York*
*Friday, 4:24 p.m.*

Marc and Claire rang the bell at the front door. Claire was calling on her inner strength and forcing an aura of calm, although they could both hear the moans of pain coming from inside.

A young woman who they recognized from the photo as Mia opened the door, looking frazzled and upset.

"It's not a good time…" Her eyes narrowed quizzically when she saw who her visitors were. "Do I know you?" she asked. "You look familiar."

Marc made the initial introductions, adding that they were from Forensic Instincts. He knew there had been leaks about FI assisting in the capture of Oliver Steadman.

Even as Mia cringed from her mother's lingering whimpers, she said, "You helped the NYPD find out who really killed my father. The detectives didn't tell me that outright, but I saw articles and photos on the blogs I follow. How can I thank you? And what brings you here today?"

Claire spoke up. "Your mother. She's in terrible pain. How can we help?"

"I don't understand…"

"I'm not sure how much research you did on our firm, but Claire is what's known as a claircognizant," Marc said. "She senses emotions and events that the rest of us mortals don't. We were nearby, at the 111th Precinct, finalizing some paperwork. Claire got a horrible sense that your mother was in excruciating pain, and she insisted we come by to check on her."

"I apologize for the intrusion," Claire said, letting her anguish show. "But I was terribly worried."

Mia opened the door wide. "Come in. I don't know if you're aware of it, but my mother has cancer. Sometimes the pain gets severe. My brother just changed her fentanyl patch. But once I explain who you are…I think it will help."

She guided Marc and Claire into a cozy living room where she seated them in two matching armchairs. "I'll tell my mother and brother what's going on. Then I'll put up a pot of coffee."

Once Mia had left the room, Claire said, "Isabel's pain has eased, but the darkness hasn't. If anything, it's growing stronger. So is the rage. Marc, something is very wrong here."

"Then let's find out what it is," he replied.

Sounds of heated discussion drifted down the hall from the rear of the house. Those sounds were clearly coming from Mia and Franklin, because Isabel was already making her way slowly and shakily into the living room.

She looked at Marc and Claire, tears in her eyes.

"I had no idea you aided the police in the hit-and-run that killed my Frank." She reached out her hands and squeezed each of their arms. "I don't know how to thank you."

Claire spoke up first. "Please sit down. You've just been through a horrible bout of pain."

Isabel complied, looking relieved but puzzled. "Did Mia tell you that?"

"No." Again, Marc went through the brief explanation of Claire's gift.

"I was terribly uneasy," Claire concluded. "I needed to see for myself that you're okay."

Isabel was staring at Claire in fascination. "You actually sensed my pain?"

"Yes," Claire replied.

Isabel gave an amazed shake of her head. "That's an astonishing gift. I so appreciate you checking up on me." She frowned. "Did Mia make coffee?"

"Doing it now, Mother," Mia called out from the kitchen.

"Thank you, dear." Isabel was clearly an excellent hostess. "Also, please bring out the plate of cookies you brought me earlier. They smell heavenly."

"Of course."

Marc frowned. "None of that is necessary, Mrs. Vicario," he said politely, counting on the fact that she'd ignore his words. He and Claire needed to be inside that house for a lot longer than five minutes.

"It most definitely is," Isabel countered. "I owe you so much. Coffee and cookies are hardly inconveniences."

As she spoke, Mia returned to the room, accompanied by a tall, solid-looking man who both Claire and Marc recognized from his photo as Franklin Vicario. He shifted on his feet and didn't look the least bit pleased to see them.

"Franklin, these are the Forensic Instincts people I told you about," Mia said in introduction. She turned back to Claire and Marc. "And this is my brother, Franklin."

"It's nice to meet you," Franklin said, shaking each of their hands as if it were an order. He looked totally thrown by their presence. "And I really appreciate everything you've done. But my mother is in no condition—"

"Franklin, stop," Isabel interrupted. "The new fentanyl patch is already working. I'm feeling better, and I want Claire and Marc to stay." She gestured at the empty love seat. "You and your sister join us. And thank you, Mia, for bringing in our coffee and sweets."

"Of course." Mia placed the tray on the coffee table, ready to serve.

Reluctantly, Franklin gave in to his mother's request and sank down on the love seat.

Marc edged a glance at Claire, who'd gone sheet white the instant she'd touched Franklin's hand. Now she was visibly controlling herself, but it was clear she'd connected with the anger and the darkness she'd been sensing.

Marc decided to go with that and push things a bit further.

"You've all been through a terrible time," he said. "I'm just relieved the correct guilty party is being punished. I realize it won't bring your husband and father back, but hopefully it will give you some measure of peace."

A muscle twitched in Franklin's jaw. "Some. Not enough. There's still so much we had…have to take care of ourselves. There are all different kinds of guilt."

Mia glanced at her brother, hoping he wasn't going to start going on and on about the insurance companies. That was a private family matter.

"How do you take your coffee?" she asked Claire and Marc, trying to nip that rant in its tracks.

"Black is fine," Marc said.

"Cream and sugar for me, please," Claire managed. She customarily drank herbal tea, but she didn't want to cause any delays in this conversation.

Franklin took the cup his sister offered him. He still looked agitated, and Marc could swear there was fear in his eyes.

His next words confirmed the agitation.

"My father's death…my mother's health…some things can't be made right," he said, talking more to himself than to them. "They say there's justice, but there isn't any. Except for the rich and entitled. Somehow, they come out unscathed. They have money and they have power. We don't stand a chance against them, even if they're scum."

"Franklin…" Mia began, appalled by her brother diving into the very diatribe she feared.

"What? It's true. I'm not going to sugarcoat it just to make everyone feel more at ease. Has your pain lessened, Mia? Mine hasn't. In many ways, it's getting worse."

"We have guests, Franklin." His mother stepped in, giving him a disapproving look. "I know how badly my pain is affecting you, but this isn't the time or place." She turned to Claire and Marc. "I apologize for my son's outburst. He took Frank's death very hard, and he's taking my illness just as hard."

"Yes, I am." There was a muscle twitching in Franklin's cheek as his control started to slip. "You don't deserve this. *We* don't deserve this. And we wouldn't be in this position if—" He cut himself off.

*If what?* Marc wanted to ask. This is the part where he always closed in on his prey. Not this time. This time he kept his mouth shut. *This guy's on the brink. It won't take much to push him over the edge. But that's not my or Claire's job to do—unfortunately.*

Marc took the next necessary step. He slid his hand into his pocket and tapped his cell phone to begin recording. He kept his hand poised and ready, waiting for the sliver of proof that would make him notify Casey.

He sure as hell got it.

Abruptly, Franklin changed the subject in a most damning way. "I saw that the president of your company was shot. It sounded serious. I hope she'll survive. It only takes one bullet to kill."

*One bullet? How did Franklin know that piece of information? No details of the shooting had been released.*

Marc's hand inched back into his pocket. They had enough to go on.

In that second, Franklin leaned forward to pick up his cup of coffee.

There was a triangular-shaped birthmark on his wrist.

Claire bit back her gasp.

Marc pressed the button on his Bluetooth key fob, activating a shortcut on his iPhone to send a text message to Yoda.

Casey would take it from there.

# 39

Burt Ogden swerved into the left lane of the LIE, swearing under his breath. "It's fucking rush hour. *This* is when all this had to go down?"

Lorraine frowned. "We had to get the warrant. You're doing a great job of weaving in and out of traffic. We'll be there in twenty more minutes. Which is good, because I'm still trying to figure out what direction to come at Franklin Vicario from. Casey only knew what a panic button could tell her."

Ogden slanted her a look. "How much of her whole story do you believe?"

"A good portion of it, actually. From what I understand, Claire Hedgleigh has a lot of visions, or whatever you call them. But the NYPD doesn't work with psychics, at least not officially. Given Claire's track record, I'm beginning to think we should take her more seriously."

Burt scowled. "I'm still not sure I'm buying it." He paused. "But, if we ever do change our minds and use her, we're going to have to stay way under the radar."

"Yup," Lorraine agreed. "Anyway, we're not ready to deal with all the red tape that kind of decision would require. So the point is moot. For now, we can't act on her metaphysical stuff. Casey knows that. And she did call us the minute Marc Devereaux signaled that Franklin Vicario was starting to incriminate himself. Then again, we don't know how much he's said. We're going to have to feel our way into a confession."

"We will."

Burt found a hole in the traffic and zoomed through it.

***

*Vicario Residence*
*South Bayside, Queens, New York*
*Friday, 5:58 p.m.*

From the moment Marc pressed that button, he knew that he and Claire had to buy time. Any aggressive push was out. So he'd made sure they just danced on the edge, mixing casual conversation with the occasional comment that kept that nervous expression on Franklin's face.

The goal was to keep themselves in that house until Banks and Ogden arrived.

That moment was imminent.

***

*Vicario Residence*
*South Bayside, Queens, New York*
*Friday, 6:01 p.m.*

Marc heard the stealth gliding of the detectives' car turning into the driveway. Quickly, he spoke over the sound, making sure none of the Vicarios was aware of the detectives' arrival. Plus, this was the time to prime the pump for them, to reignite Franklin's fear and anger.

"Franklin, you're an auto mechanic, right?" Marc asked.

Franklin eyed him. "Yeah, why?"

"Just thinking that you probably work long hours. It must be hard to find enough time to be with your mother."

"I manage."

Claire took over for Marc, knowing just where he was headed. "Is it dangerous at your shop when there are late-night pickups?" she asked in a concerned tone. "This is a crazy world. Do you at least keep a gun on hand to protect yourself?"

Now, Franklin was starting to sweat. "A gun? I don't... I mean...I did...but I got rid of it."

"When did you get rid of it?" Marc asked.

"I don't remember the exact date." Franklin wiped the sweat from the back of his neck.

The doorbell rang.

"I'll get it," Marc said, rising and striding to the front door before anyone could question him.

"What the hell...?" Franklin, who was already off-balance from Marc and Claire's probing, half rose from the chair, looking like he wanted to bolt. Instinct was clearly telling him that there weren't kids selling Girl Scout cookies on the other side of the door.

Marc opened the door, glanced at the warrant, and muttered a few words to the detectives. He then led them into the living room.

"I'm sure you all remember Detectives Banks and Ogden," he said, staring straight at Franklin.

All the color drained from Franklin's face.

"We have some questions for you," Burt said.

"For us?" Mia looked totally at sea.

"No," Lorraine corrected her. "For your brother."

Franklin croaked out his words. "About what?"

Lorraine shot a quizzical glance at Marc, asking for a lead-in as to where she should start.

Marc gave her what she needed.

"Franklin was just expressing concern about Casey and about the fact that even the one bullet could have killed her," Marc informed Lorraine. "Also, he doesn't seem to be sure of whether or not he has a gun."

Lorraine ran with that. "How did you know that Casey Woods was shot once? We made no reference to that in our news conference."

"I just…I mean, I must have read about it—"

"It wasn't published anywhere," Burt cut him off. "Only the police and the shooter would have that information. And do you or don't you own a gun?"

Franklin snapped, starting the downhill path. "I don't have a gun."

"Did you cut it into pieces at your auto shop?" Burt kept the pressure on.

"Why would I—?"

"Because you shot Casey Woods," Lorraine said. "Did she know something about you and Christopher Hillington? Is that why you tried to kill her?"

"Tried?" Franklin blurted. "You mean she's going to make it?"

"Oh, yeah, she is," Burt answered. "And she's already supplying us with answers that will ensure your conviction."

"Conviction?" Franklin was practically shrieking. "For seeking justice? Yeah, I shot her. She had to die. It wasn't what I originally planned. It was easier when she was the prime suspect. Her name in blood—hell, she should have been locked up."

Mia gasped, and all the color drained from Isabel's face.

"Franklin, what are you saying?" Isabel whispered.

"He's saying he not only shot Casey Woods, he killed Christopher Hillington," Lorraine said.

"I never said that," Franklin bellowed, desperate to fight his way out of the trap he'd created.

"You didn't have to. No one knew any of the crime scene specifics you just rattled off."

Seeing Franklin eyeing the distance to the door, Lorraine whipped out her pistol and aimed it at him.

Burt followed suit. "Don't even think about it." He didn't miss a beat. "Why did you kill Hillington? Did you think he was responsible for your father's death?"

"Of course I did," Franklin snapped, anger replacing the fear in his eyes. "My father was my mother's whole life. And the thought that that bastard took him away..." Franklin swallowed, tears abruptly welling up in his eyes. "He was her support, and not just financially. She's ill. She needed him. She needed his health insurance. And now we need money so badly. I've done whatever I needed to, but still—it's just not enough."

As Franklin was spilling his guts, Claire was getting a kaleidoscope of images, like scenes from a movie.

"You blackmailed him," she said, lost in the visions she was seeing. "You demanded money in exchange for keeping your mouth shut."

"It was the least my mother deserved."

"You targeted him, followed him to see why he was in your neighborhood that night," Claire continued, her gaze faraway. "And you found his family—his *other* family. That was the foundation of your extortion."

Franklin blinked away his tears, fury replacing them once again. "So Casey Woods told her whole fucking team about Hillington's mistress and bastard daughter." He turned to Banks and Ogden. "I saw her bring the two of them into your precinct. So you all know. But you didn't when I got to Hillington. No one knew. Only me."

"So you blackmailed him, and when he didn't come up with whatever ridiculous amount you demanded of him, you killed him," Burt said.

"That's not how it started!" Franklin was on total meltdown. "I called him, but I never accused him, not then. Even though I knew he did it. I told him how my family was suffering. I told him about my mother's cancer. I poured my heart out, and he agreed to see me. He told me we'd be alone. I only brought that sledgehammer to shake him up if he didn't come through."

*The murder weapon that no one knew about*, Marc thought. *Another nail in Vicario's coffin.*

"He thought you were looking for compassion and a little help getting your family through a tragedy," Lorraine prodded, never lowering her weapon.

Franklin was breathing hard, and his gaze shot daggers at Lorraine. "*A little help?* Do you know how much my mother's medication costs? And she has no insurance now. Our family was drowning. I tried everything to bring in more cash. I had to get us a lifeline."

Claire spoke up again in that faraway voice. "He was sympathetic. He even offered you money. But it wasn't enough. So you told him you were going to tell his wife and children about Natalie and Morgan. You tried to squeeze him out of millions."

"So what happened, Vicario?" Burt demanded. "Hillington didn't jump on your idea of forking over millions?"

"Jump on it?" Franklin was wild. "He said he'd throw me out and call the police. To turn *me* in. When he was the one who killed my father. The one who had the most to lose, including his legitimate family. I wasn't letting that happen…it couldn't happen. So when he went to grab his phone, I grabbed my sledgehammer and beat the shit out of him. There was no other way."

Wild-eyed, realizing where this was headed, Franklin took an insane risk. He made a dash for the front door.

"Stop right there," Burt ordered, feet planted, finger on the trigger as he quickly assessed whether the bastard would obey.

Franklin didn't hesitate. He kept going.

Marc crossed the room in two strides and tackled Franklin to the floor. Ignoring his sharp cries of pain, Marc pinned him in place and jerked his hands behind him, keeping his own knee firmly planted in the center of Franklin's back.

"You shot Casey," he ground out as Burt dashed over with his handcuffs, simultaneously reciting Franklin's rights. "And you killed a man in cold blood. The only reason you're not dead is because these two detectives are following proper protocol. That protocol doesn't apply to me. You'd better thank your lucky stars that Detective Ogden is cuffing you. Otherwise, I wouldn't be responsible for my own actions."

With that, Marc rose and Burt yanked Franklin to his feet. "Freedom's not in the cards for you, you sick bastard. You're coming with us."

Franklin fought with everything in him. "You have no proof... It's my word against yours."

Lorraine walked straight in front of him, pistol aimed dead-on, and held up her phone.

"No," Lorraine said. "It's your word against yours."

Marc flashed his own cell. "And I have the rest of what was said before the detectives got here." He purposely stepped away, letting Lorraine and Burt take him away to get the written confession they knew that, given Franklin's state of mind, he would crumple and supply.

"Franklin," Isabel called after him in a small, broken voice. "Oh, God, Franklin."

Mia was openly sobbing, turning away from her brother and holding her mother's hand tightly in her own.

Claire left the love seat and knelt in front of them. She knew they were both in shock and beyond grieving.

"I'm sorry," she said, gently covering their joined hands with her own. "I wish we hadn't further shattered your lives."

Mia shook her head. "You have nothing to be sorry for. I just never in a million years imagined that Franklin could...would—" She broke off, her worried gaze going to Isabel. "Mother? Please hold on—for me. I need you."

Isabel squeezed her eyes shut. "And I need you. I just don't know if I can withstand this, not after losing your father, my failing health, and now your brother..."

"You can and you will," Claire said, conveying to them that, through her gift, she somehow knew. "You're both survivors, and you have each other. That will be enough to fight your cancer into remission, Mrs. Vicario. And enough for both of you to find life is worth living." A heartbeat of a pause. "Your husband and father want that for you."

"Yes," Isabel said softly. "He does."

# 40

*Casey and Hutch's Apartment*
*Battery Park City, New York*
*Monday, 11:30 a.m.*

Casey sat back in her favorite chair and smiled. Lord, it was good to be home.

She'd had a busy morning. She'd had breakfast with Hutch, done all her pre-dawn PT, and her aide was on hand for anything she might need.

William Donnelly, Esquire, Christopher Hillington's trusts and estates attorney, had called her at ten thirty to report in. It was the second time Casey had spoken to him since she arrived home from the hospital yesterday. Now that Hillington's killer had been arrested, the attorney could be more open.

On Sunday afternoon, he'd called to fill in the pieces she'd already suspected. Before Hillington's unexpected murder, he'd planned to contact Casey and ask if she would get in touch with Natalie and Morgan and, with his input, to figure out the best timetable to announce their existence to his current family and to the world at large. His biggest concern was for their well-being, since he knew the explosion that this announcement would cause. He was counting on Forensic Instincts to act as both contact and protector.

He, of course, had no idea he was going to be killed.

Fortunately, he'd already drawn up his new will, which, as Donnelly carefully told Casey, provided handsomely for the Evanses. Casey understood that he hadn't been able to say more, not with the will reading scheduled for first thing Monday morning.

As requested, immediately after she'd concluded that first call, Casey had contacted Natalie and Morgan to fill them in. They were overcome with relief and gratitude, and ready to attend Monday morning's will reading with their heads held high. This tragedy had strengthened both of them.

That fact was proven by Mr. Donnelly's second call to Casey, the one he'd made right after the will reading—and the angry verbal exchange that had accompanied it. The bottom line was that the new will was ironclad. Natalie and Morgan would now officially be acknowledged in public, and the entire extravagant chunk of Hillington's estate would belong to them.

Casey had heaved a deep sigh of relief. Finally, closure on all fronts. Answers, too. She'd been right about Hillington. He'd written her name in blood to warn her what Franklin was about and hoping she could stop him from harming Natalie and Morgan. FI had even ensured closure for Isabel and Mia. Despite all protests, they'd insisted on depositing a large sum of money in Frank and Isabel's joint account each month to help cover medical expenses, plus extra for Mia to put herself and her mother in a better financial situation.

Casey had a few minutes to enjoy that satisfaction, before her cell phone rang.

Casey answered, "Hi, Angela."

"Hi to you" was the reply. "Are you home, safe and sound?"

Casey's lips curved. "I'm sure William Donnelly already supplied you with that information—plus a whole lot more."

"You and your team have been quite busy, and you really lived up to your reputation." A chuckle. "You do know the police have taken full credit for Franklin Vicario's arrest, I assume."

"That's how my team and I arranged it. It beat being brought up on obstruction charges."

"Makes sense." Angela paused. "Did you manage to keep your affiliation with my firm out of it?"

"Never mentioned," Casey assured her.

"Good." Another pause. "Are you up for a proposition?"

"Sounds intriguing. Sure."

Angela didn't miss a beat. "Your track record with the NYPD sucks, and is always hanging by a thread. You need inside legal counsel as much as your clients do. Someone who'll push the boundaries as you require, who knows how to color outside the lines. You'll keep your outside counsel for the straight-up stuff. But I need a change. How about my joining Forensic Instincts? I'd be an incomparable asset."

Casey's jaw dropped, just it had the first time Angela called her weeks ago. "Are you serious?"

"As a heart attack. I'm sick of defending scum. They don't deserve me. I want to use my skills in more rewarding and challenging ways. Such as, keeping you out of jail."

Now Casey was laughing. "I give my team tons of latitude, but you do realize I'd be your boss?"

"I can respect that. Doesn't mean I won't argue with you."

"I welcome the challenge. Also, I have to run this by the whole team. We need a unanimous vote."

"Do it now. I'll be at your place in an hour with a celebratory lunch."

Casey grinned, feeling a powerful rush of adrenaline.

Life was about to get a whole lot livelier.

# ACKNOWLEDGMENTS

My deepest thanks to all the extraordinary professionals with whom I consulted. By offering me their time and their knowledge, they added realism and authenticity to *Struck Dead* and, as a result, helped me to create an even better book.

Laura M. Zartman, FBI Special Agent, former senior team leader of Evidence Response Team, Newark Division (ret.).

Deborah Macy, Nurse Practitioner, MBA, MSN, manager of Level One Trauma Center and director of Level Two Trauma Center. Assisted in development of the first emergency helicopter program for Level One Trauma Center. Former director over Critical Care and Emergency Services, worked with the FBI.

James McNamara, Captain of Marines, Supervisory Special Agent, Behavioral Analysis Unit, FBI (ret.).

Bradley H. Zartman, FBI Special Agent Bomb Technician, who is knowledgeable in even more FBI areas and a great go-to professional.

Ted Polakowski, whose sharp eye and even sharper mind find each and every detail I miss.

And last, but truly first, my innermost team:

LP, for being the quintessential gem of an editorial partner.

My wonderful, one-of-a-kind family. You mean the world to me. Both your commitment to my books and your love for their author are immeasurable:

My husband, Brad, whose skills help me enhance Ryan's talents, both real and fictional. His scientific yet creative mind lends so much fullness to my characters. And his partnership, love, and support never fail to make me a better writer.

My daughter, Wendi, for being the best and most caring brainstorming partner, and the most creative master at getting past stumbling blocks.

And my granddaughter, Laci, who's mature way beyond her years. She's a constant challenge, who always brings love and laughter into my life. She's so proud and excited about the fact that I create books, but would prefer that it happened by magic, rather than by my having to work.